Diplomatic

Immunity

★ ★ ★

A NOVEL BY

TAD SZULC

SIMON AND SCHUSTER

NEW YORK

Copyright © 1981 by Tad Szulc
All rights reserved
including the right of reproduction
in whole or in part in any form
Published by Simon and Schuster
A Division of Gulf & Western Corporation
Simon & Schuster Building
Rockefeller Center
1230 Avenue of the Americas
New York, New York 10020
SIMON AND SCHUSTER and colophon are trademarks of Simon & Schuster
Designed by Eve Kirch
Manufactured in the United States of America

1   3   5   7   9   10   8   6   4   2

Library of Congress Cataloging in Publication Data

Szulc, Tad.
Diplomatic immunity.

I. Title.
PS3569.Z8D5   813'.54   81-5811
                              AACR2
ISBN 0-671-25095-7

This book is for J. S.

Contents

Prologue

THE bomb went off, suddenly and deafeningly, just outside the huge window facing the tarmac of Malagua International Airport, and shards of glass, vicious daggers, slashed through the cold, musty air of the excessively air-conditioned VIP lounge. A large sliver hit the plump, short Chief of Protocol on the left side of his face, shattering his eyeglasses and drawing blood. Fat red drops appeared on the man's cheek, quickly dripping down onto his dark suit and the collar and front of his white shirt.

"*¡Coño!*" he screamed. His hands flying to his eyes, he dropped a bouquet of red roses to the thick carpet. "*Por Dios . . .* I'm blind. *Oh, cabrones, hijos de la gran puta . . .*" There was an instant of silence, then a small crash. The oversized portrait of the dictator and owner of the Republic of Malagua, a well-posed smile on his fleshy, mustached mouth, came down from the wall.

Julia Savage, her arms out to accept the flowers, froze when the bomb burst, her smile dying. The shower of glass missed her, but the thud, the panic now erupting in the room, and the blood covering the swarthy little man riveted her to the ground. She noticed that the Chief of Protocol's blood had splattered the sleeve and the skirt of her white suit. Julia stood there for an infinitely long moment, defenseless, waiting for her composure to return and telling herself an Ambassador Extraordinary and

Plenipotentiary of the President of the United States of America, which was her freshly minted title, must act with bravery.

The airport's public-address system crackled, and a triumphant young male voice shouted in accented English: "The Malaguan Front of National Liberation welcomes the imperialist American Ambassador. Long live the People's Revolution!"

The Chief of Protocol, his voice trembling with terror, turned to Julia Savage: "Oh, my God, Madam Ambassador. Are you well?" She forced a smile, and picked up the bouquet at her feet. "Yes, I am, *señor*," she said evenly in Spanish. "I'm so grateful for your courtesy. The flowers are lovely."

★

"We don't need any more Cubas." This had been the Secretary of State's farewell message to Julia Savage, and these words raced through her mind as she was escorted from the bomb-shattered lounge to the black Embassy limousine awaiting her on the tarmac. It had been parked there so that she would not have to walk through the terminal. William "Mac" McVeigh, the Deputy Chief of Mission, who had acted as *chargé d'affaires* pending her arrival, explained the security arrangements to Julia as they walked to the Chrysler.

"I didn't want to take any more chances than necessary," McVeigh said. "The Frente, or whoever does those things, evidently wanted to greet you in grand revolutionary style. This morning, our Cultural Center downtown was firebombed—some damage, but nobody hurt—and now they've staged the airport blast. That poor bastard Moreno, the Protocol Chief, really got it, but it could've been you, Julia."

She shuddered and, involuntarily, quickened her step, moving with confident grace. Her thick black hair felt damp against her neck, and she narrowed her deep-set green eyes to cut the glare of the noontime July sun. She was thirty-six, and her face had a strong Celtic beauty. As they approached the car, Julia shifted her heavy attaché case from one hand to the other. McVeigh had offered to take it, but she said, "Thanks, Mac, you're an angel, but I'd rather carry it myself. I'm used to it—I feel almost undressed without it."

Julia and McVeigh had been friends for years, and she had requested that the State Department let him stay on as DCM—Deputy Chief of Mission—for at least six months, until she became familiarized with the Embassy and Malagua. She trusted his political judgment, unlike the former Ambassador's, and several weeks earlier, in Washington, Mac had given Julia a solid rundown on the Malagua situation. For the past year Julia had been reading, in her office next to the White House, lengthy telegrams from the Embassy in Malagua and estimates from the Central Intelligence Agency. Those reports were insistently optimistic and, she suspected, rather unrealistic. However, Mac—emphasizing that Embassy telegrams were drafted by the Ambassador in coordination with the CIA Chief of Station—offered Julia his private assessment. The Frente Malaguista de Liberación Nacional, the militant opposition movement against the country's dictatorial régime, had to be taken with utmost seriousness, Mac had said. And the FMLN, as the Frente was known, was savagely anti-American because the United States had undeviatingly supported the dictatorship for decades. In fact, General Juan Ferrer Berrio, the present Malaguan dictator, still enjoyed Washington's virtually unreserved backing. He was fervently anti-Communist, an attitude that served him well with many American politicians. His father, General Anselmo Ferrer García, had proved the ruling family's anti-Communism and pro-American stance when twenty-two years before, in 1961, he had allowed the use of Malagua's territory for the secret training of the CIA's exiles' brigade for the invasion of Cuba that ended so disastrously at the Bay of Pigs. His grandfather, Bolívar Ferrer Valle, the founder of the Ferrer dynasty, had been the creature and the protégé of the United States.

Juan Ferrer, now the President of Malagua as Anselmo Ferrer's natural and constitutional successor (the Malaguan constitution had been framed to meet the family's requirements), was a West Point graduate. Military experience was essential in his role as commander-in-chief of the American-trained National Guard, and the Ferrers never relinquished their personal control of the army. He spoke excellent colloquial English, with a predilection for four-letter words. He had devoted friends among conservative congressmen and heads of large American corporations that did business in Malagua. A half-dozen or so congressmen, mainly from the South and the Southwest, had partaken of his generosity: free trips to Ciudad Malagua aboard the Ferrer airline's Boeing 707 and pleasant weekends at his Pacific Coast hideaway, which was stocked with caviar, champagne, lobster, and young women (flown in from Miami or Caracas). Some lawmakers had quietly accepted unsecured loans from the dictator. And Ferrer was the silent partner in all the American companies operating in the republic.

This was political power, and the Administration in Washington comprehended it perfectly. Malagua was invariably overlooked in the days when the United States preached its human-rights sermons to the world. There had always been successful amendments exempting Malagua from legislation banning foreign aid to countries where human rights were being violated. As far as the Pentagon and the State Department were concerned, Malagua was the linchpin of American security in this turbulent region. The Panama Canal was an hour away by supersonic jet. Mexico and its oil were even closer to Malagua in the northern direction.

Of course, even the current conservative-minded Administration wanted Malagua to *appear* more democratic, but as the Secretary of State cautioned Julia Savage in his official instructions, the last thing the United States wished to see in Central America was the emergence of imitations of the Cuban revolutionary model. There already was plenty of turmoil in the region. Thus Julia's instructions were to work *with* Ferrer toward a gentle democratization—certainly not *against* him. The historic relationship between the United States and the Ferrer dynasty was to be maintained.

★

"We have to take all possible security measures," McVeigh was now saying, holding the limousine's door open for Julia. "We don't want you dead the first day in town. And speaking of security, meet your driver and your bodyguard. This is Salvador, the best man behind the wheel in Malagua, and this is Gonzalo, the fastest gun south of the border."

Salvador and Gonzalo turned around in the front seat to smile and shake hands with Julia as she got into the car. She smiled back, studying the two men, and said, "I see I'm in good hands here." They nodded in proud appreciation. Salvador was a trim man in his fifties, with a dark Indian complexion in stark contrast to his snow-white hair and white goatee. He was wearing a white short-sleeved *guayabera* shirt, and Julia saw the outline of a holstered gun under this loose garment. Gonzalo was younger and stocky, with the impassive face of a highlands Mayan and granite-hard eyes. He wore a flowered Hawaiian sport shirt and tan slacks, and a submachine gun rested across his knees, his right hand on the trigger. Julia noticed that three hand grenades had been fitted in metal brackets under the dashboard on Gonzalo's side.

Mac had followed her glance, and shrugged. "I'm afraid this is the required security for the Ambassador's car," he said. "And there's more than meets the eye. There's a submachine gun under the carpeting here in the rear—that bulge near your feet. Tomorrow the Embassy security officer will teach you how to use it, unless you already know how. There are two cans of Mace in this compartment under the right armrest. You should always sit on the right-hand side of the car, behind Gonzalo. See that little button on the floor, near your right foot? Well, in a kidnap situation, if Salvador and Gonzalo have been neutralized, you are to step on the button. It activates a radio transmitter in the car, which is monitored and taped by the sergeant of the Marine Guard at the Embassy. If you're kidnapped, try to keep a conversation going, because it makes it easier to triangulate by radio the location of the limousine."

"I see you people have thought of everything," Julia said woodenly, and reached into her purse for a cigarette.

"No smoking in the car," Mac said quickly. "That's a no-no. The windows are permanently sealed—as you can see, they're double windows—and they can't be rolled down. You get air from the air conditioner, and you don't want to poison it with cigarette smoke. Of course, the car is reinforced with armor plate, which can't be pierced by bullets and should be resistant to hand grenades. By God, I *do* hope we've thought of everything. You remember what happened to John Trax, don't you?"

Julia did remember. John Trax, another friend, was the American Ambassador to Guatemala who had been kidnapped and executed by the local underground three years before, after the Administration in Washington had refused to meet the *guerrilleros'* demands: $1 million in cash and the release by the Guatemalan government of a dozen of their imprisoned comrades. It was United States policy not to negotiate with terrorists, not to give in to their requests. The Secretary of State himself had warned Julia about it.

"Tell me, Mac," she now said, "how bad *are* things in Malagua? Are we in the middle of a civil war, a revolution? What do *you* see?"

McVeigh took a deep breath. "Well, the truth is that anything is possible here. I don't know about this being 'another Cuba,' as they say back home; no two situations are exactly alike. But yes, this *is* the beginning of a civil war, or a revolution, or whatever you want to call it. The ruling family is facing its strongest challenge; but I'll be damned if I'm going to play prophet about Malagua. The CIA people are doing enough of that—though I wonder more and more whether they're not being false prophets, or should I say bad prophets, with their 'all's-well-here' attitude so long as we keep supporting Ferrer in every way."

★

Salvador, the driver, picked up the microphone under the dashboard, and called in English: "This is Number Six to Number One and Number Two. This is Number Six to Base. We're ready to roll." The radio receiver crackled, and one voice after another answered: "Roger, Number Six." A green sedan that had been parked in front of the Chrysler started down the tarmac. Salvador put the car into gear and followed. Julia saw that a blue sedan behind them began moving at the same time. McVeigh said, "Oh, I forgot to tell you that you'll have a lead car and a follow car with you at all times. They're in radio contact with Salvador, with each other, and with the Marines' shack, which is Base. There are four armed guards, all local police sharpshooters, in each security vehicle, and you are never to get out of the limousine until they have parked in front of you and behind you, and formed a screen on foot to cover you."

The motorcade drove past helmeted National Guardsmen, their submachine guns at the ready, posted every fifteen yards on the tarmac and all the way to the exit gate from the airport. An armored car stood by the shattered window of the VIP lounge, a dozen troopers cordoning it off from the rest of the field. The Guardsmen had shot it out with the guerrillas, who had seized and briefly held the control tower with its public-address system just as they detonated the bomb, but the attackers had fled unscathed. The soldiers looked angry and frustrated.

More Guardsmen manned a roadblock at the gate, and an officer waved on the ambassadorial convoy. A small crowd had gathered behind the soldiers, chatting excitedly. A scarved woman peered into the passing limousine over a trooper's shoulder. "*¡Ay, qué guapa!*" she exclaimed loudly, pointing at Julia. The others were silent. Her anxiety lifting, Julia asked McVeigh lightly: "Mac, don't I get to fly the Stars-and-Stripes and *my* flag on the fenders of the limousine? You know, the flags were the main reason I wanted to be Ambassador."

"No, here you don't," McVeigh said. "Here we keep our profile low, and the flags furled and covered. We don't want to give people ideas. Don't forget, Julia, you've come to live in a real state of siege in Malagua."

BOOK ONE

★ ★ ★

Malagua

1

THE President of the United States and the members of the National Security Council were assembled in the White House Cabinet Room to discuss the situation in the Republic of Malagua and elsewhere in Latin America. Edward R. Masterson, Jr., the Secretary of State, was obsessed with Cuba and Fidel Castro, and now he was expressing his acute concern over Malagua, reading from notes prepared by his experts. It was the message he would later deliver to Julia Savage, after failing to block her appointment to Ciudad Malagua.

A new revolutionary surge was sweeping Latin America—this now occurred every few years—and the President had decided the time had come for another White House review of the whole problem. The President, a conservative thinker, tended to see Cuba, the Caribbean, and Central America in the larger context of the East–West contest. He saw the expansion of Cuban influence in the Hemisphere as a definite plus for the Soviet Union—after all, the Cubans and the Russians were military allies—just as Masterson did. But the President had a greater sophistication than his Secretary of State about Latin America, where he had traveled extensively as a senator, and he thought the problem was manageable if the United States played its cards right—if it was less excitable and supported existing governments, even the

dictatorial ones—he had said publicly that "moderate dictatorships" were not anathema—while pushing them toward a
modicum of democracy and sensible social and economic
development. He was convinced such policies would do the
trick, and prevent the emergence of "new Cubas." Today he was
annoyed with Masterson for making an issue over the ambassadorial appointment in Malagua, and he lit a cigar with a touch of
irritation.

"I fear Malagua has all the makings of a new Cuba," the Secretary of State said gravely. "What's happening there is extremely serious and dangerous—even if we're being assured by
our Embassy and the CIA that General Ferrer remains in full
control. We must therefore proceed with the greatest care." He
cleared his throat and glanced at the President. "This is the fore-
most reason the State Department finds it highly inadvisable to
send Julia Savage as ambassador to Malagua. Yes, I know she is
both highly intelligent and well motivated. I am aware of her fine
work on the staff of the National Security Council. But the fact
remains that she isn't sufficiently experienced for the Malagua
assignment. We need a tough, seasoned Foreign Service officer
there. I'm sure, Mr. President, that we can find a more suitable
little embassy for Miss Savage. Perhaps something on the quiet
side—the Bahamas, for example."

It was most unusual for the National Security Council to be
reviewing an ambassadorial nomination. But Masterson was
under powerful pressure from his top people at State to kill Julia
Savage's appointment to Malagua; there was something of a rebellion rising against it among career officers. He was anxious to
keep peace at the State Department, where there was growing
unhappiness over the frequent bypassing of deserving professionals (Masterson had been led to believe that they were indeed
deserving) in favor of political appointees for the ambassador-
ships.

And the Secretary himself did not trust the bright young people
the White House kept foisting on him as ambassadors in important places. A Wall Street lawyer with impeccable international
connections through his New York firm, Masterson was the most

conservative member of the Republican cabinet—he had been brought in to erase the impression created during the campaign that the President was "a bit too internationalist"—and he had genuine political doubts about the wisdom of the proposed Savage nomination. He was sincerely worried about the events in Malagua. No, Miss Savage simply was not the person for the job. The Secretary repeated it once more for the President's benefit. "And Malagua isn't safe for a woman with all that terrorism going on," he added.

After Masterson finished, the President went around the table for comments. The National Security Adviser, a political scientist from Stanford named Thomas Morelli who had roomed with the President in college, had made it a practice to remain silent at NSC meetings, and now he said nothing. But privately he had warned the President that he would have a problem with both the State Department and the CIA over Julia Savage.

Morelli was personally in favor of the appointment: Julia had worked for him for nearly a year as the senior NSC staffer in charge of Latin America, and he had grown to respect her judgment. Like him, she was liberally inclined (the President had refused to load the Administration with right-wing ideologues), but hardheaded and not romantic about leftist revolutions. She understood that the problems of Latin America—economic underdevelopment and revolutionary patterns—were interrelated. Morelli thought Julia would do well in Ciudad Malagua, particularly if she was supported by clear and firm instructions from the White House and the State Department. And finally, her nomination would help the President politically in next year's reelection campaign with women's groups and the liberals whom he needed. While she was doing postgraduate work at Georgetown University in Washington, Julia had had friends who were active in the New Left, as it was called in the early days of the Vietnam war, some of them belonging to the SDS—Students for a Democratic Society. She had made no secret of these associations when she came to work at the White House, and both Morelli and the President knew about them. It had been such a long time ago that the friendships posed no political problems for the White

House, though they served to enhance Julia's standing with the liberals.

"Fuck them," the President had said when Morelli mentioned Masterson's and the CIA's objections to Julia Savage.

Michael Creighton, the crotchety Defense Secretary, was saving his ammunition for a future showdown with the President over more ships for the Navy in the next budget, and kept silent. He quietly filled his pipe, thinking that there were higher bureaucratic priorities than Julia Savage. Besides, he was confident that the U.S. Government could cope with any situation in its Latin American backyard. If it came to the worst, he thought, we can always turn to the Marines, as we did in the Dominican Republic under Lyndon Johnson.

Only the CIA Director, Lieutenant General Henry B. McCullen of the Air Force, joined Masterson in objecting to Julia Savage. McCullen, who had an overblown reputation as a military intellectual because he had published a treatise on World War I aerial-combat tactics and had served briefly as Commandant of the Air Force Academy, had been named to head the CIA after a stint as Commander-in-Chief, United States Air Force, Europe (USAFE). He had been chosen as a compromise when the President was dissuaded from naming a Washington lawyer with a White House adviser background on the ground that he was too liberal. McCullen, however, knew little about the intricate art of intelligence and its politics; he tended to miss nuances, and neither the President nor Tom Morelli trusted his judgment. He was a bureaucratic accident, but the President's exaggerated loyalty to his nominees prevented him from making a change at the CIA. In addition, McCullen was a hard-line conservative, and the President did not want to do battle with the military establishment and the right-wing groups who had supported him.

Choosing his words carefully, so as not to offend the President, McCullen said a woman might react too emotionally in Malagua's tense atmosphere. He refrained from saying that she was too liberal (a view passionately held within the Agency), and that because she had once been married to a Latin American, a Colombian, she might be a security risk. There might be emotional blackmail from the ex-husband, whoever he was (McCullen had not bothered to read the Colombian's CIA file and was unaware that it was kept with the Agency's most sensitive documents). In any case, McCullen decided to couch his reservations in political terms.

"You see, Mr. President," he said, "we have some rather sensitive operations running out of Malagua, and I'm not sure Miss Savage, qualified as she may be diplomatically, is equipped to understand them. You always insist, and rightly so, that the Ambassador must be the head of the Country Team in a foreign capital—which, of course, includes my people, my Station Chief —and I just fear that all this may be too complicated for such a young and inexperienced person."

The Vice President, George Mill, who had originally recommended Julia for the Malagua job, leaned over to whisper something to the President. Julia had worked for Mill when he was the junior Senator from Maine, handling foreign policy-matters, chiefly Latin America, and the Vice President and his wife had grown fond of her; and when the new Administration took office, Mill had proposed her for the NSC staff. When, some time later, the decision was made to remove the then Ambassador to Malagua, a holdover from two Republican administrations and the last Democratic Administration (which had wanted to appease Senate Republicans), the Vice President urged that Julia Savage take his place. The President liked the idea, though he was vaguely aware that Julia, using her NSC influence, had long pressed for a change in Malagua despite the opposition of the State Department. She felt that the man was incompetent and too close to the dictator and his family, and when she succeeded in convincing Tom Morelli, word went out from the White House to Secretary Masterson. Ambassadors serve at the pleasure of the President, and Masterson had to give in.

Examining briefly a folder before him, the President said: "I think, gentlemen, that we've already spent too much time on the Ciudad Malagua Embassy and Miss Savage. We have other questions to discuss—particularly Mexican oil. And I see from this file that Miss Savage is eminently qualified to be Ambassador to

Malagua. She has lived in Latin America, she speaks Spanish fluently. Her writings, notably her Ph.D. dissertation, show that she understands the area. The Vice President tells me that she is well attuned to my brand of human-rights policies. Besides, I want younger ambassadors, and I want more women ambassadors. In a place like Malagua, a young woman, enjoying my full confidence, will go over extremely well. I believe the *latinos* will sit up and take notice of a liberated American woman. I don't want a hidebound Foreign Service type, and so tomorrow I'm sending Miss Savage's nomination to the Senate.''

Glancing at General McCullen, the President said with a little smile: ''And I also see in the file that Miss Savage is the daughter of a former Deputy Director of the CIA. I'm sure you can't object to her family background.''

Thus Julia Savage, age thirty-six, was appointed Ambassador to Malagua—not the youngest United States ambassador ever, but the youngest American *woman* ambassador; one of thirteen women chiefs of mission serving at that time. She was certain that she understood Latin America and its problems better than most people in the government. Better than Terence T. Terhune III, the Assistant Secretary of State for American Republics Affairs, a pedantic career officer who had spent twenty years in Latin America—twice as ambassador—without learning very much about the region, presumably because of his intense preoccupation with the social life and the interests of the American business communities. And with the profound crisis unfolding in Malagua, she was sure that she could change old policies to fit the new reality. The Malaguan dictator had to be persuaded to lessen repression and to move his country toward democracy if an explosion—and a Communist takeover—were to be averted.

A rebel victory would clearly be a disaster for the United States, she believed—in total agreement with the rest of the government, which saw nothing but the shadow of Marxism behind the Malaguan Liberation Front. Julia thought, however, that Washington tended to oversimplify issues, and she was not convinced that Marxism was all that was involved in Malagua. Evolution toward democracy was something the former Ambassador, the dictator's poker-playing crony, had never accepted for Malagua. "Don't rock the boat," he would tell his superiors when he visited Washington on consultations. "Do you want Fidel Castro in Malagua?" And the State Department, even under the Democrats, did *not* rock the boat.

The President and Tom Morelli had been too busy with negotiations with the Soviet Union and China, with the chain of crises in the Middle East, and with the new wars in Indochina (this time without Americans) to pay much attention to Latin America. The only Latin American problem for which the White House had a sustained attention span was Mexico and its oil—the stubborn Mexicans would not agree to guarantee the United States long-term supplies at stable prices—and this was primarily an American domestic matter. The dismissal of the Ambassador in Malagua was the single concession on Latin American policy that Julia had been able to wrest from Tom Morelli and the President.

Now she hoped to build on this victory, and impatient by temperament, she wanted to get started. A compulsive worker—seven days a week at her desk in the Old Executive Office Building across the alley from the White House—Julia Savage was a totally self-assured person, or so she believed. Her only failure, a failure she acknowledged to herself and others, had been the end of her marriage seven years earlier. Of course, the memories of her disastrous marriage to Enrique Palma Rioseco were painful, but Julia's great dedication to her work helped to keep away thoughts about her private life. Because she had not been a success in marriage, even if it had not been wholly her fault, Julia was determined to be a success professionally—and she was, by Washington's exacting standards, *that*.

Julia was powerful and she was beautiful: an extraordinary combination in the jaded capital. And she wore her background well. With the additional advantage of being a single—"extra" —woman, she was on almost every important invitation list, from Georgetown to Embassy Row, and she regularly made the society pages of *The Washington Post* and *The Washington Star*.

Julia knew many Washington bachelors—congressmen; State

Department, Pentagon, and CIA officials; foreign diplomats; and ranking journalists—but she refused to engage in a permanent relationship. The truth was that Julia was afraid of lowering her emotional guard, afraid of falling into sexual dependence, afraid of again losing control over her life. And she knew she was vulnerable—emotionally and sexually.

A few months after going to work on Capitol Hill, Julia had met a congressman from California, an intelligent man in his mid-forties, full of charm and self-assurance. He was separated from his wife, and as he told her over their first dinner, he was about to initiate divorce proceedings. Basic incompatibility, he had said, and no way of repairing the marriage. Not having been to bed with a man since she left Enrique, Julia found it easy to be seduced that evening. She had been unspeakably hungry for sex for years, frequently catching herself fantasizing about lovemaking as she sat in her office or spent occasional lonely evenings in her small apartment, surrounded by books and reports. Julia, however, rejected the idea of casual affairs, one-night stands. It would be demeaning, she told herself.

The Californian was different. Julia was immensely attracted to him—an older, mature man; a tender and experienced lover. The relationship was superbly satisfying, and Julia began to think, if not hope, that he would propose to her after his divorce. But one winter evening, the Congressman blurted out that he had decided to go back to his wife—because of the children, and reelection problems in California. Julia did not flinch. "I understand," she had told him quietly, despising him. "It was good while it lasted."

Afterward Julia made certain that there would be no involvements. She ached emotionally, and sexual abstinence after months of almost nightly lovemaking left her empty and off balance. No, Julia promised herself, she would never again become so dependent on a man. It had already happened twice in her life. She would be better off with a monastic existence, repressing her powerful sexual drives, sublimating them into her work. That was before Malagua.

★

The ambassadorial assignment became another rung on Julia Savage's ladder of success. "Father would be so proud of you," her mother told Julia at the swearing-in ceremony in the Benjamin Franklin Room on the eighth floor of the State Department. She had come down for a week from Boston, again her home since Randolph Savage, the CIA's dashing Deputy Director for Plans (DDP, as it was then called, was the Agency's clandestine "black" side), had been killed in 1968 in a mysterious shooting incident in Amman, Jordan, a year after the Arab–Israeli "Six-Day War."

Eleanor Savage was never told exactly what had happened. The CIA Director, a family friend, had come unexpectedly one morning to the Savage home on Dumbarton Avenue in Georgetown and, with no preamble and no elaboration, had told Eleanor that "Randolph was killed yesterday in Amman in the line of duty. That's all I can tell you." A CIA wife for more than fifteen years, she had asked no questions. In the intelligence service, one does not ask or inquire or insist. One accepts in silence and secrecy, as Eleanor Savage did, the CIA's Intelligence Star awarded posthumously to her husband. Star awards are never announced, nor are reasons given. Julia was in Cali, Colombia, a new bride, when Eleanor telephoned her the news: "Your father was killed. I don't know anything else. I don't ever expect to know." Many years later, working for Senator Mill, Julia discovered that her father's death had somehow been connected with the secret operations of the CIA in providing nuclear-weapons technology to Israel.

Randolph Savage would have been proud of his daughter. He loved success, had achieved success himself, and admired success in others. He adored intrigue, and he was mesmerized by international politics, the never-ending and often lethal game that nations play. He would have envied Julia's going to Malagua and being in the midst of it all—and as the American Ambassador to boot.

The State Department ceremony was a fine Washington social occasion. Secretary Masterson, now all smiles, administered the oath of office to Julia on the Savages' family Bible. Vice President Mill was on hand, along with Tom Morelli from the White House, all the senior State Department officials (with Terhune in special prominence), and a scattering of invited foreign ambassadors, among whom the envoy from Malagua, a first cousin of the dictator, was the most loudly cordial to Julia.

The government of Malagua had granted Julia Savage *agrément* without hesitation. In the first place, the régime would never have thought of offending Washington by rejecting an ambassadorial appointment—much as General Ferrer would have preferred that his old friend Wilbur Breck stay on indefinitely. It had been an exceedingly convenient arrangement for more than ten years. The Presidential Palace in Ciudad Malagua, to be sure, was taken aback by the nomination of a young woman identified with some of the American Administration's more liberal policies; but Ferrer had been promptly reassured by a discreet visit by the CIA Station Chief in Malagua, Jim Morgan, who enjoyed total and immediate entrée to the dictator.

"I wouldn't worry too much about this Julia Savage, Señor Presidente," Morgan said softly. "I can promise you she'll be no trouble. We can keep her in line, if necessary. In a crazy sort of way, this may even be a lucky break for us."

★

After calling on the President, the Vice President, Secretary Masterson, Assistant Secretary of State Terhune, officials at the Pentagon concerned with hemispheric defense, and the tight-lipped men at the Drug Enforcement Agency who reluctantly explained to her the narcotics-traffic problems in Malagua and Central America, Julia Savage drove to the CIA headquarters in Langley, just outside Washington, for her intelligence briefing. This was routine procedure for all new ambassadors, who had to be acquainted in a general way with the workings of the CIA stations attached to their embassies, the identity of the Station

Chief and his deputy, and the overall intelligence picture in the country of their assignment.

Julia received her briefing in the conference room in the seventh-floor Executive Suite, where the offices of the CIA Director and his Deputy are located. Kingsley Duke, the Chief of the Western Hemisphere (WH) Division of the Agency, described and analyzed at length the revolutionary groups in Malagua, their leadership, their strength, and their potential. He was a retired colonel with long service as an Air Force attaché in Latin America, and he spoke with absolute assurance. "The opposition is *completely* controlled by the Cubans and other Marxists," he said. "But the Station in Malagua doesn't believe they have much popular support. Besides, the régime is quite strong. Still, we must watch the opposition, its contacts with Cuba, the flow of funds and arms and propaganda. And we have adequate assets for *that*. You'll meet Jim Morgan, our Station Chief, when you arrive in Ciudad Malagua, and I'm sure you will enjoy working with him. He's first class—one of the best we have."

"I have two questions," Julia said. "First, how do we know that the opposition is 'completely' controlled by the Cubans and the extreme left? Isn't there *any* opposition that is moderate, democratic, or whatever? And second, how do we know that the opposition doesn't have much popular support?"

The Colonel was flustered. Few new ambassadors questioned the accuracy of CIA assessments. "Why," he said with an edge of irritation, "that's what the Malagua Station reports. The boys there know what they're talking about. They have excellent contacts."

"With whom?" Julia asked pleasantly.

"Well, with the G-2 of the National Guard, which is the secret police. They are very good, because they were trained at the U.S. Army School in Panama as well as by the Agency. And the Station has access to the confidential reports prepared for the President of Malagua every day. As I told you, it's a hell of a good operation we're running there. Every time a Cuban agent turns up in Malagua, I hear about it in a matter of hours. Yes, Ambassador Savage, we certainly keep track of them."

"That's very interesting, Colonel," Julia said, "but do you—does the Station—have any contacts with the opposition to make independent assessments? Does the Embassy?"

"Certainly not!" he sputtered. "Certainly not. General Ferrer wouldn't stand for it. We have a clear understanding with the government that all information concerning the internal political situation in Malagua can come to us only—and only—through them."

"You mean as you had in Iran when the Shah was about to be overthrown?"

Colonel Duke gave her a withering stare. "I wouldn't know about Iran," he said icily. "We're very compartmentalized here at the Agency, and that doesn't fall into my area of expertise. I *do* know about Malagua. What I'm trying to tell you, Madam Ambassador, is that we would be interfering in Malagua's domestic affairs if we did any poking around on our own. And you know that the CIA is not supposed to interfere in the politics of foreign countries. The Congress says this is *verboten*. Anyway, the fact is that we aren't permitted to have contacts with the opposition. For that matter, I wouldn't want to have any. I trust the local boys. They know their own country. Obviously, we help them when they ask for it—you know, tracking foreign contacts and that sort of thing."

"Does this ban on opposition contacts apply to the Embassy as well?"

"Sure it does. The rules apply to everybody."

Julia lit a cigarette and stared pensively at the Colonel. "Do you mean to tell me, sir," she said slowly, "that our people, CIA or Embassy, have *no* contacts of any kind among university students, among professors and intellectuals, among any independent-minded Malaguans?"

"No, ma'am—not with any of those people if they are known to oppose the government. They are off limits to us, and I think it should be kept that way. Don't you see that any contacts by United States officials with the opposition, which is Marxist, would only encourage them? And surely you know that it isn't in the national interest of the United States to encourage Communists who are against the established government?''

"Yes, I do see," Julia said, rising from her chair. "This has been a most enlightening conversation. I want to thank you for your time, Colonel."

★

As soon as the door closed after Julia in the conference room, Jim Morgan, the CIA Station Chief in Malagua, walked in through another door from an adjoining room. A tall, lean man just fifty years old, with strong features, reddish hair, and blue eyes, Morgan slumped in an armchair, relighting a cold cigar. Colonel Duke, still seated at the conference table, smiled and asked, "So what did you think of my little chat with the lady Ambassador, Jim? I take it you heard it all."

"Yep, I sure did. Every fucking word of it. It looks like the bitch is out to give us a hard time down in Malagua. All this crap about contacts with the opposition. I think I know what's coming. Fucking liberal bleeding-heart, wanting to play footsie with the Commies. But we'll put a stop to that. Thanks for not letting her know I was here. It's better that we meet in Ciudad Malagua, on my turf."

"How are you going to stop her? After all, she *is* the Ambassador; she has some leverage. She can lean on the White House."

"Bullshit. You know exactly how we're going to play it. Remember the contingency plan we developed after the President announced he was sending Savage to Malagua?"

"You mean using her ex-husband?" the Colonel asked.

"Yeah," Morgan said. "Yeah. Her ex-husband, that guy Enrique Palma Rioseco. We own him, and he knows it. He'll do what I tell him. Anyway, he's volunteered his services in this. And as a matter of fact, I've already sent word to him to meet me next week in the Virgin Islands. I'm going to stop there on my way to Malagua to brief him—and to check on my other operations there."

"Will the Director approve of what you have in mind, Jim? Let's not forget that she's Savage's daughter."

"So? Savage's been dead for a long time. And the Director, bless him, is so busy with other things that I don't think we ought to disturb him with details. You have line authority as the WH boss, and your okay, my dear Colonel, is good enough for me. Do I have your approval?"

Kingsley Duke looked out the window. The CIA park was dark green in the afternoon sun, and he could see Tom Paine's statue, just off the main entrance. "Yes, I suppose you have my approval—orally."

LEAVING the airport access road, Julia Savage's limousine and the two security cars turned right onto a four-lane highway. A large sign proclaimed:

CARRETERA PANAMERICANA—TRECHO MALAGUA
OBRA DEL GOBIERNO DEL SEÑOR PRESIDENTE DE LA REPUBLICA
GENERAL JUAN FERRER BERRIO
EL BENEFACTOR

The Malaguan segment of the Pan American Highway between Guatemala in the north and Nicaragua in the south—the republic forms a triangle, with the Pacific Coast on one side and the Guatemalan and Nicaraguan frontiers on the two other sides—had been built with United States funds, but the Ferrer family was in the habit of taking credit for everything positive and important in the country. The highway had been started by President Anselmo Ferrer, and his name had then appeared on the signs. However, the work was completed under his son Juan Ferrer, who promptly put *his* name on them. This was an example of the Ferrers' sense of continuity: allegiance by the four million Malaguans must be to the *present* ruler—not, sentimentally, to his father or grandfather.

The "Benefactor" title also was hereditary: it went back to the first Ferrer, who had conceived the notion of making political paternalism a principle of modern government. Mayan emperors and the Spanish Crown, the precursors of independent republican Malagua, had practiced paternalism as well, but not with the aplomb of the Ferrers, who had elevated it to the status of an art and a science.

Paternalism in its simplest and historical Latin American sense, certainly as practiced in Malagua, meant that—by definition—all decisions affecting the lives of the people were taken by the ruler and his advisers. To put it another way, those who were governed were regarded as children, destined always to remain children, and strenuously discouraged from learning decision-making even on the most elementary level.

The way early Indian societies were organized, intensely tribal and hierarchical, this control was easily sustained, being further consolidated by the power of the Mayan priests and the mystery of pagan religions. But if rulers exercised total control, they had to offer their subjects parental—or paternal—protection, and in Indian countries of the New World this form of feudalism was more deeply embedded than in medieval Europe. The Mayan emperor, for example, always saw to it that the villages had adequate corn supplies, even in times of drought and flood, from the huge stocks he would amass through taxation. He presided over great religious ceremonies and feasts, providing gifts of food and fermented beverage.

The Ferrers, with Mayan blood in their veins, applied this paternalism to the requirements of a twentieth-century society. Thus medical care, to the extent to which it existed in Malagua, was free to the people, and the régime never tired of reminding them of it through its propaganda organs. Education was also free, though its quality left much to be desired. Social legislation was remarkably advanced, at least in theory. If an urban worker was fired, no matter how miserable his job might have been, the government was supposed to pay unemployment compensation —though in practice, it was virtually impossible to collect. What counted was appearances, and the Ferrers were very good at maintaining them. In an uneducated society, this was not too difficult.

Then there were special occasions. Every year, for instance, a child would be chosen "Best Scholar of Malagua" and, in front of television cameras, be awarded a sum of money by the dictator for further education. Soccer and basketball teams received free equipment from the Ferrers, then competed for the "Benefactor Cup." On high national and religious holidays, the dictator—all three Ferrers did it—appeared at a military parade with uniformed schoolchildren marching behind the soldiers, chanting *vivas* to the ruler. Pomp and circumstance were extremely important in the trappings of Ferrer paternalism, and the dynasty knew how to display it well. It was the art of manipulating the nation.

Julia Savage had read about how the Ferrers ran Malagua, but she had not realized how highly orchestrated the system had become, what a superb act of political deception it was. Now she noticed a smaller sign, pointing to the north, reading:

CIUDAD MALAGUA—35 KM

General Bolívar Ferrer, the first dictator of the dynasty, had once toyed with the idea of renaming the capital "Ciudad Ferrer," but he did not wish to be accused of aping Generalísimo Rafael Trujillo in the Dominican Republic. Juan Ferrer had given some thought to naming the new international airport after himself; he was dissuaded by the New York public-relations firm that advised his government—it would look silly to Americans, he was gently told.

As it was, the main runway extended the length of a narrow valley, and although the new airport had up-to-date electronic equipment and navigational aids, commercial pilots considered the final approach to Malagua one of the most dangerous in Latin America, particularly during the rainy season when clouds and fog hugged the mountains on both sides of the descent path. Clouds and rain usually came in the afternoon during the May–October period—the annual time of bad weather—and airlines scheduled their flights into Malagua during the morning hours. Julia Savage's plane touched down just before twelve o'clock on July 7, when the valley was still bathed in the sun (and at Malagua's altitude of 5,000 feet, the sun burned as strongly in the rainy season as in the dry months), and during the approach she had a breathtaking view of the hilly city nestled between diamond-blue Lake Taxchilán and the Mixull volcano. The pilot smoothly banked the DC-9 jet at 1,500 feet over Mixull—looking down, Julia saw the darkish vapors curling malevolently inside the crater—then headed the aircraft into the valley. The plane was tossed by a crosswind in the canyon and slammed by a downdraft, but the captain gave the turbines a little more power and stabilized it. Then they were on the ground, the wheels hitting the runway hard. Julia's seat companion, a florid American priest with whom she had chatted intermittently during the flight, crossed himself, and said, "You know, it's always tough to get into Malagua, but I guess God watches over us every time."

★

The souped-up lead car leaped forward on the highway, and Salvador gunned the Chrysler's engine to keep pace. Within seconds, the motorcade was traveling at nearly 70 miles per hour, whizzing past slower traffic. "Do we always drive this fast?" Julia asked McVeigh. "Well, we try to," he said. "If we go more slowly, we're a better target for sharpshooters, if there are any around. Salvador here handles the car so well he could win at Le Mans, and we don't want to be sitting ducks."

There were rows of coffee trees climbing up the hillsides of the valley, and here and there, small *finca* houses, painted pink or blue or white. A man in a leather hat and a short jacket was riding his small *paso fino* horse along the highway, the animal lifting its forelegs gracefully. "It's so lovely and peaceful here," Julia remarked, glancing at the coffee plantations. Above the neatly spaced coffee trees, whose beans were turning dark red, a thick forest covered the mountain ridges. "Right," Mac said, "it *looks* peaceful in daytime; but the forest up there is thick with *guerrilleros* the National Guard simply cannot flush out. It's a war zone, and it reminds me of the Mekong Delta, full of the Viet Cong when night fell. I'm getting this *déjà vu* feeling; maybe it's time for me to get out of here."

Mac sighed and closed his eyes. He was a heavyset man in his late forties, normally full of life and fun; totally dedicated to the Foreign Service, he had taken one hardship assignment after another. He had agreed to stay on with Julia for a while, both out of friendship and out of residual hope that with his help she might be able to turn things around a bit. But now McVeigh was exhausted and depressed. His three years in Malagua, serving under an ambassador for whom he felt personal and intellectual contempt, an ambassador with whom he disagreed on practically every major point of assessment and policy, had drained the DCM. He knew he was simply going through the motions; he had begun to think that the whole effort was pointless and that he probably should call it quits, going for early retirement. However, Julia had a direct line to the White House through Tom Morelli, and, of course, the Vice President. So McVeigh resolved to wait a while longer.

But his family life was deteriorating under the force of Malagua's violence. The Embassy staff worked long hours and thus had an escape from the ceaseless terrorism, bomb explosions, shoot-outs, and kidnappings—the overwhelming reality of Malagua. But for dependents, especially wives, it was hell around the clock. It was not safe for American women to go shopping alone —to the city's fruit-and-vegetable markets, or downtown stores —and there were no security personnel available to protect the dependents. All children had been sent to Stateside schools, and the wives were virtually imprisoned at home, behind the high walls of the villas, with nothing to do except brood and, increasingly, drink alone while their husbands were away at the office. There was not much social life in the evenings, because it was too dangerous to venture out after dark.

Mac McVeigh's wife, Sonia, once a charming, outgoing woman, often broke into sobs when a car or a motorcycle backfired. "Christ, I'm afraid—I'm scared sick—can't you understand that?" Sonia would ask Mac. "I just want out, out of this

God-damned place.'' And Mac had, in fact, decided to send
Sonia back to Washington on a compassionate basis, though he
disliked the example it would set for other officers' wives. He
would have to discuss it with Julia after she got settled.

Soon, the green countryside gave way to the dirty ugliness of
the suburban apron of Ciudad Malagua's southern *barrios*. Boxlike concrete and wooden houses, each just large enough to shelter a family (and Julia remembered from her briefing that a
Malaguan family had, statistically, 4.3 children), lined the Pan
American Highway. More windowpanes were broken than not,
the jagged glass held together with tape or covered over with old
newspapers. The doors stood ajar to catch a breath of breeze in
the early-afternoon heat. Dark-skinned and copper-skinned and
white-skinned children loitered in front of their dwellings, watching the traffic, or splashing in slimy puddles from the rain of the
night before. Naked or wrapped in rags, the children had the
telltale appearance of severe undernourishment: distended bellies, stick-thin limbs, heads too large for the bodies, and vacant
eyes. This was the sprawling and labyrinthine Barrio del Sur, a
vast realm of misery, receding away from the Highway and covering a good square mile.

Women, barefoot or shod in wooden clogs, sat listlessly by the
doors. The young ones all seemed to be big with child, motionless
madonnas in torn calico dresses. The men sat in languid idleness
at open-door *cantinas,* drinking beer, or tiny glasses of sugar-
cane *aguardiente.* The younger men crowded around bar juke-
boxes, from which emanated earsplitting disco sounds. It was at
least a touch of life.

But the concrete pillboxes were not the worst among the *barrio*
dwellings. Farther back, toward the mountains, was the domain
of shacks: thrown-together huts of wood planks or plywood sections, with cardboard flaps for windows, frayed curtains for
doors, and wide banana leaves for roofs. Scrawny chickens and
black snouty pigs were masters of the refuse-filled alleyways.
Zopilotes, black birds of prey, circled low and lazily overhead.

"This is where the rebels recruit quite a few of their fighters,''
Mac McVeigh remarked. "The *barrio* kids—the tough, street-

wise ones who can't or won't find jobs, who finish primary or high school and have no place to go in life, or those who drop out for whatever reason. They're the kids the National Guard picks up when they hang around in town, and beats the shit out of. They are bitter, frustrated, disenchanted, full of hate. I guess they watch their parents rotting away, and want something better for themselves. So when the Frente sends recruiters down to the *barrios* to tell them that life can be better if *only* Ferrer can be overthrown, they find very receptive listeners. And by now there's prestige, a badge of honor, attached to being a *malaguista,* to having a gun and a purpose. There's a *machismo* element in all of this, and why not? It's part of the culture here, as it is elsewhere in Latin America. In the end it all comes together, and the Frente are very clever about the whole thing."

"But the *malaguistas* are not just *barrio* kids, are they?" Julia asked.

"No, of course not," McVeigh said. "They come from everywhere in the Malaguan society. No matter what you've been told in Washington, the Frente is quickly growing into a national movement. An important segment are university students, students who have just graduated, and young professionals. That's where you find your leadership. And intellectuals, too. And very secretly, the Frente even has sympathizers among young businessmen who feel, and rightly, that they are being screwed by the Ferrer family. There are peasants in the mountains who help the *malaguistas*—the very poor Indian peasants belonging, and I mean *belonging,* to the rich farmers. Whenever the peasants try to protest, to get more than starvation wages from the *hacendados*—and the Ferrers are among them—the National Guard or the rural police are summoned, and they get killed.

"To tell you the truth, Julia, I'm not sure whether the régime is more scared of the Frente or of the peasants. A lot of rich people here still remember the peasant uprising in 1934, when the Indians marched on the *haciendas* and the towns, and massacred scores of landowners and their foremen. I guess the big fear is that the Frente will attract the peasants to its cause. Finally, the rebels get important support from segments of the Catholic

Church. One of them, as you know, is Bishop Pepe Vargas; but there are young parish priests in the villages who cannot stomach the social injustice and the brutality, and there are pro-Frente Jesuits here and there. For example, there is a Jesuit around we've been hearing a lot about lately, a Father Rolando Asturias.''

Julia noticed that the *barrio* houses, the concrete boxes and the shacks, all had electricity and television aerials on the roofs. "How can they afford it?'' she asked. "Well,'' McVeigh said, "this is the Benefactor's idea of the Roman circus in the modern Central American environment. The only reason, as far as I can make out, why the government provided the *barrios* with electricity—but no water or sewerage, mind you—is so that the people can have television to be kept down, quiet and passive. In the evening, they have *telenovelas*—you know, soap operas—from Mexico, or something like *Kojak* dubbed in Spanish. On Saturdays and Sundays, it's soccer games. Television here is dreamland—much more so than back home in the South Bronx or in the slums of San Antonio. Television is supposed to keep the good people of Malagua mentally occupied and in line, not thinking of poverty and hunger and lack of decent jobs, or any jobs—and certainly not thinking of revolution.''

McVeigh grimaced and went on: "President Ferrer says, approvingly, of course, that television is the opium of the people. He contributes to this national unreality when he makes a TV speech. Listening to him, you'd think Malagua is the happiest land in the world—thanks, of course, to the Benefactor. And by the way, the General has nothing against the real thing in the way of opium, which here is marijuana—very high quality, I'm told. I wouldn't be surprised if he had a hand in the drug traffic; he's in every other kind of business here. That's what our narcs think, but God forbid the Embassy should ever say a word about it officially. He would scream all the way to Washington, so we just keep our mouths shut. But you'll get your briefing from the Drug Enforcement Agency guys here. . . .''

"Yes, I've heard something about it in Washington,'' Julia

said. "But tell me, Mac, where do these people get their TV sets? They must cost an arm and a leg."

"Oh, they buy them on the installment plan—a few malaguas a month, which everybody can come up with, one way or another. The annual interest is around one hundred percent, and needless to say, the Ferrer family controls all the distributorships and the financing. So the boss man has it in every way: he puts the poor bastards into lifetime debt, makes a fortune from it in the process, and sees to it that television keeps their minds numbed. Neat, isn't it? You've got to admit the man is a genius."

"I guess he is," Julia said. "I can't wait to meet him."

"You will in a week or so. Your presentation of credentials is tentatively set for July 25. Tomorrow I'll confirm the date with my friend Moreno, the Protocol Chief, if he has recovered from the airport scene."

★

The American motorcade slowed down and turned right onto a downtown street that linked the Pan American Highway with the city. Gonzalo, the bodyguard sitting in front of Julia, tensed and cocked his submachine gun. McVeigh said, "This is the part I don't like at all, driving through the town. There are no alternative routes, and it's no secret that you've arrived today."

Suddenly, the car radio came alive: "This is Base to Number Six. Over." Salvador picked up the microphone and acknowledged the call. A Marine sergeant at the Base spoke over the static: "Mr. Anders in Political Section has a message for the Ambassador or the DCM. The message is: Colonel Saavedra was killed by unidentified gunmen in front of his house an hour ago. There are no other details. Okay? Over and out."

"My God!" McVeigh exclaimed. "Manuel Saavedra was chief of G-2 in the National Guard—the head of Ferrer's secret police —and the President's closest friend. There'll be hell to pay. Ferrer will avenge Saavedra's death even if he has to kill a thousand people. The creep probably deserved it, but I never thought the Frente could pull off a coup like that. Saavedra never went anywhere without a half-dozen bodyguards. This could be a whole new ball game. Let me drop you off at the Residence, Julia. Then I better hightail it to the office and get busy.''

"Are you going to call Washington?'' Julia asked, glancing down at the dried blood on her white suit.

"Absolutely. Unless Anders has already thought of it. He's quick on his feet.''

"Do you think the Station Chief can find out quickly just how it happened, and what comes next?''

"You mean Jim Morgan? No, he's in Washington. Hasn't come back yet. I thought you knew he was away.''

"As a matter of fact, I did *not* know,'' Julia said, her green eyes flashing. "When I went for my briefing at the CIA three days ago, I was told that Morgan was in Malagua, and I would meet him on arrival here. Hell, I didn't even know he was away at all. What's going on, anyway?''

"Well, Julia, this Jim Morgan is a very mysterious gentleman who plays it close to the vest. About two weeks ago he told me he was leaving—Langley had called him for consultations, or whatever—and I haven't seen him since. Luckily he has a competent deputy, a fellow named Crespo, who should be able to get the dope for us. I'll talk to him as soon as I get back to the office. But I have no idea why they lied to you.''

"I don't either,'' Julia snapped. "But believe me, I mean to find out. Either I run this Embassy or I don't. It's as simple as that. And I *do* propose to run it, whether Mr. Morgan and the CIA like it or not. He'll find that out soon enough.''

★

They were now on Avenida Bolívar, Ciudad Malagua's principal commercial thoroughfare, two lanes wide, and almost empty during this lunch and siesta hour. Climbing rather steeply toward El Cerro, the city's highest point, where the Presidential Palace stood, Avenida Bolívar had nearly been restored from the devastating earthquake just before Christmas of 1972, the powerful tremor that leveled the capital's hillside working-class section. To help rebuild the city, foreign funds, mainly from the United

States, had poured into Malagua—and the U.S. Army Corps of Engineers had decontaminated Lake Taxchilán, in which hundreds of bodies were awash—but though more than a decade had passed, President Ferrer had made no effort to reconstruct the poorer areas. He insisted that there were other and greater national priorities (one of them was a luxury hotel-and-casino on the lake). Virtually every citizen of Malagua believed that the President and his friends had pocketed the relief funds; it was the kind of thing they expected from the Ferrer family.

The merchants of Avenida Bolívar, many of them General Ferrer's business partners, had collected enough in insurance payments to fix up their area. Besides, easy and cheap loans were available to them from local banks, always eager to please the dictator and his associates. A new cinema had recently opened on the Avenida; the film being shown this day was *Close Encounters of the Third Kind*. Next to the theater, Yamaha motorcycles were on display behind a huge window. Malagua's *jeunesse dorée*, the sons of the country's rich and powerful men, raced on these machines from party to party through Ciudad Malagua's nighttime stillness, the backfiring sounding to the shuttered-in citizens like a fusillade between the National Guard and the *guerrilleros*.

Then there was, on a corner, Ciudad Malagua's leading Chinese restaurant—"The Smiling Buddha"—with a five-foot ideograph sign. There were scores of Cantonese eating establishments in the city, a reminder of the fact that at the turn of the century British railroad builders had imported thousands of coolies from southern China to lay the line from the capital to the Pacific Coast port of San Pablo. (Malagua's Indians were not considered adequate for the task, being thought to be too lazy.) The Chinese families had stayed on, turning to commerce, restaurants, and truck farming in and around Ciudad Malagua. One of the most notorious anti-Ferrer *guerrilleros*, a mixed-blood *malagueño* who had been killed in an affray with the National Guard several years ago, was called "El Chino." Malagua also had a scattering of other races; a dentist of East Indian extraction personally attended the Ferrer family, and quite a few prosperous stores were owned by descendants of immigrants from what had been British India.

Avenida Bolívar led to El Cerro and its plaza—and the Presidential Palace. Normally the limousine would have crossed the wide plaza and then proceeded downhill, past the Cathedral, to the opulent district on Lake Taxchilán where the Embassy residence was located. But this afternoon the entrance to the plaza was blocked by two armored cars, their machine guns trained down Avenida Bolívar, and by a dozen National Guardsmen. The murder of the secret-police chief must have caused the dictator to adopt stringent security measures. For all the régime knew, McVeigh told Julia, Saavedra's slaying might have been intended as a signal for a major uprising.

"Christ, we *must* get through," McVeigh said. "I don't want to get lost in those narrow streets below the plaza, but we can't just sit here. The Frente's urban guerrillas are on the loose, and all we need is to be spotted by them." Salvador, the driver, was already urgently talking on the radio to the lead sedan, which had stopped at the roadblock. One of the bodyguards got out of the car ahead, his submachine gun in hand, and spoke to the National Guard officer in charge, pointing to the Chrysler. The officer nodded, the security man got back into the sedan, and the motorcade moved forward.

The plaza was deserted, except for armed soldiers standing in a skirmish line in front of the Palace, a sprawling white-stucco colonial structure. The men belonged to General Ferrer's elite military unit, his praetorian guard. He trusted them implicitly; their officers were on his personal payroll and enjoyed special privileges, such as duty-free imports of cars, liquor, and whatever else they desired. In Malagua, this was one way to ensure absolute loyalty.

They drove across the El Cerro plaza, and a short stretch of street took them to the Ciudad Malagua Cathedral, unfinished and inhospitable. Except when Don Pepe Vargas Merino, the tough fighting bishop from the northern highlands, made an appearance to preach a sermon on social justice and political freedom, people tended to stay away from the House of the Lord.

The Church, symbolized by the Cathedral, had little to offer them. The Roman Catholic hierarchy of Malagua, headed by Archbishop Jesús María Ledesma, an unctuous and self-indulgent prelate, was firmly in Ferrer's camp. The General's hatred of Communists, the proponents of Antichrist, had won him the respect and admiration of the higher clergy. In him they saw a leader who could control the growing number of Malaguans who were turning away from the true religion, undermining secular and ecclesiastical authority, and daring to advocate heresies like birth control.

Bishop Vargas—who frequently said, "I'm accused of being against the government, but that isn't true; it just happens that I am *for* the people and the government is *against* the people"— was a great irritant to these self-righteous clerics. He simply had to be in cahoots with the Communists, the other bishops told each other and the Archbishop. Letters denouncing Don Pepe had been sent to the Vatican by the Archbishop, but the Holy See, disturbed by deep splits in the Church everywhere, was reluctant to become involved in a controversy in Malagua.

Meanwhile, the Cathedral was often a battlefield. Only the summer before, for example, Julia remembered from newspaper stories, thirty or forty persons had been machine-gunned to death by Ferrer's armored cars as a crowd surged out of the sanctuary in a demonstration for *pan y libertad*—bread and freedom—following a fiery sermon by Don Pepe Vargas. Several months before, the dictator's sharpshooters had flushed out two young *guerrilleros,* one a girl, from the Cathedral's bell tower, where they had sought refuge after spraying midtown walls at night with anti-Ferrer slogans. They had been executed on the spot.

Now oppressive heat and emptiness hung over the Cathedral. Yes, the usual beggars and old women—the *pordioseros,* who mumble, *"Por Dios, por Dios"* as they whine for alms to every person hurrying past—had sought shelter under the portico, as they did every day and every night. *Pordioseros* always slept on the steps of the church, in clement and inclement weather, covered with their rags, piling up old newspapers for pillows, cursing each other, preferring to share bits of dry bread with mangy dogs rather than with one another, scratching their fleabites, and shouting maledictions at Miguel, the idiot, whose piercing cries for his mother disrupted their fitful sleep. Among the *pordioseros* there were invalids with amputated limbs, shriveled men displaying bleeding stumps and festering wounds. Blackflies buzzed over their wounds and their faces in a low, irritating monotone. A *mestizo* who had once earned a living as a puppeteer lay on the steps in drunken stupor, his arms and hands jerking nervously now and then as if in memory of his lost art.

On a clear day, one could see the Pacific Ocean from the Cathedral square, as from El Cerro, and, below, the oblong outline of Lake Taxchilán, on whose shores the Mayans had built one of their holy cities during the Golden Age of the old Empire in the fifth century after Christ. But the beauty of Malagua held no interest for the mendicants.

A narrow street of the old colonial town descended from the Cathedral to the lake. This was the poor peoples' downtown district known as "La Culebra" (the cobra), and this was where the last earthquake had wrought the greatest damage. Hardly a house along the fetid street was intact. Some houses were gutted from the roof down to the ground floor, entire façades gone as if they had been sliced off by a giant machete. Makeshift curtains of blankets and tarpaulins protected what was left of rooms on each floor from the weather and the eyes of neighbors and passersby. Here and there a staircase was left standing, like a fleshless spine. Elsewhere ladders had to be put up for the inhabitants to reach their lairs.

But people lived in these caves of smashed masonry, for these were their homes. Some of the caverns had been fashioned into pathetic shops—*bodeguitas* and *farmacias* (where ancient Indian remedies were sold along with aspirin and Alka-Seltzer) and butcher shops where flies stuck to dark red slabs of meat like large grains of pepper. A Coca-Cola sign flapped in the rising wind (the afternoon rain was approaching) over one *bodega;* a poster promoting Cerveza del Rey, produced in a brewery owned by the Ferrer family, was plastered over the crooked door of another shop. The strains of a *mambo* blared from a radio in one of the hovels. A superannuated prostitute—a *puta*—with flabby breasts and a painted face stared blankly from a window. She sat there from habit: she had no customers in La Culebra. And in what remained of doorways, people snoozed and snored in the afternoon heat, just as at the House of the Lord.

"My God, this is *awful*," Julia said to McVeigh. "Maybe we can embarrass the Benefactor by printing some postcards showing La Culebra—the real Malagua? It'd be quite a contrast with all that pretty stuff, blue lakes and majestic volcanoes, they're cranking out for the tourists. Maybe this would be a nice covert-action project for Mr. Morgan of the CIA, to have pictures taken of where Malaguans sleep. Oh, I know I shouldn't be sarcastic, but I just don't know what to say about this horror." Foolishly, she was reminded of an old story about Tegucigalpa, in Honduras. An American visitor, driving in the evening from his hotel to a dinner party, asked his taxi driver why so many people were asleep in doorways. "Because it's night, sir," the man replied.

"I doubt Ferrer will do much about the *barrio*," Mac told her. "He's spent the relief money on God knows what—you know, he's borrowing money abroad again. Tourists probably think this is picturesque, the natives in their habitat. Anyway, nobody in his right mind expects any rebuilding to be done."

"Well, I'm going to take this up with the President," Julia said stubbornly. "After all, American taxpayers' money was sent to Malagua for reconstruction."

"Good luck. I'll be interested in hearing what he says."

★

At the bottom of the hill, the *barrio* gave way to a middle-class neighborhood. The houses were intact, the pavement reasonably clean, and cars were parked in front of two- or three-story apartment buildings and tidy private homes. The small businessmen, less-than-successful lawyers and doctors, teachers, and bureaucrats who lived there were described by optimistic Embassy reports as Malagua's "growing middle class," the guarantors of its social and political stability. The former Ambassador had written in a recent dispatch, Julia remembered, that "too many Malaguans have now acquired too much of a stake in the country's prosperity, and their own prosperity, to let themselves be manipulated by a small group of Marxist agitators. Democracy is on the march in Malagua, slowly but surely."

A half-mile farther south, there was a small park planted with ceiba and hibiscus trees. Children liked to play in the park, watching the tame sloths on the ceibas and the domesticated five-foot-long black-and-gray iguana, almost all tail, that lived in the shrubs. In the center, General Bolívar Ferrer had erected a statue of himself, a thoughtful statesman in military uniform, peering into the distance. Most of the children playing in the park had no idea who this bronze hero was.

Avenida Ferrer, the most exclusive boulevard in Ciudad Malagua, bisected the plush residential district as it ran from the park toward Lake Taxchilán. Fifty years before, it had been called Avenida Libertad, but the first Ferrer had been keener on memorializing the dynasty than on commemorating the achievement of independence from Spain. The residential area, known as Las Brisas, was the preserve of embassies' residences and opulent private mansions surrounded by high walls, some topped with barbed wire. Ceiba trees, which had been sacred to the Mayans, lined the handsome boulevard. Avenida Ferrer was expensively cool and quiet, and entirely empty, except for an occasional passing car, and for National Guardsmen with submachine guns standing or pacing in front of many of the great houses. It was a different face of Malagua, a different world.

"See all the soldiers?" Mac asked. "We've had so many kidnappings and bomb throwings that the government had to assign the National Guard around the clock to protect the residences of ambassadors, and for that matter, of all the friends of the Ferrers who live in this district. Some of them also have their own bodyguards, like private armies. You'll be living in an armed camp. It's not pleasant, but there's no other way. State of siege, as I was telling you."

The motorcade stopped at the heavy iron gates of a walled house, the United States Residence. There were bunkerlike observation posts atop the yellow outer walls, Malaguan policemen peering down at the cars through the slits. A searchlight was mounted next to each bunker. National Guardsmen stood outside the gates. Three security men leaped out of the lead sedan, fanning out in a protective screen as the electrically operated gates opened to let in Julia's limousine and the follow car. A concrete guardhouse sat inside the walls, an incongruous sight in the midst of lawns and flower beds, and a young Marine in a blue tunic and white cap and gloves stepped out and smartly saluted the new Ambassador.

"This is home," McVeigh said as Salvador eased the limousine into the semicircular gravel driveway, bringing it to a stop in front of the door of the Residence. Julia saw the Stars-and-Stripes on a flagpole in the garden. The mahogany door opened, and an elderly black man in a white jacket bowed gravely. "Welcome, Madam Ambassador," he said in English in a lilting West Indian accent. "I am Dudley, the principal butler." Turning to Mac, he said, "Mr. McVeigh, would you please call your office at once? Mr. Anders is most anxious to speak with you, sir."

"I hope," Mac said, "it's not more bad news." He disappeared into the library, rejoining Julia in the foyer of the Residence a few moments later. Julia looked at him questioningly. "Anders says that Ferrer has just decreed modified martial law for thirty days because of the Saavedra killing. The Congress will confirm it tomorrow—they always go through constitutional motions, and the President will have a free hand for a month to try to clean up the place. It's going to be something, all right. Yeah, it's bad news again."

3

In Malagua the news was almost always bad. It had started
with the name. *Malagua* is a contraction of the Spanish words
mala agua, which mean "bad water." The bad water must have
been a reference to Lake Taxchilán, as Mayan Indians had called
it for centuries, if not millennia, before the Spanish Conquest.
The meaning of the word *Taxchilán* is obscure, but scholars do
know that the suffix *chilán* stands for "priestly diviner." Archeological studies have determined that in the fifth century the
Mayans built a city named Taxchilán on the shores of the oblong
lake of the same name. This was the beginning of the Early
Mayan Classic Period, and nearby Palenque and Pestac were
erected roughly at the same time.

Long prosperous, Taxchilán was destroyed three or four centuries later by an unknown catastrophe, though historians believe
that a volcanic eruption in the lakebed created a tidal wave which
engulfed the city. Culturally and scientifically advanced as the
Mayans were, they believed that the end of the world would be
marked by an inundation. Thus they were convinced that there
had been three worlds prior to their world, each destroyed by a
natural catastrophe. The first world was ended, according to ancient Mayan lore, by *haiyococab,* which means "water over the
earth"—a vast deluge. The inhabitants of that first world were

dwarfs, who built great sacred cities and temples in absolute darkness because the sun did not yet exist. And when the sun shone for the first time, the dwarfs—the *saiyam uinicob*—turned into stone figures. Then came the deluge. The next two worlds too were swept away by deluges. In the eighth or ninth century, it was life in the *fourth* world. But the Mayans knew that this one as well would be swept some day by a new *haiyococab,* in which the waters of the lakes and the oceans would swallow forever the land and the people.

The Mayans, possessed of extraordinary religious superstitions, may have well concluded, historians say, that the *chilán*'s spirit that inhabited the lake was an evil one, exacting the terrible punishment of the destruction of the city of Taxchilán. Thus the lake's waters were *bad,* and the *haiyococab* prophecy had come true once more, ending the *fourth* world. And as far as the Mayans were concerned, it had to be so: in their superstitions, more things were thought to bring bad luck than brought good luck.

Mayan religions, like other religions, firmly forecast the ultimate end of the world as it was known, because nothing in creation could be eternal. The descendants of the Mayans were also fatalistic about life and death; it really mattered little what humans did, for their destinies were held by deities. If one did not die today, the end could come tomorrow at the hands of Ah Puch, the Mayan god of death. Earthquakes alternated with hurricanes, and after the Spanish conquest, in about the year 1525, smallpox decimated the Yucatán Maya. All one could do was try to placate the angry deities—they *always* were angry at man— and to please the good ones in the Mayan pantheon. Thus human sacrifice, then as now.

★

The Indians passed on their superstitions and lore to the first Spanish *conquistadores,* who reached the plateau where Ciudad Malagua now stands in the first quarter of the sixteenth century —more than five hundred years after the disappearance of the city of Taxchilán. The first known mention of "Mala Agua" appears in the chronicles of Frei Bienvenido Mosca, a monk-scribe who accompanied one of the early Spanish expeditions to the mountains of Central America. The Spaniards were in quest of gold and silver and precious gems, and Frei Bienvenido noted that "there exist vast treasures in the sands near the shores of the very blue [*muy azul*] lake, in which the natives claim there lives bad water [*mala agua*]." Frei Bienvenido's chronicle, along with subsequent reports from the territory, have been preserved in the Archive of the Indies in Seville.

Mala Agua became *Malagua,* and the name stuck. Perhaps because *conquistadores* had a morbid, if defiant, sense of humor, this was the name they gave to their first settlement on Lake Taxchilán. Or perhaps in part it was because "Malagua" sounded like "Málaga," reminding the Andalusians among the settlers of their ancient Mediterranean. In any event, on August 27, 1535, the settlement was formally named Ciudad de Nuestra Señora de Malagua. The Spaniards professed to be very religious, and most of the towns they founded in the New World were named after saints and madonnas, sometimes invented for the occasion. In the case of Malagua, it may have been spiritual insurance against Ah Puch and the *chilán.* To this day, a dark and rather crude *Madonna and Child,* said to have been painted in 1567 (perhaps by Frei Bienvenido himself), adorns the altar of Ciudad Malagua's unfinished Cathedral. She is Our Lady of Malagua.

As it turned out, however, Our Lady of Malagua was not much of a protector. Despite Frei Bienvenido's enthusiastic reports, there was precious little gold and silver around Lake Taxchilán. Most of the gold ornaments the good friar had observed on the local Indians had come from further north, from the Yucatán Peninsula, and from around Copán and Tikal, where the great temples of the Mayan empire once dominated the land. The adornments filtered down southwest to Taxchilán over centuries of wars, migrations, and tribal marriages.

What Taxchilán had was maize—the Mayans' staple food— the maize to whose gods the copper-skinned Indians prayed the year around, and which the Spaniards learned to live on, in addition to what they could hunt and fish.

Malagua had few riches, few heroes, little romance. Even at the apex of Mayan glory, the area never had great metropolises like Uxmal, Tikal, or Chichén Itzá—just second-class cities like Taxchilán. And under the first centuries of Spanish rule, Malagua attracted chiefly impecunious adventurers, sentenced criminals, and lost souls. Yet the colonizers found Malagua to their taste: the country was stunningly beautiful, with its peaks and valleys and lakes and lush vegetation; the climate of the *altiplano* was pleasant—hot but dry, except for the rainy season; there was plenty of water for drinking and irrigation from the big lake (and other lakes) and from mountain streams; and the Indians (whose tribal societal fabric and advanced culture, including an astounding knowledge of astronomy and geometry, were summarily destroyed) were excellent farmhands and workers. Pagan Indians lived in coastal jungles—only the Pacific Coast port of San Pablo, where Spanish galleons visited twice a year, was "civilized" and had a mule trail to the capital—and in the rain forests of the north. They seldom ventured out, and missionary priests were content to confine catechization of Indians to the settlements.

After several generations, a creole aristocracy emerged in the towns, and the families with the greatest business acumen began to accumulate fortunes from sugar and coffee that, for Malagua, were quite respectable. A social life developed, and soon there were dancing evenings at the homes of the Governor and of the leading citizens. At the court in Madrid, Malagua was something of a joke, but the Malaguans—that is, the Spaniards and the creoles—were not unhappy. Indians, on the other hand, kept degenerating more and more as a race. The Spanish men savored the bodies of the maidens who descended from Mayan kings and princes, and Malagua became in time something of a *mestizo* land. The Indians lost their culture and identity, but they were recompensed with Christianity and an admixture of Castilian, Andalusian, and Huelvan blood.

European conquest, in this case Spanish conquest, is usually held accountable for the disappearance of the great American civilizations: the Mayan, the Aztec, and the Inca. The colonizers, with their penchant for introducing Christianity and their way of life along with the importation of disease strains from the Old World, are generally believed to have killed the superb ancient cultures of the Americas, cultures that with the Mayans went back many millennia before Christ. That was when the Mayans developed their extraordinary agricultural system, based on maize, which still prevailed, though only in a fragmentary fashion, in modern-day Malagua.

Actually, modern research shows that Mayan history began about 9000 B.C. Between 3300 B.C. and 2500 B.C., the period known as Progreso, Mayans started engaging in farming. Sometime about 250 B.C., the Mayans' culture entered into its most glorious epoch. In rain-forest lowlands they constructed a far-flung and highly complex system of irrigation canals, which made possible extensive maize agriculture and, in turn, the supplying with food of the great temple cities. It took the use of airborne radar surveys in the late 1970s—two millennia later—for scholars to realize how magnificently the Mayans had mastered the art of irrigation.

But a closer look at Mayan history, Julia Savage discovered as she did her homework before flying to Malagua, suggested that the civilization of the Maya was already under fearsome pressures even before the first Spaniard set foot in Middle America. Something had gone awry—perhaps the eternal curse of Ah Puch, the God of Death, being inexorably fulfilled—long before the Conquest, and the Spaniards simply completed what Ah Puch had already set in motion. The fate of the Maya may be one of history's strangest mysteries.

The late Sylvanus G. Morley, probably the leading authority on the subject, has written that the Mayans had produced the "greatest native American civilization," that their maize cultivation system was "one of the world's most notable agricultural experiments," and that the numerical system devised by Mayan priests for their incredibly complex sacred-year and civil calendars in the fourth century B.C. "even today stands as one of the brilliant achievements of the human mind." The conception of the mathematical quantity of zero was a "notable intellectual accomplishment" of the Maya.

The Mayans who inhabited the mountain ranges and plateaus of the Central American *cordillera,* where Malagua lies today, were not the most advanced among their brethren (it was always the same story with Malaguan history), but Taxchilán produced masterpieces of low-relief sculpture on temple tablets in the seventh and eighth centuries after Christ, the climax of the Golden Age. To this day, Malagua was a treasure trove of archeological findings, and as Julia Savage knew, the Embassy had to look after absentminded American archeologists constantly getting themselves into trouble with the authorities for trespassing and similar minor sins.

In the eighth century, however, the civilization of the southern Maya, the forefathers of Malaguans, began to decline. Late in the ninth century, their territory was invaded by Nahuatl-speaking warrior tribes from Mexico. About the end of the first millennium, Toltec from Tula, in northwest Mexico, overran Mayan lands, doing away with the classic culture. The Toltec's Lord Kukulcán, the "Feathered Serpent," imposed his rule on the Maya; Mayan cities were destroyed and abandoned.

What historians call the "Period of Mayan Disintegration" began in 1461, when the great city of Mayapán ("The Standards of the Maya") was leveled by another wave of northern invaders. In 1464, it was the great hurricane that flattened maize fields and villages. The first Spaniards came to the lands of the Mayans in 1520, their first gift to them being pestilence, "great pustules that rotted the body" of the Indians, as a contemporary chronicler put it. With or without the Spaniards, the Mayan civilization was collapsing under the deluge of disasters. Frei Diego de Landa, the first serious Spanish historian of the Maya, summed it up in these words in 1556:

> Since the last plague, more than fifty years have now passed, the mortality of war was twenty years prior, the pestilence of the swelling was sixteen years before the wars, and the hurricane another sixteen years before that, and twenty-two or twenty-three years

after the destruction of the city of Mayapan. Thus according to this count it has been 125 years since its overthrow, within which the people of this country have passed through the calamities described.

Small wonder, then, that the Mayan culture and civilization had reached a point of such total exhaustion that the society was rent asunder as well. It was left to the Spanish *conquistadores* to pick up the pieces of that ancient civilization, and grind them further into dust. Officially, the Mayan "Disintegration" period ended in 1717, with the Mayans totally subjugated to the Spaniards as chattels and impoverished farmhands, their astounding heritage buried by history and their monuments overgrown by the jungle.

★

And the gods stayed angry with Malagua. Earthquakes came often in this geologically unsettled volcanic region, often most devastatingly. Earth tremors caused tidal waves on the large lakes and on the Pacific Coast. Nominally Christian, the Indians of Malagua—deep inside—still believed in their Mayan myths. The tidal waves were, clearly, *haiyococab*. If the Christian God was "good," as the Spanish priests said, He could not cause such grief and havoc among His flock. It simply made no sense, and neither did priestly explanations that the catastrophes were God's way of "testing" his people to determine whether they were worthy of Paradise in the Hereafter. The priests always fell back on these unintelligible assurances when they were unable to explain the simplest things. Mayan religious traditions, on the other hand, were perfectly logical: there were Ah Puch, the god of death, and Chac, the god of rain, who was crucially important for maize crops, and in the end, everyone knew exactly where he or she stood. The evil Ah Puch brought disaster, and had to be assuaged with animal and human sacrifice. The good Chac brought felicity, and all he required was prayer and dance. But one never knew what to expect from the Christian God.

In any case, Ciudad Malagua was hit by thirty-four major earthquakes between 1600 (the first quake recorded by the Spanish came that year) and 1972 (the last one on record). In the interval, the city was completely destroyed five times. In 1756, when the capital had a population of forty thousand, an awesome quake struck. According to historians, some fifteen thousand people died. But Ciudad Malagua was always rebuilt, such was the tenacity of its citizens, though the Cathedral, started in 1780, was never finished. Only the clergy complained.

Over the years, in part because of the earthquakes, the city developed chaotically, without a plan. Malaguans built where and how the spirit moved them. Around the turn of the century, the régime then in power built an opera house in the middle of the city, off Avenida Bolívar. But since Malaguans had no money to attract touring troupes, and local talent was not up to the challenge of staging an opera production, the rococo structure fell into disuse. A few theaters were erected in the 1920s, but the thespian arts never caught on seriously in Malagua, and one of the theaters was turned into a cinema. Culture was not Malagua's strong point.

Under the Ferrers, Ciudad Malagua went from bad to worse. The family was interested in real-estate profits, and the first Ferrer had been able to acquire land in and around the capital cheaply. His successors sold off parcels of land along Lake Taxchilán at highly inflated prices: this was the birth of the tree-shaded residential district and the embassy row. The *barrios* were allowed to expand in their filth and misery as migrations from the countryside began in earnest in the 1940s. In the late 1950s, Anselmo Ferrer constructed a sports stadium, chiefly for soccer, between the midtown section and the southern *barrios*. Thus Ciudad Malagua turned into a crazy and ugly mosaic. The few modern buildings erected in the business district in recent years had only added to the urban confusion. Except for the lakeside, Ciudad Malagua, unlike most Latin American cities, was wholly devoid of charm.

★

Malagua gained its independence in 1827, one of the last Latin American colonies to sever their ties with Spain. It was the most beautiful of the very beautiful Central American nations, but also the poorest. Yet it was fought over by Malaguans and everybody else. Between independence and Malagua's occupation by United States Marines in 1918 (ordered by President Wilson to impose peace in the little republic and to guarantee the repayment of debts to New York and Boston banks), Malagua had fifty-one presidents, three full-fledged civil wars, and more revolutions and *coups d'état* than anyone could count. There may have been as many as one hundred *pronunciamientos* to announce an uprising or revolution. The strife involved a continual contest for power between the Liberal and Conservative parties, although the only notable difference between them was the identity and personality of the leaders. Sometimes these leaders switched parties, and sometimes Liberals stood for conservatism, and Conservatives for enlightened nineteenth-century liberalism. It was the age of *personalismo* at its most outrageous. In the three civil wars, the opposing armies were composed almost entirely of Indian peasants with flintlock rifles and machetes, having not the slightest idea of the cause for which they were fighting. But refusal to be conscripted usually meant execution by the warlords and the burning of whole villages. At the same time, however, Malaguan Indians were not altogether averse to violence, this too being in the Mayan tradition, and war often meant plunder and rape by the victors.

Then there were foreign wars. Malagua was invaded on seven occasions by Nicaragua and four times by Guatemala, its two neighbors, during the first ninety years of its sovereign existence. Most of the invasions were in support of one or the other of the Malaguan political factions. Nicaraguan–Guatemalan competition was a permanent feature of Central American politics, with Malagua, caught in the middle, usually emerging as the victim.

The occupation by United States Marines put an end to both the internal violence in Malagua and the foreign wars (although in 1968, Malagua and Guatemala battled on the border for a month as a follow-up to a bloody brawl during a soccer match between the two national teams: each country's honor was thought to be at stake). In addition to peace, the Marines provided Malagua with a telephone system and with a National Guard, which they trained. Before finally departing in 1933, on orders from President Franklin Roosevelt, who advocated a "Good Neighbor" policy toward Latin America, the Marines installed Colonel Bolívar Ferrer Valle as National Guard commander. Colonel Ferrer had worked his way up through the ranks from sergeant, and he was the toughest and wiliest soldier in the country. When the last Marine went aboard ship in San Pablo, the colonel promoted himself to general and, with the blessings of the American Minister in Ciudad Malagua, proclaimed himself President for life. The scenario, of course, had been written in Washington by the State Department, which had mixed feelings about the whole "Good Neighbor" idea.

★

Bolívar Ferrer's ascension to Malaguan presidency marked the birth of the Ferrer dynasty. This first ruler, who kept a magnificent jaguar in a cage on the grounds of the Presidential Palace, was succeeded, after his assassination by a lone gunman (who was killed on the spot) in 1961, by his son Anselmo Ferrer García, who, in turn, was replaced in 1965 by Juan Ferrer Berrio, the present dictator. Anselmo died of cirrhosis of the liver, though the official announcement claimed it was cardiac arrest. The ruling family grew enormous over three generations: brothers, sisters, nephews, nieces, sons- and daughters-in-law, fathers- and mothers-in-law, brothers- and sisters-in-law, first, second, and third cousins, godfathers and godchildren. The Ferrer presidents provided generously for all the relatives, no matter how remote, and it was no exaggeration to say that the Ferrer clan *owned* Malagua.

Interestingly, however, the Ferrers also had a sense of Malaguan—or Mayan—history, at least to the extent to which it suited them. They liked to compare themselves to the legendary ninth-century Xiu dynasty of Mayan warriors, the rulers of the Tutal Xiu nation, which had held power for five generations, from Ah Xupan Xiu to his great-great-grandson Ah Ziyah Xiu. President Juan Ferrer, whose son Pedro was being groomed for succession, boasted that the Ferrers would beat the Xiu record by the twenty-first century. And General Ferrer was not being entirely unrealistic: the dynasty had already ruled, without serious challenge, for half a century. It had survived, unscathed, the antidictatorial wave that swept Latin America in the 1950s, sweeping away Juan Perón in Argentina, Manuel Odría in Peru, Gustavo Rojas Pinilla in Colombia, Marcos Pérez Jiménez in Venezuela, Fulgencio Batista in Cuba, and finally Rafael Trujillo Molina in the Dominican Republic. The Nicaraguan dictator Anastasio Somoza was overthrown by a revolution in 1979. But the Ferrers stood firm—it still was high noon of dictatorial darkness in Malagua, and would be for years to come.

Ironically, Fidel Castro's seizure of power was a boon to the Ferrers, particularly when the Soviet Union started shipping sophisticated arms to Cuba and the "Maximum Leader" proclaimed himself a "Marxist-Leninist." President Anselmo Ferrer, still alive at the time, busied himself denouncing the perils of Communism in the Americas, but privately, he was delighted. After listening to Castro's ideological confession speech over Havana radio (senior officials in Malagua reserved for themselves the right of tuning in Cuban stations; citizens caught doing it were subject to arrest and imprisonment), the aging dictator howled with joy.

"Bueno, chico," he shouted across the room to his son Juan. "This is the best news I've heard in a hundred years. Now that this filthy *barbudo* says that he's a Communist, the Americans, even that *inocente* John Kennedy, will protect us all the way. I'll bet they're scared out of their pants. If there's one thing the United States will not stand in its backyard, it's Communism. And God be blessed, this idiot Fidel *admits,* can you imagine, that he's a Communist! Mark my words, Juanito, there will be no more of this liberal shit about democracy coming down from Washington, all this nonsense about teaching us how to run our own country. *Sí, señor,* that's now behind us. The Yankees simply *must* protect us. They can't afford to have fucking Communists popping up in Malagua and Central America. *Oh, gracias, Fidel.''*

Anselmo Ferrer clapped his hands for the dwarf Fabio, his valet and bodyguard, who was hovering, as usual, in the background. "Eh, Fabio, give me a drink of Scotch," he said. "We're celebrating today." Actually, the General always had his first drink of the day exactly at noon, his glass being refilled regularly by Fabio through the afternoon and evening, but he liked to joke about "celebrating." It was an established ritual, and Fabio never failed to respond, "*Sí, mi General*, this *is* a celebration," when he served him. On his own time, Fabio engaged in other rituals. He held the rank of major in the secret police, the G-2 of the National Guard, and he often put himself in charge of torture squads in the dungeon of the Presidential Palace. He liked to bite off prisoners' testicles with his sharp, filed-down teeth; then he ejaculated in his trousers. Malaguans referred to him as "Snow White." When Anselmo Ferrer died of cirrhosis, Juan Ferrer kept Fabio in his employ, a faithful family retainer.

The Ferrers, father and son, had an extraordinary capacity for alcohol. Neither of them ever seemed drunk, no matter how much they ingested. On the night of Fidel Castro's speech, the two men put away a fifth of Chivas Regal, with much laughter and knee-slapping. They were off the hook politically as far as the United States was concerned, and it was great fun to see that the know-it-all Americans now had no choice but to play the game the Ferrers' way. They chuckled appreciatively when the Kennedy Administration invented the Alliance for Progress, the economic and social aid program, running into billions of dollars annually, designed as a pillar of Latin American democratic institutions, because this meant extra American assistance to Malagua.

In the first two years of the Alliance, over $150 million was earmarked for Malagua, mostly in food on a grant basis, with the idea that it would be sold cheaply to the half-starved population in local currency—malaguas, which were on a par with the dollar —the income thus generated being used for development projects like schools, low-cost housing for Indian peasants, and the like.

Anselmo Ferrer laughed uproariously after the signing of the first aid agreement under the Alliance, when the American Ambassador had left the Palace following ceremonial champagne toasts (the Moët et Chandon was on Ferrer). In his speech, the President had praised the United States for its generosity in "improving the lot of the people of Malagua," but when he and Juan were alone, the dictator said, "I just can't believe how naïve these Americans are. Do they really think I'm going to waste all that money from food sales on some crazy social programs? They've got to be insane. I'll tell you, Juanito, what we'll do: we'll build two elementary schools here in Ciudad Malagua where they can be photographed by Yankee newspapermen. We'll name one after John Kennedy and one after Anselmo Ferrer. This will symbolize that Alliance of theirs. The rest of the money—well, Juanito, you know how we can use it. And it's going to take the Americans a thousand years to audit our books. The *gringos* will never know the difference, the fools." He asked Fabio for a "celebration drink."

Anselmo Ferrer died early in 1965, missing what would have been his greatest political vindication: the landing of American Marines and airborne troops in the Dominican Republic to put down a rebellion that President Johnson claimed was led by Communists. But Juan Ferrer, the new President, at once offered a battalion of Malagua's National Guard for the inter-American force the United States was organizing in the Dominican Republic to erase the impression of a purely American military intervention. Washington thought better of it, preferring Brazilian and Paraguayan units, but Johnson sent Ferrer a handwritten letter thanking him for his support in the battle for democracy and against Communism. Ferrer had the letter framed and hung on his office wall, above his desk. "Now I'm a hero of democracy," he told the dwarf Fabio.

Juan Ferrer felt so good, in fact, that the following year he organized a presidential election, with himself on the Liberal Party ticket (it was the official party). He was overwhelmingly elected to a six-year term, the opposition candidate having suffered a fatal automobile accident on the eve of the balloting and there being no time to find a replacement. In 1972 and 1978, General Ferrer was reelected without difficulty (opposition leaders were jailed and exiled before the 1972 election on charges of maintaining secret contacts with Cuba and "international Communism").

When Julia Savage arrived to take up her duties as American Ambassador in Ciudad Malagua, President Ferrer was serving the penultimate year of his third "constitutional" term. In the National Congress (he, like his father and grandfather, insisted on preserving the outer trappings of a legal régime), the Liberals outnumbered the Conservatives by two to one, but all Ferrer legislation was approved by near—though not total—unanimity: on less crucial matters, the General liked to have a few dissenting votes. In this fashion, he could tell foreign diplomats and visiting foreign journalists that a "democratic opposition" existed in Malagua. Of course, he planned to be reelected in 1984.

★

The dictator was confident that he had the power to outlast and smash the resistance to his rule that had been building for the past several years. This time, however, he realized that a victory would be neither quick nor cheap. The FMLN, the clandestine liberation front, could not be dismissed out of hand: it was the first time in nearly a half-century that a paramilitary opposition movement, with obvious support from younger people, had come into being in Malagua. The FMLN, the General knew, was well organized and highly motivated and, most important, had access to funds and arms.

With money, he knew so well, you could buy everything: from arms and munitions to people. The Frente had the funds from at least two major sources: bank assaults, a time-honored revolutionary technique which had been mounting in frequency and daring over the last two years or so, and ransoms from kidnappings, a fairly novel revolutionary practice. Hardly a month went by without the kidnapping of a Malaguan millionaire or a foreign businessman, and families and corporations had paid as much as $1 million, usually in American currency, for the release of hostages.

At first, General Ferrer sought to discourage ransom payments (not on principle, as with the United States and Israeli governments, but for practical political reasons of his own), but it soon became evident that the payoffs would continue. Families would not sacrifice their loved ones, nor corporations their executives, to the Ferrer régime. This was a fact of life that the Frente understood as well as Ferrer. That criminals also went into the kidnapping business, under the guise of revolutionary action, further complicated matters, because in the end the régime had no way of knowing who was getting the blood money. Nevertheless, the President was aware that the bulk of it was going to the Frente.

The money, in turn, bought arms. The *malaguistas* were thought to keep secret bank accounts in Panama, the Bahamas, and Grand Cayman to make payments to international arms dealers and brokers. It was a rather sophisticated operation—so sophisticated, in fact, that Ferrer had been pressing his friend Jim Morgan, the CIA Station Chief in Malagua, to provide Agency resources in tracking down the Frente's financial network abroad so that it could be cracked. The CIA kept trying, out of its own interest as well, but it had made little progress. The discretion of Panamanian and Caribbean bankers is even greater than that of the Swiss, and local governments are neither capable of discovering nor interested in who is laundering whose money. The important thing was for the money, no matter how mysterious, to keep flowing through the banks. Besides, the CIA, a detail that Morgan omitted to mention to Ferrer, had to be careful not to blow its own, and equally mysterious, financial dealings in the region.

Actually, it was an embarrassment for Ferrer to have to ask the CIA to assist him in investigating the Frente's financial affairs. Ferrer had to rearm and modernize the National Guard. He needed more aircraft for counterinsurgency operations, helicopters, and even tanks—in addition to small arms: M-16 automatic rifles, submachine guns, pistols, and so on. The big items were hard to procure on the open market—the United States, for one thing, had suspended sales of modern aircraft to most of Latin America—and Malaguan agents had an increasingly difficult time procuring the weapons General Ferrer needed to survive. They were able to buy a dozen obsolete armored cars from Israel, shipped via South Africa and Antigua with false documents, and six French Alouette helicopters belonging to the Gabon government—all for exorbitant prices.

The President believed that vastly superior firepower and air power and the capability to raze *guerrilleros'* bases, if they could be found, would liquidate the rebellion. This strategy had failed in Vietnam and Rhodesia, but Ferrer often told his commanders that those conflicts were not analogous to the strife in Malagua. In Vietnam and Rhodesia, the established régimes had had to fight foreign-based foes. Ferrer, on the other hand, was facing his fellow *malagueños,* and he was prepared to destroy much of the country in order to quell the rebellion. But to succeed, he saw that he must persuade the United States to change its policies and to sell him, preferably on credit, the military equipment needed for the National Guard.

But the General was also aware that the Americans would do so *only* if he could convince them that he was an anti-Communist threatened by *malaguistas* who were funded and armed by Cuba and Eastern Europe. In public speeches and in private meetings with American officials, Ferrer always emphasized the Communist origin of the Frente's money and weapons. It made no difference that this was not true to any important extent (the Frente did not require much Cuban help, though some of its younger leaders had been trained and indoctrinated in Havana)—so long as Washington believed it.

Asking Jim Morgan for assistance in locating the rebels' bank accounts abroad thus weakened President Ferrer's argument: it tacitly acknowledged that the Frente did not really depend on Cuban sources. But no great damage was done. Morgan knew as well as Ferrer where the FMLN obtained its funds and arms. He and the CIA were willing to go along with the charade, the Station Chief having easily sold Headquarters on the notion that it was essential to maintain the Malaguan dictator in power and that therefore modern arms should be given him. The Communist ploy, it was generally agreed at the CIA, would be helpful with the State Department and the White House, which, after all, did not know any better.

General Ferrer made his big pitch for American arms when Wilbur Breck, the departing Ambassador, accompanied by Jim Morgan, paid his farewell call at the Presidential Palace. The Ambassador, happy to accept Ferrer's Communist-conspiracy theory as the sole explanation for the rising rebellion in Malagua, was all for providing the dictatorship with everything it needed to put down the guerrillas. With Morgan's concurrence, he had recommended it on numerous occasions to the State Department, but the Administration remained reluctant about changing its policies.

As they sat drinking Scotch in the presidential office, with the dwarf Fabio dancing attendance, Ferrer told Breck, "My final request to you, my good friend, is to tell your President the truth about Malagua when you return to Washington tomorrow." Lowering his voice, he added: "I don't know if I will be able to speak as frankly with your successor as you and I have talked together for these ten years. I doubt that I will. For the Republic of Malagua, you will always be the *real* ambassador from the United States, and you must help us, even if you're away—because this will always be your home, *amigo. . . .*"

Breck, who a few minutes earlier had been given the Grand Cross of Merit of Malagua, said emotionally: "My dear Mr. President, my friend, you know you can always count on me. I have already drafted my final recommendation to the Department, and I have appended the list of military equipment that the Minister of National Defense was kind enough to deliver to me yesterday. I shall speak about Malagua to our friends in the Congress. I am confident the United States will not abandon Malagua to international Communism. As for my successor, Ambassador Savage, there is little I can tell you, but Jim here, I am sure, will know how to interpret your thoughts to her. God bless you and God bless Malagua, Señor Presidente."

4

JULIA Savage had read the final recommendations of The Honorable Wilbur R. Breck as she prepared to leave Washington for her post. His proposals for substantial military assistance to the Ferrer régime had been discussed at some length in the office of the Assistant Secretary of State for ARA, just before Julia's departure for Ciudad Malagua, and she had participated in the meetings. To be sure, General Ferrer's requests for American arms—and Breck's supporting dispatches—were nothing new. They recurred every six months or so.

However, the difference this time was that the Malaguan President was facing a serious challenge, and senior officials in the ARA Bureau at State felt that Ferrer's ouster would not be in the best interests of the United States, in part because of the concern in many government quarters that a Cuban-type régime might emerge to fill the void in the little Central American republic.

The consensus in the Bureau, snugly hidden away in a corner of the State Department's sixth floor, was that Ferrer was probably right in claiming he could defeat the Frente rebels if he were given arms. There was general agreement, based more on CIA reporting than on telegrams from Ambassador Breck (who even at the Department was thought to be essentially a mouthpiece for the dictator), that the Frente was not yet an imminent threat to the *status quo* in Malagua, but could become one if, as the CIA warned, the Cubans threw all their resources into the fray.

Still, supplying weapons to a Central American tyrant, which was Juan Ferrer's outstanding reputation in liberal circles, was an awkward proposition for an Administration publicly committed to better relations with Latin America. Assistant Secretary of State Terhune was well aware of it, and he knew he could not recommend arms for Ferrer to the Seventh Floor (the Office of the Secretary) or to the White House without some redeeming political feature. Finally, the group concluded that the solution, the classical bureaucratic solution, would be a compromise, a *quid pro quo*. Thus Ferrer would be given arms, but in exchange, he would be asked to offer public assurances that political prisoners would be freed from Malaguan jails, that tortures and brutalities would no longer occur, that censorship of local newspapers would be lifted, that the Inter-American Human Rights Commission would be invited to inspect Malagua, and that a new presidential election would be held ahead of time, before 1984, when Ferrer's present term would expire.

"This is the only way we can sell the package upstairs," the Assistant Secretary told his colleagues and Julia. "If Ferrer accepts our conditions, it's entirely possible—in my opinion—that the antirégime movement would be defused and the National Guard could take care of the hard-core elements of the Frente. But this calls for tough negotiation in Ciudad Malagua. At the outset, it seems to me, Ferrer should be carefully sounded out, and this will be Julia's first piece of business there."

He looked pleased with his strategy, and his deputies nodded vigorously, having no better ideas. Taking off his glasses, Terhune turned to Julia. "But let's have the new Ambassador's comments," he said soothingly.

"Well," Julia said, "I think I want to reserve judgment on this whole package until I get to Malagua and I get some sense of the situation there. Frankly, I have little confidence in Wilbur Breck's views, and by the same token, I don't find the CIA's reporting fully convincing."

"Are you skeptical about what we're proposing here today?" Terhune asked pointedly.

"No, I didn't say that," she said with care. Julia was genuinely open-minded about policy in Malagua. She was inclined to think that, for broader international reasons, Ferrer probably should stay in power. But if he were to be armed by the United States, he would have to pay for it politically—to get the Administration off the hook. She was not opposed in principle to the plan devised by the ARA, but she simply had to take the measure of Juan Ferrer before deciding in her own mind whether the *quid pro quo* approach made sense. On the other hand, there was no advantage in antagonizing the ARA Bureau. Bureaucracies have a way of quietly but effectively undermining ambassadors.

"What I am saying," Julia went on, "is that I need a little time, and certainly a meeting with Ferrer, to be able to give you an intelligent answer."

"That's fair enough," the Assistant Secretary said. "We'll wait to hear from you. In the meantime, get settled in Malagua."

★

At the Residence, after they arrived from the airport, McVeigh introduced to Julia Mark Starek, the Embassy's security officer. Starek, a pleasant young man with a brisk manner, took her on a tour of the house. "There are some security features here you should be familiar with," he said. "I know it's a hell of a way to make you feel at home, but that's Malagua for you.

"For one thing," Starek continued, "you are the only American living at the Residence. The Marines are assigned to protect you day and night, but they are housed elsewhere. The domestic staff, however, do live in. You have Dudley, who is the butler, and he's really in charge of the household. Then there are a woman cook, who's not bad, and three maids to clean, do the laundry, and help serve at the table or at cocktails. They've been here for quite a while, and they're experienced. The gardener works full time, but he lives away. Dudley, I think, is completely trustworthy. He is from Grenada, and he despises Malaguans; he wouldn't have any contacts with them—you know, political contacts—with either side. But I'd be a bit careful with the Malaguan staff: they could be under pressure from the government or the rebels—so be discreet when they're around.''

The Residence, purchased by the State Department after the war, was a spacious single-story structure in what is commonly known as the Spanish style: white rough-plaster walls, red-tiled roof, ceramic-tile floors, curved archways and windows. It had belonged to a Ferrer uncle who had decided to live out his years in Paris, and it had been built for comfort—and for safety. But the house, Julia saw with a sinking feeling, was shabby and run-down. Wilbur Breck, a bachelor, had been content to live with the basic furnishings with which the State Department equipped residences around the world, and he had resisted the efforts by Department decorators to refurbish the mansion. Breck seldom entertained at the Residence, except for his men friends in the Malaguan government, and those were usually hard-drinking occasions. His favorite pastime was poker, at which he was exceedingly good, and he often presided over all-night games at the Residence when he was not playing with Ferrer at the Palace. Occasionally the dictator would drop in for a game at the Residence, a sign of friendship for Breck. A good deal of official business between the President and the American Ambassador was transacted, between hands, over the poker table. And nobody cared about the appearance of the Residence.

There was no touch of color in the rooms, Julia saw. Breck had shipped home whatever paintings he possessed, having refused to accept on loan American art from museum collections that the State Department made available to embassies under a special program. Breck did not think his Malaguan friends cared much about, say, Robert Motherwell or Larry Rivers. Julia saw that the house would have to be put into shape quickly. She simply could not live in the dirty, empty rooms—much less receive guests. And she wanted to entertain as many Malaguans as possible, all kinds of Malaguans.

The property itself, a rectangle of park surrounded by high walls, extended between Avenida Ferrer on the northern side and Lake Taxchilán on the south. There were large private homes on either side of the Residence, but privacy was ensured by the expanse of the grounds around the American mansion. The tall trees that had once screened the outer walls had been cut down several years before when a team of State Department security experts had concluded that they could conceal trespassers. At night, powerful reflectors set in flower beds cast their beams on the walls: an intruder attempting to climb over would have been bathed in intense light, presenting a perfect target for the guns of the Marines on night patrol. An electric alarm system had, of course, been installed on the walls.

"You will notice that in Malagua, unlike most other places, we use the Marines to guard the Residence as well as the Chancery," Mark Starek said. "Since kidnapping has become the most popular outdoor sport here, we require top security for the Ambassador at all times. And just between us, I'm not too impressed by the Malaguan police. I'm paid to anticipate the worst, and I have a feeling that if the *guerrilleros* ever attacked the Residence, the local cops would just vanish in the night. We use them to man the walls and the front gate, in coordination with the National Guard sentries outside, but I prefer to have armed Americans *inside* the compound, which is okay because it's U.S. territory."

Starek continued his briefing: "The Marine detail in Ciudad Malagua is also unusually large for an embassy of this size. We have eighteen men, including the staff sergeant in command. Twelve Marines are assigned to the Residence, patrolling in three four-man shifts of eight hours. So you're guarded around the clock. The off-duty men are at the Marine House, a villa four blocks from here, and they're available at a moment's notice. There's phone and VHF radio contact day and night linking the Residence, the Chancery, and the Marine House. Six Marines are on Chancery duty, which is sufficient because, as you know, the Embassy is in an office building downtown. Naturally, we rotate the men between the Residence and the Chancery."

"I understand," Julia said, the fear that she had felt at the airport returning. My God, I'm already catching the Malagua syndrome, she thought. I had better watch myself, not let it get to me. Julia swallowed hard.

"Yes, I understand," she repeated, "but why do you trust Salvador and Gonzalo, who are not Americans, in the car?"

"That's a different situation," Starek replied. "Salvador and Gonzalo were trained at the International Police Academy in Washington in the Sixties. They're professionals, and I trust them more than anybody else in Malagua. Besides, their families live in the United States, in the Miami area, and if you'll excuse the expression, we own them. They're totally loyal and as experienced as any security agents anywhere in the world."

The entrance hall of the Residence opened directly into an ample living room. At the far end, sliding glass doors separated the living room from a patio, a U-shaped area, and with the doors open, the entertainment area could easily accommodate well over a hundred cocktail guests. The residential and service wings were on either side of the patio. Beyond, Julia saw a large swimming pool and gardens running down to the wall facing on the lakeshore. "The glass in the sliding doors is bulletproof," Starek said reassuringly.

To the left of the living room, through a wide arch, was the dining room, with a mahogany table that could comfortably seat twelve persons. Julia, who preferred rather small dinner parties, where she could talk easily to all the guests, noted the size of the table approvingly. The table could be extended with extra leaves, on formal occasions, for another twelve. The pantry, the kitchen, and the servants' living quarters were beyond the dining room, in the left wing of the house. To the right of the living room, in the corner, there was a small library with a desk and telephone. Framed photographs of the President of the United States and President Ferrer were the sole adornment on the bare walls. The windows in the dining room and library were barred by what looked to Julia like decorative wrought iron. "Actually, those bars are solid steel," Starek told her. "We had them painted black to fit into the Spanish décor. Now let's go to your living quarters."

An archway led to a corridor fenced off by a heavy gate of thick steel rods, and Starek explained to Julia that it could be opened manually with a key from either side, and electrically from the bedroom. "It's absolutely essential that you lock this gate from the inside when you retire for the night," the security officer said. "Never forget it. If the Residence is attacked and penetrated, you are sealed off in your wing of the house, hopefully long enough for help to arrive. It would take a charge of TNT to blow off the gate. Only you, Dudley, and the Marines have keys to the gate. Either Dudley or a Marine will let the maids into the residential section when they come to do the rooms."

Three guest bedrooms opened off the corridor. The master bedroom was at the end of the right wing of the mansion, but a massive steel door, next to the bedroom entrance, led to the patio. "This is your emergency exit, if you don't want to—or cannot—get out through the corridor and into the living room," Starek said. Julia's bedroom was large, with a steel door, and its steel-barred windows looked out on the patio and on the gardens on the side of the house. The windowpanes were bulletproof as well, Starek said. Three telephones and a radio transmitter/receiver stood on the bedside table.

"Let me explain the communications system," the security officer said. "One telephone, the black one with the buttons, is a regular phone for outside calls, though you can also use it as an intercom—to the library, the kitchen, the pantry, and the swimming pool. The red phone is a direct line to the Marine guard post at the Chancery, which is manned twenty-four hours a day. You just pick it up, and the Marine will answer it at once. The green phone is the same thing, except it goes to the Marine House. The radio—it's VHF—connects you on the same frequency with the Chancery and the Marine House. If phone cables are cut, you use the radio . . . Oh, yes. In the drawer of the bedside table you'll find a thirty-eight-caliber Smith and Wesson revolver, and boxes of extra ammunition. If you don't know how to use it, I'll show you later. Also the submachine gun in the car. Is it all clear, Madam Ambassador?"

"Yes, it is," Julia said. "Now I know what it means to live in a gilded cage."

How extraordinary, she thought. God knows that *nobody* will ever share this bedroom with me. You can't make love in a steel box, surrounded by guns, radios, and telephones, and watched over by Marines. Of course, an ambassador, especially a woman, mustn't use the American Residence for trysts. And probably I never would anyway. But it's the idea that you simply can't, no matter what. I wonder if isolation isn't worse than bombs? I guess you could go over the edge if you stayed here long enough. But Christ, what kind of thoughts are these? You have just arrived and you have a job to do. Come on, get hold of yourself.

★

Julia went to the Embassy a few minutes before eight o'clock in the morning to move her papers into the office, glance at the overnight cables (nothing interesting), and, purposefully, make the best possible impression on Ann Mestre, the Ambassador's secretary, whom she wanted to stay on. Ann, a woman in her forties, who had worked for Wilbur Breck for four years and detested him, had had enough of Malagua and its tensions, and she had put in for a transfer. She was a solid, bilingual State Department secretary, and Julia did not want to start out with an inexperienced assistant. When Ann brought her a cup of coffee, Julia asked her to sit down for a chat. Ann Mestre was tall and thin, her hair in a severe bun, but her tanned face easily broke into crinkles of good humor.

"Look, Ann," she said. "I won't beat around the bush. I know you've asked for a transfer. But I would very much like to have you stay with me for a while. I've also asked McVeigh to stay on. Obviously, I need help, and I need your experience. I think you and I will get along splendidly, and we'll have fun working together. Now, don't give me an answer right away. Give it some thought. But I'll respect whatever decision you make. Okay?"

Ann Mestre glanced at Julia. She had felt a liking for her from the moment Julia had entered the office, lugging her attaché case, and she was no longer sure she wanted to leave. Working for

Wilbur Breck had been an exhausting job—he was extremely demanding, and as fussy as only aging bachelors can be—but it had been an empty and unrewarding one. Breck was cold and remote, and Ann had never had the sense she belonged to a team working together. Breck did not particularly like people—except, it seemed, General Ferrer. But the idea of working for—with—a young woman intrigued Ann.

"Madam Ambassador—" she began.

"No. I'll call you 'Ann' and you'll call me 'Julia.' It makes life easier."

"Okay, Julia," Ann said softly. "I promise to think about staying on."

The staff meeting was held in a conference room adjoining the ambassadorial office on the sixth floor of the building of the Quetzal Insurance Company on Avenida San Martín in downtown Ciudad Malagua. It was the street of banks and insurance companies, just one urban block on the eastern slope of El Cerro, an area the government was trying to develop into a business center. The Embassy occupied the top two floors of the seven-story structure (the British Embassy was on the third floor). The American Chancery took up the sixth floor. The seventh floor was the domain of the CIA Station, and it included the Embassy's communications facilities. As a matter of convenience, the Station handled all the Embassy communications, though it had its own direct "back channel" lines to CIA Headquarters at Langley. In practice, it meant that the Station Chief saw the entire Embassy traffic, but the Ambassador did not have automatic access to the CIA traffic. Anyway, Wilbur Breck had never asked Jim Morgan to let him see the Agency's incoming and outgoing messages. He had no interest in CIA business, trusting Morgan without reservation.

Julia walked into the conference room at nine o'clock, and the men stood to greet her. "Everybody please sit down," she said with her best smile. She felt good this morning; a sound night's sleep had dissipated the fears and tensions of her first day in Malagua. She had the sense of being in command, of being exhilarated. She had decided to wear today a dark blue silk-foulard dress, a Bill Blass she had not been able to resist buying. It was discreet, feminine, just right for the office. She sensed that the men were appraising her as a woman, a desirable woman. And indeed, why shouldn't they? This too made her feel good.

"My name is Julia Savage, as you probably know," Julia said, and there was a nervous titter of laughter in the room. The men were tense. "I already know Mac—I've known him for years— and I met Mark yesterday. Now I'd like to meet everybody else." She went from chair to chair around the table, shaking hands and matching faces and names in her mind. Rick Anders, the Political Counselor, short and intense. He had a good reputation, and his two subordinates, Max Schmidt and Leo Bass, were young and eager. The Economic Counselor, Sam Miller, a serious man in his fifties. The Administrative Officer, Stanley Smith, nondescript. The Public Affairs Officer, George Maxwell, elegantly dressed, but vacant-eyed. The Information and Cultural Officer, Henry Clark, bright and alert. The Defense Attaché, Colonel Victor Brown, a spit-and-polish type. Finally, John Crespo, the CIA Deputy Station Chief, the thinker.

"I have no speech to deliver," Julia said, taking her seat at the head of the table. "All I want to say is that I'm happy to be here, to have an opportunity of working with you. I know that we'll work well together, and I'm counting on your help. You know that I'm a political appointee, not a career officer, but I hope you will not hold it against me too much." Again, there was a round of nervous laughter, but the room now was more relaxed, Julia noted.

"So, let's get down to business. I'd like to ask John Crespo to give us a fill-in on the Saavedra situation, the martial law, and the rest. We'll have to draft an updating telegram to Washington later this morning."

Crespo cleared his throat and consulted a note pad on the table before him.

"Information is very fragmentary," he said. "Colonel Saavedra was killed by three masked gunmen using submachine guns. They made their getaway in a waiting car. G-2 has a description of the car, but that isn't much help. The bullets, according to G-2, came from FALN automatic rifles, the kind used by the Cubans in the Sixties and now floating all over Central America and the Caribbean—wherever Cuba has been arming rebel movements. Obviously, Colonel Saavedra was shot by urban guerrillas of the Frente, and the ambush was very carefully planned—his escort never had a chance to react."

"Why the killing?" Julia asked. "What does it tell you, and what does it tell G-2?"

"Well, it's hard to say. You can read it several ways. It may have been a way to show President Ferrer—and perhaps you, Madam Ambassador—that nobody is safe here."

"And it *has*, hasn't it?" McVeigh commented.

"Sure. That's why the President has decreed modified martial law—to have more freedom to hit back at the Frente. But this could be only a partial interpretation. Shooting Saavedra in broad daylight may also have been meant to show the population that the Frente is getting stronger and bolder, and that people had better start getting behind it. This fits into guerrilla strategy: carry out a number of dramatic, spectacular acts to create the illusion that you're really powerful. This would be my personal view. The rebels simply have to keep up the tension in order to attract supporters before the Frente is smashed by the National Guard. You'd be surprised how much can be accomplished in this way by two dozen determined terrorists, making people believe there's a whole rebel army behind them. But it isn't the way to take over a country."

"So you don't think this is the start of something big, like a general uprising?" Julia asked.

Crespo shook his head. "No. The Frente doesn't have enough popular support to launch an uprising. We're dealing with a terrorist movement, not yet a national revolution. Sure, Madam Ambassador, there'll be more and more terrorism, but President Ferrer can handle it. This is the official evaluation in our office . . . particularly if Ferrer gets the arms he needs to mop up the leftists. Don't underestimate his staying power."

"Okay, but let me play the devil's advocate," McVeigh said. "By all means, let us *not* underestimate General Ferrer. But aren't we running the risk of underestimating the opposition? I disagree with John's catchall description of the Frente as 'terrorists.' It's too simple. Quite a few young Malaguan businessmen —the comers—are tired of Ferrer and are sympathetic to the Frente. Hell, our best friends at the American–Malaguan Chamber of Commerce have been telling us this for months. The British, who, unlike us, *are* in contact with all the Malaguan factions, also think that the Frente is gaining a much broader base than we realize. What I'm saying is that we ought to reexamine our assessment of the situation."

"I don't see anything wrong with the assessment I've just outlined, and which has been the Embassy's official assessment all along," John Crespo said, a bit too stiffly.

Julia broke in. "My suggestion is that at this point, we simply draft a reporting telegram to the Department on Saavedra and the martial law, with such details as we have," she said firmly. "I'm sure the Political Section and John Crespo can pull it together this morning, and I'll go over it during the lunch hour. For my part, I'd like to hold off on the interpretive stuff. At least until I've met the President."

★

On July 25, a muggy Monday, Julia Savage drove to the Presidential Palace on El Cerro to present her credentials to General Ferrer. She had dressed carefully—there was no precedent for a woman foreign ambassador in Ciudad Malaga, where exaggerated formality prevailed on official occasions—choosing a fawn-colored silk-linen suit, black-and-white silk blouse, black ballibuntl straw hat, fawn kid gloves, and fawn-and-black Chanel pumps. McVeigh, weighed down by a morning coat over striped pants, accompanied her.

President Juan Ferrer Berrio received them standing in the ornate Independence Room, portraits of Jesús María Tierno del Valle, Malaga's first colonial governor, and of selected Malaguan presidents, with the first and second Ferrers the most prominently displayed, staring down from the walls. Juan Ferrer, a tall and powerful figure in a white suit, towered over the Foreign

Minister, on whom Julia had already called, and Señor Moreno, the Protocol Chief, her companion at the bloody airport baptism. As Julia and McVeigh entered the room, Señor Moreno intoned, "The Honorable Julia Savage. . . ." Ferrer stepped forward, a warm smile lighting up his face. Photographers' flashbulbs popped, and television cameras came alive.

"Madam Ambassador, welcome to the Republic of Malagua," Ferrer said in his perfect English, ignoring the Foreign Minister and the Protocol Chief. "We are happy to have you with us." With a twinkle in his eyes, he added in a lower voice, out of hearing of the TV and radio microphones, "and I hope you don't judge us by the unpleasantness at the airport on your arrival last week."

Julia smiled back, and proceeded to deliver the short message from the President of the United States she had memorized. Then she handed Ferrer her credentials. As the General took them, white-gloved waiters with trays of champagne moved up to the group. Ferrer picked up a glass and gave it to Julia with a graceful slight bow. He took another glass for himself, raising it in a toast: "May I drink to you, Madam Ambassador, and to the excellent relations between the United States and Malagua, which I know will improve even further during your stay among us."

She tasted the champagne and raised her own glass in turn: "And may I drink to your health, Mr. President, and, of course, to the best possible relations between our two countries."

Ferrer leaned over and said to Julia in a conversational tone, "Okay. Now that we're over the ceremony, let us—you and I— get acquainted. Won't you join me in my office for a chat— alone?" He strode toward the door of the Independence Room, his hand lightly holding Julia's left elbow. He led her down a corridor to the door of his office, where two National Guardsmen in dress uniform stood at attention. Ferrer held the door open for Julia, letting her into the enormous room, the windows looking out on Lake Taxchilán and the Mixull volcano. He motioned her to a leather sofa, and sank into an armchair to the side of the jacaranda coffee table.

"Do you mind if I light a cigar?" he asked Julia.

"No, if *you* don't mind if I smoke a cigarette," she answered, taking one from her black patent-leather handbag.

Ferrer laughed, getting up to light her cigarette with his gold Dunhill. "At least we have the tobacco vice in common," he said, "but I hope that we'll have much more in common than *that*."

Julia was surprised to find him both attractive and charming—quite *simpático*. She had carefully studied his background and history in State Department files and in a biographical sketch, marked SECRET, prepared by the CIA, but the dossiers had omitted all aspects of his personality. At the age of fifty-one, Juan Ferrer was overweight, though his big athletic frame—six feet two—carried it well. His face and lips were fleshy, and the slightly curving black mustache gave him a sensuous *latino* look he evidently wished to cultivate. His brown eyes, behind gold-rimmed glasses, conveyed amusement. He must have a sense of humor, just as he has a sense of cruelty, Julia thought. He is both warm and sinister. But now, with her, the General was friendly and relaxed. His manners were impeccable: he had gone to Choate, then spent two years at Harvard before entering West Point. His *latino* demeanor could instantly change into American demeanor, and now he sounded wholly American as he inquired politely how Julia liked Malagua so far and whether she was comfortable in her new home.

His movements were quick, and he radiated magnetism and self-assurance. Under his polished veneer, his casual American-ism, Julia detected a formidable toughness. And you have to be tough, she thought, to run a country like Malagua for eighteen years. The CIA sketch had mentioned in passing that Ferrer had an interest in ancient Mayan religious traditions, that he dabbled in Mayan occultism, and that he appeared to identify more strongly with Mayan culture and identity than had his father and grandfather. The CIA sketch made no attempt to relate these penchants to the totality of Ferrer's personality. They were just facts, or alleged facts, culled by CIA analysts from the Ferrer legend. Julia knew she had to discover the real man, the full man, in Juan Ferrer before being able to make the judgments necessary to recommend American policies toward Malagua.

And this would be extremely difficult, she realized as she listened to his small talk. Juan Ferrer evidently was a complex creature, a man totally in control of himself, knowing exactly what he wanted and, thus far, how to get it. He was not the classical Latin American dictator Julia had expected to find in Ciudad Malagua. And there was the eternal question in Julia's mind: could a North American woman ever understand a Latin American man? Julia was never certain, for example, whether she had even begun to understand Enrique, her husband.

As if reading her thoughts, Juan Ferrer, his voice still soft, said: "Let us be frank with each other. I want to cooperate in every way with the United States, and your country will need us again as the Cuban offensive continues in Central America and the Caribbean. But the United States must cooperate with me too. Life, my dear Ambassador, is a two-way street."

"Oh, we certainly realize that in relations between nations, especially friends, one hand washes the other," she said cautiously. "But sometimes a situation can arise, for a variety of political reasons, when you may have to help us to help you, Mr. President."

Ferrer shifted his bulk in his armchair and laughed in genuine mirth.

"I know exactly where you're going, Madam Ambassador— oh, hell, do you mind if I call you by your first name?—and believe me, I do understand American politics. You know, I've been around for a long time. Okay? So the idea is that the United States will consider giving me arms if I introduce what you might call 'democratic reforms' in Malagua. Am I right?"

"You are very well informed," Julia said, trying to conceal her annoyance. She had blown what she had planned as a long-term negotiation in her first five minutes with the Malaguan President. Ferrer had assumed control of the conversation, and he was not even bluffing. He *was* very well informed, and he knew the business of diplomacy. And above all, he knew Americans.

She sought to keep her composure, flashing a bright smile at
Ferrer.

She heard three short and one long beeps, a disconcerting
sound. Ferrer heard it too, and laughed again. "Oh, this," he
said, producing a wafer-thin Casio computer from his suit's
breast pocket. "I have this gimmick set for seven minutes before
the hour to remind me it's time for my next appointment. It
usually ends a meeting. But obviously, it doesn't apply to you.
My time is yours, and I must apologize for having forgotten to
turn it off. Will you forgive me?"

"Certainly, Mr. President," Julia replied, thinking that some
informality between them would be in order. After all, Ferrer
was thoroughly Americanized. "And I would be honored if you
called me by my first name. And would you please go on with
your analysis of relations between our governments? I'm finding
it extremely useful."

"All right. You know my problems. I need arms, lots of arms,
to deal with the situation here. You must have read old Wilbur's
reports on the way I see things. But I don't take you for a fool,
Julia. I'm aware that you're not going to endorse every request
of mine the way poor Wilbur did. Oh, he was so devoted to us!
But we've checked your background—you expected that, I'm
sure—and we know that you are an independent thinker. I also
know that you were behind Wilbur Breck's removal from Malagua. But that's neither here or there—Wilbur is gone and you are
here. So now my job is to persuade you that unless I get these
weapons, Malagua will turn into a mini-Vietnam, and sooner or
later, the United States will be sucked into it, probably too late
to do any good. You Americans always come too late with too
little or, the way you did in Vietnam, with too much too soon.
And even if some liberals in your Administration hate my guts,
you can't afford to let Malagua go down the drain. Not after
Cuba and Vietnam and Cambodia and Angola and Ethiopia and
Iran and Afghanistan. Not after Grenada, in the Caribbean. Not
after Nicaragua. Do you agree?"

Julia nodded. This was not the time to argue.

"Fine," Juan Ferrer went on. "Now, your job is to persuade

me, the 'dictator,' to let up a bit so that your government can't be accused of supplying a tyrant with arms. I want you to know that I appreciate the American position. I would like to help you, as you put it. But have you asked yourself, Julia, how much I can relax my rule? I don't put people in prison just for the hell of it, and the National Guard doesn't go into the hills to kill the *malaguistas* just for the fun of it. I'm not a fool. I know that I'm engaged in a war, and I know my people. The one thing we Malaguans despise is weakness or the appearance of weakness. If I released political prisoners, it would be taken as a sign of weakness—not conciliation—and it wouldn't get me any points with the opposition. The Frente, you see, doesn't simply want 'democratic reforms.' They're out to destroy me, my family, my régime, our way of life, everything we stand for. They want a complete social revolution, top to bottom, on the Cuban model. I'm not making this up. Surely, Julia, you have read the *malaguista* manifesto?''

"Yes, I have."

"Then you must understand what we're up against. I never expected Wilbur Breck to read the Frente literature—it was too complicated for him—because all he had to know in order to support my requests in Washington was that the Cubans are behind the Frente. But you're more intelligent and sophisticated, Julia. You have a Ph.D. in Latin American affairs. You understand history and you understand ideology. You must see that what I have on my hands is an honest-to-God revolutionary movement. And I must act accordingly.''

"I'm interested to hear, Mr. President, that you take the Frente seriously," Julia said. "Some of the reports we've gotten in Washington suggested that you thought the rebels, whoever they are, are nothing but terrorists with no popular support."

"You are very clever, Julia," Juan Ferrer told her. "You are clever enough to see why I have to behave as if I were dealing *only* with terrorists. If I openly admit that they are more than that, I will have played right into their hands. But with you, I can be frank. This is a very difficult situation, one that can only be resolved militarily. There's no room for compromise in Malagua:

we're already too polarized. But if the United States provides me with arms—counterinsurgency aircraft like the Bronco, for instance, and other things—I can wear them down and beat them to a bloody pulp. Once they're beaten, as they will be—at great cost to both sides, and with a great deal of destruction in the country—then I can afford to embark on your 'democratic reforms.' Can't you be pragmatic; can't you wait?''

"I can't say, Mr. President. The final judgment must be made by the Administration.''

"But you can, and will, make recommendations, won't you?''

"Yes. That's my job.''

"Okay. I'd like to ask you for one thing. Keep an open mind about Malagua. Try to understand all our harsh realities before you form an opinion. It is hard for a North American to come to terms with our cultural problems and the way they influence politics here. Yes, I know that you are a student of Latin America, but the Latin American reality has to be lived, not just studied from a distance.''

"I'm sure, Mr. President, that you know that I have lived in Latin America; in fact, as you must also know, I was once married to a Latin American,'' Julia said. "I don't claim, of course, that this has given me all the necessary insights, but—''

"Well, here I must sound a note of caution,'' Ferrer broke in, laughing. "My own sense is that the worst way for a North American woman to understand Latin America is to marry one of us. Latin American husbands aren't good teachers of anything, I'm afraid. But let me go on: you must understand that with the killing of Colonel Saavedra I can't even think of relaxation. I had to impose martial law to show that I am the boss. Otherwise, there would be a killing of this kind every day. Now, I think I can bloody the Frente just enough, and then we shall see. . . . But will you promise me to keep an open mind?''

Julia stood up and extended her hand to Juan Ferrer. "That *is* one promise I can make, Mr. President. I'll try to learn as much about Malagua as I can.''

Ferrer nodded and broke into a grin.

"It's so nice to have you here, Julia," he said lightly. "It's a welcome change to have someone as intelligent as you to discuss our problems. We'll be seeing a lot of each other. Remember, my door is always open to you. . . ."

The General walked Julia to the door. He took her hand in his two hands, and said, "*Hasta muy pronto.* And by the way, did you know that your father was a friend of mine for many years? It went back to the Bay of Pigs, when *my* father had designated me as liaison with the CIA. I was really fond of Randolph. And now I'm getting fond of Randolph's daughter."

★

Back at the Residence that evening, sipping a Scotch-and-water in the library, Julia scribbled on a yellow pad her impressions of Juan Ferrer. She liked to jot down notes about people, events, ideas, and problems in preparation for the drafting of a position paper or a telegram. She had about an hour to play with ideas about Juan Ferrer before having to dress for dinner.

Tonight, Mac and Sonia McVeigh and Rick and Betty Anders were coming over for what Julia hoped would be a quiet, relaxed evening. She had told Dudley that she hoped they could have dinner at nine o'clock, but she knew that the cocktail hour would run much longer—Sonia and Betty were overwrought and tense, and it would take at least three drinks before they were at ease —and that they would not go to the table until much later. Julia was getting used to the *hora malagueña:* dinner at ten, to bed well after midnight.

She also knew that a decision about sending home Sonia and, possibly, Betty had to be made soon. Both husbands, separately, had brought it up with Julia. The women, of course, were free to leave whenever they chose, but the emotional and political implications of their departure had to be considered. Panic at the Embassy was the last thing Julia needed at this point. She expected to get a better sense of the situation at dinner. But she realized that inevitably, they would talk the whole time about Malaguan politics, in effect holding a staff meeting at the Residence. In Ciudad Malagua there was no other subject of conversation but Juan Ferrer and the Frente.

Returning to her notes, Julia thought about her meeting with Ferrer. In his pleasant and friendly outward fashion, he was very good at being brutally frank.

Okay, frankness was a plus. Ferrer had made his position absolutely clear, and no more time had to be wasted in sounding him out on the State Department's "package deal." The next question was where United States policy went from there. He had probably been right in saying that no room was left for compromise with the opposition, that Malagua had become utterly polarized. The Embassy had had no contact with the opposition prior to Julia's arrival, but to McVeigh and Anders, for example, it was clear that the Frente shared Ferrer's assessment of the polarization. And this was the way the Frente wanted it. One had to be blind not to realize it. Even the most conservative businessmen were telling the Embassy that accommodation was out of the question. It was turning into a battle to the death. And if proof were needed, Colonel Saavedra's assassination had provided it just over a week ago.

"Polarization," Julia wrote in large letters on her yellow pad. Polarization that could go on for years—as it had in Nicaragua, Guatemala, and El Salvador—with the opposing forces escalating the violence, and the Malaguan population being caught in the vortex. Since martial law had been imposed by Ferrer, the secret police had detained some one hundred persons, including several well-known intellectuals, to be interrogated about Saavedra's death. Rumor had it that the prisoners were being tortured, and such rumors were seldom wrong in Malagua. Four students at the National University had been found dead in recent days, their mutilated bodies dumped in the small hours of the morning at the doors of their parents' homes. The University was a hotbed of antirégime sentiment, and Ferrer believed in teaching by example. A letter from the mother of one of the slain students, addressed to Julia, had arrived at the Embassy two days before. *"From woman to woman,"* it said in elegant handwritten English, *"I beg you to help us find and punish the mur-*

derers of our sons." Julia stared long and hard at the letter, feeling cold and paralyzed inside.

She was intellectually and emotionally repelled by the dictatorship, but she had to consider the Malaguan drama from the viewpoint of American national interest. Ferrer, from his perspective, was quite rational about his attitude in the emerging civil war. His survival was at stake. *"No change possible,"* Julia scribbled. In the end, she thought, the United States had only two options: it could refuse to help Ferrer, or it could actively support him. There seemed to be no middle ground. Refusal, Julia was inclined to believe, would lead to increased conflict, with the Frente gathering more power and support as the régime grew more repressive. And this, in turn, could make Juan Ferrer's prediction of a "mini-Vietnam" come true.

In the meantime, Juan Ferrer was assuming the initiative. Colonel Brown, the Defense Attaché, had reported the day before that the National Guard was preparing "search and destroy" operations to eliminate Frente bases in the highland forests. This, he said, would mean burning down whole villages. "And if the President had more and better equipment," Brown said, "he could do it better and quicker." Brown was all for it.

Ferrer, as Julia noted on her pad, was convinced he could win in a civil war. But she could not discard the possibility that ultimately, the Frente might prevail. The British Ambassador, who ran an excellent intelligence operation in Malagua, had told Julia that the Cubans were not yet in control of the Frente. But as the rebellion progressed, he said, they would become increasingly involved. Havana's method in recent years was to go all out only in support of sure causes; marginal causes received marginal support. This was the Chinese and Vietnamese international guerrilla doctrine—and Che Guevara in Cuba had spelled it out in his guerrilla manual. This, naturally, was Juan Ferrer's argument, and much as Julia abhorred his dictatorial practices, she could not ignore it altogether.

Should the United States, then, provide Ferrer with military support? If the Cuba theory were to be accepted—the theory that Ferrer's fall would inevitably result in a Cuban takeover—

the answer probably would have to be in the affirmative. The geopolitics of Central America and the Caribbean dictated such a conclusion. But could the United States be sure that Ferrer would really prevail, *even* with American weapons? American clients had seldom won civil wars in the past. And if this were to be the case in Malagua, no dialogue would be possible for a very long time with a revolutionary régime. Had not the time come, then, to abandon conventional policies and try a new approach? But how? One way, Julia concluded, would be to establish contacts with the opposition, so that at least, Washington would have a complete picture of the situation. Contacts with the opposition, however, would require permission from Washington. And would the State Department grant it to her? Probably not.

"Ghastly dilemma," Julia scribbled on the pad. There was a discreet knock on the door, and Dudley entered the library. "Madam Ambassador," he said, "your guests are here." Julia looked with alarm at her wristwatch; she had lost track of time, and now she would not be able to change for dinner. "Damn," she said.

★

Across town, at the Presidential Palace, General Ferrer was dining with General Amador Mujica, the Chief of Staff of the National Guard. They had graduated together from West Point, and were close friends. Ferrer was telling Mujica of his morning meeting with the new American Ambassador.

"It's just what I thought, Amador," the President said, slicing his steak. "She certainly won't be putty in our hands the way *el viejo* Wilbur was. She may have been a bit shaken by the way I presented the Malagua picture, but I don't think she's ready to recommend arms for me. I'm afraid it's going to take some time and effort to turn her around."

"But Juancito, you've made quite a start with the Saavedra business."

"Yeah, Fabio here did a great job, didn't he?"

"He certainly did. Poor Saavedra never knew what, or who, hit him. I don't think he even had time to realize that Fabio had switched bodyguards on him when he walked out of the house right into the bullets of Fabio's boys. *¡Carajo!* Of course, I made sure there were no Guard patrols around when Saavedra was being hit.''

Juan Ferrer chewed pensively on his meat. ''Amador, I'll bet you that the liquidation of the chief of the secret police gave the fucking *gringos* something of a pause. We'll have to worry less about Miss Savage, and our friends in Washington will have more ammunition in pushing our case. And Jim Morgan tells me that there are other ways of putting pressure on Ambassador Savage. By the way, Amador, something tells me that she's dying to get laid, and I sure as hell wouldn't mind getting in there. Anyway, I'm sort of sorry about Saavedra, but he was getting a little too greedy and a little out of line. Chasing the Frente had gone to his head. But he has served his purpose well, dying for his country. Well, let's hope our unwitting martyr rests in peace.'' The General smiled sardonically.

5

THE day Julia Savage arrived in Ciudad Malagua, Jim Morgan was aboard a commercial airliner from Washington's Dulles International Airport to San Juan, Puerto Rico. The four-hour flight was bumpy, but the CIA man, his long legs stretched out in the first-class cabin and a Bloody Mary in his hand, was preoccupied by "Operation Enrique," as it was called among the few men at the Agency's Western Hemisphere Division who knew of the enterprise.

As usual, information about highly sensitive operations such as this one had been circulated on a "need-to-know" basis, and even General McCullen, the CIA Director, had no knowledge of this project. There were occasional "autonomous" projects run out of Langley, projects initiated by individual divisions that were best left unknown to the top people: the Director, his Deputy, and the Inspector General. This procedure gave the option of "plausible denial" to these men; thus when a politically embarrassing operation was suddenly brought to light, the Director could honestly state that he (and his superior, the President of the United States) had known nothing about it. Those "autonomous" projects covered a wide range of activities—operatives in Counter Intelligence Staff had secretly provided Israel with technology to develop nuclear weapons (in violation of United States laws); the Western Hemisphere Division had conspired with the Mafia to murder Fidel Castro in Cuba; and the Technical Division had carried out illegal experiments with LSD on unwitting subjects as part of "mad-scientist" mind-control programs.

Operation Enrique was a classic autonomous project, and for Jim Morgan it was the latest highly sensitive undertaking in his twenty-five-year career in the CIA. It also was political dynamite, but Morgan did not have the slightest doubt that it had to be done—for the Agency and for the United States, which, to him, were one and the same. Actually, Morgan never had doubts about what he did in the line of duty; he was a "true believer," as they said at Langley.

Jim Morgan had just reached his fiftieth birthday, and his prestige in the CIA's Directorate of Operations, the Agency's clandestine side known as DDO, was immense. He had been through the mill, had done nearly everything in terms of undercover assignments since he'd joined the CIA after a stint as an Army intelligence officer at the outset of the Korean War, and despite certain eccentricities, he was supremely dependable. Born in Argentina of American parents (his father had managed a sheep *estancia* in Patagonia), Morgan had learned Spanish as a child. After he finished high school in Buenos Aires (Patagonian schools left much to be desired), his Irish Catholic father had sent him to college in the United States. Jim Morgan had been accepted by Notre Dame, where he played football for four years —he was an outstanding quarterback—and majored in psychology. Following graduation, he spent an unrewarding year in New York, working at odd jobs and going through nine months of marriage to an Alabama girl he had met at a Greenwich Village party. Discovering one day that his wife was sleeping with a *Daily News* reporter, he beat her into unconsciousness and walked out forever. Having battered his wife, Morgan spent four days and nights drinking whiskey. He left it to her to sue for uncontested divorce, and he never spoke to anyone afterward about his marriage.

The central fact about Jim Morgan in those days was that he did not know what to do with himself. He was angry much of the time, at society and at himself, a failure. The Korean War saved him. He volunteered for the Army, and was commissioned a second lieutenant within six months. Shipped out to Korea early in 1951, he was assigned to the G-2 section—intelligence—of the Twenty-fourth Infantry Division, which included a large number of Puerto Rican soldiers. Morgan's Spanish came in handily. Wounded in action when the Chinese overran the divisional headquarters during the winter offensive—it was a bullet in the thigh—he was discharged. In Korea, however, Morgan had met several CIA officers through his intelligence work, and presently he was offered employment by the Agency, then barely five years old. He accepted at once, and the CIA became Jim Morgan's home and destiny. From then on, he knew exactly what he wanted his life to be.

Not being an Ivy League graduate or a wartime Office of Strategic Services veteran, then the two principal sources of manpower in the strongly elitist Agency, Morgan was initially looked down upon by his superiors. But quickly the men who ran the "black side" realized that he was a natural intelligence officer— tough, taciturn, and brilliant in his own mean way. In 1954, when the CIA prepared to overthrow the leftist government in Guatemala, Jim Morgan was assigned to the project. His responsibility was to assemble in Honduras the CIA-equipped ragtag army of Guatemalan refugees who, at the proper time, invaded their homeland. Morgan was commended for his efforts.

Afterward, he served at CIA Stations in Uruguay and Venezuela, specializing in agent recruitment. In 1958, after seeing the Venezuelan dictatorship overthrown by a revolution, he concluded that it had been the work of Communists. When Fidel Castro took over Cuba the following year, Morgan became convinced that the United States faced a Communist conspiracy, directed from Moscow, throughout Latin America. Hearing through the Agency grapevine that an invasion of Cuba by CIA-organized exiles was being prepared, he asked to be attached to the operation. At first, Morgan worked out of Miami, trying to put some order into the recruitment of volunteers for the invasion brigade. When the CIA opened secret training camps in Guatemala and Malagua, he was sent to Ciudad Malagua to act as one of the permanent liaison officers with the local régime, the overall political liaison being conducted from Washington by Randolph Savage, then a Deputy to the Director of Plans (the old name for the Directorate of Operations). Morgan reported directly to Savage, but the two men disliked each other, Savage being a suave, well-born buccaneer and Morgan a rough-and-tough field operative.

In Ciudad Malagua, Jim Morgan struck an acquaintanceship, which soon developed into friendship, with Juan Ferrer. The two men often drank together, spending more and more time in each other's company. When liberal-minded members of the exiles' brigade revolted against the way the CIA directed the training, favoring former army officers of the ousted Batista dictatorship, it was Morgan who rounded them up with a hand-picked squad of CIA paramilitary personnel and had them flown to a remote village in the Malaguan highlands where they were kept under detention until the invasion. At the Bay of Pigs he went ashore with the first wave of the amphibious brigade (defying White House orders against direct involvement in the invasion by Americans), and made his way back from the beach in a dinghy to a United States destroyer standing miles offshore.

Morgan remained engaged in Cuban operations for four years, organizing CIA infiltration-and-sabotage teams, mostly of Cuban agents, that were dispatched almost nightly to the island. Late in 1965, he was posted to Vietnam, where the CIA was setting up "pacification" programs. Morgan was attached to Operation Phoenix, a secret project managed jointly with the South Vietnamese National Police and designed to eradicate Viet Cong agents. This was done largely through assassination, and Morgan was in charge of one of the principal Phoenix teams. He rapidly earned a reputation for efficiency as well as cruelty, personally supervising the interrogation and torture of suspected Viet Cong. His colleagues joked that Vietnamese mothers in the village scared their children by telling them, "If you're not good, Morgan will get you." After each torture session, Morgan withdrew to his quarters, usually a commandeered Vietnamese house, and put away a bottle of whiskey. The next day, he was ready for more Phoenix work.

Jim Morgan remained in Vietnam until 1970, when the CIA named him Deputy Station Chief in Spain. Opposition to the Franco régime was mounting, and the Agency was anxious to infiltrate the antigovernment Workers' Commissions. His knowledge of Spanish again helped Morgan, who worked closely with the Dirección Nacional de Seguridad, the secret police. The Spaniards often let him watch interrogations of political prisoners (he did it through a two-way mirror in a room at the Puerta del Sol headquarters, because it was undesirable for an American to be seen by the prisoners), but Morgan shared little of his own information with the Dirección, on the theory that what the CIA did was its own business.

Early in 1974, Juan Ferrer, now president of Malagua, visited Washington, and meeting the CIA Director at a dinner, he asked about his old friend Jim Morgan and remarked that ''he is just the kind of man I'd like to have helping me in Malagua.'' This hint was not wasted, and a month later Jim Morgan was appointed Station Chief in Ciudad Malagua with additional top-secret responsibilities in the region. Instantly, he reestablished his intimate relationship with Juan Ferrer, becoming the *de facto* American ambassador, bypassing and ignoring Wilbur Breck. With Jim Morgan in Ciudad Malagua, all the important business between the two countries was conducted through the CIA.

★

It was raining hard when Morgan's plane landed at Isla Verde Airport in San Juan, and the clouds were dark and menacing. Coming out of the gate, his Val-A-Pak over his shoulder, Morgan was met by a tall, meaty man wearing a sport shirt, slacks, and a Panama hat.

''Hi, Jim,'' he said in a Southern drawl. ''D'ya have a good trip?''

''Yeah, I guess so. How you're doing, Johnson?''

''Okay, okay. Let's get out of this mess and find your plane,'' the man replied. Sam Johnson was the head of the CIA's field office in San Juan, a most discreet presence. Theoretically, the Agency was not supposed to be running clandestine operations on American territory, which Puerto Rico is, but with the investigations of past years safely behind it and with a new political climate in the country, the CIA was quietly rebuilding its capabilities. The San Juan office was important as a logistics base for Caribbean operations, along with a crucial secret "Support East" office in Miami. Both offices were subordinated to the CIA's Western Hemisphere regional command located in Mexico City.

Because of Cuba's backing for Puerto Rican independence, the CIA's San Juan office also concerned itself with tracking down Cuban connections with Puerto Rican terrorists. Finally, San Juan was one of the main gateways to the Caribbean from Europe, and CIA officers carefully watched passengers arriving on direct flights from Madrid, Paris, Amsterdam, and Frankfurt. Intelligence agents from the Soviet Union and Eastern Europe were known to use San Juan as a transit point for the troubled independent island states of the Caribbean; they simply changed planes at Isla Verde, without having to clear U.S. Immigration. Most of the islands could not be reached directly by air from Havana. Other agents jumped off from San Juan to South America.

Johnson led Jim Morgan, sweating in his business suit (he had an aversion to casual garb), through the crowded terminal—it was July, and thousands of vacationers were arriving and departing—and opened a side door with a key he took from his pocket. Nobody paid any attention to them in the terminal's noisy throng; they were assumed to be airport or airline employees stepping out to the tarmac. Outside, the rain was still coming down, and the two men were soaked when they reached a red-and-white single-engine Cessna. It was one of the small fleet of CIA aircraft used in the area. (The planes were registered in the name of several air charter and taxi services, which were CIA "fronts.") The Malagua Station Chief said goodbye to Johnson and climbed over the wing into the plane, closing the door and tossing his bag into the back seat. The flier, a young man in a green baseball cap and dark sunglasses, said, "Hi" and switched on the engine. It coughed and turned over.

"In this weather, when do you estimate arrival in St. Thomas?" Morgan asked.

"Oh, shit, I guess we can make it under forty minutes, unless we run into a bad squall or something," the pilot replied.

He did not know Morgan's name—he had no "need to know" —and his orders for the day from Johnson were to fly a passenger to the U.S. Virgin Islands, drop him there, and return to San Juan. He was strictly a technician, a Caribbean aviator, and his only concern was to deliver his passengers safely to their destinations in the ever-uncertain Caribbean weather. The CIA paid well for this type of work, and the only injunction to the pilots was to keep their mouths shut about when, where, and with whom they went. A pilot who was known to drink excessively off duty was subject to instant dismissal and loss of his flying license: the Agency had ways of getting the Federal Aviation Administration to lift the licenses. Operationally, the practice, with extremely rare exceptions, was to file correct flight plans to avoid unnecessary problems with air-traffic controllers.

Now the pilot identified the Cessna by its number to the control tower and asked for takeoff clearance. Turning the plane's nose into the northeasterly wind—the Caribbean trade wind, which was about ten knots stronger than usual—he said to Morgan, "Okay, here we go." The aircraft raced down the wet runway and lifted off the ground. It was briefly buffeted by the wind, then steadied as it climbed through the low clouds. At 10,000 feet, they broke through the cloud cover into sunlight and leveled off. The pilot checked the compass for the correct heading—Zero-Six-Zero—and relaxed. "Make it a half-hour from now," he said. Morgan lit a cigar.

After twenty minutes of cruising, the pilot called the St. Thomas tower for landing instructions. They sliced through a bank of fluffy clouds, and Morgan saw the jagged outlines of St. Thomas. Crown and St. Peter's mountains rose majestically in front, Morgan spotting the tall radio antennas on the top. In another minute they bounced on the ground.

Avoiding the main terminal building, the plane taxied toward a cluster of small hangars at the far end of the field. This was standard CIA procedure in St. Thomas: arriving and departing without being noticed. St. Thomas was a tight little community, aside from the swarm of tourists, and it was just too easy to be seen and identified, especially if one came to the island as frequently as Jim Morgan did.

Morgan jumped out of the Cessna, shouting, "Thanks" to the pilot, and strolled over to a yellow minibus taxi waiting behind the hangars. There were so many taxis on the island to serve the hordes of tourists coming off daily cruise ships and planes that, as a security measure, the CIA Base in St. Thomas had all its vehicles disguised as cabs. The drivers occasionally accepted fares to make their operation look normal, the money going for the beer fund. The driver awaiting Morgan was black, but he spoke without the island accent when he greeted Morgan, asking, "Up the Hill?" He was a regular CIA officer, a New Yorker, and the two men knew each other well. "Yes, up the Hill, Joe," Morgan answered.

★

The CIA taxi drove along the harbor's Veterans' Drive, battling through the heavy afternoon traffic, then passed the green Legislature building, and began the steep climb up St. Peter's Mountain. In a few minutes, after several sharp twists and turns, they were high above the deep blue harbor, the cruise ships, and the old Danish town of Charlotte Amalie. At a gnarled tree just above Mafolie Chapel, the taxi made another left turn and kept going in low gear, passing expensive homes surrounded by gardens. At the top of the mountain, the cab came to a large parking lot, next to a vast flat-roofed structure serving as a tourist bar with the most striking view of the Caribbean—strings of smiling islands dotting the sea west of Sir Francis Drake Channel, the rays of the setting sun painting them, the sky, and the water in pastel shades.

Joe, the driver, parked the taxi at the far end of the lot, away from the jabbering tourists and near a chain-link fence enclosing television and microwave antenna towers. No tourists ventured here. Walking down a narrow path past the enclosure, now out of view of the parking lot, they came to a gate in another chain fence, this one surmounted by barbed wire. A deeply tanned young man in shorts and a Virgin Islands T-shirt, a .45-caliber pistol in a holster hanging loosely from his leather belt and a walkie-talkie in hand, came out from behind a tree and waved at Morgan. "Hey, Jim," he said, "good to see you again." He unlocked the gate, and the men walked another fifty yards downhill to a point where thick shrubbery concealed the entrance to a house, as did a stand of mahogany trees. A hummingbird was dancing on its head on a hibiscus flower. Another young man in shorts, a submachine gun slung over his shoulder, lounged at the door. Seeing Morgan, he grinned and unbolted the door.

Built into a cliff, a sheer drop of jungle vegetation below it, a large house with terraces and balconies looked over the sea. From the terraces, one could see fat pelicans circling slowly and gracefully over the bay beneath the house, then suddenly diving vertically into the water at the sight of a fish. Constructed after the war by a retired corporate executive, the house had been bought from his widow by the CIA to serve as the Agency's clandestine-operations base in the eastern Caribbean. It was home and "office" to twenty-five hand-picked experts in every field of intelligence, occasionally reinforced by special units. Its very existence was highly classified information, because it was on American territory and, even more, because of the nature of the operations the Agency ran out of St. Thomas.

The Virgin Islands base was the communications center for the entire Caribbean, and most of the classified Agency traffic in the region was routed through St. Peter's Mountain. Its sophisticated listening devices also monitored Cuban and Soviet air and maritime radio traffic in the eastern Caribbean. Agents in the Caribbean—Americans and natives—were debriefed on the island, although only Americans had access to the mountaintop installation. Others were handled in hotel rooms the CIA rented all over St. Thomas. Clandestine-operations teams were assembled and instructed at the St. Peter's Mountain base and flown from Harry

S. Truman Airport to their destinations aboard CIA "black flight" aircraft based in Puerto Rico. Occasionally, teams left St. Thomas aboard Agency helicopters, usually at night. The chief of the base was a former Special Forces major named Riordan Jordan who had worked with the CIA in Vietnam and Laos. But St. Thomas was directly under Jim Morgan's supervision. Major Jordan reported only to him and to Headquarters at Langley, bypassing the San Juan field office and the regional command in Mexico City.

This was so because Morgan, in addition to his duties as Malagua Station Chief, coordinated all the clandestine operations in the Caribbean, Central America, and Panama. The Malagua job gave him the cover for his wider operations, though the State Department (station chiefs technically worked under ambassadors) was unaware of Morgan's double function. Currently, Morgan was directing an investigation of the flow of *malaguista* funds in the Caribbean, and case officers assigned to the project worked out of St. Thomas, where they collated and compared the information they picked up in their travels through the region. Not long ago, they had discovered that some *malaguista* money was moving through several small banks on the island of Tortola in the British Virgin Islands, just a few minutes by air from St. Thomas. A discreet request by the CIA to MI-6 in London had quickly shut off this channel.

Morgan's other active project involved the infiltration of agents into Grenada, a former British colony in the southeastern Caribbean now governed by a revolutionary régime whose army was trained and equipped by Cuba. Morgan was convinced that a successful *coup d'état* could sooner or later be mounted in Grenada, and he was putting considerable resources into its preparation. Infiltration teams were flown from St. Thomas to tiny islands in the Grenadines, and then transported to Grenada in small boats under cover of darkness. The St. Thomas base was also responsible for monitoring drug traffic in the Caribbean, something in which Morgan had a very special interest.

Finally, a scientific team was attached to the Hill; its purpose —and this was the most secret of the base's activities—was the study of ciguatoxin, a powerful and lethal poison found in fish caught in Caribbean waters. The CIA had been involved in toxin research in the 1950s and 1960s, when its Technical Division came up with a variety of poisons, including a shellfish toxin. The idea was that these toxins, fatal even in tiny doses, could be used for assassinations that would escape detection. They could be surreptitiously slipped into food or beverages, or used as coating for small darts to be fired at a victim from special pistols. This research had been abandoned even before investigations of the CIA were launched in the mid-1970s, and stocks of toxins supposedly destroyed. But some years later, permission was quietly granted to undertake "theoretical" studies.

The working assumption among the base's scientists, stemming from accounts by fishermen, health officials, and marine biologists in the Virgin Islands, was that fish—groupers of different types, snappers, parrot fish, and doctorfish—absorbed coral poison as they fed at reefs and coral heads off eastern Caribbean islands. Then the organism of the fish transformed it into ciguatoxin. When ingested, the contaminated fish caused what doctors called ciguatera poisoning, whose symptoms ranged from severe nausea to mental disorientation, paralysis, and, often, death. A neurotoxin, the poison attacks the central nervous system, and no cure or antidote exists for it.

Their task therefore was to isolate the ciguatoxin from the fish —the St. Thomas base purchased daily pounds and pounds of freshly caught fish—and analyze its chemical structure to determine whether the toxin could be extracted and stored for some future use.

Jim Morgan came to St. Thomas several times a year—always telling the Embassy in Malagua that he had been called to Washington or Mexico City—to check up on his operations in the Virgin Islands. This time he came to St. Peter's Mountain on a delicate mission.

Drinking a Heineken beer out of a frosty bottle in Riordan Jordan's office, Morgan read two telexes that had just arrived from Malagua via Langley. Both had been sent by his deputy, John Crespo. One reported the bomb explosion at the Ciudad

Malagua airport when Julia Savage had landed earlier in the day. "Good," Morgan remarked to the Base chief. "This helps to create the proper atmosphere for the lady Ambassador." Crespo's second message told of Colonel Saavedra's assassination. Morgan whistled appreciatively as he reread the telex. "Well, well," he said softly to himself. "I didn't believe old Juanito had it in him. And what timing! Yeah, it looks like Uncle Jim's advice still counts for something."

★

An hour later, Morgan was back in the yellow CIA taxi, driving downtown. A rainsquall had just swept over Magens Bay, on the north side of St. Peter's Mountain, and a perfect rainbow lovingly kissed the water, a momentary illusion of ethereal beauty. The long summer's day was ending, and the evening was now descending quickly on St. Thomas.

Riordan Jordan had filled Morgan in on the details of the arrangements tonight, and the Station Chief directed the driver to take him to the Frenchman's Reef Hotel, on the rocky tip of land at the western entrance to St. Thomas harbor. The Reef was the biggest and busiest hotel on the island, always full of package-tour tourists, its lobby and bars teeming with people. Another good place to avoid recognition. Morgan checked a piece of paper he had taken out of his pocket, and took the elevator to the third floor. He walked down the dimly lit corridor, looking at room numbers. When he reached Room 314, he knocked twice.

There were hurried steps inside, and the door, its chain lock still in place, opened a few inches. "It's okay, Enrique. It's me," Morgan said impatiently. A man stepped aside to let him into the room. Unmistakably Latin American, he was tall and handsome, in his early forties, and immaculately dressed in a Pierre Cardin sport shirt and slacks. Well bred and well educated, he looked like one of those wealthy Latin playboys who are seen at the Carlyle in New York, at the Connaught in London, or at the Carlton in Cannes and who are at home everywhere. Another man, a heavyset American in a blue *guayabera* shirt, sat in an armchair. Morgan acknowledged his greeting and said, "All right, Jack, why don't you wait out on the terrace?'' The man nodded and left the room. Morgan slid the glass door closed behind him and sat on the double bed.

''Enrique, I'm delighted that you were able to come and meet me here on such short notice,'' he said, lighting a cigar and staring at him over the flame. ''And I trust you've brought the goods with you. You know, I need it badly.''

Enrique Palma Rioseco flashed a self-satisfied smile at the CIA man. He walked over to a small bar, asking in barely accented English, ''Jack Daniel's okay, Jim?'' He poured the bourbon for Morgan and refreshed his own Scotch.

''It's always a pleasure to be of service to you,'' he said in a tone that was more subservient than companionable. Enrique was clearly uncomfortable with Morgan, who, just as clearly, was the boss in the room. ''Anyway,'' he added, delivering the drink, ''I was getting bored stiff in Colombia. God, what a stinking hole my country is! Your call, Jim, was a great excuse to break away.''

Morgan tasted the whiskey, grimacing approvingly. ''All right, Enrique,'' he said, ''let's cut out the shit and get down to business. I haven't got all night. What else have you got on her?''

''You mean, on Julia?''

''Who the hell do you think we're talking about? Eleanor Roosevelt?''

''Sure, Jim. On Julia. Yeah, I do have a few more things.''

''Like what? Let's have it. Remember what you told me over the phone after the Savage appointment was announced?''

''Yes, I do,'' Enrique said.

And Enrique did remember with absolute clarity that day late in June when he had seen Julia's picture on the front page of the morning newspaper in Cali, Colombia, over a report that his ex-wife had been named United States Ambassador to Malagua. Enrique's first reaction had been one of annoyance—even anger—mixed with envy. God damn her, he had said to himself. The bitch had walked out on him, Enrique Palma Rioseco, a member of a premier Colombian family. He chose not to remember the reasons why Julia had left him—Enrique was not a man ever to consider that he might have been wrong. And now she was a big deal, an American ambassador and, at that, to a country where so much of his business was centered. She was a *somebody* while he, basically, remained a *nobody*. The thought rankled. The newspaper story had mentioned him in the last paragraph as Julia's former husband, and this made matters even worse. He had received numerous telephone calls from his friends and relatives, calls that were ostensibly meant as congratulations ("Isn't it great that your ex-wife is an *ambassador?*" and "Of course, you two have remained friends"), but Enrique knew they were put-downs, sly comments that he was nothing but a wealthy jet-setter entering middle age. To be sure, they did not know the truth about him, which was naturally the way it had to be, but Enrique felt miserable, betrayed, and furious nevertheless.

His second reaction was sudden concern that Julia's presence in Ciudad Malagua might interfere with his Malaguan ties and operations. Why, of all places on earth, had she had to be sent to Malagua? That evening, after several drinks, he decided that he had to act to protect his interests, and he did the only thing that occurred to him: he telephoned Jim Morgan in Ciudad Malagua.

Guardedly, he conveyed his fears to the Station Chief, asking what, if anything, he should do. There was a long silence at the other end of the line; then Morgan said he would get back to him. The CIA man did so the following morning, from a phone at the office of the new chief of G-2 of the Malaguan National Guard—he did not want to call from the Embassy—and he had a question.

"Concerning the person we discussed last night," Morgan said, "it would be important to know whether, by any chance, you are in possession of derogatory or damaging information about that person. You know, embarrassing stuff."

For Morgan, it was a shot in the dark. Everybody, he assumed, had a skeleton in the closet, something never to be revealed, innocent or not. Experience had taught him that such shots were seldom off the mark.

Enrique thought the question over. Suddenly, it triggered a memory, half-forgotten images from the past.

"Now that you ask, Jim," he said, "I do know an interesting story about her. But I never thought it would be of any value to you."

"Well, now it is. Everything is of value. But you better be sure of your facts."

"Of course I am," Enrique replied with new self-assurance.

"Okay. I want to hear it. But this is an open line, so mention no names. I'll understand what you're saying."

Enrique's mind went back many years, to when he and Julia Savage had been graduate students in Washington, started the affair that led to their marriage, and been in the thick of the nascent antiwar movement. Julia had had friends—bearded and blue-jeaned young men and intense young women affecting long skirts and peasant blouses—who were called "peaceniks" or "hippies" by the serious people. They smoked pot when Julia brought them over to Enrique's house for endless discussions of the war and "Fascist America," though she never accepted a joint, preferring to sip wine.

It was about that time that newspapers began reporting mysterious bombings of military installations across the United States, university research laboratories with defense contracts, and ROTC offices on campuses. Enrique noticed that some of the young men and women began missing the nocturnal sessions at his house, never to be seen again. When he inquired about them, Julia dismissed their absence casually, saying, "Oh, they're SDS people, as you know, and they must have gone into hiding somewhere to do their political work. Maybe they're in Michigan with Mark Rudd, or something."

One night, Julia had called Enrique in a state of agitation. "Listen," she had said, "there's a friend of mine who's in trouble and who needs protection. I'm bringing her over now to your place so we can figure out what to do next . . . but look out the window to make sure there are no cops or strange-looking cars in the street. If you see anything suspicious, turn off the porch light and I'll know."

The girl Julia brought to Enrique's house was scared but defiant. He remembered her muttering, "The pigs will never get me ... they'll never get me alive. ...." Julia made several phone calls, then told the girl, "The only safe place I can think of in Washington is my house. I doubt anybody will check on my father's home—the FBI and the CIA don't get in each other's way."

The next morning, *The Washington Post* carried a front-page story with a picture of the girl, describing her as a "Weatherman Bomber" and as the object of a nationwide search by the FBI. She had been linked, the story said, with the bombing of a physics laboratory at the University of Wisconsin in Madison. A young instructor had been killed in the bombing.

"Now you know who she is," Julia said to Enrique that evening. "Yes, she does belong to the SDS Weatherman Movement. Yes, she was involved in the Wisconsin bombing. Yes, I'm opposed to violence and bombings, but she's a friend of mine, and she needed help. She's scared out of her wits, and she needs time to get her head together. That's why I took her home. You should have seen my father's face this morning—we were all having coffee in the kitchen when he saw her picture in the paper. Christ, I never saw him so angry and confused! He said that as a government official, he couldn't abet crime, and he went to the phone to call the FBI. I began to cry and plead with him, and finally, I persuaded him not to do it—for me—so long as she left the house by noon. I guess he didn't want in the end to make me a traitor to my friends, which is what I would have been if she had been arrested at my house."

Speaking to Jim Morgan from Cali, Enrique had described the incident in great detail though, as ordered, omitting names.

Morgan was astounded and forced himself to speak calmly. "You're sure of all this?"

"Absolutely. I couldn't make up that wild a story."

"No, I guess you couldn't. Okay, we'll have to talk more about it, but in person. I'll let you know when and where to meet me. In the meantime, pull all that stuff together; try to remember all the details."

Morgan whistled as he hung up the phone. God, shots in the dark can certainly pay off! And this was serious stuff: an Ameri-

can ambassador who had aided fugitives from justice—a friend
of bombers and killers. And her fucking father, the CIA hero,
covering up for her. Christ, this will blow Ambassador Savage
right out of the water!

Making a quick trip to Washington, Morgan informed Colonel
Duke, the CIA's Western Hemisphere Chief, of what he had
learned from Enrique. The two men spent hours discussing how
best it could be used against Julia Savage. First, they had agreed
to keep the information to themselves for the time being. There
was no point in involving the Director. Then, they concluded that
it would be unwise to hit Julia with Enrique's material during her
Senate confirmation hearings. Leaks to senators or the press
could backfire against the CIA, raising the awkward question of
why the Agency wanted to sabotage her confirmation. Besides,
there was no proof. The girl was still missing, Julia Savage could
deny everything, her father was dead, and her mother, if she had
ever known anything, was an alcoholic and not a credible wit-
ness. It was better, Morgan and Kingsley Duke had decided, to
hold their weapon in reserve and to activate it—through Enrique
—once Julia Savage was installed in Ciudad Malagua. In fact,
Morgan had said, this approach would produce even better re-
sults, with Julia a pawn of the CIA. This, then, was the genesis
of "Operation Enrique," a very closely held secret at Langley
Headquarters.

★

Now Jim Morgan was facing Enrique in the St. Thomas hotel
room, anxious to launch him like a missile against Julia Savage.
This alone, Morgan thought, was worth the whole investment the
CIA had made in the Colombian.

Swallowing the bourbon, Morgan repeated, "You do remember exactly what you told me about Julia Savage?"

"Yes, naturally I do."

"Do you have any doubts about any of it? Do you remember
anything else?"

Enrique nodded. "A few more details. The girl telephoned

Julia at my place several times that year, and I think that once or twice she asked for money."

"Did she get it?"

"I don't know, Jim. Julia never said anything about sending money."

"Okay. What about her father? You said he had agreed not to turn the fugitive over to the authorities? Are you positive?"

"Well, that's what Julia told me. But now that I've thought about it, something else about Mr. Savage sticks in my mind. It's not very clear, but it has to do with his death, back in 1968, when Julia and I were first married. Her mother called her in Cali to say that Savage had been killed. Julia cried a lot after the phone call, then told me that it had had to happen because the old man might have been playing games with the other side. I think that's the way she put it."

"You mean he was a double agent, or a mole, or something of that kind?"

Enrique shrugged. "I'm not familiar with those expressions, but Julia did say, as I recall, that he had had to be finished, or whatever you call it."

"Terminated?"

"Right. That's the word. Terminated."

The CIA man considered it carefully, puffing on his cigar. Outside, a cruise ship sounded its foghorn, summoning passengers back aboard after the day's shopping in St. Thomas. If the Colombian was telling the truth, it was dynamite. But, he asked himself, where would Julia have gotten this information? If Randolph Savage had indeed been a mole, he would hardly have told his young daughter about his double life. No, it made no sense. He suspected that Enrique had invented the story to make himself more important, but he had no interest in verifying it. The Agency had been torn for years by suspicions that the Soviet KGB had planted a mole in Langley, and Morgan did not want such flimsy evidence to bog him down in this witch-hunt. It was something to be tucked away in his mind for the future, but nothing to be touched now. He did believe, however, the account of the Weatherman fugitive: what Enrique had told him about the girl was corroborated in its main outlines by the FBI. That was enough for Morgan's immediate purposes.

"Well, Enrique," he said, "now you've got your work cut out for you."

"Meaning?"

"Meaning that you are to warn Julia Savage that you'll spill the beans about her little bomber friend unless she's prepared to cooperate."

"I don't understand."

"I'll draw you a picture," Morgan said impatiently. "Julia Savage is now Ambassador to Malagua, which is my territory. Theoretically, she's my boss there. But Miss Savage doesn't seem to care for President Ferrer, who is a friend of mine and whom I don't want to see kicked out by fucking revolutionaries. Neither does the Agency. Therefore the name of the game is to change Savage's mind and her policies."

"You want me to blackmail her, Jim? Is that what you're saying?"

"Oh, shit, Enrique," Morgan said wearily. "Blackmail, that's a nasty word. Let's say I want you to *persuade* Miss Savage to mend her ways."

"Jesus, I can't do it. It's one thing to tell you about it, and it's another to blackmail her. You don't know her—you're asking me the impossible."

"I'm not asking you: I'm ordering you."

"But Jim," the Colombian sighed, collapsing into a chair, "what if I can't do it or won't do it?"

"Very simple," Morgan told him quietly. "In the first place, you're the one who called me for advice. How to protect your business. In the second place, I *own* you, and you know it. What if I were to take the cocaine routes away from you and give them to someone more deserving? What if I were to drop a word about you to our Drug Enforcement Administration boys, or the Colombian authorities? What if I told Ambassador Savage that her ex-husband, one of the biggest cocaine dealers in South America, is doing business in Malagua? She would have no choice but to inform Washington, because it affects her territory. And it would make her look good to report on you."

Morgan pointed his finger at Enrique and continued: "And what about your sideline of smuggling illegal immigrants into the United States? You'd get a real nice prison term in either the United States or Colombia—and I would see that you're extradited from Malagua if you hide there. No, Enrique, you have no choice. What I'm offering you is a fair business proposition. You owe me, and I can destroy you."

"Well, it's not like it's a one-way street," Enrique Palma said with a flash of bravado. "You and your people get plenty out of our partnership too. Let's not forget that. And you know, *I* could blow the whistle on you and the CIA."

"What we get out of it is none of your fucking business, pal," Morgan replied. "And don't kid yourself about blowing the whistle on us. Who the hell would believe you, a no-good Colombian drug smuggler? Your own Miami contacts would come down on you like a ton of bricks if you opened your mouth. Come off it, boy. . . ."

Enrique rose and paced, swearing in Spanish, *"¡Coño, carajo!"* He faced Morgan.

"Suppose I'm willing to take a chance that you won't dare to expose me because, in the end, you'd be exposing yourself? In Latin America, you know, the word of the CIA doesn't carry much weight. And I have friends. . . ."

Morgan examined his cigar with intense interest. "Well, if that's what you want to do, I won't argue with you," he said. "But I wouldn't like to see you meet with an accident, Enrique. You travel so much. You do business with such peculiar people. . . ."

"You wouldn't dare!"

"No? *¿Quién sabe?*"

"¡Carajo!"

"Well, my dear Enrique, I must go now," Morgan said, getting up from the bed. "Why don't you think over our conversation? You have a perfectly legitimate reason to turn up in Malagua— you make trips there all the time—and it would be quite proper for you to pay a call on the American Ambassador who happens to be your ex-wife. Then you can lay it all out for her: either she gets off Ferrer's back or that whole business about her and her father sheltering a Weatherman bomber becomes public. I'll see to it that it does.''

Enrique Palma remained silent, and Morgan smiled thinly at him.

"You can stay here, at the Reef, as long as you want. You should get some sun on the terrace. It'll be good for you. Jack will make sure that you're safe and that all your meals are nicely served in the room. And all the booze you want. By the way, you should try the banana daiquiri—it's very smooth. We'll be happy to pick up the tab for your vacation in the Virgin Islands. Then, when you've made up your mind, you can send me a message through Jack, and we'll be in touch again. I know, Enrique, that you'll make the right decision.''

BOOK TWO

★   ★   ★

Julia

6

"I HAVE heard that you were once married, Madam Ambassador," the wife of the Chairman of the National Assembly, Señora Marisol Duarte de Vega, said conversationally to Julia Savage as she filled her plate with shrimp *à la créole* and rice at the buffet table in the dining room of the Residence. She was a tall woman with her hair in a chignon, her beauty not yet wholly dissipated by age that comes so quickly in the tropics. Taking a fork, she added, "And did your husband die?"

"No, we were divorced seven years ago," Julia replied politely, knowing full well that Señora de Vega was aware of that, but wanted to pretend innocence. In Malagua, conversations were charades with subtle messages.

"Oh, really," Señora de Vega said. "How interesting. Malagua, you know, is a very Catholic country, and we have no divorce here." She looked around, and added quickly, "Which is a pity. . . . Maybe someday we'll have it too. . . . And other things. . . ."

It was the first reception given by Julia, four weeks after her arrival in Ciudad Malagua, and with the help of McVeigh, Ann Mestre, and the Embassy's Public Affairs Section, she had drawn up a guest list representative of the Malaguan government, society, the press, and a few intellectuals who had never before been invited to the American Embassy. The latter had been suggested by Henry Clark, the Information and Cultural Officer, when Julia told him that she wanted to meet some of his contacts. Delighted, Clark had proposed ten names, but she had cut down the list. "Let's start with just five," she said, "and then we'll go on from there."

There had not been a single refusal on the 110-person invitation list—an exceptional level of attendance at a diplomatic affair in Latin America—and Julia and Ann Mestre agreed that it was as much from a desire to show courtesy to the new American Ambassador as from curiosity in meeting the woman envoy. "I know I'm something of a freak," Julia told Ann that morning, "but there are times, I suppose, when it helps to be a freak." She laughed. Ann said, "That's right: remember you're on display tonight."

Julia displayed herself with elegance, but without exaggeration. In the *nouveau-riche* Ferrer society of Malagua, it was important to be stylish without overdoing it, lest some of the women present feel put down by the American. And unlike many American women in high official positions, Julia had learned in Washington the importance of cultivating the wives of the men with whom she dealt professionally. They should be friends and allies, not enemies put off by Julia's official standing and youthful attractiveness. A resentful wife could be a lethal foe: she could turn her husband against Julia. A successful woman had to protect herself from all sides. Not that Julia was coldly calculating; she simply happened to like women—and to understand their reactions—and she acted with tact and sympathy.

Tonight, she dressed in a below-the-knee pale green silk-chiffon dress, with a high neck and butterfly sleeves—quite chic but not overbearing. Her earrings were small cabochon emeralds set in gold, and she carried a gold *minaudière*.

"What gorgeous earrings!" exclaimed Señora de Moreno, the wife of the Protocol Chief. "May I ask where they come from?"

"They are Colombian," Julia said patiently, "and they were a present from my ex-husband." She assumed that the Señora would instantly spread the word among her friends in the room, and that there would be no more pointed questions about her past marital status. This would take care of at least one item of gossip about her—though inevitably, there would be others. Julia had become resigned years before to gossip flying about her life. Still, Julia felt annoyed that the subject of her marriage had become a topic of conversation at her reception. To be sure, this was Latin America, but she would not allow it to spoil her party. In fact, she would preempt further gossiping by facing the issue squarely. Flashing her best smile at Señora de Moreno, Julia said, "And you know, I find that being divorced isn't such a bad thing. It does give you a great deal of freedom to act and think as a woman. To tell you the truth, I doubt that I'd want to get married again—even if I found the ideal man." Señora de Moreno looked her in the eyes, and she knew that Julia meant it. "Yes, I understand," she sighed. Julia touched her arm, and made her way across the crowd in the dining room to the living room, where Henry Clark was deep in conversation with an elderly man sporting a goatee.

"Madam Ambassador," Clark said in Spanish, "do join us for a moment. I know Professor Merino would enjoy chatting with you. He's the greatest living authority on the Malaguan culture and society. He's the chairman of the department of social anthropology at the National University."

The professor bowed over Julia's hand, and said, "I'm not sure whether being 'the greatest living authority' on the Malaguan society, if that's indeed what I am, does carry any extraordinary credentials. Malagua is a small and poor society, which once knew the greatness of the Maya, but today . . ."

Julia now remembered his name from the list of intellectuals Henry Clark had proposed for the reception. Luis Merino Caña, according to Clark, was one of the most interesting and independent minds in Malagua, a respected teacher and a prolific writer. He was the author of the three-volume *Mayan Influences,* a Central American classic, and had been a close friend of Guatemala's Nobel Prize novelist Miguel Ángel Asturias. Clark had told Julia that Professor Merino was considered to be a quiet critic of the Ferrer régime. He had never publicly participated in politics, even in 1966 when Ferrer engaged in his brief flirtation with democracy, and whatever he thought of the government, he kept it to himself and a few intellectuals in his immediate circle of friends. It was assumed that Ferrer was aware of Professor Merino's discreet opposition, but regarded him as a politically harmless old man—Merino was sixty-eight—whose international prestige among men of learning served to enhance Malagua's standing. He was a short, copper-complexioned man, dressed conservatively in a dark suit, and now he was peering at Julia with a touch of amusement through his horn-rimmed glasses. His goatee gave him a benign air.

"I'm most honored to be your guest, Madam Ambassador," he said, "but I should tell you that this is the first time I have ever been invited to the American Embassy, and of course, I can't help wondering to what I owe this distinction."

"Actually, Professor Merino," Julia said, looking him straight in the eyes, "*you* honor *me* by coming to my house. It has been a loss of this Embassy that you have not come here before. And I hope that from now on we'll be seeing a great deal of you."

"You are very kind, madam," Merino told her, sounding unconvinced.

"No, I'm being selfish. I want to learn about Malagua, and I intend to squeeze every bit of knowledge out of you. You may be sorry you came because now that I've met you, I'll pester you all the time to explain your country and your people to me."

Merino stared at Julia for a moment; then an impish smile lit up his dark, wrinkled face.

"I can promise you that I shall never regret coming to your house," he replied. "Not only are you beautiful, Madam, but you have appealed to the vanity of an old teacher. Of course, I'm at your service, if there's anything I can really do to interpret Malagua for you. But you know, it's so unexpected to find an American ambassador who seems so seriously interested in us. I daresay it's refreshing. . . ."

"Thank you," Julia said. "In fact, I was wondering whether I might have my first lesson tonight. Why waste time? If you are not too busy or too tired, I would love for you to stay late. I think most of my guests will leave around ten o'clock—let's see, it's already close to nine—and you and I could have a quiet talk together."

"I'd be delighted. I'm neither tired nor busy, and I told you I'm always at your service."

★

The rest of the evening, Julia moved from group to group, chatting brightly and making mental notes about those she thought she wanted to see again—for lunch, a small dinner, or drinks—to have a chance for serious conversation. Official contacts with Cabinet ministers or members of the National Assembly had, naturally, to be kept up, but Julia did not expect to glean much from them. If she were to understand Malagua, it was absolutely vital to broaden her circle of acquaintances. Beyond the banality of dictatorship in a backward Central American nation and apart from all the political implications of the present crisis for the United States, there was a special dimension of mystery and things locked behind the façade of what Malagua was supposed to be. Julia had felt it instinctively from the day she had landed in Ciudad Malagua. Was it the Mayan influence Professor Merino had written about; was it something unique yet elusive in the Malaguan character?

Ever since Julia had become involved in Latin American affairs, even before her marriage to Enrique Palma, she had been exposed to the eternal complaint that North Americans did not understand Latin Americans, that they would never understand them, that the cultural differences were too profound to bridge. Latin American intellectuals, artists, and diplomats Julia knew usually said it patronizingly, with that irritating condescension that an earlier generation of North Americans had learned to expect from Europeans. Often, to "understand" Latin America was equated with the total and uncritical acceptance of whatever view a Latin speaker was expressing at a given time, no matter how demonstrably foolish.

Briefly, during her marriage crisis, Julia had almost come to believe that indeed it was this mystical *cultural* difference that had destroyed her relationship with Enrique. But that was in her younger period of self-doubt. Now she had developed a sounder sense of these differences, making the points in her conversations with Latin Americans that, in the first place, there was no such thing as a monolithic Latin American reality (a notion expressed by Latins themselves when it was intellectually convenient); that, in the second place, Latin Americans themselves knew little about one another's countries; and finally, that in the past quarter-century Latin American studies had flowered in American universities to an extraordinary degree. The Latin Americans, of course, remained unconvinced, and Julia's conversations with most of them remained essentially mutually accusatory dialogues. But, she thought, Luis Merino seemed like a man who was anxious to teach and share rather than to hector. Julia was not an expert on Malagua—there really were not any in Washington—and she knew that running an embassy would leave her little time to learn alone.

As a rule, an American ambassador does not have much time to read anything beyond official materials and newspapers. The demands on his or her time are frightful. The day-to-day running of an embassy even as small as Julia's in Malagua is a vexing and time-consuming process, although a first-rate deputy, like Mc-Veigh, can take on much of the administrative burden.

In a typical day, an ambassador reads, or should read, the stream of classified and unclassified telegram traffic from Washington. There are "Action" telegrams from the State Department, requesting political information on some specific point; instructing the Embassy to carry out some *démarche* or other at the Foreign Ministry; announcing the visit of a Congressional delegation or a fact-finding official; or passing on messages from other Government agencies seeking data on, say, the size of the next sugar harvest, the country's international balance of payments, or the prospects of the fishing industry next year. Then there are general circulars concerning administrative matters in all the embassies in Latin America. Routinely, the Malagua Embassy also received copies of reporting telegrams sent to Washington by other posts in the region, on the correct theory that they were of interest to Julia and her colleagues. Dealing with the Ferrer crisis, she wanted to be informed of developments in neighboring tension-ridden countries in Central America and the Caribbean. One situation could have an impact on another situation next door.

All telegrams from the State Department to the embassies are addressed to "The Ambassador" (and they are signed by the Secretary of State), but Julia quickly learned to be selective about what she really had to read every morning when she reached her desk. The first line or two of the telegram told her whether to keep reading it or refer it to one of her staff. Still, glancing through telegrams took up too much time, particularly when the Malaguan crisis was growing increasingly acute. Preparing outgoing telegrams to Washington also consumed hours. Julia drafted personally only the most important dispatches, but she was responsible for every scrap of paper flowing from Ciudad Malagua to the State Department, each telegram bearing the signature SAVAGE. This meant perusing all the telegrams drafted by Embassy officials, sometimes insisting on changes and arguing about them. She disliked overruling her staff, preferring to reason with them and, as often as not, yielding points. Still, she had to be in control.

Daily staff meetings and discussions with individual officers of the Embassy on topics of their special responsibility commanded additional hours. So did telephone calls to and from the Assistant Secretary of State, his deputies, and the Malagua Country Director (it used to be called Desk Officer) in the Department. But all this was only the "inside" part of the ambassadorial job. At least once a week, especially in the beginning, Julia had to call on the Foreign Minister and other ministers at their offices, to become better acquainted and because of previously neglected items of business—such as economic aid to Malagua—requiring a top-level approach. Julia's mornings and afternoons at the Embassy were also broken up by visitors: Malaguan government officials; resident American businessmen and their visiting bosses from the States; American journalists in town for two or three days, believing it was the Ambassador's duty to receive them at once and give them the "inside information" about Malagua; and assorted private citizens passing through and whom the State Department, usually on behalf of a senator or a congressman, had asked Julia to see.

Congressional delegations were the worst. They had to be met by Julia at the airport; put up at the Residence, if possible; fed and wined at her personal expense (the State Department's "representation" budget does not begin to cover an ambassador's basic entertainment expenses); given long briefings; and fixed up with appointments with local high officials. Every congressman wanted to be received by President Ferrer, and failure to arrange an audience was counted personally against Julia. Actually, public-relations-minded as Ferrer was, he tended to comply with most of the requests, and Julia had to go time after time to hear the General's smoothly delivered explanations why the United States should give his régime unqualified support. And as Julia found out, Ferrer's pitch usually worked. Before departing, more conservative congressmen would tell her, as one senator from the Southwest did, that "I don't care if this fellow Ferrer is a dictator or not, he's a true friend of the United States, and I hope you State Department people realize it." Liberal congressmen who came to Malagua seldom rated a Ferrer audience (the General knew who stood where in the Congress), but they were equally full of advice for Julia. Their hope was that the State Department would let the tyrant fall.

Julia's evenings were almost never her own. There were official dinners and receptions at other embassies—despite Malagua's nocturnal terrorism—and her attendance was *de rigueur*. No high-level official Malaguan function could be ignored. When Embassy officers had parties at their homes for Malaguans who were their contacts and they invited her, Julia made a point of accepting. It enhanced the prestige of her staff and, occasionally, provided a good, quiet chat. When she was not going out, Julia used the evenings to entertain at the Residence, usually at small dinners.

Diplomacy's social requirements had forced Julia to redecorate the Residence almost as a top priority. The condition in which she had inherited it from the reclusive Ambassador Breck rendered self-respecting entertainment virtually impossible. Using her own money (and hoping to be reimbursed someday by the State Department, notoriously slow in approving this kind of funds), Julia had the Residence painted in light colors. She replaced Breck's furniture with elegant sofas, chairs, and tables belonging to the Savage family that had been stored for years in a Washington warehouse. And through arm-twisting in the State Department's Interior Design and Furnishings Branch in the Office of Foreign Buildings, Julia had obtained rapid delivery of a half-dozen modern American paintings. At least, the American Residence in Ciudad Malagua looked comfortable, lived-in, and a presentable setting in which Julia could suitably perform her diplomatic person-to-person duties.

Tonight, at her first reception, Julia was surveying the crowd for interesting guests. She spotted Nestor Cruz, the owner and editor of Ciudad Malagua's oldest newspaper, *Clarín,* who was known to be less than enthusiastic about Ferrer, and artfully managed his editorial page to get across some of his criticisms. Julia put him down mentally for a dinner invitation soon. The young economist Fernando Silvestre, trained at the Harvard Business School and now in charge of Malagua's National Development Board, a new agency created by Ferrer to attract foreign investment, was another candidate. So was Manuel Schneider Belmonte, an MIT graduate, who had inherited his father's automobile distributorship (though it was partly co-owned by Ferrer), the largest in Malagua, and who spouted ideas about the need to modernize the country's economy. But Julia was also deeply interested in María Carmen Escalante, a woman in her mid-twenties, with intelligent, outspoken eyes. Despite her youth, she was Malagua's most important painter, and Julia had admired at several homes and embassies her portraits of Malaguan peasants, works that had touches of Orozco and Guayasimín.

All these contacts, Julia hoped, might make up at least in part for her absolute lack of time to read up on Malagua. In a month, she had been able to go through only forty pages of a book on

Malaguan history; dog-tired, she would drop off to sleep after two or three pages of the volume she kept on her bedside table, next to her bank of telephones.

Julia realized, of course, that she *could* be less compulsive about her work and that she could do less. Wilbur Breck had led a life of comparative leisure, doing the bare minimum. Ambassadors from smaller countries, particularly from Latin America, seldom worked more than three or four hours a day. The Bolivian Ambassador, for example, spent most of his time working on his new novel. He was a noted writer, and his government, believing —probably wisely—that art took precedence over diplomacy, had awarded him the Malaguan ambassadorial sinecure so that he could work in peace and comfort, unconcerned about money.

This was a nice Latin American trait, Julia thought, of naming outstanding writers as ambassadors to encourage their creativity. The Guatemalans had done it for Miguel Ángel Asturias, the Chileans for Pablo Neruda, and the Mexicans for Carlos Fuentes. But the United States was involved in everything and everywhere—certainly in Malagua—and the American Ambassador, even a less compulsive one than Julia Savage, was given no opportunity for serious reading, let alone writing. She was reminded of the old State Department dictum that "nobody above the rank of an Assistant Secretary has the time to think."

Julia could not read to her satisfaction, this was evident, but she had sworn to herself that she would not abdicate her thinking functions no matter what the pressures of the daily work. And among these pressures was the problem of Jim Morgan, the CIA Station Chief.

★

The difficulties had begun with their first meeting. Morgan had returned to Ciudad Malagua four days after Julia Savage's arrival. He had lingered an extra day at the St. Peter's Mountain Base, going over current operations with Riordan Jordan, and then flown back to San Juan to spend a day with Sam Johnson. Checking with St. Thomas, he learned that there were no messages for him from Enrique Palma Rioseco, who was remaining in his hotel room. Taking the weekly Iberia DC-10 flight from San Juan to San José, Costa Rica, Morgan spent the evening drinking with the local Station Chief, an old friend. Finally, he caught a LACSA BAC-111 flight to Ciudad Malagua. His driver met him at the airport and drove him home, where Morgan lazed away the afternoon and the evening, reading an espionage paperback —he was an *aficionado* of this kind of fiction, always marking passages where *he* would have done things differently—and drinking bourbon. He was interrupted once by a phone call from John Crespo, his deputy, reporting that all was relatively quiet in Malagua. Finishing the paperback, he fixed himself a cold roast-beef sandwich (his maid had orders to keep the refrigerator always stocked) and opened a fresh bottle of bourbon, now concentrating on his meeting the next day with the new Ambassador. He went to sleep around midnight, heavy with whiskey, tossing restlessly amidst erotic dreams about Julia Savage. Over the weeks, Morgan had studied photographs of Julia with great attention.

The next morning, he had his secretary call Ann Mestre to say that he would like to see the Ambassador. Ann suggested ten o'clock, right after the staff meeting, and Morgan, who almost never attended the meetings, said it would be fine. This gave him an extra hour to nurse his hangover with cups of black coffee. Finally, he lit his first cigar of the day and took the elevator to the floor below.

Julia Savage awaited Morgan with anger mixed with nervousness. She was angry that the CIA in Washington had lied to her about his whereabouts; that he had not been in Ciudad Malagua when she arrived, contrary to what Colonel Duke had said; and that Morgan had been mysteriously absent for four more days. With the Saavedra murder and the martial law, she thought, the Station Chief should have been on the job. Julia was nervous about the meeting with Morgan because this would be her first test of authority as Ambassador and because, instinctively, she knew that he would be an adversary. She was ready for confrontation.

The first thing Julia noticed as Morgan walked into her office was the cigar in his hand. Bad manners or deliberate discourtesy? The second thing she saw when he approached her desk and she rose to greet him was that his pale blue eyes were unbelievably bloodshot. Julia started to extend her hand, but Morgan ignored it, plunking himself down in the chair facing the desk.

"I sure could use a cup of black coffee," he said flatly.

"Of course," Julia said, sitting down and depressing the intercom key. "Ann, a cup of black coffee for Mr. Morgan, please." She was taken aback by the man's rudeness. The Station Chief was looking at the ceiling, blowing cigar smoke, and clearly waiting for her to open the conversation. Ann came in with the coffee, setting the cup on the desk in front of him. Morgan did not thank her.

"Mr. Morgan, I was disappointed that you were away when I arrived in Malagua," Julia said, moving to the offensive. "It was indicated to me that you would be here."

"Is that so?" he asked, taking a gulp of coffee.

Controlling her fury, Julia said, "Mr. Morgan, I know that you have special responsibilities, and I'm not interested in the details, except as they affect the running of this Embassy. I insist on being notified when you leave your post and when you return to it."

"There were no such rules under Ambassador Breck," Morgan said harshly. "I don't see why there should be new rules now."

"I am *not* Ambassador Breck," Julia replied, trying to keep her voice even. "And this is a rule that applies throughout the Foreign Service. I intend to implement it here."

Morgan looked bored. He shrugged his shoulders. "Okay, if you insist. I'll see to it that my secretary advises your secretary when I leave town and when I get back. Is there anything else we have to discuss this morning? I have a lot of catching up to do."

"Yes, there is, Mr. Morgan. Since I'm in charge of this Embassy, I want all the reports from here to be coordinated. You are free to dissent from the Embassy's conclusions, either with me or through your own channels to your direct superiors, but I must know the essence of what you report to the Agency. We can't work at cross-purposes. And there is one other thing. I don't care who your contacts are at the Presidential Palace or elsewhere in Malagua, but I want you to keep in mind that the Ambassador is the only *authorized* United States Government contact with President Ferrer. He should not get a different impression. It could mislead him, and have serious consequences."

"Well, I guess there are ways and ways of doing business," Morgan said, in a conciliatory tone which surprised Julia. "Breck had his ways, and you have yours. I agree that we shouldn't work at cross-purposes, and I'll see to it that you'll have no complaints about how I run my shop."

After Morgan left, Julia thought over their conversation. No, he does not want a showdown, certainly not yet, she decided. But Morgan will go on doing what he has always done, except that he will be more discreet. She was convinced that he regarded her as an adversary too. She would have to watch him as carefully as he watched her.

In the days and weeks that followed, Jim Morgan's behavior was above reproach. He attended the daily staff meeting, instead of deputizing Crespo, and provided detailed reports on the Malaguan situation, some quite incisive. He showed deference to Julia, in private and publicly. But now, as Julia chatted with her guests at the reception, she could see Morgan out of the corner of her eye, standing against the living-room archway, drink in hand—watching her.

★

"Paternalism is an important feature in Malaguan society, and therefore in Malaguan politics," Professor Merino was saying to Julia in Spanish as they sat in the Residence library. All the guests had gone by shortly after ten o'clock, Jim Morgan being among the last, and the professor was comfortably installed on the sofa, a glass of wine in his hand. Dudley had brought them cold plates and a bottle of Beaujolais, and they had settled down to a quiet conversation. She was instantly at ease with Merino, who in turn dropped his earlier formality. "You know," he said, "you remind me very much of my daughter Dora." Then, abruptly changing the subject, he asked, "You wanted to talk about my country, no?"

"Yes, of course I do," Julia answered. "Let me start with one question, if I may. What would you say is the most important single thing about Malagua, its society, and its politics—if it's possible to single out one element—that someone like me should understand?"

Merino stroked his goatee reflectively. "I think I have to answer as an anthropologist, because that's what I am, not a politician. We don't really have many politicians in Malagua, as you must have discovered. I look at my country and my people in terms of the physical and cultural forces that have affected and molded them. I'll tell you what I think as a scientist, and then you are free to extrapolate whatever present-day conclusions seem to make sense to you."

"Fair enough."

"I'd like to mention first a phenomenon probably applicable to much of Latin America, although I'm not sure my historian colleagues would necessarily agree. I'm talking about paternalism. Whatever you may have heard about our individualism and sense of independence, which, naturally, do exist, we have a powerful paternalist tradition going back to Mayan days. I've written extensively about it in my books—which, possibly for all the wrong reasons, has made them publishable in Malagua."

Julia nodded, and poured more wine.

"Well. The Mayan history demonstrates that even in the Golden Age, the people had no leadership inclinations. They were essentially happy and sociable, they liked to talk, joke and laugh, but it was almost in a childlike manner. . . ."

"Why childlike?" Julia asked. "What does it mean?"

"It means that, as a nation or a race, Mayans tended to shy away from responsibilities of adulthood. We cultural anthropologists sometimes find it hard to explain precisely why a human group would behave in a given fashion, particularly in societies that vanished thousands of years ago. We lack the proper data, and in the end, we depend on early Spanish chronicles that describe—and I must say, with an astounding eye and ear for detail and nuance—what the *conquistadores* and their scribes have observed in their initial contacts with the Mayans. The study of this civilization through archeology, the deciphering of the *stelas,* and broader cultural patterns identified after the conquest are helpful in reconstructing the Mayan personality. In the end, then, the picture that emerges is of people who willingly accepted authority imposed by the handful of leaders, often hereditary leaders, that every society produces.''

"Was it, then, a passive society?''

"In a sense, yes,'' Merino said. "It was a society that, despite the amazing talents and skills of its members, was highly responsive to authority. I suppose that if nothing else, the people were spared decision-making on almost every level. In one dimension, I imagine, it added up to a happy society. But the weight of authority was immense. First, it was represented by the panoply of Mayan gods, the evil ones and the good ones. One didn't question the wisdom of the gods. One accepted the divine will while, at the same time, one tried to buy off the gods with prayers, dances, and human sacrifice. . . .

"This is an important point for you to remember. On the level immediately below the gods, the Mayans recognized the authority of the priesthood and the nobility. Thus peasant artisans built the temples, the pyramids, and the great palaces with no thought of complaint or revolt—most of the time. I expect they accepted this system as a divine social and political order. Therefore the Mayans were rather fatalistic about what they must have seen as a foreordained mechanism of life, in relation both to the gods and to the established civil and ecclesiastic hierarchy. Am I making myself clear?''

"Yes, superbly so,'' Julia told him.

"Fine. So to continue. In my view, the Spanish rule reinforced these characteristics. Roman Catholic priests and monks replaced the Mayan priests as a source of authority, though for a long time, I'd say until today, we have had a bizarre mix of Catholicism and paganism in Malagua. In the highland villages and among some elderly people here in the slums of Ciudad Malagua, Jesus Christ is honored, but so is Ah Puch, the god of death; Christmas is celebrated, but so is Cimi, the day of death in the Tzolkín, the Mayan sacred-year calendar. I'm not so sure Malaguans really understand Christianity, and at the risk of blasphemy, I have my doubts whether they're missing an awful lot.

"But that's another story. As I was saying, Catholic priests took the place of the pagan religious men, and Spanish governors and generals supplanted the ancient nobility. In this way, paternalism and the eschewing of individual responsibility went on being accepted as a way of life. No rebels or native leaders emerged in Malagua during the Spanish days. Our *próceres*, the fathers of our national independence from Spain, were mostly Creoles, the new aristocracy. They too exercised paternalism when they held power. They made the decisions, and they saw to it that the people had enough to subsist.

"In fact, as far as I'm concerned, *caudillismo*, as we know it in Malagua and other Latin countries, was a paternalistic phenomenon. It still is. . . . The rulers tell the people what's good for the people, tolerating no questioning of the established order. So what we see here is much more complex than just a question of political form of government. You understand me, Madam Ambassador?"

"I believe I do, Professor," Julia said. "But I wish you wouldn't be so formal with me. My friends call me by my first name, and I already think of you as a friend."

"This would be a pleasure," Merino said, raising his wineglass. "To your health, Julia." He pronounced it softly, in Spanish fashion, "Hulia." "You know, I never thought I'd be drinking a friendly toast with the American Ambassador. Maybe the world is changing. But let me get back to my thesis, if I'm not boring you."

"You know you're not. Please go on."

"*Bueno.* In general, the great masses, especially the peasants, do not really resent paternalism. It's too deeply inculcated in them. To put it another way, they don't hate dictators, whoever they may be, because the dictators are graven images of the paternalism cult. The political system—such things as the absence of political freedoms—don't really touch their lives. It's an abstraction when compared with the maize crop or the price of a bottle of beer. Politics here has always been an elitist preoccupation. The masses respond to economic pressures. For example, our great peasant uprisings of the early 1930s were not a political movement, but an economic protest against the landlords who were trying to absorb Indian lands into their *latifundios*. This is something the paternal ruler, the wise dictator, or, if you prefer, the 'Good Prince,' should understand. It's in his bones; it's part of the Mayan heritage. So he will prevent the landlords from grabbing land from the peasants; he will see to it that the price of corn doesn't go down for the farmer, even if the government has to subsidize both the grower and the consumer, and that the price of beer and rum doesn't get out of hand. He will show himself in his grandest uniform with all his medals to the peasants in the villages once or twice a year, and the people, who love pomp and ceremony, will cherish and respect him— with awe.

"The first President Ferrer, who came from peasant stock, knew all this from instinct. That's why when he died, thousands and thousands came to Ciudad Malagua to pay their last respects to him, weeping and wailing. This is something our intellectuals couldn't comprehend. . . . But I'm not certain the present ruler understands it. He's too much part of the new economic structure."

"Are you telling me, then, that this paternalism here is so profound that nothing will ever change in Malagua? That you are prisoners of history and anthropology?"

The professor laughed, and wagged his finger at Julia. "That, my dear Julia, is a leading question. We're getting into dangerous waters. But I will answer you. I think it's important that someone like you understand the Malaguan reality.

"No, I'm not saying that nothing will change in Malagua. Things are changing already because the world around Malagua is changing, and because our society is in flux. Migration to the cities, which is a fairly new thing here, is making a difference and affecting attitudes. We have more well-educated young people than ever before, and they see the problems of the present and the future differently from the way their parents did. It would be foolish to deny that the Cuban revolution did have a significant impact on our young people; I see and hear it every day at the University. There is a new consciousness in the *barrios* and the villages, the consciousness that the *present* system of paternalism no longer suits the societal needs. So the old values are breaking down, and we are witnessing the dying days of the old order. It may take years, but it will happen. Even young Catholic priests in the villages are pushing it, as are Bishop Vargas Merino, who happens to be my first cousin, and quite a few *barrio* curates.''

"All right, but what will emerge instead?'' Julia asked.

"I don't know,'' Merino said. ''I don't think I would want the traditional paternalism to give way to a form of Marxist paternalism. A clever Marxist leader could, I suppose, play on the inherent Malaguan need for paternalism of one sort or another to impose a new, perhaps harsher authoritarianism.''

"Is there such a danger?''

"Oh, my dear Julia, you have no idea how many dangers there are in the Republic of Malagua. . . .''

★

Professor Merino took a taxi home from the American Residence. His modest two-story house was in the middle-class district of Ciudad Malagua, an area that was clean but ill-lit at night. His wife was waiting for him in the parlor.

"Dora is home,'' she whispered as he walked in. ''She came about an hour ago. She will not be spending the night—she doesn't think it's safe for us—but she wants to see you. She's in the kitchen, having something to eat.''

Merino rushed to the kitchen. A petite, pretty woman, her hair cropped short and her face creased with fatigue, was sitting at the table, voraciously eating a roast chicken. She appeared to be in her mid-twenties. A black beret lay on the table. Seeing her father, she wiped her hands on her slacks, and ran up to him.

"Oh, Papa," she cried, "how glad I am to see you!"

"No happier than I am to see you, *niña*."

Father and daughter embraced silently for a long moment. Then Dora drew away.

"I can't stay very long," she said, "but I had to deliver a message to somebody in the city, and I decided to take a chance and come to see you and Mother. It's been two months, and I wanted you to know I was in fine health, and that things are going really well for the Frente."

"My daughter, the *guerrillera*," Professor Merino said in bewilderment and admiration. They both laughed.

"Don't worry, Papa," she said, "I'm very careful. Nothing will happen to me."

"May God hear you," Merino replied.

"But where were you so late? Mother said you'd gone to a party, and I was afraid I wouldn't see you."

"I see your mother wanted me to tell you the awful news myself. I was at a reception at the American Embassy."

"You *what?*"

"I said I was at the Residence of the American Ambassador," the Professor said calmly. "I had a most interesting evening."

"But Father, how could you? That's enemy territory—you know that."

"I'm not sure. Not with the new Ambassador, the woman. I liked her, Dora, and she reminded me of you. I think she might be the kind of person who would listen to your people."

Dora raised her eyebrows, then kissed Merino on the cheek.

"You know how much I respect your judgment," she said, "but what have you got in mind? Nothing must be done to violate our security. This woman may be all right, as you say, but I wouldn't trust any other Americans at the Embassy. It could be terribly dangerous to our cause."

"I have an idea in the back of my mind," Merino answered. "Let me play with it for a few days, and then let's see what I can come up with. I need not say that nobody will be endangered by my little idea. . . ."

★

At the Residence, Julia Savage barricaded herself in her bedroom for the night. She undressed, but not feeling sleepy, she sat on her bed, smoking a cigarette and thinking about Professor Merino. Julia felt extremely pleased with the evening—and with herself.

7

Sitting at her desk the morning after the Residence reception, Julia Savage allowed herself a moment of daydreaming before tackling the overnight cables and going to the staff meeting. She had no intention of mentioning her conversation with Professor Merino or the hopes it had aroused in her of establishing a quiet contact with the opposition. Julia was convinced now that this was vital if she was ever to arrive at a rational judgment about Malaguan politics on which to make sound policy recommendations.

But she knew that she might be embarking on a perilous and slippery enterprise. Should Jim Morgan, for example, find out about it, the CIA in Washington would be instantly informed—behind her back—and word would reach the State Department and the White House that Julia was in effect violating standing policy on Embassy contacts in Malagua. She would become extremely vulnerable, strict instructions would be issued to her to refrain from further meetings with General Ferrer's critics, and for all practical purposes, she would be immobilized, neutralized, and indeed, finished in Malagua.

Inviting the five intellectuals to the Residence was in itself a risk—she remembered Morgan watching her at the party—and henceforth Julia would have to act with the most extraordinary care. It was strange, she thought, how difficult it was to carry out what she regarded as normal ambassadorial duties: to be fully informed about a situation. And how politically dangerous the whole thing had become. The slightest slip, she realized, could result in her being recalled after the shortest decent interval, and dropped like a hot potato by the State Department. They would enjoy doing it to a political appointee. And Washington was full of forgotten ex-ambassadors.

Still, Julia told herself, it was her obligation to do her job the best she could according to her lights, even if she jeopardized her future and her dreams. It was the old Savage trait of independence in her, the Yankee stubbornness, her own habit of self-discipline.

★

The Savages were an old Boston family both in tradition and in wealth. Julia's first childhood memories were of the house on Beacon Hill, an early-nineteenth-century structure on the park, purchased by her grandfather, who was the first Roman Catholic to establish himself on the Hill. He was also the first Catholic investment banker in Boston, setting up shop just before World War I, and the first Savage to attend Harvard. By the time he died, the Savages were solidly part of the Boston Establishment, the sin of their English Catholicism being forgotten or forgiven in Back Bay.

Julia's father, Randolph C. Savage, went to Exeter and then to Harvard after the start of the Great Depression and Franklin D. Roosevelt's election. The Depression had little effect on the Savage firm—the canny old banker had sold all its stockholdings three weeks before Black Friday. He was a prominent Democrat, and Julia remembered seeing engraved invitations from the White House, requesting her grandparents to take tea or dine with President and Mrs. Roosevelt.

Within forty-eight hours of Pearl Harbor, Randolph Savage enlisted in the Navy, a handsome young man of great charm, intellectual accomplishment, and considerable ambition. After graduating from Harvard, he served as assistant to his father at the House of Savage, taking time off for big-time yachting and winning the Newport–Bermuda race. The day he was to report for Navy duty, Randolph married Eleanor James, a Smith graduate from Oyster Bay and a Catholic.

But the Navy was a disappointment to Randolph Savage. He had been tapped by Naval Intelligence, presumably because his file showed that he had visited Europe frequently, on holidays and on bank business; spoke French and German; and had useful international financial contacts. And sitting behind a desk at the Navy Annex building in Washington was not Randolph's idea of fighting the war. One day, a former Harvard classmate and now a Wall Street lawyer called him to propose a mysterious meeting at a Washington hotel. He told him that a New York attorney named William Donovan was organizing a special wartime operation called the Office of Strategic Services. "I can't tell you much more about it, but with your background, you're a natural for the OSS."

Savage agreed enthusiastically, and presently he was detailed by the Navy to the OSS to undergo intelligence, sabotage, and weapons training at a secluded farm not far from Washington. By Christmas, 1942, he was in England as part of an OSS detachment working closely with the British Special Operations Executive. He was dropped in southern France with two OSS and two SOE officers one night in the spring of 1943, spending three months with French *maquis* groups. Then he was exfiltrated through Spain and Portugal, and sent back to the United States as an OSS instructor. This gave him the opportunity of seeing Eleanor almost every weekend at a small apartment she had rented in Washington. In the spring of 1945, Randolph was transferred to an OSS detachment operating behind Japanese lines in southern China. While he was busy blowing up bridges and harassing Japanese forces, his father died in Boston.

Discharged from the service with an OSS lieutenant colonel's rank, Randolph, as his father had always planned it, took over the House of Savage. Julia was born a little over a year later, in January, 1947. But after the excitement of the war, he discovered that banking was anticlimactic. He craved more adventure.

Three years later, the call came. An OSS colleague invited him to join the infant Central Intelligence Agency, the successor to the OSS, and Randolph jumped at the chance. His colleague was the CIA's Deputy Director in charge of clandestine operations, and he wanted Randolph on his personal staff. "You know, this is a real elite organization we're putting together, and a man like you has the patriotic duty of serving his country even in peacetime."

Turning over the chairmanship of the House of Savage to his brother Tom, Randolph simply announced to his friends and relatives that he would be working "for the government" in Washington. No questions were asked, and Randolph told Eleanor that his new work was of a confidential character and he preferred not to discuss it. Eleanor accepted that, as she accepted the fact that he would be living in Washington alone, because his job required frequent foreign travel and it made no sense to move the family away from the Beacon Hill house he had inherited from his father. He would try to visit as often as possible.

★

Julia Savage grew up in wealth and comfort. Though a nurse looked after her full time, Eleanor was always around, talking with the little girl, often joining her for lunch, taking her shopping, and later, driving her every morning to nursery school. Eleanor was a doting but exacting mother. From earliest girlhood, Julia was taught manners—as behooved a Savage, as her mother put it—even how to curtsy. And Eleanor would tell her, "You must learn, as you get older, to do everything by yourself." A quick learner and a bright child with a sunny disposition, Julia seldom got into trouble. When she did, she would be punished by being deprived of ice cream on Sundays or of a shopping trip.

The Savages being practicing Catholics, Julia was exposed to church and religion from the age of four, when her parents took her for the first time to Mass on Sunday. She loved the liturgy and the mystery of Mass: the genuflections, the crossing of oneself, the ringing of the altar bell in the silent church, the choir singing, and the smell of incense, though her attention often wandered during the sermon, when she didn't understand the words from the pulpit.

Julia's life changed radically when Randolph signed up with the CIA, and his disappearances became longer and longer. He was attached to the Agency's "Quarters Q" headquarters in the temporary wartime buildings, an esthetic eyesore next to the Lincoln Memorial in Washington (the massive building in Langley, Virginia, would not go up for another decade), but his services were increasingly required abroad.

In the aftermath of Korea, the Cold War was now in full swing, and the CIA was busily setting up and augmenting stations and bases in Europe and Asia, launching massive operations everywhere. Randolph Savage, as the principal assistant to the Agency's Director for Plans, the "black side," became the field supervisor of all these new enterprises, racing by plane from Vienna to London, from Bonn to Helsinki, from Europe to Washington, from Washington to Tokyo, Manila, and Bangkok, and round and round again. He managed to hit Boston five or six times a year, usually for a few days at a time, including Christmas. He missed three of Julia's birthdays, which made her cry despite his long congratulatory telegrams or phone calls from mysterious spots in the world, never saying from where he was calling.

Deprived of her father, Julia was also seeing less and less of Eleanor. Having turned eight, she was attending a private grade school, and she was picked up and brought home in the school's station wagon. And returning home, Julia would often find her mother in a strange, word-slurring condition. Eleanor had acquired what was delicately known in Boston society as a "drinking problem"; she was rapidly turning into an alcoholic. Randolph's absences may have played a role. To Julia, the sight of her mother in varying stages of drunkenness—the vacant stare; the fixed, mindless smile; the stumbling from room to room and up and down the stairs; the thick speech; and the occasional bursts of anger—was devastating. It scared her. She did not know how to act, how to respond, or what to say. She became afraid of Eleanor, though when sober, her mother was her normal loving and attentive self.

Eleanor's problem taught Julia a new dimension in self-discipline. It had been her habit in the first years of grade school to bring home in the afternoon one or two of her friends: Julia made friends easily. But as her mother's drinking grew worse, Julia made the decision to stop inviting them. When Eleanor asked her one day why the friends were no longer coming, Julia replied, "Oh, Mother, it's just that I have too much homework to be able to play in the afternoon." And actually, Julia concentrated with fury on the homework, winding up the year with straight A's in all the subjects. She had been a compulsive worker ever since.

Her relatives brought some solace and amusement into Julia's life, but fundamentally, she had come to terms with her father's absences and her mother's condition increasingly delineating her own life. She remained warm, friendly, and sociable—everybody's favorite—but she developed the ability to separate herself emotionally from others.

★

In 1955, shortly after Julia's eighth birthday, Randolph Savage was named Deputy to the CIA's Director for Plans; now he would spend most of his time in Washington. The Savages bought a rambling old house on Dumbarton Avenue in Georgetown, and Julia was enrolled in an exclusive girls' school in suburban Maryland. Eleanor threw herself with frenzy into remodeling and furnishing the house. For nearly a year, until the project was completed, Eleanor gave up drinking.

The Washington years were happy for Julia, chiefly because her father was home most of the time. She had a pleasant but somewhat reserved relationship with Eleanor, and she quickly made friends at the new school, though she remembered the Boston days too well to risk inviting them home. Julia wanted to be absolutely certain that Eleanor was over her drinking problem, waiting a month, then another month, and still another month. Eleanor did relapse into alcoholism within the year, and Julia was glad she had once more exercised her self-discipline.

But Randolph Savage began vanishing again in 1960, for weeks at a time, under the pretext of urgent foreign travel. This time his involvement was in the preparations for the Bay of Pigs invasion of Cuba, a tightly held CIA secret. Randolph was engaged in the Cuban project at the highest planning level in Washington, but he had the additional responsibility for personal liaison with President Anselmo Ferrer of Malagua, who had agreed to allow the Cuban exiles to be trained for the invasion on his territory. This had required complex negotiations with Ferrer and his son Juan, who acted as the chief coordinator on the Malaguan side. Randolph was in and out of Ciudad Malagua, usually taking a CIA "black flight" from the Opa-Locka field on the outskirts of Miami to the Malaguan Air Force base next to the old civilian airport. There he was picked up by Juan Ferrer's limousine and taken to his well-guarded villa on Lake Taxchilán. No outsider, including the American Ambassador, was aware of Randolph's presence in Malagua. The CIA Station Chief called on him at the Ferrer house for nightlong conferences.

The Ferrers were tough negotiators. In exchange for the use of secret Malaguan training bases, they demanded a flat payment of $100 million from the United States plus the refund of highly inflated costs supposedly incurred by Malagua in the course of the operation. When Randolph Savage first informed the CIA Director of the Ferrers' request, it was met with incredulity at Headquarters. He was instructed to advise the Malaguans that $10 million was the absolute limit for their cooperation, in addition to the refund of the costs. "Who does this tinhorn dictator Ferrer think he is?" the Director, who had contempt for all Latin Americans, had said. "We're supposed to be allies in the fight against Castro. In the long run, it's his neck too, if Castro isn't kicked out. Ten million is *it*. Not another cent. . . ."

Randolph conveyed the message to Juan Ferrer over dinner after he flew back from Washington. Roaring with laughter, Ferrer slapped Randolph on the back and poured a fresh drink. "Boy," he said, still laughing, "do you Yankees really think you can always get something for nothing? We're taking a helluva chance on this fucking invasion; we're conspiring with you to attack a sovereign country, and you want to screw us. You know I love you like a brother, but I won't even pass this on to my dad. He'd throw me out of his office. You can tell your people that it's one hundred million or it's no deal. And we won't spend months haggling with you, Randolph. If we can't come to terms right away, I'll have the National Guard round up your God-damned Cuban recruits, put them on the first plane back to Miami, and shut down the camps. We've already done plenty for the CIA just out of friendship, after you and I shook hands on it.''

Savage knew Ferrer well enough to realize that this was no bluff, and the next evening in Washington he told the Director that "the Malaguans have us over a barrel.'' Swearing loudly, the Director called the White House to ask for an immediate appointment with President Eisenhower. He explained the situation, and Eisenhower said, "I guess it leaves us no choice.'' He authorized the payment, and the Secretary of the Treasury was told to arrange for a $100-million deposit from unvouchered contingency funds in a numbered bank account in Geneva. It was a Top Secret matter of national security, the President said. No questions were to be asked or answered.

The 1961 Bay of Pigs invasion, with John Kennedy inheriting the operation from Eisenhower, was an absolute fiasco. But the friendship between Savage and Ferrer remained intact. Malagua continued to be helpful to the CIA in a variety of clandestine undertakings against Castro. And it became firmly established that henceforth all sensitive dealings between Ciudad Malagua and Washington would be conducted through the CIA, bypassing the Embassy. Nobody bothered to inform successive American ambassadors of this agreement, not even Wilbur Breck when he took up his post. It was sufficient for the Agency and the Ferrers to know how the system worked.

★

After the abortive invasion, Randolph Savage felt more strongly than ever that *fidelismo* was an enormous danger to the United States and Latin America, and that it had to be eliminated. A cold warrior, he tended to place worldwide events in the context of the Soviet–American rivalry. And when it came to Cuba, he believed that only the CIA, acting more intelligently than it had at the Bay of Pigs, was equipped to do away with Castro. The deal between Kennedy and Khrushchev after the missile crisis in 1962 was that the Russians would not again introduce offensive nuclear weapons into Cuba if the United States committed itself to refrain from new invasions. So, Randolph reasoned, this left only the CIA and its clandestine paramilitary activities as an instrument to smother the Cuban revolution.

While he opposed bizarre plans developed under Operation Mongoose at the White House to assassinate Castro, even enlisting the Mafia to hit the Cuban Premier, Savage was all in favor of sustained sabotage and political action against him. He was convinced that sooner or later, it would work. And the best base for these operations, he insisted, was Malagua. What was required to achieve this objective, Randolph told the new Director, was an intimate and confidential relationship with the ruling family, which had to be maintained by the Agency.

The Embassy and the State Department had to remain ignorant of this secret link. Otherwise, they might oppose the whole-hearted support for the Ferrer régime that Randolph argued the CIA should provide. And such support, he pointed out to the Director, had to exclude any contacts between the Embassy in Malagua and the anti-Ferrer opposition. The State Department had had sporadic contacts with the opposition over the years in its *pro forma* attempts to encourage democracy in Malagua, but in Savage's judgment that was tantamount to undermining the Ferrers. "We can't have it both ways," he said at an Agency meeting. It was not that Randolph Savage was ideologically in favor of dictatorships. He was simply being pragmatic and practical. Friendship with the Ferrers happened to serve the American interest.

Two decades later, Julia Savage inherited the political machinery her father had devised and, entirely unaware of its history, set herself the task of dismantling the CIA–Ferrer relationship.

8

Julia's political education had begun at home, when she was
still in preparatory school. Randolph Savage no longer had to
keep his association with the CIA secret. Times had changed,
and ranking Agency officials were becoming more and more vis-
ible. Randolph liked to entertain, and several evenings a week
the house on Dumbarton Avenue was filled with senior CIA people, State Department officials, congressmen, and journalists.
Georgetown had not turned against the CIA, even after the Bay
of Pigs catastrophe, and Julia was not troubled by her father's
job. She had not been aware of his role in the invasion—he
never discussed his work at home—and she was too busy
with the approaching spring exams to pay much attention to
press and television reports about the failure at Girón Beach.
Once she did ask him if the invasion had been a mistake; he
shrugged, saying, "Well, I guess that's life," and dropped the
subject.

The first serious criticism of the invasion and its deeper implications was expressed in Julia's presence by an athletic Jesuit, a
contemporary and tennis partner of Randolph's, who taught political science at Georgetown University. Father Peter Malone
had lived in Latin America for several years, and he felt very

strongly that the Bay of Pigs had done incalculable harm to the prestige of the United States.

Malone had come home with Savage for a cold beer after a tennis game—it was Savage's first free weekend after long months of involvement with the Cuban enterprise—and the two men talked politics as they relaxed in the garden. Julia made a lemonade for herself and joined them under the trees.

"I assume, Randolph, that you had some part in this mess," Father Malone was saying, "and I must say I'm surprised that a man of your intelligence and experience went along with the Bay of Pigs."

"You see, Pete," Savage said defensively, "it was a Presidential decision to go ahead with the invasion, and we were assigned the operational responsibility. So the CIA had to do it. And I still think that had it succeeded, the Castro cancer would have been extirpated, a liberal but anti-Communist government would have been put in place—as we had planned it—and public opinion in Latin America would have swallowed it, sooner or later. Then the Alliance for Progress could have proceeded on a more solid basis. The problem was that it didn't work."

Julia, curled up in her chair, broke in: "But Father Pete, wouldn't you say that the fact that no American forces participated in the invasion makes it look a little different? I mean, it wasn't as if *we* invaded Cuba."

"No, Julia," the Jesuit answered. "The hand of America was behind it, for everybody to see, and that's something the Latins will remember for a long time. Sure, they will take the Alliance money—why not?—but I'm not sure that it's going to buy us very much."

"Oh, come off it, Pete," Savage said. "You know as well as I do that in their heart of hearts most of the Latin American governments and politicians would have been delighted if we had overthrown Castro. They just can't say it publicly. Face it, Pete, you're a hopeless idealist in a predatory world."

"I won't deny it, but you're too much of a cynic," Malone told him. "You know, cynicism has a way of catching up with people.

I'm just looking beyond the immediate consequences of this whole thing. I'm a practical idealist.''

"Okay," Savage said. "You've made your point. How about another beer?''

★

Father Malone became a frequent visitor at the Savage home. Julia took a great liking to him, and often they spent hours chatting about politics, which was turning into her favorite topic. She kept plying the priest with questions about Latin America and his experiences there. One day, Malone told her that when she went to college the following year, she might find it rewarding to go into Latin American studies. "I think Latin America today is the most interesting part of the world," he said. "You ought to think about it.''

But before Julia could give it adequate thought, she found herself *in* Latin America. She had planned to apply to Smith, but her plans went awry before the year was out. Eleanor was sliding rapidly into total alcoholism, and Randolph, who opposed the idea of hospitalization, decided that there simply were too many pressures for her in Washington. It was an illusion to which he wanted to cling. Coincidentally, the CIA's top officials, including Savage, had decided that the Agency's Latin American operations should be considerably beefed up to cope with what they regarded as the mounting danger of Cuban subversion in the region. Thus Mexico City was designated a "Regional Command" for the Western Hemisphere. The CIA Director, who was aware of Eleanor's problem and Randolph's desire to get away from Washington, suggested that Savage take over the new Command. His official title would be that of Station Chief at the Embassy in Mexico City, but in practice, he would outrank the Chief of the Western Hemisphere Division at Langley. Savage agreed at once.

Julia took up life in Mexico with zest and enthusiasm. She loved the sprawling, noisy, pulsating city on the high *mesa*. She was excited by the ancient land of the Aztec and Maya, by its mysterious beauty, its bloody but romantic revolutionary history, its complex people. She went to Mérida in the south and the Mayan pyramids of Chichén-Itzá, and she visited the great museums of Anthropology and Modern Art in Mexico City. Wholly new perspectives opened for sixteen-year-old Julia.

The family had rented a luxurious home with a swimming pool in the Lomas de Chapultepec, a new suburb of the capital, and as she had when they moved to Washington, Eleanor stopped drinking. Randolph traveled occasionally around Latin America (Julia would remember later his mentions of visits to Malagua) and to Washington, but the trips were relatively infrequent.

At an Embassy reception, to which she was specifically invited at Randolph's request, Julia met the American Ambassador. Afterward, at home, she told her father how disappointed she had been. The Ambassador, a slim, intense Texan who had come up through the ranks of the Foreign Service, had struck her as an arrogant little man, contemptuous of Latin Americans in general and Mexicans in particular, and unabashedly critical of the Alliance for Progress. He thought it was a waste of money, and he favored a tough approach to the Latins. Turning to Randolph and Julia, he remarked that it was a "shame" the Bay of Pigs had failed. "It would have been so much easier for me to put the fear of God into the Mexicans if the invasion had succeeded," he said. "As it is, all I hear is bitching about the United States, and the Mexicans keep rubbing my nose in the Cuban thing. They think they are the only ones who know what the relations between the United States and Latin America should be." Julia wondered why the President kept in Mexico an ambassador so hostile to the country where he served.

In Latin America, and especially in Mexico, political education comes quickly. And so it did for Julia. She graduated from the American High School in Mexico City six months after their arrival, and she persuaded her parents to let her enroll at the National University of Mexico instead of going to Smith. She wanted to improve her Spanish, she said, and she wanted to learn more about Latin America.

At the University, Julia became known as the "good" *gringa,* and was accepted by her Mexican peers. It was known that her father was a diplomat at the American Embassy, but somehow his CIA connection never surfaced in Mexico, though Randolph was open about it in Washington. The National University being quite radicalized, Julia was exposed to anti-American sentiment, although it was never personally directed at her. Fidel Castro was a great hero among the students, and Julia's friends sought to convert her to the revolutionary cause. "We had our revolution in 1917, the Cubans in 1959, and now it's the turn of the rest of Latin America—and even the United States," a student leader named Jorge Solís told her. "Decent people don't have to be afraid of revolutions . . . only imperialists, exploiters, and the CIA."

Julia was torn by the opinions she was hearing. She had attended lectures by Octávio Paz and Edmundo Flores on social and economic inequity between the United States and Latin America, about the *yanqui* inability to understand the Latins, about the cultural gulf between them, and she sympathized with the arguments. Oscar Lewis' *Children of Sánchez* had just been published, and Julia read it avidly, learning about the misery and the culture of poverty in Mexico City slums. She spent long hours in the slums, usually with Jorge Solís, seeing the reality on which Lewis had based his arguments. Yes, she understood what the young Mexicans were trying to tell her, but she was not convinced that violent revolution was the cure for the ills of Latin America: two hundred years of her pragmatic New England heritage made her reluctant about embracing new revolutionary theories.

She often tried to discuss her doubts and impressions with her father, but he was impatient with them. "I think all this revolutionary talk is so much poppycock," he told her. "Your friends are 'parlor radicals'; they won't put their money—or their lives —where their mouths are. They're not about to give up their upper-class privileges, their sports cars, and the rest of it." On one occasion, as if out of professional habit, Savage asked Julia to give him the names of the principal pro-Cuban leaders at the University. Julia, who loved and respected her father, was absolutely indignant. "I'm not going to do your job for you!" she shouted in anger—the first time she had ever raised her voice at him. "Let your spooks do it. And don't ever ask me again to be an informer." Randolph had the grace to apologize, and he never again brought up the subject.

In November, 1963, John Kennedy was assassinated, and Julia wept bitterly. Jorge Solís, now a close friend, offered his condolences, as did the others. "We too have lost something in Dallas," Solís, who had often excoriated Kennedy for the Bay of Pigs, told Julia.

Early in January, 1965, Anselmo Ferrer died in Malagua, and Savage quietly slipped into the city on Lake Taxchilán to tell Juan Ferrer, the new President, that he could count on his old friends in Washington. Three months later, civil war erupted in the Dominican Republic, and Savage coordinated from his Mexican command post the CIA's operations in conjunction with the American military intervention. For Julia, who was unaware of her father's involvement, the Dominican episode was a traumatic experience. She had to sit silently as her Mexican friends irately denounced the United States and rioted at the American Embassy.

That was also the year Julia Savage graduated from the University and, not quite nineteen, lost her virginity. She had engaged in her share of passionate kissing and petting, felt strong sexual urges, thought frequently about being in bed with a man, as so many of her women friends were doing, but she always drew back at the last moment, always fearing an involvement she did not desire. Then one weekend Jorge had driven Julia to Cuernavaca in his Alfa Romeo. After a long evening of dancing, kissing, holding hands, and drinking too much *tequila* and wine, Jorge took her to his room at the hotel, and knowing perfectly well what would happen, Julia said to herself, The hell with it . . . why not? and let Jorge deflower her. Except for a touch of initial pain, Julia enjoyed it hugely. She was sober enough to be aware of the passage of every moment, and she had a deep and satisfying orgasm the second time Jorge made love to her. They stayed in bed the next day, and Julia again responded joyfully to his lovemaking.

Back in Mexico City, Jorge talked of marriage when he finished law school the following year. This, however, was where Julia, the self-disciplined Bostonian, drew the line. She was not in love with Jorge, much as he excited her in bed. Jorge was insistent beyond endurance, accusing her of feeling superior to him, a *latino*. What saved Julia from further problems with Jorge was Randolph Savage's transfer back to Washington as the CIA's Deputy Director for Plans—clandestine operations. It made him Number Three in the Agency. Julia told her friends that she was going home with her parents to work on a graduate degree in Latin American affairs at Georgetown University, a student of Father Peter Malone.

★

Pete Malone, now a little stouter and a Georgetown dean, remained passionately devoted to Latin American causes, his liberalism not having flagged. He was delighted to have Julia at the University, personally designing her curriculum for the two-year Master's program. He thought that afterward she might work toward a Ph.D. in Latin American studies, then perhaps join the Foreign Service. "You're the kind of person we can use on Latin America in the State Department," he told Julia. "Someday you will make a crackerjack Political Officer at some embassy in Latin America."

But one day late in May, 1967, just before the end of the academic year, Julia came to Malone's office and announced that she was getting engaged the next month and expected to be married before Christmas. "You're the first one to know," Julia told the priest. "Tonight, I'll break the news to my parents. I plan to return to Georgetown for the fall term; that way I'll be three-quarters of the way to my Master's, and I can finish it up once I'm settled. What do you think, Father Pete?"

"I imagine that first I ought to wish you happiness, and I do so most sincerely," Malone replied, recovering from surprise. "God be with you. Secondly, I hope that you will indeed go back to your studies. It would be a shame to throw it all away. But once you start having babies and so on, it may be a bit difficult to buckle down again to the routine of studies. Still, quite a few women have done it, so I don't see why you wouldn't be able to get back to academic work in your own good time."

"Well," Julia said, "this is precisely where I need your advice. You're not my confessor—in fact, I don't have one—but I think of you as a friend, Father Pete. You see, the man I love, the man I'm going to marry, is a Latin American, a Catholic. His family is very close to the Church. I know that I'll be expected to start having children right away. But the thing is that I don't want children yet. I want to get my degree. I have to have some freedom for a while. God's knees, I'm not even twenty-one. Can you advise me?"

"Christ, you're putting me on the spot," Malone told her. "You know what the teachings of the Church are on birth control, so I don't have to repeat the official line for you. Personally, as you may have suspected, I have my doubts about the wisdom of Holy Mother Church's stand on this issue. So my advice is to let your conscience be your guide. Now tell me more about your young man."

★

In mid-June the engagement of Julia Savage and Enrique Palma Rioseco was announced at a small reception on Dumbarton Avenue. Enrique was a twenty-five-year-old Colombian, the scion of a leading industrial and ranching family in Cali, who was spending a year at Georgetown's Foreign Service School. He was tall and handsome, with extraordinary charm, and his professors said he was the most brilliant Latin American ever to attend Georgetown. Julia had met him at a party at a friend's house, and they were soon inseparable. They had nightlong conversations about the Vietnam war and the problems of Latin America. They were always in agreement, opposing the war and deploring American policies in the Hemisphere. They discussed the evolution of the Roman Catholic Church under John XXIII, wondering how it would affect Latin America.

Often, they were joined by Julia's leftist friends from Georgetown and elsewhere, most of them activists in the antiwar movement. Several of them were women. One was Sally Kleben, whom Julia had first met in Mexico, and who described herself as a Trotskyite. Sally was a student at American University, and she was a busy member of Students for a Democratic Society. She tended to disappear and reappear in Washington at irregular intervals, never explaining her absences.

On weekends, Julia and Enrique played tennis, went horseback riding in Potomac, floated from party to party, and made love at his house, Julia marveling at her lover's thoughtful tenderness and almost dazed by the sharpness of the pleasure she felt with him. When they spent the night together, Julia, always first to awaken, brought Enrique out of his sleep with caresses —at first gentle, then more insistent—until he opened his eyes, stretched with pleasure, and turning to her, made her cry out.

Julia had soon realized she was in love with Enrique. It was more than sex, more than their serious conversations, more than their attunement to each other. It was absolute love. Julia was convinced of it. Several evenings later, they sat in Enrique's living room over wine and cheese. He was agitated, pacing up and down the room. Finally, he said, "Look, Julia, there's something we must talk about. I've been thinking it over for weeks, and now I have to say it: I love you, *yo te amo,* and I want to marry you. Will you marry me?"

Both families were pleased with the match. The Palmas were as established and well respected in Colombia as the Savages were in New England. Being Catholic, Julia was even more acceptable to the Palmas; Enrique's great-uncle had been Archbishop of Cali. Randolph Savage had some initial reservations about Julia's marriage to a Latin American—he mentioned the dangers of "transcultural" marriages—but he too was taken with Enrique.

After the engagement party, Julia spent two weeks at the Palmas' Cali mansion, meeting Enrique's parents and two younger brothers and a procession of aunts, uncles, and cousins. Parties were given by the Palmas to present Julia to Cali society. Her fluent Spanish and her knowledge of Latin American culture, art, and literature made her an immediate success. Don Miguel

Palma, Enrique's father, told her fondly that in her God had finally given him a daughter. Doña Marta, his mother, chatted with Julia for hours about wedding plans.

The wedding was held in Washington in December, shortly before Julia turned twenty-one, and it was a major social event in the capital. Julia and Enrique were married by a bishop at St. Matthew's Cathedral, and the reception at Dumbarton Avenue was attended by 150 guests. For their honeymoon, they went to the island of Moustique, in the Grenadines, where the Palmas' Venezuelan cousins owned a hotel. The principal private bungalow was placed at their disposal, and there they spent ten blissful days.

★

After the honeymoon, Julia and Enrique made their home in Cali, in a luxurious, palm-fringed villa which was a wedding gift from his parents. The first year of their marriage was marred only by Randolph Savage's death in Jordan. Julia and Enrique took the first plane to Washington to be with Eleanor when Randolph's body was brought back from the Middle East. A private funeral was held in Boston—small notices in the newspapers stated only that "Randolph Savage, a senior government official, died suddenly at the age of 52 while traveling abroad"—and the young Palmas returned to Cali.

Before their marriage Julia had told Enrique that she wanted no children for two or three years, and he had agreed. "There's no hurry, darling," he said. "Cali and Colombia can wait a little longer for the new Palma generation." From time to time Doña Marta talked softly of how she looked forward to the joy of grandchildren. When Julia said, "Ah, but we *are* trying," her mother-in-law would smile with gentle encouragement. She never suspected that Julia was taking birth-control pills.

After a year in Cali, Julia realized that she knew little about Colombia except how the *oligarquía* lived. From hearsay and occasional newspaper stories she had learned that there was unrest at the universities, that leftist guerrillas were fighting the Army in the mountains, and that the country was in economic trouble. Frustrated, Julia asked Enrique how she could find out more about the realities of Colombia. Enrique, increasingly preoccupied and frequently away on trips he explained merely as "family business," had no suggestions for her. He became impatient when Julia insisted. "All you have to know is what goes on around you in this house and this family," he snapped. "You're not an American intellectual; you're a Colombian wife."

Enrique had begun to drink heavily, often coming home late at night, too drunk to undress himself. He began to spend days away from the Palma office, sitting morosely in the villa's living room, a drink in hand, waiting for mysterious phone calls. When the telephone rang, Enrique jumped up to grab the receiver, speaking in slurred tones, sometimes in Spanish, sometimes in English. Once, when Julia answered the phone, Enrique tore it from her hand, shouting, "Don't you *ever* touch that fucking telephone when I'm here."

When she tried to talk with Enrique about his drinking, he said coldly, "Mind your own God-damned business." When she insisted, he slapped her. "Now shut up," he yelled, walking out of the bedroom. Julia's first instinct was to pack up and leave. No man had ever struck her before, and she would not tolerate it. She had heard how Latin men treated their American wives, and she was determined not to be made into a Yankee slave. But the next day, when Enrique apologized for slapping her, Julia decided to give their marriage another chance. He, however, turned away from her love and understanding. As their second wedding anniversary approached, he had not made love to her in more than six months. She could not comprehend any of it.

Then more blows came. Don Miguel Palma stopped by the villa one morning. "I know Enrique is away," he said, "but there's something I must ask you. I hate to bring it up, but I have discovered that twenty million pesos, a half-million dollars, is missing from the company. These were funds to which my son had access. Do you know anything about Enrique's finances?"

"I . . . I've no idea, Don Miguel," she stammered. "Enrique

doesn't discuss anything with me anymore." Her father-in-law said, "Thank you for being helpful. I would be grateful if you didn't mention our conversation to my son."

A week later, Enrique came home from a trip. It was evening, and although he had been drinking, he made an effort to be charming. He kissed her for the first time in months.

"Oh, I missed you so much, my darling," he said thickly. "God, these business trips I have to make are awful."

"I don't even know where you go on trips," Julia replied cautiously.

"Well . . . never mind that. The main thing is that I'm back home. But I have a request to make of you."

"What is it, Enrique?"

"I need to borrow some money from you. I think one hundred thousand dollars should do it. What do you say, darling?"

"But I don't have that kind of money—you know that."

"I know *you* don't," Enrique said testily, "but your mother does. Your family does. There must be all kinds of money in trusts. And didn't your father leave you a small fortune?"

"He did leave me some money, but it's not a fortune, and it's all tied up in trusts and things."

"Well, can't you spring it loose for your own husband?"

Julia felt sickened. "I can only spring it loose, as you put it, if I can give a good reason to the executor of the estate, who is my uncle, and to the trustees. You have to tell me what you need the money for. Is it an investment?"

"Oh, shit!" Enrique said furiously. "Just tell them it's for your husband. Isn't that good enough?"

"I'm afraid not," Julia said patiently.

"Then fuck you and your family and your trustees," Enrique shouted. "I've had enough of supporting you and putting up with your nasty little penny-pinching New England ways."

He bounced out of his chair and, smashing her across the face with the back of his hand, screamed, "That's what you deserve, you fucking bitch!" He ran out of the room, slamming the door. Julia sat alone in the living room for long minutes.

★

Enrique was gone the next morning when Julia, who had stayed up all night, finished packing and called for a taxi to take her to the Cali airport. She was dry-eyed, but something was dead inside her. I may fall in love again, she told herself, but I'll never live with a man again. Julia spent that night in Bogotá and flew to Washington the next morning.

The year was 1969, and Washington was a crisis city as Julia sought to reconstruct her life. The Vietnam war raged, Martin Luther King and Robert Kennedy had been assassinated the year before, Czechoslovakia had been invaded by the Russians, and Richard Nixon was President. Father Peter Malone, to whom Julia had turned for advice, counseled her to find work as soon as possible and to resume her studies. "You can't just sit and mope around and feel sorry for yourself," he said. "You still have a whole life ahead of you."

With Malone's assistance—and helped by the Savages' political connections—Julia found a job in the office of Senator George Mill, first as a clerk, then as one of his foreign-policy aides. Mill, a friend of the Jesuit priest, had a special interest in Latin America, and soon Julia was doing all the work for him in that field. When Mill became ranking Republican member of the Western Hemisphere Subcommittee of the Senate Foreign Relations Committee, she had her hands full. She also started attending night courses at Georgetown and, within a year, won a Master's degree in Latin American studies. Then she moved to the Johns Hopkins School for Advanced International Studies to work on her Ph.D.

Life had fallen into place for Julia more easily and quickly than she had expected. She lived in a small apartment on Q Street in Georgetown; she was extraordinarily busy, and extraordinarily popular. She was besieged with invitations and requests for dates from men in and out of government, foreign diplomats, journalists, and most of the town's eligible bachelors—single and divorced. Julia went out whenever she was not working at the Senate or studying, but she shied away from sexual or emotional involvements—except the hurtful affair with the married California Congressman. This had been her only lapse; afterward she inexorably kept up her defenses.

For a long time, Julia had given no thought to divorce. She was a Catholic, respecting the laws of the Church. There was no one she wanted to marry. But after five years, Julia decided that as a matter of principle, she wanted her freedom. One evening, she invited Father Malone to dinner at her apartment. Since Randolph Savage's death Malone had been her only confidant. He was an older man, and Julia felt at ease with him, quite apart from his priesthood.

"As usual, I want your advice," she said, pouring him a stiff drink of Scotch-on-the-rocks. "I've come to the conclusion that I want a divorce. It just makes no sense to go on staying married to Enrique. We'll never get together again, so what's the point of remaining Señora de Palma for the rest of my life? I know what the Church says about divorce, but I think you'll agree that I've done my penance."

Pete Malone tasted his drink. "What you want is a *tabula rasa,*" he replied. "You want to wipe the slate clean and start life anew. Yes, I can understand that. . . . I can't give you an absolution, because it goes against my vows and Church law. So what can I tell you? You don't have grounds for an annulment. The only thing is that you will not be able to be married in the Church again."

Julia filed for a divorce the next day. Uncontested, it was granted. She was now twenty-seven years old, and she was pleased she had broken the last link with Enrique, although a nagging sense of failure remained. In Malagua, many years later and at the peak of her professional success, the memory of her broken marriage still rankled.

★

Enrique Palma flew from Cali to Malagua as soon as Morgan's instructions to approach Julia Savage had reached him. The Station Chief had wanted her to get settled in the ambassadorial post before staging his coup, and a month had elapsed since his confrontation with Enrique in the St. Thomas hotel room. After two days under CIA guard there, the Colombian had concluded that Morgan held all the cards. He sent a message to Morgan accepting his proposition.

★

Enrique Palma had checked into the Malagua Inter-Continental on Lake Taxchilán, on the edge of the capital's residential section and roughly a mile from the Residence of the American Embassy. He always stayed at the Inter-Continental, which was Ciudad Malagua's best hotel, and the assistant manager greeted him familiarly.

"*Bienvenido, Señor Palma*. We got your telex yesterday, and your favorite suite is ready. You haven't been to see us in quite a while."

"That's true. I've been busy with the coffee *fincas* at home."

Enrique's dealings, however, were concerned not with brown beans, but with a white powder—cocaine. For years now, he had been a major drug dealer, leading a double life. Shortly after his marriage to Julia, he had concluded that a great and easy fortune was within his reach if he entered the cocaine world, Colombia being one of its greatest centers. It was more exciting—and promising—than helping to manage the family properties. But the beginnings were hard. He defrauded his father to buy the first raw-coca shipment from a Peruvian supplier, then tried to borrow money from Julia to secure another load.

Enrique soon found out that it was one thing to buy the leaf from wholesalers in the jungle around Letitia, where Colombian, Peruvian, and Brazilian borders converged on the Amazon River, but another to transport it to Bogotá, where clandestine laboratories transformed the leaf into paste and then into "snow," and to connect with big buyers in the United States. Besides, it was a cutthroat business, with rival gangs in Colombia fighting over shipments, routes, and customers. Men were killed mysteriously, no questions asked, and no inquiries held. And Enrique Palma was a newcomer, trying to elbow his way into one of the world's most profitable and jealously protected enterprises. He had first been approached by a friend in Cali, a former schoolmate, with a proposal to put up several hundred thousand dollars for leaf shipments. "You will get your money back almost immediately, with a hundred-percent profit or better," the friend had told him. "And in the end, you will discover that this is a real gold mine compared with your father's business. Just get the money to start the ball rolling. . . ."

But it had not worked out that way. Enrique's friend was found shot to death in his own car in Cali, and the money simply vanished. Enrique was suddenly at the end of his rope, drinking heavily and wondering how he would ever restore the funds he had stolen from his father's company. That was the time when he lost his wife, his self-control having abandoned him in a paroxysm of fear and worry. Julia was gone, but he had to survive. And Enrique needed protection to stay in the drug business, which was the only way he knew to repay Palma S.A. and to support himself. He happened to mention it to another friend whom he knew vaguely to be engaged in narcotics traffic.

Within a week, Enrique received a call from an American who mentioned the friend's name, and suggested that they meet for drinks. When he arrived at the designated hotel bar in Cali, Enrique encountered a tall, redheaded man who wasted no time on niceties. This was Enrique Palma's first introduction to Jim Morgan.

"I am associated with a company that has a lot of influence with the U.S. Government," Morgan said, "and I think I can help you with your problem. You need protection, and we can provide it so long as you deal on our terms."

Morgan, who made no reference to the CIA at their meeting, explained his proposition. His associates would put up the money for coca-leaf purchases and see to it that he went unmolested. "We have our ways," the American said. In exchange, Enrique had to commit himself to sell the pure stuff only to a buyer whom Morgan would designate. When Enrique agreed, Morgan told him to be at the Miami airport the following Wednesday, and handed him a first-class ticket. Morgan and Enrique had a drink at a bar at the Miami terminal and flew together to Ciudad Malagua. There, Morgan took him to a private home near the lake and introduced him to a short, swarthy man, Dr. Pedro Lobo. "This is your buyer," Morgan said. Lobo, who never explained his doctoral title, looked like a caricature of a banana-republic plainclothesman. But he was as sharp as a dagger.

They spent several hours at the lakeside house, discussing what Lobo called "our partnership." Coca-leaf purchases and the cost of Bogotá laboratory processing would be financed by Lobo's Malagua company, which was called *Comercio Internacional S.A.* The company, specializing ostensibly in the import of machinery from the United States and Japan, had offices in the same downtown building as the American Embassy Chancery. It would be Enrique's responsibility to buy the leaf, have it processed, and have the product hand-delivered to the offices of Comercio Internacional. He also had to arrange for couriers. Then Lobo would pay him for the cocaine, at a price considerably below the American wholesale market. Purchase money formed a revolving fund: when Enrique collected a payment from Lobo, it included dollars for new shipments, processing and delivery expenses, and his own commission. The deal was so structured that Enrique chalked up a handsome profit for his work: in the first year, he made nearly $200,000.

Because Lobo and Morgan did not trust the couriers with cash, it was necessary for Enrique to fly to Ciudad Malagua every month or so to pick up the money. To justify the trips, Morgan set up a Comercio Internacional branch office in Cali, with Enrique appearing as a vice president of the parent company. Occasionally, Lobo shipped some machinery to Cali to make the branch office look legitimate. At the outset of the "partnership," Morgan had told Enrique not to worry about competitors anywhere along the line in Colombia. "The word is out that you're a very special person and nobody's to interfere with you." And it worked like magic: Enrique never had the slightest problem with his operations.

"It all seems too easy," he remarked one evening to Pedro Lobo as they met for drinks in the bar of the Malagua Inter-Continental. "I'm not sure I understand everything about it."

"You don't?" Lobo asked incredulously. "*Hombre,* you're being protected by the Ferrers and the American CIA. You can't beat such a combination. . . . Didn't they tell you?"

"No," Enrique replied with utter astonishment. It had never crossed his mind that he was employed, as it were, by the American and Malaguan governments. He had assumed that Morgan was a top Mafia figure. Lobo, who had had too much to drink, was now eager to display his knowledge.

"It's the only way a deal like this can work," he proclaimed with authority. "The CIA, and our friend Mr. Morgan, are interested in helping our beloved President. This man, he needs a lot of money. My own thinking, if you're interested, is that in this manner the CIA can also blackmail El Benefactor. And a coca network can be an intelligence network as well. It's a good connection to have in this nasty world. And you know, I wouldn't be surprised if our Mr. Morgan had a cut in the business himself. So Morgan has picked you to bring cocaine to Malagua. You're good family and above suspicion. Anyway, Morgan's people control a lot of Colombian policemen, which is why the law there has never touched you. The other dealers were warned through channels in the networks to stay away from your operations. They respect that big Colombian man who told them so, and they know what's good for them. Is that clear?"

"Why, yes," Enrique answered. "It explains a lot. . . ."

"*Por Dios,* you're right," Lobo went on, pleased with himself. "And at this end, who do you suppose owns Comercio Internacional? You've guessed it: General Ferrer himself. He's my boss. That's why your couriers are never stopped or searched when they arrive here. When you telex me the name of the courier, I send word to Customs at the airport to lay off him. The boys understand it's official business."

"And where does the cocaine go from here?"

"Ah, my friend, that's a trade secret. . . . Let us say that I have ways of forwarding it to buyers in the United States. And *not* to wholesalers, either. We have our own organization there, and we get the top dollar. . . . You should see the profits for Comercio and the General. Not even I know exactly what they are. . . . The money paid in the United States doesn't all come here. Most of it is deposited somewhere in Europe—in Switzerland, I guess. . . ."

The next time Enrique came to Malagua, Jim Morgan stopped by his hotel room. "I gather that big-mouth Lobo told you a lot about our business, like who I work for. . . . Well, now that you know, you'd better keep your trap shut. It's your neck too, you know. . . ."

As the years went by, Lobo encouraged Enrique to expand, adding marijuana to his traffic. "Colombian Gold," he told him, was now fetching superb prices in the United States, the fields in Mexico having been ruined by chemical spraying, and it would be a shame if Comercio and Enrique did not pick up a piece of the action. Back in Colombia, Enrique contacted an organization in Santa Marta, saying that his principals could use some shipments from the Guajira area. Offers poured in to him. Lobo took charge of hiring pilots and boat captains to ferry the merchandise to Malagua. The pilots landed undisturbed at Ciudad Malagua' airport or at smaller fields. Vessels, ually shrimp or tuna boa sailed from Colombia's Pacific coast to the Malaguan coast r San Pablo. Next, Lobo organized aerial shipments to the Uni States, sometimes through the Grenadines and the Virgin i lands, sometimes directly to Texas or Louisiana.

When Drug Enforcement Administration agents in Ciudad Malagua got wind of narcotics traffic through the country, they went to the Judiciary Police, where they were told—pointedly—that they must be mistaken. The DEA agent-in-charge reported it to Ambassador Breck, who suggested, innocently, that the matter be taken up with Jim Morgan because of his liaison with Malaguan intelligence services. Morgan said, yes, he would take it up with the proper authorities; but nothing further was heard about it. The agent-in-charge, who was extremely bright and understood Malaguan politics, raised the problem with McVeigh. "I think I know what you're talking about, Steve," McVeigh said, "but I'm not the man to help you. My hands are tied. If I were you, I'd start bugging your own superiors in Washington. . . ."

Presently, Enrique Palma branched out into the smuggling of aliens into the United States, another of Lobo's ideas. This too was beautifully profitable. Sometimes it fetched as much as $5,000 per head, with a thousand or so "clients" annually, and Enrique had boats and planes available all over the Caribbean. The expenses were tremendous, but so were the profits. When suitable yachts or motor cruisers could not be bought or bare-bottom yachts chartered in the Caribbean, they were hijacked, renamed, repainted, and put to use for drug or alien smuggling. Yacht piracy was growing alarmingly.

Lobo had suggested that Malagua would be a good staging area for aliens from Colombia and Central America anxious to enter the United States, and that Enrique would get all the necessary help—in exchange, of course, for a very fat commission. From Malagua, the aliens were flown to the British Virgin Islands, with intermediate stops, and then to St. Thomas or St. Croix. The coasts were not well guarded in any of the Virgins—British or American—and the illegal immigrants were then landed by boat in Puerto Rico, vanishing in the Spanish-speaking population. Fake identity papers were obtainable in San Juan, and the aliens could pass for Puerto Ricans for entry in Miami or New York. It worked at least half the time, the payments being collected before departure.

Enrique was getting wealthier and wealthier. He was a millionaire, a jet-setter, spending his free time on the Côte d'Azur, in St. Moritz, and in Paris and New York. Enrique having taken over Palma S.A. on his father's death six years before, it was generally assumed that his great affluence was derived from the booming family business and from Comercio Internacional. Palma S.A. was an excellent cover for Enrique, and nobody questioned the affairs of the handsome Cali aristocrat.

The business had to be protected, and so after he unpacked, Enrique Palma called the American Embassy. Julia was out, and he left word that he was in town and would call again. He had taken the first step, and there was no turning back. He was frightened, but he knew he could not fight the CIA. Too much was at stake.

When Julia returned from the Foreign Ministry, Ann Mestre handed her Enrique's message. Going into her office and closing the door, she sank into her chair and angrily drummed her fingers on her desk. What could he possibly want? It seemed unlikely that he simply wanted to pay a courtesy call on an ex-wife who had become an ambassador. And how would she react to a meeting? She realized abruptly that she was eager to see Enrique.

★

At the Inter-Continental, Enrique Palma was having second thoughts about his enterprise. Not having found Julia at the Embassy on the first call, he was thrown off balance. He had prepared a little speech, asking to come to see her, and now he was frustrated and confused.

He mixed himself a drink, and thought about what he faced. He was not a brave man, and the idea of blackmailing an American ambassador terrified him. It couldn't possibly work, he told himself.

My God, he thought as he poured himself another drink, how am I going to get out of this terrible trap? He could not go back to Morgan to say that he had changed his mind, that he wouldn't play the game because they had no chance of winning.

But he was convinced that she would not be blackmailed, and that she would probably initiate legal action against him. What, then, was the solution? Could he tell her the truth and ask that she change her political views to save him from disaster? For old times' sake? It was ridiculous.

But, Enrique reflected, perhaps there were alternatives. He could gently broach the subject of the fugitive girl in Georgetown years before to test Julia's reaction, then drop it if the initial response was wholly negative. Yes, he could probably risk that. If it worked, fine. If not, he would back out gracefully, then tell Morgan that the ploy had failed and Julia simply would not be blackmailed. There would not be much the CIA man could do about it. Feeling more encouraged, Enrique concluded that Morgan would have no way of determining what had gone on between him and Julia. And with luck, he could pump her for some political information to pass on to Morgan. Yes, that would help to reduce the damage. *¡Carajo!* Enrique said to himself as he lifted the phone to call Julia again, this time at the Residence.

But it occurred to him that a bit of suspense for Julia would do no harm. It would be better to put off his call until tomorrow. He always knew how to handle women, didn't he?

★

Julia was dining alone at the Residence, reading a Malaguan history book as she ate her salad, when the telephone rang. She stiffened. Dudley, the butler, came in and said, "It's for you, Madam Ambassador. . . . He says it's urgent." Julia walked over to the extension in the living room.

"Julia?" a man said, pronouncing the "J" of her name as an "H." She recognized Professor Merino's guttural Spanish tone. "Julia, it's your new friend. I'm calling from a public telephone. I would very much like to see you."

"I think," she said after a moment's thought, "that it would be best if you contacted tomorrow the person who introduced us the other night. He'll put us in touch."

9

Aᴀfter the staff meeting the following day, Julia asked Henry Clark to come by her office. "Look, Henry," she said, "I had a call at home last night from Professor Merino. He was calling from a pay phone, and wouldn't even give his name. Anyway, the point is that he wants to see me. I think I should see him, but we ought to be very careful. I told Merino to get in touch with you to work out the arrangements. I suggest that you bring him to my office, but make it look casual."

"Right. I'll handle it," Clark told her.

Just before noon, Merino called him at the Cultural Section. "Señor Clark," he said, "I'm calling to ask about that book on American Indian anthropology you thought you might be receiving this week. I'm most eager to see it."

"Well, Professor, this is a happy coincidence. I was going to call you to say that the book has just arrived. If you happen to be in town this afternoon, why don't you stop by my office at the Embassy—*not* at the Cultural Center—and pick it up? I'll be there until late. Okay?"

★

Julia spent the rest of the morning reading her mail. The State Department courier had dropped off the pouch for Malagua dur-

ing the weekend, and she was now going through official corre-
spondence, routine things, addressed to her. But she was also
wondering when Enrique would call again. Realizing that she
was irritated by his silence, she decided not to think about it: if
he calls, that's fine; if he doesn't, that's fine, too.

In her mail, Julia found a letter from Father Malone.

"Dear Julia," he wrote.

> *I'm sending this through the State Department rather than
> regular mail, which I'm sure is read in your city. It has
> occurred to me that you may find it useful in your work in
> Malagua to get to know a friend of mine, a fellow Jesuit
> whom I have known for some years. His name is Rolando
> Asturias Puix, and he's an extraordinarily interesting and
> intelligent man. For reasons that you will understand, I am
> not writing Father Asturias directly about you. But I am sure
> that you will have no trouble in locating him. And please use
> my name when you meet him.*
>
> *I trust that all is well with you.*
>
> *God bless you—and lots of love—*
>
> Pete.

The name sounded vaguely familiar to Julia. Then she remembered that McVeigh had spoken of a Father Rolando, a priest
who was said to be a supporter of the anti-Ferrer Frente. Politically minded as Pete Malone was, it had to be the same person.
He meant well, and Julia was grateful for his thoughtfulness, but
it was clear that she could not go around tracking rebel priests.
She was already running a risk by meeting with Professor Merino
in what amounted to a clandestine fashion. Julia crumpled the
letter and put it in the "Burn" bag under her desk. She hoped
Jim Morgan did not go through her "sensitive" trash before the
Marine on duty burned it every evening.

★

"Julia," Ann Mestre said over the intercom, "Señor Enrique
Palma is on the line. Will you take it?"

"Yes," Julia answered. It was near one o'clock, and she had

subconsciously delayed going to lunch, though she knew she would be late to join the British Ambassador at his residence. It was their weekly note-comparing session on the Malaguan situation, and Sir Malcolm Knox was the host today. Now Julia took a deep breath and picked up the phone.

"Hello, Enrique," she said as lightly as she could. "What a surprise—"

"*Ola,* Julia . . . I *did* want to surprise you. I just happen to be in town on business, and I thought I'd give the American Ambassador a call. . . . I hope you don't mind . . ." She thought she detected a note of strain in his casualness.

"No, of course I don't mind," she said carefully. "It's nice to hear your voice."

"Thank you. It's good to hear yours. . . . Ah, I'm not sure what the protocol is, but I was hoping to invite you to dinner. Is it all right for an Ambassador to have dinner with her ex-husband? Could we dine here at the Inter-Continental?"

Julia had already made up her mind that she would see Enrique if he suggested it, but it would not be a good idea to be seen in public with her former husband. They would be spotted at once, the dining room at the Malagua Inter-Continental being the favorite place of Malaguan society, and someone would make sure to find out the identity of her dinner companion. Then gossip and tongue-wagging would start.

"Protocol is not a problem," she said at length. "But I have a better idea. I'm free tomorrow, so come and have dinner with me at the Residence. This is my town, so you should be my guest." Actually, Julia could see on her desk calendar that she had a reception at the Mexican Embassy. But Ann could take care of it, offering one excuse or another.

"I accept, I accept," Enrique roared with boyish joy into the phone. "It's a marvelous idea, Julia, and I can't wait to see you. . . ."

"Eight o'clock, then?"

"That's perfect. I'll be there right on time. . . . *Ciao, querida.*"

Enrique Palma replaced the receiver, and whistled softly to

himself. It had gone better than he'd hoped. He was prepared for a brush-off, even for Julia's refusal to take his call. He had never expected a dinner invitation at her home. "Oh, boy!" he said aloud. It was just possible that it might work.

★

At four o'clock that afternoon, Professor Merino was ushered into Henry Clark's office by a secretary. They shook hands, and Clark said, "You know, the Ambassador borrowed that book you wanted. It's upstairs in her office. Why don't we go to get it there?"

"*Muy bien,*" Merino answered. They smiled at each other.

Julia greeted the Professor warmly, motioning him to the leather sofa, taking a seat herself in an adjoining armchair. She leaned forward expectantly. Henry Clark waved at Merino and disappeared.

"I hope I wasn't being melodramatic with my call last night," Merino began. "But I assume that your phones are tapped by the government, and one must be very careful."

"You were absolutely right," Julia told him. She was feeling she was becoming part of a conspiracy. "Is there anything special I can do for you?"

"Yes, and let me get straight to the point," the Professor said, pulling on his goatee. "After I left you and returned home, I gave a lot of thought to our conversation—and to you. Then an idea came to me. You see, Julia, the most serious problem the opposition in Malagua has always had with the United States, with your government, has been the inability to get its views across. The Embassy has been so beholden to the Ferrers for three generations that it simply would not even listen to the other side.

"But there *is* another side, as you know. The régime claims that the opposition is made up of Marxists, Communists, *fidelistas,* and God knows what else. Obviously, there are Marxists and other leftists in the opposition. That's only natural. But the leftists by no means control the opposition—not even the Frente. Not yet, anyway. . . . There are lots and lots of moderates who do not wish to see the Ferrer dictatorship replaced by a Marxist dictatorship. But your government seems unaware of this fact. It has always swallowed the Ferrer line and has never tried to discover what the truth in Malagua is. Ambassador Breck, for example, was absolutely unapproachable. His people had strict orders to stay away from anybody who was even suspected of oppositionist sympathies. Am I correct?''

''Well, there's something in what you say. . . .''

''But you, Julia, seem to be different. You *are* interested. We are nearing a very dangerous point here, and if the Americans fail to understand very soon what is happening here, Malagua could be the scene of a frightful tragedy. Now, I'm not an activist in the opposition, and I'm not a politician. There are limits to what I'm able to tell you. So I think you ought to listen to somebody who can give you a very accurate and up-to-date picture of the situation. I'm saying all this to you because I care for my country.''

Merino took a sip of the coffee Ann Mestre had brought in, and cleared his throat. ''This, then, is my proposition,'' he said. ''I would like to have your permission to put you in touch with just such a person. I can promise you that he isn't a Marxist or anything like that; it wouldn't make sense. I have taken the liberty of bringing it up with this person. He understands what I'm trying to do, and he's willing to talk with you. It took a little persuading, because the American Embassy here isn't very popular with the opposition, but in the end he agreed. What do you say, Julia?''

''Well, Professor, this isn't very simple from where I sit,'' she said slowly. ''You are familiar with the constraints under which I operate in Malagua. I'd be taking an awful lot on myself if I said yes to you right now. How could you arrange such a meeting? We certainly can't do it publicly.''

''We think we can find a way that would not expose or embarrass you or place my friend in danger. Julia, if you are prepared to give my friends the benefit of the doubt, someone will contact you in the most discreet manner before too long.''

Julia had the sensation of being propelled by events much faster than she could control them. She was being pushed from all sides—by the State Department, by Juan Ferrer, by Professor Merino, even by Father Malone. The State Department had not specifically forbidden her to have contacts with the opposition, but she had been ordered to work with Ferrer, not against him. On the other hand, a meeting with someone from among the moderates did not necessarily mean working *against* the dictator. She could hear out Merino's friend, and let it go at that. And it would be useful. She really knew so little about the antirégime forces. And before long, she had to draft her recommendations on whether Ferrer should be supplied with American arms. How could she make a judgment without knowing all the factors in the situation? Well, she told herself, an ambassador is entitled to some leeway. She would not be making any commitments for the Administration.

"Professor Merino," Julia said, "I've decided to take a chance. Have your friend contact me, and I'll talk with him. But it must be absolutely clear to you and to him that this does not represent any change in basic United States policy. It does not mean this Embassy supports the opposition in the slightest degree. I promise to listen, but nothing more."

"You will not regret your decision, Julia," the Professor said. "And I thank you for your courage. But shouldn't I be carrying a book with me as I leave your office? That's what I came to get."

★

As Julia was receiving Professor Merino, Terence T. Terhune III, the Assistant Secretary for ARA, was chairing a meeting at his State Department office to review again the Malaguan situation. It was an Inter-Departmental Group meeting, and Pentagon, CIA, and NSC representatives were attending.

"Gentlemen," he said, "it's mid-August, and we still have no firm policy on Malagua. The most important question, of course, is whether we will supply Ferrer with arms to deal with the opposition forces. The related issue, as you will recall, is the *quid pro quo* we proposed for these arms—political liberalization by Ferrer. Ambassador Savage has been in Malagua for over a month, she has had a meeting with General Ferrer, but we still have no policy recommendations from her. Frankly, I was hoping for quicker action on her part."

"I agree," the CIA representative said. He was Colonel Kingsley Duke, who headed the Western Hemisphere Division. "Our own sense is that the situation in Malagua is becoming critical. General Ferrer is up against serious new pressures from the leftist opposition."

"Colonel, I'm not sure I understand what you mean by 'critical,' " David Lustig broke in. A bearded young man who had replaced Julia on the NSC staff, he was a former Rand Corporation analyst and assistant professor of Latin American history at Stanford. He saw his role on the NSC as that of a devil's advocate, dedicated to picking apart State Department generalizations and CIA scare tactics.

"As I recall," Lustig went on, "the CIA has taken the view all along that the opposition in Malagua does not command popular support. Unless you've changed your mind, I fail to see the criticality."

The Colonel reddened. He disliked Lustig, often remarking to his associates at the Agency that the new NSC man was an "upstart Jew-boy."

"No *we* haven't changed our minds about that," he said testily. "We continue to believe that the opposition has virtually no popular support. The important point is that Cuban and Communist control over the Frente has now been completely solidified. You all know what a determined, well-armed minority can do in an unstable situation. With professionals like the Cubans directing the operation from inside, the subversion potential is enormous. The killing of the secret-police chief last month is a typical Cuban action, and this morning we received a corroborated report that a large shipment of Cuban arms for the Frente guerrillas has entered Malagua over the Guatemalan border. With the new arms, the Frente can soon launch an offensive in the mountains, take some villages, terrorize people in the countryside and in the capital, and create the impression—the illusion —that it's gaining the upper hand. This is why the National

Guard needs modern equipment—to smash the *guerrilleros* the moment they show their heads. Ferrer is already thinking of a 'search-and-destroy' operation, even before he gets the weapons, but that, at best, would be a holding action.''

"I see what you mean," Terhune said. "My own inclination is to okay the arms, but I know I'm going to get flak from the Seventh Floor and the White House unless we can deliver the complete package, with liberalization in Malagua and so on. I'm also being pressed by people on the Hill to get cracking with arms for Ferrer. Yesterday I had a letter from Congressman Leo Perkins from Texas—you know the clout he has on the House Foreign Affairs Committee—demanding to know why the United States isn't helping General Ferrer against the Communists. I have to draft some kind of a reply, but I know Perkins won't go along with more temporizing. He'll kick up a storm in the Committee.''

"Still, we have to face up to the fact that Ferrer isn't about to liberalize anything," Lustig said. "You've all read Julia's reporting telegram on her first conversation with him. She didn't even have a chance to put up our proposition to him. He already knew all about the package—and by the way, I'd be curious to find out how it had been leaked to him—and he preempted her. I think Ferrer means business, and as far as I can see, we have a hell of a dilemma here."

"Thank you, David, I can figure that out for myself," Terhune said. "What I need is ideas, not people sitting around and stating the obvious." The room fell silent. David Lustig stared at the ceiling, the CIA Colonel looked at his briefing notes, the Pentagon representative scribbled on a note pad, and Terhune's three deputies waited for the Assistant Secretary to speak again.

Terhune cleared his throat. "It seems to me that the next step is to force Julia to send up her formal policy recommendations. I can't go to the Secretary to propose policies without having heard from the ambassador in place. She's been wasting time; a career officer would already have presented his conclusions.''

"Now, wait a minute, Terry," Lustig said. "Julia is dealing with a very complex situation, and you wouldn't want her to cut corners and do a sloppy job. And whether or not the situation in Malagua is as critical as the Colonel here tells us, I don't think it will hurt if we wait another week or two for Julia's report. She's been sending some damned good reporting telegrams; her stuff is infinitely better than the Breck telegrams. For God's sake, let's give her a chance.''

"I don't seem to have much choice, do I?'' Terhune said with anger in his voice. "But I think we ought to make it clear to Ambassador Savage how urgent it is for her to come up with a position paper.'' He turned to one of his deputies: "Bill, get the Ambassador on the phone and tell her that her recommendations must be in within ten days.''

★

Julia was listening to the problems of an American business-man—he had not been able to get a license to build a paper mill in Malagua and clearly didn't know that he had to take the Ferrer family into partnership before anything would move—when Ann Mestre walked in and placed a typed message on her desk. She excused herself and read it:

> The office of the President just called. The General wants you to come to lunch at the Palace at one o'clock tomorrow. I accepted and cancelled your lunch with the AID people.

The next day, at one minute before one o'clock, Salvador drove the black Chrysler through the gate of the Palace on El Cerro. A National Guard aide-de-camp was waiting on the steps to escort Julia upstairs. The President, wearing a military fatigue blouse with four stars on the collar tabs, was at his desk, and he rose to greet her.

"Julia,'' he said cordially. "Julia, welcome back. I hope I didn't inconvenience you with lunch on such short notice, but I did want to discuss some matters with you. And I thought it would be pleasanter to lunch informally here in my office.''

She had been wondering what was on Ferrer's mind, and the General wasted no time in telling her. Pouring chilled white wine into her glass, he said, "I asked you here to share with you my concern over the way the situation in my country is developing. The news isn't good. Our intelligence people have discovered that a large shipment of Cuban arms was smuggled into Malagua over the Guatemalan border sometime last week. Maybe the biggest shipment yet. Cases of AK-47 automatic assault rifles, the ones made in the Soviet Union, and a dozen or so mortars. Plus ammo. We think it was landed on the Caribbean coast of Guatemala, from small boats, and picked up by the guerrillas there to be put across the frontier into Malagua. You know that Guatemalan and Malaguan terrorists work together under Cuban coordinators. Trouble in Malagua helps the terrorists in Guatemala, and vice versa. So I think a decision has been made for a big push against me."

"Were you able to seize any of these arms?"

"No. Unfortunately not. You know how our border with Guatemala is: mountains and forests, which are impossible to police from either side. We learned only yesterday of the shipment. We have some people infiltrated in the Frente, our G-2 agents, and they've told us that the arms are on Malaguan territory, being distributed to guerrilla units."

Fabio, the dwarf, dressed in a white jacket, served them a shrimp appetizer. When he left the room, the President continued to talk.

"This places me in a very dicey position, Julia," he said. "One is always at a disadvantage fighting guerrillas—as you Americans found out in Vietnam. But the disadvantage is even greater when the *guerrilleros* acquire greater firepower and the established government has to make do with obsolete stuff. I have only six helicopters, only one of which can be used as a gunship. My air force is pitiful. The National Guard is short on modern field equipment and expendables—ammunition. As I've told you before, the country is polarized. If the Frente decides to attack in a systematic fashion, and I think they will, there's going to be a bloody civil war. I believe it is in the interest of the United States that I should win in the end. I need American weapons urgently and desperately, and I must ask you if you've made your recommendations yet."

"To be truthful, Mr. President," Julia said, "I haven't, but—"

She was interrupted by the ringing of the telephone on the General's desk. "Shit!" he exclaimed. "Oh, excuse my language . . . but I left orders not to be interrupted during lunch. Let me find out what it is. . . .

"*¿Sí, qué pasa? . . . What?* Say that again. . . . *¡Por Dios!* . . .* Are you sure that he's dead? . . . Okay, call me at once with any details."

Ferrer put down the phone and stared into space for a moment. He was visibly shaken when he returned to the table, and his hands were trembling.

"It's Nestor Cruz," he said. "He's been killed. . . ."

"Oh, my God!" Julia cried. "How did it happen?" Nestor Cruz was the publisher and editor of *Clarín,* Malagua's leading newspaper, and a critic of the régime. He had been one of her guests at the first reception at the Residence, and Julia had been planning to invite him to dinner.

"He was hit by submachine-gun fire when his car stopped for a red light on Avenida Bolívar," the General said heavily. "The fire came from another car at the intersection. It took off at once. Nestor was alive for a few minutes, they tell me, but died before an ambulance arrived. Oh, God, Julia, I'll be accused of having ordered Nestor's murder because he was critical of me in his newspaper. That is how *malagueños* think. That a dictator goes around assassinating people who criticize him. But I swear to you I had nothing to do with it. I swear on my father's memory. And if Malagua is already polarized, wait and see what happens now with Nestor's death. I'll bet you the God-damned *malaguistas* had him killed to put the blame on me . . . the bastards. . . ."

★

Mac McVeigh; Rick Anders, the Political Counselor; and John Crespo, the Deputy CIA Station Chief, gathered in Julia's office that afternoon to study the implications of the Nestor Cruz assassination and to prepare a telegram to the State Department. She had asked Morgan to attend, but he could not be found. (He was in Enrique Palma's room at the Malagua Inter-Continental, instructing him on what to say at dinner that night with the American Ambassador.)

"Things seem to be getting out of hand," McVeigh said. "First Saavedra; now Nestor Cruz. I can believe that the Frente liquidated Saavedra—he was a shit and a torturer—but I can't buy their killing Nestor too, as Ferrer suggested to the Ambassador. Of course, the Frente would gain, because Ferrer will obviously get the blame, rightly or wrongly. But would they sacrifice a leading editor who was a supporter of their cause? Maybe I'm naïve, but I just don't believe they're that cynical."

"Do you think it's possible that Ferrer had Nestor shot because he was getting to be a burr under the saddle?" Rick Anders asked.

"No, I don't," McVeigh replied. "Ferrer isn't mad. This can only hurt him, and hurt a lot."

"Okay," Julia said, "if we rule out the Frente and we rule out Ferrer, what have we got? Who else had a motive to assassinate Nestor Cruz? John, what do you think?"

The CIA man shrugged. "I concur with Mac that neither the Frente nor Ferrer did it," he said. "Practically speaking, I doubt seriously that the Frente would take such a chance. They're a very sophisticated crowd, and they know that if this thing was traced to them, they'd never recover from it. Sure, the President will play the Frente angle for all it's worth, though it won't be very convincing. The people here think highly of the Frente—"

"I've never heard you say *that* before, John," Julia interjected. "And I haven't heard Mr. Morgan say it."

"No, I guess you never have," Crespo replied quietly. "I'm just giving you my personal opinion, not the Station's official assessment. Okay?"

"As far as I'm concerned, it's a big, fat mystery," Rick Anders said. "There may have been personal motives, not political. It happens. We won't solve it here today. The best we can do for now is inform the Department of the killing, try for an estimate of the potential impact of the shooting on the Malaguan situation, and let it go at that until we know more. I'll go and draft the telegram, and I'll have it ready for the Ambassador to see in an hour or so.''

As the men were leaving her office, Julia asked Crespo to stay for a minute. When they were alone, she asked, ''Have you heard about a shipment of Cuban arms that came into Malagua last week? Information that the government here obtained yesterday morning?''

''Yes, of course,'' Crespo said. ''Jim passed it on to Headquarters as a priority message as soon as G-2 told him about it— oh, I guess around nine o'clock yesterday morning. His friend called him at home. Is there something wrong?''

''No,'' Julia answered. ''It's just curious that Mr. Morgan didn't mention it at yesterday's staff meeting.''

★

Julia left the Chancery shortly before seven o'clock in the evening, giving herself an hour to dress for dinner with Enrique Palma. As she stepped into her car, Julia saw a crowd surging down the Avenida San Martín, less than a block behind her. ''Let's get the hell out of here,'' Salvador, the driver, shouted in English. He tried to pull away from the curb, but the limousine was blocked by the lead car, still parked in front. Security men surrounded the immobilized Chrysler as it was engulfed by the mob. Gonzalo, the bodyguard in the front seat, dropped his submachine gun to the floor, concealing it with his feet. ''There's no point in provoking them,'' he said to Julia. ''Don't worry. I'll be able to use it if I have to.'' The crowd, however, was not interested in the Embassy car. The chant of *¡Asesino! ¡Muera Ferrer!* rose from a thousand throats. Through the bulletproof window, Julia saw young men and women, their faces contorted with rage and grief. Some carried clubs; others had paving stones in their hands. *¡Asesino! . . . ¡Muera Ferrer! . . .* they shouted rhythmically. A crudely lettered poster urged *venganza* against the assassins of Nestor Cruz. As predicted, Nestor Cruz's death was being blamed on the dictator.

She heard the crash of breaking glass as rocks hit store windows along the Avenida. Then police sirens began to scream. Looking ahead to the next intersection, Julia saw police cruisers and gray-painted riot-squad buses forming a roadblock. Riot police, shotguns in hand, poured out of the buses, advancing in wedge formation toward the crowd. The demonstrators hesitated, but for a moment held their ground. *¡Muera Ferrer!* . . . they shouted defiantly. There were several sharp explosions, and the street began to fill with tear gas.

More tear-gas grenades landed on the pavement, and the crowd broke and ran back. But a contingent of police had moved behind the demonstrators, cutting off their retreat. They were hemmed in. The young man carrying the poster was now a foot or two from Julia's car; she heard a dry crackle and saw him fall backward from the bullet that caught him full in the chest. A police skirmish line, firing directly into the crowd, moved past the Chrysler. Looking out the rear window, Julia saw people mowed down by the fusillade. There were screams of pain, fury, indignation. Rivulets of blood ran down the pavement to the curb. She closed her eyes.

★

It was a few minutes after eight o'clock when Julia finally reached the Residence. There were riots all over Ciudad Malagua, and Salvador chose circuitous routes to avoid them.

Enrique Palma was standing in the living room. As she had feared, he was on time. His hotel on the lake was just a mile away, and he had not had to cross the riot-torn city to reach the Residence. Avenida Ferrer was an elegant enclave of peace. "Oh, Christ!" Julia said softly, catching a glimpse of herself in the hall mirror. She smoothed her hair, straightened her damp, wrinkled dress, and went in to greet her ex-husband. In a black silk suit, white shirt, and figured dark tie, he exuded quiet, conservative elegance. Yes, Enrique was still handsome; but he was heavier, there were pouches under his eyes, and his movements were slower. He looks older than his age, Julia thought.

She had both anticipated and dreaded this moment from the time she had received his first message. She wanted to know how she would react to his physical presence. She had carried the memories for all these years; she had believed for all these years that she was still in love with him, that his sexual attraction was overwhelming and eternal. And now Enrique was here, coming toward her across the room, a pleasant-looking, well-dressed Latin American man—but a stranger. Suddenly she was reminded of the Honduran Minister of Agriculture whom she had met in Washington and whose amorous advances she had politely discouraged. She felt no flicker of emotion for the tall man who had now taken her hand to kiss it warmly.

"How wonderful to see you, Enrique," Julia said in a tone she reserved, she suddenly realized, for high-ranking official guests. "And please forgive me for being late—you know there are riots all over town, and it took longer than usual to get home. Has Dudley offered you a drink? No? Let me call him. . . ."

"Oh, Julia, I can wait for a drink," Enrique said softly. He knew these first moments were crucial. He needed her help, and the old charm had to be given a chance to work. "First, I want to see you, to take a good look at you. God, you really haven't changed. It's incredible. I saw your pictures in the papers when you were appointed, but now I'm seeing the real thing."

Julia gave him one of her sweet smiles, looking him straight in the eyes. She was still searching for something she knew was no longer there. "How very nice of you, Enrique," she said. "I see your manners are as perfect as ever, and I thank you for the compliments. Now, what will you have?"

"A Scotch-on-the-rocks would be just fine," he said. "Maybe double; it's been a long day."

She rang for the drinks and said, "Dinner should be ready in half an hour. Do sit down and tell me about yourself and about what you're doing in Malagua."

Taking the chair opposite her, Enrique felt a twinge of annoyance at Julia's direction of their conversation. In Cali, the last time Enrique had seen her, Julia had been a spirited young woman, but deferential to him. Until the day when she walked out on him. Now she was poised and mature, almost regal.

"Well," he said, "I must say I'm doing quite well. I'm not as famous as you are, Julia, but business has been very good. My father—you remember him—died eight years ago, and now I'm the head of Palma S.A. We've expanded rather considerably in a variety of fields, and it's been a success. I've turned out to be a better businessman than I seemed to be in Cali in your time. And I don't go around asking for loans."

Julia said, "I'm delighted to know that," and Enrique was furious with himself for this allusion to their final fight. God, this was a bad start. He drained his glass and got up to refill it. She sat quietly, smoking a cigarette and watching him. She had not touched her wine.

Sitting again, he smiled a little too broadly and said, "You asked what brings me to Malagua. Well, I'm vice president of a Malaguan company, and among other things I do, I run its branch office in Cali. It's called Comercio Internacional, S. A. The main office is in the same building as the American Embassy, so we're neighbors of sorts. Anyway, I have to come to Ciudad Malagua several times a year, and when I read in Cali that you were the new American Ambassador here, I said to myself, 'I must see Julia the next time I'm in Malagua.' You know, it's been such a long time. I often thought of calling you in Washington, when I came through, but it seemed awkward. Maybe you still would not want to see me there. But this is a marvelous coincidence and opportunity, Julia. Here, at least, we have something in common—our interest in the prosperity of Malagua. And I do want to be friends with you again. You know, divorced people *can* be friends."

"Yes, perhaps," Julia said flatly, nodding to Dudley, who had appeared to announce dinner.

At the table, Dudley poured white wine to go with the cold soup, a Malaguan variation of *gazpacho,* while Julia made small talk about the condition in which she had found the Residence and her plans to refurbish it even more as soon as she had time.

"I imagine Malagua keeps you pretty busy," Enrique ventured. Morgan had told him to sound out Julia's attitude toward Ferrer.

"Well, it does, Enrique," she replied. "You know, I'm very

new at the business of being Ambassador, and there's so much to learn about running an Embassy. And of course, we maintain very active relations with the government of Malagua. So I have very little free time."

"I imagine you have met President Ferrer," Enrique said. "What's he like?"

"I met him when I presented my credentials and once since then. I think he's an extremely interesting man. He was educated in the United States, as you know; he understands Americans, and his English is as good as yours and mine."

"Do you think he's in trouble here—politically, I mean?"

"You're asking the wrong person, Enrique. I've been here such a short time that I wouldn't dare express an opinion. But you should know all this better than I. I'm sure your business associates here can tell you more than I can."

Dudley served the main course, roast beef (the meat flown from U.S. Southern Command stores in Panama), and Julia poured Enrique red wine. It was a Cabernet Sauvignon from California, and she gracefully turned the conversation to a discussion of its merits. American wine was supposed to be served at American embassies. Damn her, he thought with rising irritation, she won't give me a chance. Over the dessert of fresh fruit, Enrique returned to General Ferrer.

"I'm very concerned about him," he said. "I've been doing business here for a long time, and I feel he's been very good for the country. And the United States could help him, if it wanted to. Julia, what are the chances that the Americans will come through with some kind of help for the President?"

Julia looked at him coldly. "I'm really not at liberty to discuss United States policies with you," she replied, getting up from the table. "Shall we have coffee in the living room?"

"Yes, thank you." The arrogant bitch is really asking for it, he thought, and I'll give it to her. No more hesitations—I'll do it Morgan's way.

As Dudley offered him a cognac, Enrique said quietly, "Julia, there's something I want to ask you."

"Certainly, Enrique, what is it?"

He waited for the butler to leave the room. "Julia, do you remember a girl named Sally Kleben? Back in Washington, before we were married?"

"Of course I remember her. Why?"

"You remember bringing this Sally Kleben to my house, telling me she was in trouble, and then hiding her at your father's house? And the next day it came out that the FBI was after her because she had something to do with a bombing?"

Julia stared at him silently.

"You surely realized that you were harboring a fugitive from justice," Enrique went on, hating her for the way she had treated him this evening, for what she was making him do. Julia still said nothing.

"Okay," Enrique exploded in exasperation. "How do you think it would look if it became known that the American Ambassador to Malagua has a dirty secret, that she and her patriot father had helped a criminal escape? You can imagine what the networks and the newspapers would make of that. But it *doesn't* have to come out if you decide to cooperate."

"If I support Ferrer?" Julia asked calmly. She lit a cigarette.

"Right. If you—"

Julia interrupted him: "Enrique, you have exactly one minute to leave this house—or I shall call the Marine guard. And don't you ever, *ever* try to contact me again. Even in Malagua there must be a law against blackmail."

★

Jim Morgan was waiting for Enrique Palma at the Malagua Inter-Continental.

"How did it go?" he asked as soon as Enrique closed the door.

Enrique decided to tell the truth. He could not risk lying.

"I brought up the matter of the girl," he said, "and the fucking broad threw me out of the Residence. She said she would call the Marines."

Morgan grimaced. "So you failed, didn't you?"

"But, Jim, I did my best . . . I followed your instructions. . . ."

"Obviously not well enough," the Station Chief told him. "You poor bastard." He got up and left, slamming the door behind him.

★

The Feast of Our Lady of Malagua on August 27 marked the anniversary of the founding of Ciudad Malagua in 1535 and was therefore both a religious and a national holiday. A Solemn High Mass was celebrated at the Cathedral by the Archbishop, and it was the custom of President Ferrer and his family to attend it. Then the General held a reception for the diplomatic corps and other notables at the National Palace.

This year, however, there was no *fiesta* mood in the capital. The riots sparked by the assassination of Nestor Cruz had left twenty-three demonstrators dead and more than one hundred seriously injured. Appearing on television the following day, President Ferrer stated that the city would remain under martial law, warning that "law and order will be maintained at all costs" and that "Communist-led disturbances will not be tolerated." During the next week, shopkeepers and businessmen on Avenida Bolívar were nervous, closing down before darkness fell on the city. The *barrios* were sullen, and the police and National Guard patrols stayed out of them during the night.

In the days before the Feast, rumors began to circulate in the city that "something" would happen on that day. Julia Savage sent a telegram to Washington reporting the tension and the rumors, and Terhune responded with a Top Secret message: because of the danger to American citizens and property in Malagua, troops of the U.S. Southern Command in Panama had been placed on low alert. "They're overreacting again," McVeigh said to Julia.

★

A slim figure in dirty slacks and a T-shirt under a plastic raincoat slipped into a dimly lit bar on a back alley in Barrio del Sur late on the evening of Thursday, August 25, and joined two young men at a corner table. It was raining hard, and Dora Merino's face was streaked with water as she removed her soaking black beret. The owner and other customers were watching a *telenovela* on the bar's TV set, and paid no attention to the new arrival. One of the young men brought her rum with water from the counter, and the three of them huddled together, Dora speaking in whispers despite the noise of television.

"These are the orders from the Jefe Militar," she said. "All the cells are to be advised immediately that there will be a confrontation after the Mass at the Cathedral on the day of the Feast. The mobilization is to start the night before. The Jefe wants fifty militants inside the Cathedral, one-half men, one-half women, and about one hundred outside and in the back streets. A signal will be given from inside the church the moment the Mass is finished. You will recognize the signal. The militants in the streets are to start moving exactly one minute later to distract the police. Is that clear? *¡Muerte al tirano! . . .*" Dora Merino gulped down her drink, pulled her wet beret firmly down on her cropped hair, and slipped out of the bar.

★

On the eve of the Feast, the American Embassy received a circular sent by the Malaguan Foreign Ministry to all the diplomatic missions. It read:

> Because of the unrest currently prevailing in the Capital of the Republic, His Excellency, General Juan Ferrer Berrio, President of the Republic, has regretfully decided to cancel most of the celebrations on August 27, the Feast Day of Nuestra Señora de Malagua. His Excellency will *not* attend the Mass of Thanksgiving at the Cathedral. Chiefs of diplomatic missions accredited to the Government of the Republic of Malagua are therefore not expected to be in attendance. His Excellency has decided to cancel the annual reception at the National Palace out of respect for the memory of the citizens who lost their lives as a result of recent events.

"It looks like the old man is expecting trouble," McVeigh remarked as he read the circular and passed it back to Julia. "And there goes your day in church, Madam Ambassador."

Julia replied, "Not at all, not at all. I have every intention of attending the Mass tomorrow."

"You're mad," McVeigh told her. "You know there's going to be some sort of disturbance at the Cathedral. It may be dangerous. Come on, Julia, use your head. . . ."

"That's precisely what I'm doing," she said. "I've got to see for myself what the sentiment is among the people, and how the General is going to handle it. I'm tired of second- and third-hand reports on the situation. Once in a while, even an ambassador has to do some legwork. Don't worry—Gonzalo and company will be there to protect me."

Julia had decided not to mention Enrique Palma's blackmail attempt to McVeigh or to report it to Washington. After much thought, she had concluded that Enrique was only part of a complex intrigue reaching far beyond Malagua, possibly all the way to Washington. But whom was he working for? Ferrer's secret police? Jim Morgan? Julia was not concerned about the Kleben incident; its publication could cause her some unpleasantness, but no real harm. She was far more interested in knowing who was so determined to ensure her support of Ferrer. The game was far from over, she knew, and she decided to let her adversaries make the next move. She had things to do in Malagua, and going to the Cathedral on the day of the Feast of Our Lady of Malagua was one of them.

★

The Mass on Saturday, August 27, was to be celebrated at eleven in the morning. At ten o'clock, Julia Savage, wearing a black dress and a black lace *mantilla* over her head, stepped into her limousine at the Residence. Fifteen minutes later, she reached the Cathedral plaza. Armored cars stood at every corner, their guns trained on the steps of the Cathedral. Helmeted National Guardsmen in battle dress, submachine guns at the ready, formed a phalanx in the center of the square. The faithful were allowed to march to the church down a narrow passage between two rows of riot policemen. The *pordioseros* and other usual denizens of the plaza had been evicted by the police.

National Guardsmen at a roadblock at the northern entrance to the square waved on Julia's car and the escort vehicles. She got out of the car at the Cathedral's steps and, discreetly followed by Gonzalo and three security men, entered the church. She dipped her fingers in the holy-water font, crossed herself, and walked down the aisle through the half-empty church. She genuflected at a pew close to the altar and sat down. Gonzalo, his pistol and walkie-talkie concealed under the *guayabera* he wore today, sat next to her. Looking around, Julia observed that most of those already in their seats were casually dressed young people.

By eleven o'clock, when the small altar bell rang for the Mass, the Cathedral was entirely filled. Julia went through the motions of worship, watching the congregation out of the corner of her eye. Nothing unusual. The young and old and the middle-aged were praying, kneeling, crossing themselves, and chanting responses. The celebrants came and went at the altar, and the fat Archbishop Ledesma, the friend of the President, delivered the sermon. The Mass ended with the singing of the *Te Deum*. Then, after a moment of silence, a voice shouted, *"¡Muerte al tirano!"* The cry was taken up and roared through the Cathedral. The center aisle filled with men and women chanting, *¡Muerte al tirano! ¡Muerte al tirano!* Brandishing their fists, they moved swiftly toward the main door.

Gonzalo whipped out the walkie-talkie from under his flowing shirt, and spoke urgently into it. Three of her security men closed around Julia. The crowd had broken out the door and onto the steps of the Cathedral. Julia heard more shouting, some of it coming from farther away, then the staccato chorus of machine guns. And screams of the dying and the wounded, and the chant, now weaker, of *¡Muerte al tirano!* . . .

"This way, this way," Gonzalo said, grabbing her elbow. "To the back door. An escort car is waiting there." They fought their way to the altar and slipped behind it into the sacristy. Julia heard a whisper: "Madam Ambassador, Madam Ambassador."

Looking over her shoulder, she saw a tall priest. "Yes?" she said impatiently as Gonzalo kept leading her to the sacristy door.

"I am Rolando Asturias Puix, the friend of Professor Merino," the priest said in English. "May I ride with you to your Residence? We have a lot to talk about."

10

As Julia's car pulled away, bursts of gunfire and wild screams and shouts echoed through the narrow streets around the Cathedral. Crowded between security men, she and the priest rode in silence. Now, sitting on the patio of the Residence, he said, "I assumed that you would be attending the Mass with the rest of the Diplomatic Corps, and I decided to introduce myself discreetly at the church in the hope that we could set up an appointment. When I heard that the diplomats would not be coming to the Cathedral, I feared that I would have to find another way of getting in touch with you. I could not just walk into your office and say, '*Señora,* I am Rolando Asturias and I am here to tell you all about the opposition to General Ferrer.' "

He laughed, and Julia liked the rich baritone of his voice. "In any event," Asturias continued, "I thought that so long as I was in town—my parish, you know, is up in the hills—I might as well go to the Cathedral just in case you came after all. Besides, I smelled trouble, and I wanted to be there."

"So you are the mysterious person Professor Merino wanted me to meet," Julia said. "It never crossed my mind that it would be *you.*"

"I beg your pardon?"

"Well, not long ago I received a letter from a friend in Washington suggesting that I look you up. You know Pete Malone, don't you?''

''Good heavens!'' Asturias exclaimed. ''I cannot believe it. I haven't seen Pete in years, but I often think of him. He was very helpful to me when I studied in the United States. I had no idea that you were friends.''

Julia studied the priest as he talked. He had taken off his black jacket and rolled up the sleeves of his shirt, and she saw that his lean body was well muscled. He appeared to be in his early forties, and his narrow face, dominated by an aquiline nose, was strong and smooth. He had lively deep blue eyes and a shock of light brown hair.

''Are you a native Malaguan?'' she asked. ''You don't really look it.''

''Actually, I was born here,'' the priest said. ''But my parents came from Spain. My father was an immigrant from Galicia— from La Coruña, to be exact—and my mother was a Catalán. That explains the 'Puix' matronymic of my name. They both emigrated during the Spanish Civil War and met here in Ciudad Malagua. I was born a year after they were married. My father got to own a *bodega* in the city, a very good one, but he died a few years ago. My mother still lives in our little family house, not far from the Cathedral. I'm going to visit her after I leave you. She's close to seventy now, and since my exile from the capital I don't see her very often.''

''Your exile?''

''Yes, that's what I call it. Early this year the Archbishop removed me from the University, where I was teaching, and sent me to a small parish up in the mountains, where the old pastor had died quite a while ago. I was supposed to be a radical; my ideas were said to be too dangerous for the young people at the University. As a Jesuit, I should not theoretically be ordered around by an archbishop, especially a fascist like him, and I protested to the Order in Rome. But Rome doesn't want any trouble with the people who run Malagua, so I was told to shut up and obey. The Archbishop thought I could do no harm up in the hills, but I may surprise him. But that's enough about me. Luis Merino said I should be talking to you about the Frente."

The telephone rang, and Julia picked up the patio extension. She listened carefully, nodding her head, her face turning somber. "That was my office," she told him, "with the preliminary casualty count at the Cathedral. It seems eighteen persons were killed by the National Guard, and there are so many wounded that the hospitals are too busy to try to get a figure."

"The murderers will pay for it, I promise you," Asturias said. "The madman has gone too far. Just kill, kill, and kill. That is all he knows. Well, Madam Ambassador, maybe this will make you understand better why there is a Liberation Front in Malagua!"

He spoke about the Frente for a long time, Julia listening in silence. It had been organized in 1966, he said, by six intellectuals and students from the University law school when it became clear that Juan Ferrer, upon inheriting the presidency from his father, had no real intention of instituting democratic reforms. The example of the Cuban revolution was still fresh, and the founders of the Frente believed they could organize a guerrilla force in the mountains, as Fidel Castro had done, and link it to an urban resistance movement. But Malagua, he said, was not Cuba, the level of political consciousness in the country was abominably low, and Ferrer's National Guard was far superior to Batista's army. Thus for years the Frente was essentially insignificant. Three of its founders were killed in shoot-outs with the Guard. One had languished in prison, *incommunicado,* for the last three years, but his freedom had recently been engineered by the guerrillas. The other two, in desperation, had fled Malagua.

In recent years, however, a new generation of leaders had emerged to pick up the pieces of the Frente. Some came from the University and intellectual circles, as had the Glorious Six, the founders of the Frente. Others were young professionals: a number of lawyers, several doctors. Some Frente members led full-time guerrilla lives in the mountains and forests of Malagua. Others, especially in the cities, led double lives. But the most important aspect of the new struggle, the priest said, was that the anti-Ferrer movement now had a solid backing in the rural population on the one hand and in Ciudad Malagua business groups on the other.

"And finally," Asturias said, "more and more priests have joined the people in the battle against Ferrer—and some are even leading it. You have heard, of course, of Don Pepe Vargas Merino, the bishop from the highlands who is the most prominent of the régime's ecclesiastical critics. Obviously, he's not an actual member of the Frente, but he is crucial to the movement. In the villages, there are *curas* who have made it possible for the rebellion to survive and grow. Their principal concern is the exploitation of the Indian peasants by the landlords. Both the landowners and the government are deathly afraid of the peasants—they remember the uprisings of the 1930s—and consequently, propeasant priests have become targets of repression too. In the last year, five village priests have been mysteriously murdered."

"Would you mind, Father, if I asked what part *you* play in all this? You told me you have been exiled from the University for radicalism, whatever that means in Malagua. Surely you are doing something. . . ."

"Well, right now I'm talking to you, which is not unimportant," he said laughing. "But let's not waste time on me. . . . There's one more point I would like to make."

"I'm sorry; I was being unfair," Julia told him. "I have no business asking you that kind of question."

"No, that's okay," he replied. "I just want to concentrate on the broad picture. And this picture includes the fact that a split exists in the Frente. Generally speaking, the Frente is a collection of prodemocratic elements, although many of them have leftist leanings—I would say, in the Western European sense of socialism. But there is an important faction, still in a minority, which is unquestionably Marxist, and in a rather extreme fashion at that. They make no secret of it, and they are quite busy proselytizing within the movement. They claim they are part of the Frente, but, for ideological reasons, they refuse to be represented on the Directorate. . . . It's important that you know this."

"Who are they?" Julia asked.

"Basically, the faction called Ejército Guerrillero de los Pobres—the Poor People's Guerrilla Army; and it is quite important militarily in the hills, in the *guerrilla*. Their leader, perhaps the best military mind in the movement, is Comandante Máximo Landino. The G-2 know about him, so there's no harm in telling you. . . ."

"Landino?" Julia broke in. "Is he related to—"

"Yes, he's the grandson of General Máximo Landino, who was killed by Bolívar Ferrer when Ferrer became President after the departure of American Marines. Landino fought a guerrilla war against the U.S. occupation and Ferrer's National Guard. Ferrer wanted to get Landino and his army out of the mountains, so he invited him to join a government of 'national unity.' Landino, who should have known better, agreed. He came down to Ciudad Malagua to have dinner with Ferrer, and he was killed when he left the Palace. Young Máximo, the *comandante,* hates Americans because he's convinced they were behind his grandfather's assassination. I imagine this has influenced his political philosophy."

"But—" Julia began.

"Please let me get to my point. Máximo and the EGP are tremendously important to the Frente, particularly as a military confrontation with Ferrer approaches. But the Frente should not be turned over to him. The EGP is committed to what they call a 'prolonged war,' leading to total military victory and a radical revolution in Malagua. The majority in the Frente, however, think a political solution is still possible—that is, that Ferrer can be ousted through the right mix of rural and urban guerrilla warfare and irresistible pressure by the moderate economic groups, mainly the urban middle class. They hope to establish a social democracy without the horror of a civil war. Then there are Frente elements in the middle, still undecided between these two roads. What I'm telling you is that the revolutionary movement is in the midst of a very dangerous crisis. This is why I've accepted Professor Merino's suggestion to meet with you."

"You have a purpose in telling me all this," Julia said.

"Obviously. I believe that if the United States goes on supporting Ferrer, Máximo's faction will gain in strength and will probably prevail. He will have proved that only extremism can carry the day. And I warn you, people will go along with him. But if you Americans drop Ferrer, and Malaguans recognize this reality, we'll have an alternative. Do you understand?''

"I see your point," Julia answered, "but I'm not sure I can say anything right now that would encourage you. . . ."

"I realize that," Asturias said. "All I'm asking is that you see the situation as it really is. Still, my word is not enough. You must, Madam Ambassador, meet some of the leaders of the Frente if you are to make a proper judgment for yourself. It's been discussed, and they are eager to communicate with you. . . . Máximo Landino, however, is not one of them. He doesn't know about any of this—naturally."

There was a sudden gust from Lake Taxchilán, and the wind chimes on the walls of the patio played a quick melody. Julia said, "How do you propose to do it?"

"Evidently, I cannot bring the whole group to your house," the priest replied, a twinkle in his blue eyes. "So you shall have to come to see us in the hills."

"You can't be serious," Julia said. "I'm accredited to the Ferrer government, and I have no business meeting with rebel leaders somewhere in the mountains. You know that. . . ."

"Well, it's not for me to tell you what to do," Asturias said. "But I want you to think about it. Look. I've brought a little map to show you how to find my church. It shouldn't take you more than a couple of hours to get there. If you decide to come, send a message through Professor Merino, saying that you will have tea with him on such and such a day. I'll get the word, and will be expecting you."

Getting up, he handed her a folded piece of paper. "These are the directions," he said. "I hope to see you before too long."

★

My God, Julia thought after Asturias left. Pressures and more pressures. Ferrer pressing for arms. The State Department pressing for a recommendation on the arms question. Professor Merino and now this Jesuit imploring her to see *their* side of the Malaguan conflict. Enrique trying to blackmail her. Morgan playing his private CIA games around her. People being killed in the streets and on the Cathedral steps.

Finishing her coffee, she considered the priest's invitation to visit his mountain church and meet with Frente leaders. She had already overstepped the line of her authority in agreeing to see him. To seek out the rebel leadership in the hills would be a clear violation of her instructions to work with Ferrer, not against him. But the split in the Frente, as described by Asturias, was a new and important element in the Malaguan crisis. It should be explored, Julia thought, because, indeed, it might provide a long-range option in the limited policies the Administration had been considering. Would she be wise to reject out of hand the opportunity that was being presented to her? Did an American Ambassador always have to comply with conventional wisdom, with narrowly couched instructions, and remain extra-careful and extra-conservative? Did Americans always have to fear new ideas and experiments, always toe their own party line? Wasn't there something to be gained from greater flexibility and independence? She would have to give it more reflection.

★

At the Embassy the next morning, Julia asked Rick Anders if the Political Section had a file on a Rolando Asturias Puix. Anders called back in a few minutes to say that he had no file on Father Asturias, but the CIA Station did have one, and he would get it from John Crespo. Anders and Crespo had a good working relationship, and they helped each other—unofficially—whenever they could. Morgan disliked sharing his files, or anything else, with Embassy officers, but Crespo, who had a mind of his own, felt his chief often exaggerated the need for Station secrecy.

Anders read from the *dossier:*

Rolando Asturias Puix, a Jesuit priest, was born in Ciudad Malagua in 1939. . . . Parents were Spanish immigrants, father owned *bodega,* etc. . . . Asturias went to elementary school and *liceo* in Ciudad Malagua. . . . Graduated from National University in philosophy in 1960. . . . Spent two years at a Jesuit seminary near Ciudad Malagua, then went to Georgetown University for a year's graduate work, sponsored by the Rev. Peter Malone. . . . Then two years at a Jesuit seminary in Boston. . . . Father Asturias was ordained in Boston in 1965 at the age of 26. . . .

"All this stuff comes from his U.S. visa applications at the Consulate here," Anders said. "Let's see what we have here on the Father's later years. I bet the source here is G-2; that's where Station gets most of its stuff. Let me give it to you verbatim: 'In 1965, the subject was sent to Rome by the Jesuit Order to study at the Gregorian University. While in Rome, the subject established contacts with subversive elements in the Roman Catholic Church, notably with other Latin American theological students. Still in 1965, he wrote an open letter to friends at the National University in Ciudad Malagua in favor of the so-called pro-democracy movement, following the death of General Anselmo Ferrer. In 1968, the subject received a doctorate from the Gregorian University. . . . He returned to Ciudad Malagua the same year, joining the faculty of the National University as instructor in medieval theology and philosophy. The subject is believed to have Marxist, Communist, and Castroite friends as well as tendencies. He may have ties to the 'Liberation Front,' and he is regarded as being anti-American and pro-Cuban. This year Asturias was dismissed from the University, and appointed parish priest in the Ubique district.' "

Anders closed the file and said, "It looks like Father Asturias is one of those progressive priests who are springing up all over the place. But I must say he sounds interesting—a doctorate from the Gregorian University and all that. I certainly wouldn't mind meeting him; but I don't think you would clear it, would you?"

"No, Rick, I wouldn't," Julia said. "And thank you for bringing me the file."

★

Julia Savage had another altercation with Jim Morgan, and it was an unpleasant one. She had received a visit from a noted

American archeologist, a specialist on Mayan *stelas* from the Carnegie Institution in Washington. The archeologist, Dr. Stephen Gaudier, was the leader of a Carnegie expedition that had been excavating in the northern highlands for the past two years. Dr. Gaudier, in a state of considerable agitation, complained to Julia that he and his fellow workers had recently been approached by CIA officers from the Embassy in Malagua with a request to provide information on any sightings or movements of *guerrilleros* in the area where they were digging. A CIA man had, in fact, offered him a radio transmitter to communicate with Malagua.

"He insisted that it was our patriotic duty as American citizens to make such reports," Dr. Gaudier said. "What does this man think we are? God-damned spies for the CIA? We are scientists, and I resent being treated in this fashion. . . ."

Julia assured him that it would not happen again and, in cold anger, asked Ann Mestre to have Morgan come down to her office as soon as possible. The Station Chief appeared forty-five minutes later. "Yes?" he said. Without inviting him to sit down, Julia read him the riot act.

"Listen, Mr. Morgan," she said, "I've received a complaint from a Dr. Gaudier of the Carnegie Institution that you or your people have been trying to recruit the archeological team as agents. Are you out of your mind? The CIA has no business tracking local revolutionaries or anybody else in Malagua. Private American citizens are *not* to be involved in your type of activities. I don't want this to happen ever again. Do you understand me, Mr. Morgan?"

Chewing on his cigar, Morgan replied, "Now, let's take it easy. . . . My operational methods and sources are none of your business, or the State Department's. It's Agency jurisdiction. And don't tell me what is or is not going to happen again."

"Mr. Morgan," Julia said, controlling her fury, "I'm just going to say it once. *I* am the head of the Country Team in Malagua, and I'm responsible to the President of the United States for everything that goes on here in terms of official U.S. personnel. I forbid you to engage in activities that are clearly illegal and damaging to this Embassy. If I find out that you're violating my instructions, I promise you that a top-priority telegram will go out at once to the White House. Not the State Department, but the White House. Good day, Mr. Morgan.''

There was more irritation for Julia later that week. The Embassy had received from the State Department an extradition order, signed by a Federal judge, for Louis Metcalf, a fugitive American millionaire and stock manipulator. Julia was instructed to deliver the order to the Foreign Ministry and to press for rapid extradition.

This was a hard nut to crack. Metcalf was settled in a luxurious mansion on the lake, apparently under General Ferrer's protection. The word in the American business community was that Metcalf had been buying grazing land in Malagua and making other large investments, the supposition being that he was in partnership with the ruling family, and the Embassy had credible reports that Metcalf was about to be granted Malaguan citizenship. This would enormously complicate extradition procedures —if, indeed, they were ever initiated. Julia had delivered the order to the Foreign Minister, and had to send a telegram to the State Department giving all the reasons why Metcalf might never be available to U.S. courts. The Metcalf case, with ramifications to the Watergate scandal of the Seventies, had received ample publicity at home, and Julia detested the idea of being unable, as she suspected, to obtain the extradition.

★

It was in this frame of mind that Julia went, after her Foreign Office *démarche,* to a black-tie buffet dinner at the home of one of Malagua's richest men, Silvio Brejas. She had been informed that Señora de Ferrer, the wife of the President, would attend because Brejas was a heavy contributor to her favorite causes, among them the Ballet Malagua, and Señora de Ferrer was determined to bring culture to Ciudad Malagua. Never having met her, Julia felt duty-bound to go to the Brejas house, though she knew that the host was a boorish type who had made his fortune in unexplained ways, prospering in the shadow of the Ferrers.

It was common knowledge in Malagua that the President had a never-ending succession of mistresses, but it was accepted as normal in the country's culture and political and social order. However, if this troubled Silvia Palos de Ferrer, she did not show it publicly. Being presented to her, Julia discovered in her a warm, forthcoming personality, certainly not a *resentida*. Before dinner, they sat together—alone—for some twenty minutes, chatting about life in Malagua. Señora de Ferrer was extremely intelligent, well read, and quite irreverent. She referred to her husband as "my poor Juan." Julia said that she was hoping to see her more often, and the President's wife replied fervently, almost gratefully, "Oh, I hope you will find time. . . . Do call me anytime. . . ."

The rest of the evening was an abomination for Julia. Silvio Brejas, obese in his purple dinner jacket, made a point of showing her around the mansion, a symphony in expensive poor taste, she thought. Every inch of wall surface seemed to be covered with paintings, most of them unrecognizable and bad, although Brejas did have one Matisse in a place of honor over a fake mantelpiece in the spacious living room. In the basement recreation room, which led to the swimming-pool area, where small tables were set up for dinner, a huge bar, complete with stools, covered one wall. Everywhere there were display cases with ancient weapons, *chinoiserie,* Fabergé snuffboxes, and just about everything money could buy at New York or London auctions with no regard to how it fitted, or not, in the house.

Except for her chat with Señora de Ferrer, Julia found the evening's conversation boring and desultory. Silvio Brejas, at whose table she sat with the President's wife, kept urging Julia to persuade the Administration in Washington to help save "our way of life," becoming more insistent with each glass of wine. Señora de Ferrer said nothing. There was a lot of talk about the "Communists" and their "subversion," and Julia had the distinct impression that Malagua's rich people were nervous and uneasy. She overheard Brejas telling a male guest that "my money is safely out, where the *rebeldes* cannot get their filthy hands on it."

★

Julia Savage had now been in Malagua for over two months, and she knew the moment of truth was approaching—that without further delay she had to send up to Washington her recommendations on the arms assistance to the Ferrer régime. She had had two more impatient phone calls from Terhune's office, a call from David Lustig at the White House, and even a brief formal telegram from the Secretary of State stressing that it had become urgent to reach a decision.

Yet her mind was not quite made up. It was abundantly clear to Julia that events were moving to a climax—that the Frente was increasing its strength, and that Ferrer was on the defensive. Now bombs were exploding in Malagua almost every night—at banks, at businesses believed to be owned by the Ferrer family, and randomly, at gas stations and in telephone booths. Terror was escalating on both sides, Julia having been told by Professor Merino, who came to "return" the anthropology book and used the opportunity to discuss Malaguan politics, that there were more and more arrests at the University and among intellectuals, that bodies of murdered students were being discovered three or four times a week, and that political prisoners were being subjected to extreme torture under the supervision of a G-2 major named Fabio, a Ferrer confidant.

"You simply have to make up your mind," McVeigh told Julia at lunch one day in mid-September. "The very fact that you've offered no recommendations so far and that the Administration is unable to make a decision on the arms has the effect of helping the Frente, as you must realize. In this sense, you and the United States *are* actually taking sides in the crisis. Against Ferrer. We just can't delay any more, Julia, or you'll get into trouble. You will get a reputation back home of being indecisive, which is no help."

"Yes, I know you're right, Mac," she answered. "I just must be absolutely sure that I'm doing the right thing. I've learned an awful lot since I've been here, things I had never suspected about the complexity of the situation, but maybe I'm missing one final dimension. I promise you a recommendation telegram within a week."

That extra dimension, of course, would be the meeting with the leaders of the Frente that Asturias had proposed. Julia had been struggling with a decision for three weeks—making up her mind to go through with it, then rethinking it and reaching an opposite conclusion.

On Friday, September 2, as she was preparing to return to the Residence for the evening, Rick Anders called to say that he had to see her immediately. "I have bad news," he said. "We've just learned of a massacre in the highlands. . . . Indian peasants there had started a march on the village of San Pedro de la Sierra to protest new taxation, and they were armed. . . . As I understand what happened, the National Guard platoon stationed in the village radioed for reinforcements. They held off the peasants long enough for all six of Ferrer's large Alouette helicopters to arrive with troops. They kept shuttling back and forth bringing more and more soldiers. Finally, the Guard opened fire with machine guns and mortars on the Indians. . . . We are told that at least two hundred people were killed, maybe more. . . ."

BOOK THREE

★ ★ ★

Rolando

11

T HE Land-Rover stopped in front of the Residence, and the young man behind the wheel gave the horn a discreet beep, hoping the signal had been heard through the steady drumbeat of the tropical afternoon rain. He patted the right pocket of his trousers, feeling the unaccustomed bulk of a .45-caliber pistol. On the floor on the passenger side, an Uzi submachine gun lay covered by a woolly white blanket.

The door of the Residence opened and the Ambassador stepped out. She wore slacks and a belted tan raincoat, and her black hair was covered with a blue scarf.

"God, I still can't get used to this rain," Julia said as they drove over the glistening wet gravel toward the gate. "But I suppose it's good for us today," she added. "There'll be fewer people paying attention to us."

Tom Flores, the gangling son of a *bodega* owner in Brownsville, Texas, and one of the twelve Peace Corps volunteers in Malagua, was pleased and proud that he had been chosen as Julia's driver. Only McVeigh, the DCM, and the Embassy security officer, Mark Starek, knew about this trip. The CIA Station Chief was spending a few days in Washington on consultations. When Tom had been summoned to the Residence by a call at eight o'clock that morning from the security officer, Julia had told him that she wanted to be driven to the mountains above Ciudad Malagua without being seen or recognized on the way out or back.

She did not say where they would be going—"I'll have a map to guide us," she remarked with a smile—but only that she thought it would be advisable to travel in a Peace Corps car with a Peace Corps driver. People around Ciudad Malagua were used to seeing Tom's battered yellow Land-Rover racing along the Pan American Highway and the rutted byroads, and nobody would give it another thought today. Especially on a rainy Saturday afternoon, when *malagueños* tended to stay home and watch television, except for those who ventured out to shop or take in a movie. Army and police patrols tried to stay out of the rain too, unless the guerrillas forced them to assert their presence on the outskirts of the capital. That was what the security officer had said to Tom as he showed him how to use the automatic Colt pistol and the Israeli Uzi submachine gun. Peace Corps volunteers were not weapons experts—it was standing policy for them never to use or carry arms—but as Mark Starek had pointed out, today was an exception because it was in the "national interest." Tom had repeated that phrase to himself with a touch of excitement.

★

Tom Flores stopped the car at the gate and blew the horn. The local policeman, who sat inside the observation post atop the wall of the Residence, peered out through the rain and waved him on. The electrically operated iron gate drew open, and Tom drove out into Avenida Ferrer. With the window on the passenger side rolled up and the glass splattered with rain, neither the policeman on duty at the Embassy gate nor the two helmeted National Guard troopers, Thompson submachine guns slung over their chests, posted on the sidewalk outside could possibly recognize Julia.

"Let's get out of town and take the Pan American Highway going north," she said, looking at a map she had taken out of her pocket. Tom wondered briefly who had drawn it, but decided that it was none of his business. Avenida Ferrer was empty, except for National Guardsmen in olive-drab ponchos standing or pacing in front of embassy residences and private mansions, and for an occasional car. Silently smoking a cigarette, Julia was lost in her thoughts. She was convinced that she was doing the right thing, the absolutely vital thing, if she and—more to the point—the Administration in Washington were to make the correct policy decisions.

The meeting with Frente leaders would finally enable her to make up her mind on what to recommend to Washington. Thousands of lives, to say nothing of the republic's political future, could be affected by the conclusions she would reach. To grant arms to Ferrer or not was no abstraction: it had to do with life and death for uncounted human beings. Why, she wondered, do we, the United States, *always* have to make these terrible decisions for others? Why do we go on and on living their lives for them—or causing their deaths?

Well, she told herself, stubbing out her cigarette and reaching for another, the truth is that we simply can't get away from the curse of playing and replaying our Manifest Destiny in this bloody corner of the world. Well, for God's sake, let's play it right just this once.

A child, a little girl, ran out into the street, and Tom swerved sharply.

"Shit!" he cried. "That's all we need today. An accident with you hiding in a Peace Corps car. Oh, God!"

Julia put her hand on his arm. "It's all right, Tom. Don't get upset. You're doing just fine."

Let's hope I'm doing fine too, she added silently. And what a fantastic break that Jim Morgan was away from Ciudad Malagua this weekend. With Morgan in town, today's expedition might have been impossible. He would have smelled it out, and after he had made sure the White House was informed, she would have been checkmated.

Julia Savage had spent most of the night awake, considering the pros and cons of the trip. At five o'clock in the morning, Julia had come to the conclusion that it was her responsibility as Ambassador to emerge from behind her barricaded existence and come into contact with the reality of Malagua's revolution. She knew that if she was proved wrong, she would have to resign her ambassadorship. At least she was not a career Foreign Service officer; she could always go back to other things, she thought, knowing that she had done her damnedest to make it work.

At seven o'clock, after showering and downing two cups of black coffee, she telephoned Professor Merino to tell him that she would have tea with him that afternoon. She was sorry to be calling so early, but she wanted to be sure of catching him before he left for the day. The Professor was at once alert, and, yes, he said, he would make all the arrangements for tea later on in the day.

Next, Julia called Mac McVeigh and Mark Starek, asking them to come to the Residence. They were the two men she trusted the most in the Embassy, and without too much detail, she told them what she proposed to do. In case something happened to her, McVeigh and Starek should know where she had gone. "It is *my* decision," Julia had said, "and I take full official responsibility for it."

It was a hard, pragmatic decision. But now, as Tom Flores turned from Avenida Ferrer into the midtown district, Julia was forced to admit that she had not succeeded in disassociating the priest—this immensely attractive and mature man—from his cause. She thought of seeing him with a delicious sense of anticipation. Was she on a diplomatic errand of grave importance, or on a romantic outing? Was she being absolutely honest with herself, or was she rationalizing her behavior—very personal behavior—in terms of professional duty? Julia knew that before too long she would have to face the answer. But not this instant.

They drove past the Cathedral. The square was empty except for the *pordioseros* huddled under the eaves. Entering La Culebra, Julia felt a surge of anger as she did every time she drove through the old town. The sight of the ruins and rubble, the heritage of the 1972 earthquake, made her furious. At one of her meetings with General Ferrer, she had bluntly told him that the United States Congress—and American taxpayers—expected to be informed how the Malaguan government had spent the earth-quake-relief money. Ferrer smiled graciously, and replied that of course, the Congress would be so informed in due time. "Why, my dear Julia," he asked, "doesn't the United States trust the elected President of the Republic of Malagua, a devoted and grateful friend of your great nation?"

From the business district, Tom took a two-lane road leading to the Pan American Highway. After about a half-mile they came to a roadblock where a trooper, submachine gun in hand, waved the Land-Rover to a halt. Tom rolled down his window and told the soldier, *"Cuerpo de Paz . . . carro oficial . . ."* The guard looked at him suspiciously, but gave him the sign to proceed. Four cars stood on the shoulder of the road, the soldiers checking the trunks for weapons or concealed passengers. The guerrillas were known on occasion to try to smuggle persons wanted by the authorities inside trunks of automobiles—usually when there was no time to use other methods—hoping that they would not be caught in spot checks. Sometimes it worked, but at other times, Julia knew, revolutionaries were captured in those attempts, and frequently executed on the spot.

The rain was still falling steadily as they turned onto the Pan American Highway, and Tom said, "I guess we're on our own now. You'll have to tell me what to do next."

Julia took out her map, studying it briefly.

"Okay, Tom," she said, "We'll stay on the Pan American for about thirty miles, then turn off on the road to Ubique. After that, we'll be going into the hills."

"Fine," he answered. "You're the boss. We've got enough gas to keep driving all day and all night. I've put some extra cans in the back of the car."

The highway began climbing rather steeply, away from the *meseta* of Ciudad Malagua. After five miles, they were out of the rain. Soon the sun was shining and the sky was blue. Julia glanced back at the dirty gray blanket of clouds that hung over the city. In the distance, she saw the black peaks of the Central American *cordillera* and, slightly to the right, the Mixull volcano ringed with a collar of white fluffy clouds. The volcano was still active, and it could erupt at any time. And an earthquake could come again tomorrow. Nature was not kind to the Malaguans.

Tom was whistling softly as he drove the Land-Rover up the deserted Pan American Highway. It was a habit he had picked up somewhere from the highland Indians among whom the Peace Corps volunteers had been working. The young Americans were trying to teach *malagueños* the rudiments of the agricultural arts their forebears had practiced effortlessly in the age of the Corn God.

★

At a point where the highway veered slightly to the left, a sign indicated the way to Ubique. Tom slowed down and looked questioningly at Julia. "Yes," she said, "this is where we turn." The rutted road led up toward the mountains, across savanna punctuated with volcanic boulders and covered with low grassy growth. Julia looked again at her map.

"This will take us to Ubique—it must be three or four miles from here—and we'll go through the town into the forest," she said. Tom nodded, downshifting the Land-Rover as the vehicle rumbled on from pothole to pothole. It occurred to her for the first time that she could be driving into a trap designed to embarrass a naïve American ambassador. But she dismissed this thought. The priest and his associates would not waste time on such a ploy, and they evidently wanted American understanding and support. Thinking of Asturias, Julia again was flushed with excitement. She recrossed her legs and lit a cigarette.

Ubique was a small old town—really an overgrown highland village. It must have been settled first by Indians, then by the Spaniards, and kept alive after a fashion by successive generations of impoverished people of mixed blood. They had not done well. The main street of Ubique was cobblestone, its houses shabby. A bar stood across the street from the police station, a one-story whitewashed structure, the most modern in town. A policeman sat on a chair at the entrance, his rifle leaning against the wall of the *cuartel*. He was picking his teeth and showed no interest in the passing Land-Rover. A man came out of the bar, a bottle of Cerveza del Rey in his hand, watching Julia and Tom go by. He too seemed bored. The sun was now beginning to dip in the west, and the first shadows descended on Ubique.

"Let's keep going," Julia told Tom. "There's a road into the woods on the other side of town. But drive carefully. I don't want any surprises."

The road past Ubique was a track just wide enough for the Land-Rover. The vegetation was thicker, and now they were driving through the forest, 3,000 feet high. This was Malagua jungle territory, rising above the savanna to reach the 9,000-foot tree line. The trees were tall and the underbrush dense. The afternoon was growing darker under the thick foliage. Straining, the car moved uphill. Tom's hand went to his pistol pocket, touching it lightly, and again he reassured himself with a glance that the Uzi was on the floorboard. There was a sharp turn, and Julia and Tom saw that the track was blocked by a fallen tree. Tom stopped the Land-Rover and asked, "What do we do now?"

"I don't know," Julia said. "I wasn't told anything about fallen trees. Maybe there was a storm last night and it just fell here."

Two figures appeared from the underbrush, one on each side of the log. They approached the Land-Rover cautiously, holding their submachine guns low. They were young men, in their late teens, dressed in khaki pants and free-flowing shirts. The taller of the two, clearly in charge, walked up to Tom.

"*Buenas tardes,*" he said politely. "In what way can we serve you?"

His gun was aimed directly at Tom. The youth displayed no particular hostility, but Tom sensed that he would not hesitate to press the trigger and spray him with a burst of bullets at the slightest indication of danger. Julia leaned over Tom and said, "*Buenas tardes*. We come to see the priest. He's expecting us."

"*Bueno, señora,*" the young man replied with grave courtesy. "We have been waiting for you here to show you the way." He slung the submachine gun over his shoulder and took a black walkie-talkie from under his shirt. He held it close to his mouth and spoke a few words. There was a crackle of static and a voice answered briefly. *"Un minuto,"* the youth said to Julia. He and his companion leaned down and, with surprising ease, removed the log from the track.

"We shall walk ahead, and you follow us in the car—*¿sí?"* he said.

Tom raised his eyebrows, but decided not to speak. He started the Land-Rover as Julia called out *"Gracias"* to the young men. They replaced the fallen tree and began walking rapidly uphill. The track became even narrower, and the vehicle brushed against branches. After 500 yards the track branched out in three directions. The tall youth signaled with his arm that Julia and Tom were to take the left fork. At the end of another 500 yards there was a clearing in the forest. A tiny wooden church stood at the far end, its back against a stand of cypress trees and impenetrable underbrush. A cross was affixed crookedly to its roof. The *guerrillero* motioned to them to halt. Tom shifted uneasily in his seat, and Julia held her breath.

★

The door of the church was thrown open, and a tall, muscular man appeared on the doorstep, squinting against the setting sun that bathed the jungle clearing in eerie golden light. He was dressed in white drill trousers tucked inside short black boots, in the style of Malagua highlands horsemen, and a long-sleeved blue shirt unbuttoned from the waist up. A pistol was stuck inside his wide belt. A small silver crucifix swung from a thin chain around his neck. He spotted Julia's vehicle and waved enthusiastically as he began to stroll briskly toward it. Three men, German G-3 submachine guns hanging casually from their shoulders, followed a few paces behind. Julia jumped out of the Land-Rover. She removed her scarf, letting her black hair cascade down over her shoulders. She looked attractive, fresh, and young. Tom remained behind the car's wheel, not quite knowing what to do.

"Madam Ambassador, welcome to the shrine of Santa Teresa del Monte," the tall man said formally in English, smiling warmly. His was a very Spanish face, she realized again, proud and emotional, like a Velásquez portrait. He extended his hands to Julia, and she took them. They were strong, hard, sinewy hands, accustomed to work and the handling of weapons. Julia returned his smile, and still holding his hands, said, "Thank you, Father Rolando. I'm glad to be here."

Julia introduced Tom Flores to Father Rolando—"He's absolutely trustworthy," she said—and the priest, looking him over quickly, suggested that the Peace Corps volunteer stay with his men outside while he and the Ambassador had their discussion in the church.

"They'll give you coffee and something to eat if you're hungry," he told Tom. "I imagine you speak Spanish, don't you?"

Tom grinned. "Padre, with a name like mine, what else would I speak?" Father Rolando nodded, and called out to one of his bodyguards: "Joaquín, you look after our friend here. Get a couple of *compañeros* to set up a double guard in front of the church, and make sure they have a radio to keep in touch with the outpost down the road and with me inside."

The priest took Julia by the elbow and led her across the clearing to the little church. The sun was now setting quickly, as it does in the tropics. It was getting chilly: the temperature drops sharply at sunset in the mountains during the rainy season. A bird with brilliant plumage, a toucan, flew low overhead from one tree to another. Julia turned to Father Rolando.

"You know, we should be out of here before it gets really dark," she said. "It wouldn't be a very good idea for me to be traveling back to the city in the middle of the night."

"I suppose you're right, Madam Ambassador," the priest replied, still stiffly formal. "We'll do our best to make this as short as possible."

They walked to the church. Spreading its branches protectively over the plank roof, a tall ceiba tree stood to the right, even prouder than the cypresses behind it. Father Rolando pointed to the tree:

"As you probably know, the ceiba is also known as the God tree. It was the holy tree of the Maya, who called it *yaxche*. We like to think—or at least, *I* like to think—that the holy ceiba watches over us, the *malagueños*, in our hour of need as it did over our forefathers thousands of years ago. You have to have faith in *something* when you engage in a life-and-death struggle, as we are now engaged, and for us the *yaxche* is . . .''

The church was shadowy, the only light coming through two dirty windows on either side. Father Rolando led the way down the aisle in quick strides. She thought he would cross himself as he passed the crucified Christ over the altar, but the priest hurried to the door in the back.

Two men and a woman rose when Julia and Father Rolando entered the sacristy, a narrow room with rough-hewn wood benches and a long table between them. There were kerosene lamps on the table. A wardrobe stood in a corner, its double doors ajar, showing the priest's sacramental vestments and a Thompson submachine gun hanging over them.

"La Embajadora de los Estados Unidos," Father Rolando announced. "This is Tomás Martínez," he said as a short, powerfully built man of about fifty stepped forward to take Julia's hand. "He spent three years in a Ferrer prison. He was in solitary confinement for a full year, and they kept him hooded for seven months. We obtained his freedom not too long ago in exchange for a cousin of the President we had kidnapped. In fact, we got Tomás *and* ten other prisoners for the price of one cousin. Tomás was one of the founders of the Frente in 1966."

The woman stepped up to greet Julia, and Father Rolando introduced her as Dora, a medical student who had been in the *guerrilla* for three years. She looked no older than twenty or twenty-one, but her round face was hard, and the gaze of her brown eyes pierced Julia. Her hair was cropped short; she held a black beret in her left hand. A holstered pistol hung from the belt of her jeans. The other man in the room, his features seemingly transposed from a Mayan sculpture, was introduced as Pablo. "He's one of our best *guerrilla* leaders," Father Rolando said proudly.

He invited them to sit down and reached into the wardrobe to produce a bottle of rum and a tray with dusty water glasses. Tomás, Dora, and Pablo took places on the bench on one side of the table, their backs to the wall. Julia and the priest sat across from them. Father Rolando poured the rum into the glasses, put his walkie-talkie next to a sputtering kerosene lamp, and turned to the three *malaguistas*.

"Well," he said in rapid Spanish, "it was the interest of the Frente to meet with the American Ambassador to explain its objectives. She is here now, and I suggest that you proceed with the presentation. Tomás?"

The man nodded and took a sip of rum. His voice was low and controlled as he addressed Julia in elegant Spanish. There was a sense of extreme intensity about him.

"I am told that you are fluent in our language, so I shall express myself very fully and precisely," Tomás said. "First, I would like to tell you briefly the history of the Frente Malaguista de Liberación Nacional. . . .

"When several of us decided back in 1966 that the time had come to launch the struggle against the dictatorship in Malagua," he said, "it seemed natural to name our movement after General Máximo Landino. He was the symbol of our struggle, and in a sense, we are continuing *his* struggle. He was the greatest hero Malagua ever produced. You know, of course, that Latin America produces great numbers of heroes and great numbers of poets. What we seem unable to produce is people who know how to govern justly and intelligently. It must be Spanish heritage, refined through the Creole blood. . . ."

Tomás allowed himself a small, mocking smile, and continued: "Landino was tremendously important to us, but we decided to change the name of the Frente, taking instead the *malaguista* designation. Why? Well, in the eyes of the outside world we wanted to be clearly identified with Malagua. How many people abroad have ever heard of Landino? To us, he was great; to the world at large he was, at best, parochial. Anyway, there we were in 1966, deep in conspiracy to put together our Front. We had no money, no arms. We had no people experienced in guerrilla warfare. To tell you the truth, we had no experience in politics, either. So what does one do? I shall be honest with you, Embajadora. Very quickly, we decided to seek the advice and even the help of revolutionary Cuba. The personal convictions of some of us are Marxist, but that was not why we turned to the Cubans. They had overthrown their dictatorship seven years earlier, and they understood the concept of revolution. We needed to learn from them. Learn how to get rid of the Ferrers. As far as I was concerned, ideology could come later. I should tell you that I was the emissary to Havana."

"And Fidel Castro helped you?" Julia asked.

"No, not really," Tomás replied, helping himself to more rum. "The fact is I never even saw Fidel except when he was making a speech and I was in the crowd at the Plaza de la Revolución. Fidel was extremely busy with his own problems. But I did see Che Guevara—that was shortly before he vanished—who spent an hour with me, explaining how they had organized the guerrilla war in Sierra Maestra. It was most interesting, but the Cuban experience had little in common with the conditions in Malagua. Maybe it was Che's mistake to present Sierra Maestra as the model for all the revolutions in Latin America. Look what happened to him in Bolivia. . . .

"Anyway, I met with other people in Havana—some military, some political—and everybody urged me to go on with the *malaguista* Front. But now, as I look back, it's fairly clear that the Cubans had little time for us and very little faith in our movement. When I inquired about the supply of arms, people became terribly vague. They said they could make no promises, but that I should come back later, possibly the following year. I also remember Che Guevara telling me that a real *guerrilla* should be entirely dependent on its own means and that, for instance, we should procure our own money through, say, assaults on banks. You know, Che had this thing about the independence of *guerrillas*.

"So, to make the story short, I returned empty-handed to Malagua—with only a copy of Che's book for my trouble. I made up my mind that indeed we had to be self-sufficient and couldn't rely on outside help. Today, I know it was the correct decision, and I keep insisting with the *compañeros* on the National Directorate of the Front that having gone as far as we have on our own, we must preserve our independence. I certainly wouldn't

want the Cubans to take over our movement at this point, although, naturally, we welcome help from all quarters.''

Tomás paused and looked hard at Julia. Then he went on:

''What I'm really saying to you, Embajadora—and this is the
main reason we've asked to meet with you—is that the *malaguistas* today need American help.''

''But what sort of help?'' Julia asked. ''Obviously, the United
States cannot provide arms to your movement.''

''No, of course not,'' Tomás said. ''Arms we don't need. This
country and all of Central America are smothering in arms.
Everybody has them. We have them. And money is no longer a
problem, either. We have that. We don't even have to assault
banks. Ransom from kidnappings provides us with ample funds
—although the Front doesn't kidnap people as frequently as our
friends of the EGP, the Poor People's Guerrilla Army. Extreme
as it is politically, the EGP is almost becoming a capitalist enterprise with the millions they collect in ransom. We go in for kidnappings only to get our *compañeros* released from prison or to
replenish our treasury periodically.''

''But you surely appreciate that an awful lot of people in the
world, including the United States, take a dim view of kidnappings,'' Julia interjected. ''To them, it's pure terrorism, it's banditry. So that doesn't help your image internationally very much,
especially when you want some form of American assistance.
. . . I'm being as frank with you as you're being with me.''

''Fair enough,'' Tomás replied. ''But it's important for you to
understand, I think, that guerrilla warfare and kidnappings are
the only weapons we have in the struggle against the dictatorship.
They are absolutely necessary. And why are our actions regarded—as you put it—as terrorism and banditry, but nothing is
said in the world when Ferrer's thugs massacre our Indians, execute *malaguistas* and others, and lock up people in prisons for
years without a fair trial? If your government is concerned with
human rights, as your President says it is, then why is a double
standard applied to us? And when we kidnap people, we take
immense care to ensure their safety.''

Dora broke in, laughter in her voice.

"Yes," she said, "we do take good care of our customers. I was a member of the squad that captured the West German Ambassador last year. And what did we do with him? We made sure he was comfortable in the house in the village in the hills where we kept him. We risked couriers so that he had an ample supply of medicine for his heart condition. And on his birthday—he turned sixty while he was our guest—the *compañeros* had a cake baked for him and they put on a little play with music. It was quite a *fiesta,* and I think we parted friends. We tried to explain to him why we had done the kidnapping—to liberate our friends from prisons—and he said he understood."

"That's true—we don't want to harm people in our custody," Pablo, the *guerrillero* with Mayan features, added quickly. "And we try to be extremely fair in what we do. For instance, when we take a businessman who has gotten rich with Ferrer, the ransom we set relates exactly to our calculations of how much he has stolen from the people of Malagua. There are young economists working secretly with the Front, and we get the figures from them. So we're practicing a form of social justice. And did you know that the Front often distributes some of the ransom money to very poor people in the *sierra* so that they can eat and buy the things they need to keep going?"

"You make it sound as if the Front were a Robin Hood association in the heart of Central America, taking from the rich and giving to the poor," Julia said. "But I'm still not sure that will convince people back home. Americans just don't believe in kidnappings, no matter what the cause. Even the liberals. In any event, I'd like to get a clearer idea of what sort of help you do expect from the United States."

"It's very simple," Tomás answered. "The United States created the Ferrer dynasty and has kept it alive for fifty years. Now the *malagueños* want the United States to withdraw support from the Ferrer régime. Stop arming him, for God's sake. Let us handle our destiny by ourselves. Be neutral. If you drop Ferrer, I can promise you that we'll take care of him—alone. Our motto is 'Death to the tyrant,' and by God, we mean it!"

Tomás had tears in his eyes. He bent his head and brushed

them off with his sleeve. But emotion was breaking through his self-control. He spoke urgently:

"Won't you think of the people killed and imprisoned and tortured by Ferrer? I sincerely believe that the United States has a responsibility toward Malagua after all that has been done in the last fifty years. Don't you want us to be free, just as you are? Do you really accept Ferrer's argument that he is the only alternative to a Communist takeover? In fact, if you keep supporting Ferrer, you will push the whole nation to the extreme left and to Communism. You will destroy the moderates, and even people like me, people who believe in Marxism as an ideology—a form of socialism, if you will—but who do not want a Communist dictatorship to replace the right-wing dictatorship. So in helping Ferrer, you are, in fact, helping the Communists. . . ."

Tomás lapsed into silence, exhausted by his own emotion. Julia was about to speak when Father Rolando's walkie-talkie crackled and a voice broke faintly through the static. The priest grabbed the radio, signaling for quiet in the room. He listened intensely. Julia could not make out the rapid Spanish words spoken in the highland dialect. Then Father Rolando talked into the radio:

"Okay . . . message understood. . . . Apply defensive measures. Fire only if challenged directly. If necessary, fall back toward the church. . . . Keep transmitting as required. . . . Over and out."

The Jesuit turned to Tomás, Dora, and Pablo, ignoring Julia. He spoke rapidly:

"There is a reinforced National Guard patrol in Ubique. . . . They've just arrived in the town, and they have a couple of jeeps with heavy machine guns. It's not clear if they're going to move out into the mountains, but there could have been a *denuncia*. The three of you had better leave at once. I'll stay with the Ambassador and I'll see what I can do."

12

THE three *malaguistas* rushed out of the sacristy without a word. Asturias crossed over to the wardrobe and grabbed the Thompson submachine gun. He checked the clip and placed the weapon on the table.

Lord, Julia thought, what will happen if I am caught by Ferrer's soldiers with an armed rebel priest in the middle of the jungle? It will be a major international scandal, embarrassing to the United States Government, personally intolerable to me, and, in the midst of it all, exactly the kind of propaganda General Ferrer can use so well to win support in the Congress and elsewhere in Washington.

Sensing Julia's anxiety, Father Rolando squeezed her hand encouragingly.

"I know that you're worried sick," he said, "and I know you must think all this is my fault, which it is. But nothing bad has happened yet. There is no immediate danger. The night is falling, and I doubt the patrol will venture into the mountains in the darkness. They just wouldn't chance it. You know, it's not unusual for the army to turn up at Ubique and other towns on the edge of the jungle. They do it to scare the population, to convince the people that they are in control, and that it's dangerous to give any support to the Front. . . . Sometimes they hope that by accident they might catch one or more of us in the town. What they're really doing is showing Ferrer's flag.

"It's the way it was in Vietnam: the government never controlled the countryside, but it had to make people outside believe that it did. And here, the Army never goes into the mountains, not even in hot pursuit, and there's fighting only when our *compañeros* mount an operation in the lowlands. The soldiers hate being in guerrilla territory, despite all the training they've gotten from your Special Forces and your counterinsurgency experts. The officers know it, and they don't push their men. They're happy just to keep us bottled up in the hills. So I would imagine that they'll leave Ubique very soon, unless they decide to spend the night at the police *cuartel* and get drunk—this is Saturday night—and depart tomorrow morning. . . . But whatever happens, I promise I'll take care of you—and your reputation."

"Thank you, Father," Julia said. "I *have* to hope for the best. In fact, I almost feel like praying."

The priest interrupted her. "It's evidently out of the question for you to drive back to the capital while the soldiers are still in Ubique. It would be a senseless risk. I want you to stay the night here—this is a very safe place—and you can get on the road tomorrow morning. Even if the Army is still in Ubique, there shouldn't be any great suspicions of a Peace Corps car driving in full daylight. And even if you *are* recognized, well, you have the perfect right as Ambassador to be visiting an area where the Peace Corps has been working for these years for the glory of Malagua. Don't you agree?"

"I guess I do," Julia replied. "I see no alternative. I imagine I'm stuck with you—or you're stuck with me. I just hope that all the gods of the universe, including your *yaxche,* will protect us. But what about Tom Flores, the Peace Corps boy who drove me here?"

"Well, the best thing for him will be to spend the night with our men in the woods. I'll have the Land-Rover moved out of the clearing and hidden in the jungle, just in case the soldiers get up here. But as I told you, that's highly unlikely."

"Good. Shall I go and talk to Tom?"

"No. You had better wait here. I'll explain the situation to him and brief my men."

Julia looked at him with surprise: "*Your* men? Are you the commander of the guerrillas here? I thought you were something like their chaplain."

The Jesuit laughed heartily. "Why, of course I'm their leader. I thought you realized that when you got to the church. I command all the Front's units in this part of the country. I don't think the government is aware of it, because we are very careful about concealing the identity of our commanders for security reasons. Naturally, I trust your discretion."

★

Submachine gun in one hand and walkie-talkie in the other, Father Rolando strolled out of the sacristy. Julia heard him say something to his bodyguards waiting outside the door in the darkened church, then his rapid steps up the stone aisle, and the sound of the front door opening and closing. The kerosene lights flickered unevenly, and Julia could see her dancing shadow on the wall. She looked at her wristwatch and saw that it was after seven. My people at the Embassy will be terribly concerned about me, she thought. They'll have visions of the American Ambassador being caught by the army or kidnapped by the rebels. I wish I could reassure them. But even if the transmitter of the Land-Rover radio had sufficient range to reach the Embassy, I couldn't take the chance of an intercept. So I might as well relax.

And I do admit it: I *am* looking forward to spending more time with this extraordinary priest. And let's face it, what an adventure! Now that I'm in it up to my neck, I guess I wouldn't miss it for anything. Or am I being silly and romantic about this whole thing? Yet there is something so captivating about Rolando and Tomás and the others. I suppose they are fighting a good fight. Julia lit a cigarette and drained the sweet, strong rum from her glass. Now she felt better about everything. Maybe it wasn't a mistake after all.

She heard the opening and closing of the church doors, then

the priest's steps on the stone floor, and Father Rolando walked back into the sacristy.

"Okay," he said, "I've explained the situation to Flores. My men are helping him to move the Land-Rover out of the way; then they'll all go to the tents for the night. They'll eat there. And now, Embajadora, it's time for us to get going."

"Going?" Julia asked. "Where are we going? What's wrong with staying in the church? You said it was safe."

"We are going to my very modest home, where you will do me the honor of being my guest for supper and for the night. It's more comfortable there and even safer than here. You will see."

Slinging the submachine gun over his shoulder, the priest took Julia's elbow and led her to a narrow door at the far end of the sacristy.

"This way, please," he said. "This is my private exit from the church."

They stepped into the darkness. The air was cold and smelled of flowers, and the ground was soft underfoot. A monkey screamed in the ceiba tree and its mate answered. Julia knew that the jungle sheltered jaguars. She shivered, and unconsciously drew closer to Rolando.

"You had better hold on to my waist," Rolando whispered. "I know my way up this path, and I don't want to lose you in the dark. And let's not talk. Sounds carry at night. . . ."

Julia did as she was told, and they moved slowly uphill, tips of tree branches touching Rolando's face, then hers. After fifteen minutes, Rolando stopped and said in a loud whisper, "*Bueno, we are home.*" Julia could not see anything, but the Jesuit now took her by the hand, leading her for another thirty yards. She made out the silhouette of a small structure just as they came upon it. Rolando let go of her hand and pushed the door open.

"Wait here," he told her. He went inside; she heard him strike a match, and a kerosene lamp glowed. Julia walked into the house as thunder rolled overhead, lightning rent the night asunder in a blinding flash, and rain crashed down through the jungle canopy, pounding on the corrugated-tin roof.

Rolando bowed slightly and said, *"Bienvenida. Esta es su*

casa.'' The priest's house consisted of one large room. A wide
bed, covered with a blanket in an intricate Indian red-and-green
pattern, stood against one wall. A card table weighed down by
books, papers, and the lamp was by the window. Three wooden
straight chairs were in a semicircle in front of the table, as if a
conversation had been abruptly interrupted. A smaller table held
a Coleman stove and a stack of dishes. A crucifix and a color
poster of Che Guevara in a heroic pose stared down from the
wall above the bed. Stacks of books on the floor leaned against
the walls. A bedside table was crowned with a kerosene lamp, a
smaller one than the fixture on the card table. Clothing hung from
wall pegs: shirts, trousers, a windbreaker, a *poncho,* a black
beret.

"This is my bachelor's abode," Rolando said. "A simple country priest's home. Very unkempt. Never graced by a foreign
lady. But I hope that you'll be comfortable here tonight, Madam
Ambassador."

There was a touch of mockery in his voice. He held one of the
chairs for Julia. She took off her raincoat, placed it on the back
of the chair, and sat down, looking up to Rolando.

"Yes, I shall be very comfortable," she replied slowly. "But
don't you think that under the circumstances we can dispense
with formality? My name is Julia. Please call me that . . . and
may I call you Rolando?"

He smiled, "Absolutely, Julia. Very few people these days call
me 'Padre.' I'm 'Rolando' or *'compañero.'* That's what I am."

"A *compañero*—it still seems strange to me. How does a
priest end up as a guerrilla leader?"

"Oh, my God, there is a very long tradition of it. For one
thing, we, the Jesuits, were always known as 'the light cavalry of
the Church'—that was Ignacio de Loyola's phrase—and I decided to take the title literally. Then, there is a whole history of
fighting priests. You had them in the Crusades, back to Peter of
Amiens. You had them in imperial Spain and you had them in the
Spanish Civil War—on both sides. There were fighting priests in
Mexico during various revolutions. We even had a few right here
in Malagua—and always on the side of the people. You must

have heard of Camilo Torres, the Catholic priest who led the guerrillas in Colombia before he was killed back in the Sixties. And don't forget that even Fidel Castro was educated by Jesuits. . . ."

Listening to the rain beating down on the roof, he said, "We're in luck. Now I'm positive that no one will appear at our doorstep. Not in the midst of a tempest."

The room was chilly, and Julia shivered. She reached for her raincoat, but Rolando threw her a *poncho;* "Here, take this," he said. He uncorked a bottle of rum and poured the white liquid into a glass. "And this should make you warm inside," he told her. "Drink it while I fix dinner. And why don't you curl up on the bed? You'll be cozier there."

Julia wrapped the red *poncho* around her shoulders and carried the glass of rum to the bed. The drink sent waves of warmth through her body. She felt relaxed and at peace now. I should be upset and concerned, she thought, about being here, but I'm not. I ought to worry about the people at the Embassy back in Ciudad Malagua. But I don't want to think about anything right now. I'm happy watching Rolando move around the room. Christ, I haven't felt so good in years. Not since before I was married.

"Christ," she repeated, this time aloud, glancing up at the crucifix above the bed. Her eyes met the eyes of the martyred Christ, a silver figure on a silver cross, and she read nothing in them. Julia pronounced His name again, louder than before, with a touch of impatience. Rolando turned away from the stove and the boiling water hissing in the pot, and asked, "I beg your pardon?"

"I said, 'Christ,' that's all," Julia answered. She heard irritation in her own voice.

"That's more than I care to say," he answered evenly, flatly. "Do you need Him?"

"I was brought up a Catholic. I was taught that I needed Christ. I imagine I do. Don't *you?*"

"No!" Rolando snapped like a dry rifle shot. "No longer."

"But you are a priest. . . ."

"Am I? Really?"

Rolando banged the pot on the stove, and the sound of metal hung in the air. The rain was still punishing the roof in tropical fury. At the stove, he ladled corn mush into two tin soup plates and threw hard *tortillas* on a flat plate.

"Here's the dinner," he said, bringing the food over to Julia. His voice was again calm and friendly. He handed her one plate and squatted on the floor by the bed, the other plate in his lap.

"I wish I could offer you a more elegant meal, but this is all I have in the house. It's corn. . . . As you know, maize was the basic food of Mayan Indians over the ages. They prayed to the God of Corn—he was an important deity to them—as they did to Yum Kaax, the Lord of the Forests, and Chac, who was the God of Rain, and was the most crucial of all the Mayan deities. You know, not far from this house, in the forest, I found a *stela* that depicts a very young God of Corn with an ear of maize for his headdress. He spreads grains of corn on the head of the Earth Mother. It's quite beautiful, and I wish I had time to show it to you. Anyway, our people today still pray to all kinds of gods, the ancient ones and the Christian one, for a good corn harvest. And we still eat maize to fill our bellies."

"Rolando, I'm honored to share maize with you," Julia said.

The Jesuit glanced quizzically at her as if uncertain whether she was mocking him. They ate without speaking, their eyes on the plates. Afterward, Rolando collected the plates, carried them over to the stove stand, and came back to squat on the floor by Julia. He leaned against the bed, his back to her.

"Look," he said. "I owe you an apology and an explanation. I had no right to speak to you the way I did about Christ. I had no business involving you in my spiritual problems and in my attitude toward Jesus Christ, which is my private affair, then giving you a lecture on Mayan deities. It was stupid and thoughtless of me, and I am sorry."

"Rolando," Julia said softly, "you don't have to apologize. You can tell me whatever you want or need to say. If you feel like talking about it, please do. If not, we don't have to go into it."

"Okay. Then I *want* to explain. When I said I wasn't really a priest, that I didn't need Christ, it was my angry adolescent way of telling you that I have lost faith. I cannot be a priest, because I no longer believe, no longer have that absolute faith. I took vows a long time ago, when faith lived in me—or so I thought. Now I've begun to understand the difference between truly *having* faith, which is a spiritual or metaphysical experience, and *thinking* I had it, which is an intellectualization. It's been very long since I was able to pray for myself, to immerse myself in prayer—although I do pray for the sake of others. It's expected of me. Such as when a *compañero* is killed and must be sent away with the word of God. I hear the confessions of the dying, and I give absolution. I anoint the dying with the holy oils; I still have my vials. I feel incredibly hypocritical, but I know that *they* need it. So I do it. I say the words—"O, Lord, have mercy upon us . . ."—but I don't feel the mystery. And it's been over a year since I've said Mass."

"But what happened to you, Rolando? How did you lose your faith?"

"Oh, there was no one experience I could say was a turning point. It took time—soul-searching, asking questions, reflecting, torturing myself, hating myself, doubting myself. It was a terrible process, full of pain."

Rolando fell silent, turning his empty rum glass in his hand. He shifted his position, now facing Julia from the floor.

"I've never discussed this with anyone before; I've never put it into words, but now I'll try. I think I ceased to believe that organized Christianity, as I know it, could meet the deepest needs of human beings—of my people. They deserve better; they deserve a decent life—and by God, they're not getting it. And as a priest, what did I have to offer them? Theology they could not comprehend? The promise of the Hereafter? They are hungry today, they are deprived today, they are beaten down. They are fucked over. The dictator takes care of *that*. . . .

"Christ—the Christ whose name you took, Julia—is not a living Saviour. He died on the Cross, and that crucifix hangs on my wall in remembrance of His sacrifice. But He's not with us anymore. He doesn't look after His flock. What sort of man would I be if I just kept telling my devout people, and they are so pathetically devout, that Christ died for our sins and that we must glorify Him today just for that? That we must accept oppression and injustice—in silence—because there will be a reward in Heaven?''

The kerosene lamp on the card table sputtered and died. Only the small lamp by the bedside cast a narrow circle of yellow light on Rolando and Julia. He sighed, and Julia put her hand on his shoulder. He went on: "You know, one day I went to see the Archbishop of Malagua at his palace. I asked him if it was right for us, the Roman Apostolic Church, to keep silent while the most elementary rights of the people were being so criminally disregarded by the Ferrer government. He told me that we were pastors of souls, that we should confine ourselves to the ministry of the Word, to the singing of the glories of Our Lord. Oh, God, he was so fucking righteous and sanctimonious! Of course, he's a friend and a favorite of the dictator. And his robes smelled of mothballs, which I hate, because it reminds me of embalmed corpses.

"So I asked, What about the Vatican Council, what about John XXIII, what about the social justice called for in so many encyclicals, what about the Medellín declaration of the Latin American Episcopate about making this justice a reality? Even John Paul II understood it at Puebla. . . . Well, the saintly Archbishop just laughed. The bastard *laughed*, Julia! I left without kissing his ring—I'd never done that before, and it was like slamming the door—and I said to myself, Rolando Asturias, this is the last time you're setting foot in this blessed palace.''

Julia caressed his shoulder, her fingers stroking his strong neck. She felt a great tenderness for him.

"You see, I had no place to go anymore," he said slowly. "Ministry of the Word, my ass. No more lies, I decided. Words weren't good enough any longer. Now it had to be the ministry of deed with me. So I ceased being a priest and became a man. And you see, the only deed that counts today is to fight the dictatorship—yes, in the name of Christ, if you will, or in the name of what *I* think is Christianity, in the name of our people.

Thus I took up arms, thus I joined the Front, thus I became a guerrilla commander. I have turned to that ancient tradition of fighting priests. If I have any faith today, it's the faith in my people, in their ability to decide their own destiny. Am I a priest? No, I'm not. Am I a man of God? Yes, I hope so, because I'm fighting for a just world. And you know, if I have to worship the ancient Mayan gods to make it come true, then I shall do that, too. So now, Julia, you've heard my confession. . . ."

13

"**M**Y formal recommendation is for the strictest United States neutrality in the civil war in Malagua—and we are talking about a real civil *war*—and therefore I recommend that the Administration turn down the request of President Ferrer for arms,'' Julia Savage said slowly and distinctly to Edward R. Masterson, Jr., the Secretary of State, and two of his top advisers. They were sitting at the long table in the Secretary's paneled conference room next to his office on the seventh floor of the State Department building on Washington's C Street. Outside, it was raining hard, the typical disagreeable October weather on the Potomac, but the room was windowless, the temperature controlled. It flashed through Julia's mind that the Secretary of State lived in an environment without seasons and changes, and perhaps this isolation influenced his perception of the world and his conduct of American foreign policy.

Julia had requested permission to fly to Washington to supplement her written recommendations with an oral presentation, knowing how important it was in the bureaucracy to defend one's position personally, particularly if it was highly controversial. Policy recommendations spelled out in a telegram, no matter how well and convincingly written, could be shot down easily at a single high-level Washington meeting, and once a decision was taken to overrule an ambassador, it was exceedingly difficult to have it reversed.

The Department had at first resisted Julia's request to present her own case, Assistant Secretary Terence Terhune being the most opposed to it. But a discreet call from Julia to Tom Morelli at the White House had resulted in a telegram from Masterson asking her to fly up for consultations. Being a political appointee, Julia reminded herself, did have certain advantages in dealing with the machinery of government. She left for Washington the next day, carrying her recommendations, a long and well-reasoned document, in her attaché case. Now, two days later, Julia faced Masterson, Terhune, and Marvin Black, the Under Secretary of State for Political Affairs, a tough-minded career diplomat.

★

Julia began working on the recommendations the day after she returned from her adventure—that was how she thought of it— in *malaguista* rebel territory. She warned herself about the great dangers of letting her emotions, and they were strong emotions, overshadow her political judgment. She did not lie to herself about her immense attraction to the priest—intellectual, emotional, and, yes, sexual. She knew how close they had come to the act of love before Rolando drew away and, heavily, crossed the room to the far corner where, without a word, he had dropped on the floor, pulling a poncho over himself. Had he wanted to make love to her then, Julia would have received him with hunger. Aching for him, she had lain awake in his bed, desperately alone, until the first light of the mountain dawn. But now this night was receding into an elusive dream, something that might not really have happened.

Rolando had awakened her at seven o'clock with a cup of bitter black coffee, and walked her back to the church, kissing her on the forehead before they joined the others. Tom Flores, surrounded by the armed young rebels with whom he had quickly developed a noisy friendship, brought around the Land-Rover, and the priest ceremoniously brushed her hand with his lips, bidding her farewell in front of his men. *"Hasta muy pronto,"* he said loudly with a warm smile.

The return was uneventful, even though, on Julia's orders, Tom had driven the Land-Rover as fast as he could. She was concerned that her overnight absence from the Residence would be noticed—and that the word would somehow reach Jim Morgan when he came back to Ciudad Malagua. Mac McVeigh and Mark Starek were ready with reasonably plausible cover stories, one of them being that she was spending the weekend with wealthy Malaguan friends at their country estate. But the Station Chief was unlikely to take their word at face value. He would pry and ask around and, quite possibly, come up with the truth. She had to be home as soon as possible.

The path had been cleared, the huge log having been moved aside, and Julia and Tom quickly reached Ubique. The town was empty of inhabitants on this Sunday morning, and the National Guard patrol had evidently left during the night. There was nobody in the street to see the yellow vehicle speeding down. With the sun out and the pavement drying rapidly, Tom put the Land-Rover into high gear and stepped on the accelerator as he came to the Pan American Highway. It was not even eleven o'clock when Julia Savage walked into the Residence, opening the door with her own key. Still in the Land-Rover, she had shaken hands with Tom Flores. "You're a great traveling companion," she had told him. "I'm really grateful to you."

Julia's final assessment was made coldly and impersonally. She had heard often enough the comments by career officers— men—that women ambassadors could be so easily taken in by articulate, smooth, and ingratiating foreigners, especially Latin Americans. A compliment here, an appeal to emotions there, the officers said, and the lady ambassador could be manipulated. In the days before she even thought of becoming an ambassador herself, Julia had believed that this was a monumental exaggeration. But in truth, a woman ambassador *was* more vulnerable— or perceived as being so. Therefore she had to be tougher and more questioning than the most experienced of male ambassadors.

She gave long, hard thought to the arguments presented by Rolando and his friends. The *malaguistas,* she finally concluded were not overestimating the anti-Ferrer sentiment growing in Malagua nor the ultimate potential of the Frente. Even Juan Ferrer himself had recognized in conversation with her the perils to his régime. And she saw the opportunities for the United States in the split within the revolutionary movement, if only Washington knew how to take advantage of it.

★

Secretary Masterson listened in silence to Julia's presentation, frowning from time to time, the fingers of his right hand drumming impatiently on the table. He had set 3 P.M. of that particular Wednesday for the meeting with her, carving a half-hour from a schedule that was becoming unbearably tight. A major crisis in the Persian Gulf, again threatening a confrontation with the Soviet Union, was in a critical stage, taking up the bulk of the Secretary's days and even nights. He had spent much of the morning with the President and the National Security Adviser, and he was scheduled to leave from Andrews Air Force Base that evening for consultations with NATO foreign ministers in Bonn. He still had to see the Ambassador from Pakistan and go over briefing papers for the NATO meeting with State Department experts before leaving.

Yes, Malagua *was* important; but he would have preferred that Terhune and his Latin American specialists had gone over Julia Savage's recommendations and given him a one-page memorandum with *their* conclusions. Then he would probably have okayed the memo and sent it on to the White House. That was the way Masterson liked to work, particularly in areas with which he was unfamiliar—depending heavily on staff work. It was his lawyer's approach to policy problems. Tom Morelli at the White House had insisted, however, on the Secretary's giving personal attention to Malagua—he emphasized the President's special interest in Latin America—and Masterson had had no choice but to receive Julia.

Now he forced himself to listen to her discussion of Malagua, pushing the Bonn trip out of his mind with a sense of annoyance. Why did the Secretary of State have to deal personally with *every* crisis in the world? he thought angrily. There were only twenty-four hours in a day, and Masterson could concentrate on only so many issues at a time. Sometimes he regretted having abandoned his leisurely Wall Street practice for the relative and occasionally empty glory of being Secretary of State. When something went well, which was rare these days, the credit went not to him, but to the President.

When Julia finished her presentation—it had taken fifteen minutes—the Secretary decided to make a brief comment on her recommendations, then adjourn the meeting and let Terhune take it from there.

"Your recommendations are very persuasive, Julia," he said, "but frankly, I'm not sure they are entirely convincing. Of course, as a matter of principle the United States should be neutral in other nations' civil wars. But in some cases, and I think Malagua is one of them, neutrality could result in *de facto* support for one of the sides."

Julia noticed that Terhune was nodding approvingly, while Marvin Black listened impassively to Masterson. I've lost, Julia thought. Terhune, who had read her position paper before the meeting, had obviously made up his mind that the Ferrer régime deserved American military assistance, and he must have influenced Masterson's thinking. Masterson went on:

"What I'm saying is that in refusing arms to President Ferrer, we would, in effect, be supporting the rebels. In other words, Julia, the United States would be ensuring a rebel victory, which to me means a Marxist victory, and this—clearly—is *not* in the national interest. On the other hand, I appreciate your point— the reverse side of the question, as it were—that providing President Ferrer with arms would most likely lead to the perpetuation of the dictatorship, as you call it, and impact negatively on the position of the United States in the Hemisphere. . . . Ah, I don't want to make a final decision at this point; I want to give it more thought. . . . My suggestion is that you and Terry Terhune review the problem more in depth, and Terry can give me a fill-in when I return from Bonn.''

★

Terence Terhune too was in a rush. He told Julia he had a meeting downstairs—"It's that damned Mexican oil business again," he said—and proposed that they resume the discussion of Malagua in his office the following morning.

Sliding behind his desk in his sixth-floor office, Terhune picked up the private-line phone and dialed a number at CIA Headquarters in Langley. A gruff voice answered, and Terhune said, "Good afternoon, Colonel . . . I thought I'd bring you up to date on Malagua. Well, not very surprisingly, our lady friend has recommended against military assistance there. . . . Yeah, that's right. . . . But you should have seen the way the Secretary shot her down—in flames. . . . Now it's my baby again, and I expect to take good care of it . . . You're welcome, Colonel. . . . See you soon.''

In Langley, Colonel Kingsley Duke, the Western Hemisphere Division Chief, put down the phone and buzzed his secretary. "Find Jim Morgan," he said. "Tell him I want to see him as soon as possible. . . . He should have come in from Ciudad Malagua yesterday or the day before.''

Morgan appeared in the Colonel's office at the end of the afternoon.

"Hi," he said. "What's up?''

"I just had a call from State, Jim," Duke told him. "It's exactly what you had predicted. Savage's recommendation is to deny arms to Ferrer. But Terhune says that the Secretary shot her down, as he put it, and he—Terhune—is in full charge of the matter. So I guess we've won this one.''

The Colonel took a bottle of Jack Daniel's and two glasses from the bottom drawer, and set them on the desk. "This calls for a drink," he said, pouring the whiskey and handing Morgan a glass.

The Station Chief downed the bourbon, making a grimace.

"Thanks," he said, "but the celebration is premature."

"How so?"

"You're underestimating Savage. She's tough, and she's not a quitter. She'll fight. And don't forget her White House connections. Also, the Congress has to okay the arms, and that could be sticky. That fucking human-rights legislation is still on the books. No, sir. The battle ain't won yet."

"Hmm . . . you may have a point," Duke said. "So where do we go from here?"

"We go several ways, I would say. First, the Director should be informed through channels in this building that Savage is a threat to General Ferrer's survival. This is something the Agency cannot afford, and the Director should be encouraged to take it up with the President at the earliest opportunity. This way, we can checkmate Morelli.

"Then we'll work on undermining Savage. We had a problem with 'Operation Enrique,' but it may work out after all, in a different way," Morgan said, reaching for the bottle on Duke's desk.

"What went wrong?"

"I didn't have a chance to inform you before—I couldn't use Agency communications for it because it's too sensitive—but the fact is that Palma did try to blackmail Savage with the Kleben-girl thing, but she just threw him out of the Residence, which surprised me. Enrique probably fucked it up."

The Colonel looked alarmed. "So what do we do now?" he asked. "What if she tells the White House about it? Then it could be traced to us. . . . I don't like it."

"Relax, old buddy," Morgan told him. "I'll bet you anything she won't mention it to anybody. It's one thing to resist blackmail, but it's another for her to open the whole can of worms. Anyway, I propose we beat her to it. The idea is that you advise the Director that the Agency has discovered by sheer accident that Julia Savage and her father harbored a fugitive bomber, and that given her position, the President must be personally apprised of it to avoid embarrassment for the Administration. You know, things leak in this town. But for God's sake, not a word to the Director about 'Operation Enrique' and the blackmail number.''

"I read you," Colonel Duke said. "I'll brief the Director myself as soon as I can get in to see him. The President may have no choice but to ask Savage to resign.''

"Exactly. And when I get back to Malagua later this week, I'll tell Ferrer that Savage is trying to hold up his arms shipments. He'll crank up his pals on the Hill. The combined pressure from the Director of Central Intelligence, the Secretary of State—assuming your friend Terhune keeps him in line—and a few heavy guns in Congress should do the trick. Plus a word from the Director to the President about the Kleben affair. But it's gonna take some fancy footwork and coordination—which is our job, yours and mine.''

★

Julia was going to have dinner with Pete Malone that night, and she wanted to stop at her small Foggy Bottom hotel to shower and change. First, however, she dropped by the office of the Country Director for Malagua to check on telephone messages and reporting telegrams from her embassy.

She sat down for a quick chat and a cup of coffee with Bob Robbins, the baby-faced Country Director, who was one of her quiet allies in the bureaucracy, when a secretary walked in to tell Julia that Under Secretary of State Black was on the line.

"Miss Savage," Black said, "would you have a minute to come by the seventh floor to see me?''

Marvin Black was standing by the window, watching an airliner make its final approach over the Potomac to National Airport, when Julia entered his office. In his mid-fifties, Black was the ranking Foreign Service officer in the State Department, being Number Three in the hierarchy after the Secretary and the Deputy Secretary, both political appointees. He had worked his way up through the ranks, the hard way, from vice consul in Belém, Brazil, right after the war, to Ambassador to the Philippines and Japan, Chief Delegate at the Vietnam peace talks in

Paris, and roving ambassador and troubleshooter for two administrations. He was totally professional and nonpartisan—and thus greatly admired by his peers.

A short, puckish man who was given to wearing bow ties, Marvin Black was famous in Washington for his old-fashioned Southern courtliness—he was from South Carolina—and his political courage. He had strong convictions about what was right and what was wrong, and what made sense and what did not, and he never made any bones about speaking out. In this, Black was rather unusual in the State Department, but his forcefulness and the respect he enjoyed were his strength.

He had not said a word during Julia's presentation to Masterson, though he had listened intently. Now he bowed to her, pointing to the sofa.

"My dear Miss Savage," he said pleasantly, "you doubtless realize that you're on the verge of being beheaded by the Secretary and Mr. Terhune, and I wanted to have a chat with you before the guillotine descends. Maybe we can delay or even avert the execution altogether. I'm not a Latin American specialist, but I have a gut sense of events. I read your recommendations just before the meeting, and I have a few questions. All right?"

"Of course. Anything you want to know."

"The most important thing you can tell me is whether, in your judgment, Ferrer has a real chance of winning what you call the civil war if indeed the United States gives him the arms he wants. Let's leave politics and ideology aside for the moment, and concentrate on this point."

"Look, I'm not a prophet," Julia said cautiously. "But after three months in Malagua, I'm convinced that the only thing American arms can accomplish is to draw out the civil war, postpone the inevitable—which is Ferrer's ultimate collapse. You see, Malagua today is essentially an occupied country—occupied by the National Guard, except for the expanding rebel zones. I don't think Ferrer can destroy the Frente and the EGP no matter how many planes, helicopters, and guns we give them. The best that American weapons can do is prolong the agony."

"But the CIA reports provide a completely different picture. They say Ferrer can hack it if he gets the arms."

"I can't speak for the CIA, except to say that to the best of my knowledge the Station in Malagua has no contacts other than with the Ferrer people. I don't know why the Agency people don't look deeper into the Malaguan society, but I suppose Ferrer would take a dim view of such activity. Anyway, I have made a point of broadening my contacts considerably beyond the National Palace, probably more than Mr. Terhune would have wished me to do, and my conclusion is that Ferrer can no longer win this war."

"Okay," Black said. "I'll buy that. But what happens if we remain neutral, as you recommend? I would imagine that with the Cuban arms they seem to be getting now, the rebels would sooner or later get the upper hand and, if your analysis is correct, overthrow Ferrer. Doesn't that mean a victory for the Marxists and something on the order of a 'new Cuba,' as the Secretary puts it?"

"Yes, Ferrer would fall," Julia replied, "but I don't necessarily see a 'new Cuba' coming out of it. In the first place, all rebels are *not* Marxists or *fidelistas*. The majority in the Frente, in my opinion, are democratic socialists, or social democrats. In fact, there is a split between Marxist and non-Marxist factions within the Frente, as there is between its leadership and the EGP guerrillas. And this is our great opportunity, if we can bring ourselves to play the cards being handed us. But we can mess it up if we overtly support Ferrer. If that is the case, the Marxists will emerge as the dominant force. If we maintain neutrality, we help the moderates in the Frente to keep Malagua from becoming Cubanized."

"I take it, then, that you favor dealing with the Frente moderates?"

"I'm not formally recommending that the United States take the side of the Frente's moderates; but, yes, that may be required before too long if events continue to escalate the way I think they will. Put in other words, I don't see why the United States should go down with Ferrer. We've done this kind of thing before, in

other countries and with other dictators, and you know the re-
sults. . . ."

"I think you've told me what I wanted to know," Black said.
"I can make no promises, but maybe we can get your head off
the chopping block and get ourselves a sensible policy. For now,
the best you can do, Miss Savage, is sit tight."

★

Father Peter Malone was in his kitchenette, cooking dinner,
when Julia arrived at his apartment. They embraced warmly, and
she said, "I smell something delicious; what are you up to,
Pete?"

"One of my specialties—*coq-au-vin*," Malone answered.
"But it's got quite a way to go, so let's park ourselves in the
living room and have drinks. . . ."

They made themselves comfortable on the priest's huge sofa,
close to the fireplace and its burning logs. "I see you look great,
Julia," Pete said, "and I must hear all about Malagua. . . .
What's really happening there?"

Julia leaned back and for nearly an hour, described the events
of the past three months, ending with her meetings with Masterson and Black. She spoke generally of her contacts with the anti-
Ferrer opposition, mentioning in passing that she had met some
interesting priests. She decided to let it go at that for the moment,
not naming Rolando Asturias.

"I just can't imagine the Administration providing arms to Ferrer at this stage," Pete Malone said after they had sat down at
the table. "It would be absolutely disastrous, not only in terms
of Malagua and the terrible bloodshed it would cause—and of the
certainty that afterward there would be a completely radicalized
régime hostile to the United States—but also of our entire image
in Latin America. You just can't go around preaching human
rights and democracy, and then give weapons to a bloody dictator in the name of anti-Communism. . . . Why, even the Church
in much of Latin America, except for the old reactionaries,
would oppose it."

"Of course you're right, Pete," Julia replied. "That's the point

I tried to get across in that huge paper of mine; but clearly, Masterson doesn't see it that way. Actually, I think that Terry Terhune is the real villain. I knew he favored arming Ferrer—though he realized that he had to sweeten it in the form of a 'liberalizing' package if he were to get White House support. But when Ferrer made it clear that he wasn't about to play the liberalizing game, and I reported it, Terhune made up his mind that he would push the arms deal anyway, justifying it with the old 'Red menace' rhetoric. I'll bet you that's why Masterson reacted the way he did today to my proposals. It's so depressing to see that we're deliberately missing a bet. Oh, Lord . . . But I must say I was encouraged a bit by my talk with Marvin Black. I think he's okay.''

They went back to the living room for coffee, and Julia asked, "Pete, you mentioned the Church in Latin America. How *do* you see the political position of the Church, especially after Puebla?''

"As you know perfectly well, Julia, I am totally convinced that the Church has a tremendous constructive role to play in Latin America. In fact, the Church may be the last force that can avert a complete disaster there. Yes, I think Puebla was another step forward, a logical consequence of the conference of bishops in Medellín back in 1968.''

"But,'' Julia asked, "didn't the Pope say in Puebla that priests mustn't belong to political parties, engage in politics, and so on? Doesn't that limit what the Church, and priests, can do in changing society, if that's what you're talking about?''

"Actually, the Puebla text was a pretty sophisticated piece of writing that quite a few people didn't understand at all. The Pope was ruling out a priest's *membership* in a political party or in a revolutionary movement, which doesn't trouble me at all. Priests don't have to be card-carrying members of anything. On the other hand, his emphasis on social justice was a major political statement.''

"How so? Wasn't that just a repetition of the standard line that the Church is on the side of the poor and that sort of thing?''

"Hell, no,'' Malone said. "This Pope is an activist, and that's what I like about him, and he was telling the Church in Latin

America to pull up its socks and—as an institution—to get involved in the business of promoting social justice. When he went to Brazil, he made it even stronger: he warned the rich and the powerful that unless something is done about the conditions in Latin America, all hell's gonna break loose. To me, this *is* a political statement. It pits the Church against the Establishment, and aligns it with what is known as the progressives. . . .''

"Okay, Pete, that's your interpretation. But does the Catholic hierarchy in the Latin American Church see it the same way?''

"Probably not. The reactionary bishops, and the Church in Latin America is still full of them, prefer to emphasize only the part about priests' staying out of politics. But the liberal bishops and cardinals, who are gaining more and more influence, know exactly what the Pope had in mind. In fact, there's a bishop in Malagua, Don Pepe Vargas Merino, who has spoken out against Ferrer. Have you met him?''

"No, I haven't," Julia said. "But I have met another priest— your friend Rolando Asturias. He approached me on his own, shortly after your letter arrived.''

"Great!" Malone said. "And how did you like him?''

Julia Savage was silent for a moment. "Very much, Pete," she said quietly.

"Tell me about him. . . .''

"There are many things about Rolando that may be new to you," she said. "He has lost his faith, he says, and he no longer considers himself a priest. He is a guerrilla leader, operating from a tiny church up in the hills, and he is an extremely persuasive politician. Now, this has to remain a secret between us—the State Department doesn't know it—but I went to see Rolando in the mountains to meet some top people in the Frente.''

"Fantastic!" Malone roared. "Marvelous! I knew that he was the man for you to meet.''

★

The telephone rang, and Malone answered it. "It's for you," he said.

After apologizing for disturbing her at dinner, the duty officer at the State Department's Operation Center said, "We have a priority telegram for you from Mr. McVeigh in Ciudad Malagua," he said.

"Yes?"

"The telegram says that a Professor Merino was killed today."

14

ACCORDING to an Embassy report Julia Savage read in her limousine on the way from the airport early the next afternoon —she had cancelled all her remaining Washington appointments to rush back to Ciudad Malagua—students had begun massing at about noon in front of the University's administration building, waving red-and-black Frente flags, shouting anti-Ferrer slogans, and smashing windows with rocks. The riot had been triggered by the decision of the Ministry of Education to cancel classes until the start of the next academic year, the following March, because of widespread campus unrest. The school year in Malagua normally ended in November, and the premature closing meant that there would be no final exams and no graduations for three or four more months. The government had concluded that tensions in Ciudad Malagua would be largely defused if the University were temporarily disbanded. Latin American governments often used that strategy.

The protest quickly turned ugly, and when the campus police could not control it, the rector panicked. He called the Interior Ministry asking for assistance, and within thirty minutes National Guard units in trucks and armored cars were arriving at the University. A Guard officer warned through a bullhorn that the students had three minutes to disperse before the troops advanced to break them up. At that point, Professor Merino walked out of the Administration building and placed himself between the students and the Guardsmen, appealing for calm. The Guard fired a volley into the student crowd, and Professor Merino, a bullet through his head, was the first to fall.

When she arrived at her office, Julia asked Ann Mestre to find out when and where the funeral would be held. "Tomorrow morning at the Main Cemetery," Ann told her.

★

Julia asked Salvador to unfurl the flags on the front fenders of the limousine—the Stars-and-Stripes and her ambassadorial flag —for the drive to the cemetery. It had been at least a year since the American Ambassador's car had been seen in the streets of Ciudad Malagua with its flags flying, but Salvador showed no reaction, except to raise his eyebrows ever so slightly. This time, she thought, let everyone know where the Ambassador of the United States was going. And she did not wish the lead and follow security cars to accompany her.

Ciudad Malagua's Main Cemetery, located behind Barrio del Sur, was an unkempt place, overgrown with vegetation, where for centuries the nonaffluent and the nonimportant of the capital had been buried. The affluent and the distinguished rested in peace at Los Cielos, a well-kept funeral park not far from Lake Taxchilán. Professor Merino and the seven students killed with him in the campus affray were being interred at the Main Cemetery because that was all their families could afford.

The whole cemetery area was surrounded by the National Guard, the authorities fearing demonstrations after the funeral. The University killings had raised the tensions in Malagua to a new pitch, Luis Merino now joining Nestor Cruz, the editor, in the ranks of martyrs in the anti-Ferrer cause. In life, Merino had been famous only among his fellow intellectuals and academics; in death, he became a national figure.

When Julia arrived at the gate, helmeted National Guardsmen were checking the identities of people entering the cemetery. But they drew up in a salute at the sight of the limousine with the flying flags. Julia, in a simple dark gray dress and with a black silk scarf on her head, walked alone down the path among ancient graves toward the group of mourners who had gathered under a gnarled ceiba tree.

A priest in a black cassock stood near the open grave, praying silently with his head down. There was a quiet murmur as the mourners realized they were being joined by the American Ambassador, and the priest glanced up. Julia saw it was Rolando Asturias. Their eyes met for a moment, and Father Asturias returned to prayer. Most of the mourners were University professors—middle-aged men, some with their wives—and a number of students. Merino's widow and a young woman, both dressed in deep mourning, stood behind the Jesuit.

The service was short, Rolando Asturias reading a passage from the Gospel of Mark: *"Here I send a messenger before your face, to prepare the way for you: the voice of one who cries in the desert, 'Make the way ready for the Lord, level the paths for him'* . . ." Then he said simply, "We have lost a friend . . . but he shall not be forgotten." He made the sign of the cross, and Luis Merino's coffin was lowered gently into the grave. Pallbearers threw handfuls of earth, and so did the widow and the young woman with her. Julia crossed herself, and was preparing to leave when the girl stepped over to her. "I am Dora," she said softly. "We met in the little church up the mountain, with Rolando. This is my father I have just buried."

Julia said, "I didn't know he was your father. But you knew he was my friend. . . ." She threw her arms around Dora, holding her tightly, lovingly.

As Julia walked away from Luis Merino's grave, the mourners respectfully opened the way for her. Among them, she spotted John Crespo, the Embassy's Number Two CIA man; she thought he gave her a quick, conspiratorial wink. Behind the trees, Julia saw a half-dozen men in sport shirts, just standing there: Ferrer's plainclothesmen.

★

Late that afternoon, Julia received a phone call from Terence Terhune at the State Department.

"I understand that you attended the funeral of Luis Merino today, and that you went to the cemetery in your car with the flags flying," he hissed. "I want you to know that the Department regards your actions as highly imprudent and indiscreet in the present situation."

"Are you speaking for the Department, or just for yourself?" Julia asked angrily. "If it's for the Department of State, let the Secretary reprimand me. If you're expressing your own feelings, I'll simply say it's none of your business. Professor Merino was a personal friend, and I don't expect to be told by you how to behave. If there's nothing else you have to tell me now, I'll have to hang up, because I have work to do."

That evening, Dudley brought Julia an envelope, saying it had just been delivered to the guard at the Residence gate. It was addressed to her in block letters. Inside, there was a folded piece of paper. The message, also in block letters, was two words in English: BLESS YOU.

★

In late October, Ciudad Malagua was sliding into chaos. There had been four kidnappings of wealthy Malaguan businessmen in one week alone. A National Guard outpost near the International Airport was overrun one night, three soldiers being killed and their weapons stolen. A bomb went off in broad daylight at the Education Ministry, three blocks from the National Palace, destroying the building's façade. The deaths of Nestor Cruz and Luis Merino had a powerful impact on public opinion: it had become known that the editor had been murdered by prorégime right-wing vigilantes, though there was no evidence that Juan Ferrer was personally behind it. In any case, the revolution now had new heroes and martyrs to be avenged. "As far as I'm concerned," the astute British Ambassador told Julia at lunch, "Malagua has fully entered the prerevolutionary stage. . . . The revolution itself is around the corner." Julia informed her staff that wives and other dependents were free to leave Malagua if they so desired.

Among messages awaiting Julia on her return from Washington there was one from Doña Silvia Palos de Ferrer, the President's wife. Another was from María Carmen Escalante, the painter who had come to the reception at the Residence along with Professor Merino. The First Lady of Malagua wished the American Ambassador to tea whenever convenient on her return to the country. María Carmen hoped Julia would have time to look at her paintings sometime soon, before the opening of her first show in Ciudad Malagua. Julia told Ann Mestre to advise Señora de Ferrer that the following Monday would be fine for tea, and to tell the painter that she would drop by her studio later that afternoon.

Silvia de Ferrer received Julia in her private sitting room at the National Palace, in the residential wing of the colonial structure. Julia thought her hostess looked drawn and pale. There was a silver tea service on the table, but Señora de Ferrer said, "Julia, do you really want tea, or something stronger?"

"I'll have a very light Scotch-on-the-rocks," she replied—not wanting a drink, but anxious to put Silvia at her ease. "Fine . . . I'll have one too," the First Lady said, picking up a cut-crystal decanter from a sideboard. "Let us drink to a happier future. . . ."

Putting down her glass, Silvia walked over to a radio in the corner of the room, turning it up to top volume. The room was filled with the cacophony of disco music, and she told Julia: "Please excuse the noise, but we are more private this way. Yes, I suspect that my apartment is bugged—nobody here is entirely safe. Let me sit next to you on the couch, and we can talk."

Silvia de Ferrer was so tense that her hands were trembling. She swallowed hard, tried a small smile, and said: "Julia, I'm not speaking today as the wife of the President of the Republic, but as a *malagueña,* a woman, a mother. I want you to tell me what's going to happen to us, to our country, to our people. I am terribly afraid. Please, tell me the truth."

Julia paused. Was this a trap, an ambush laid for her by the Ferrer family? But from the first time they met, Julia had had a sense of trust in Silvia. She decided to be frank: it was already so late in the game.

"I don't know what's going to happen to Malagua and to all of you," Julia said, "but your country *is* moving faster and faster toward a tragedy, which I'm not sure can be averted. Things may already have gone too far."

"But isn't there anything the United States can do? I've heard Juan talking about arms he's requested. He's afraid that you will turn him down."

So that's it, Julia thought. Ferrer is using his wife to put pressure on me. The blaring radio, the offer of a drink, the tenseness —it is all part of a clever setup, the staging of an event. She resolved to ignore the remark about the arms, waiting for her hostess to continue.

"Well," Silvia said, "I want you to know that *I* hope that Juan will get no more arms, that the Americans will stop propping him up, and think of another solution for Malagua."

The older woman saw the startled expression on Julia's face. "Yes, that's what I said. Do not, for God's sake, give him any more arms. Look, I know my country and my people. They are *against* Juan, completely. Every gun, every bullet you give him will mean more deaths in Malagua, more blood, more grief. Can't you see it?"

"I suppose I can," Julia replied guardedly. "But do you have alternatives in mind?"

"Perhaps. I'm not sure. But I have friends who think the way I do. Decent, honest people. All they want is peace, the end of the killings, a normal life for Malagua. They are not revolutionaries: they are business people, heads of families. Oh, Julia, if you could only talk to them. . . . If they knew the Americans support them, there could be a way to stop this tragedy. And there are other important people too, people I cannot talk about now."

"My door is open to everybody," Julia said. "But I can make you no promises. . . ."

"I am not asking for promises," Silvia told her grimly. "I'm just asking you, the United States, to save us. Nobody is safe here any more. Did you know, for example, that Juan had Colonel Saavedra of the G-2 murdered to make it appear the Frente did it—so that the Americans would be jolted into saving this government? Imagine, Manuel Saavedra, one of his best friends. And Juan was bragging about it here at home, how clever he was, how that horrible dwarf Fabio had arranged the assassination. Oh, Julia, you *must* help us before we all drown in blood!"

★

Julia was thoughtful and distracted when she left the palace. She was stunned not only by the revelation that Juan Ferrer had ordered the murder of his secret-police chief, but also by the fact that the dictator's wife had gone over to the opposition.

But how could she get word of her conversation to the Department? She could not use the Embassy's classified communications because Jim Morgan had direct access to them—the Embassy communicator belonged to the Station—and Silvia would therefore be placed in grave jeopardy. Wives too can suffer accidents in Malagua. And even if Julia could set up a back channel, Masterson and Terhune would probably react with skepticism—they would say that Silvia de Ferrer was a hysterical female who should have no influence on United States policy. But would Tom Morelli at the White House and Marvin Black at the Department believe what was occurring in Malagua? She must think of a way—rapidly—to get her information across to the right people in Washington.

María Carmen Escalante's studio was on the top floor of a three-story building not far from the American Embassy. Accompanied by Gonzalo and a security guard from the lead car, Julia climbed the three flights and knocked on the door of the studio. There was no response. Julia knocked again, and still there was silence. Gonzalo tried the door handle, and it opened easily. He walked in, his submachine gun at the ready, then backed out, whispering hoarsely, *Santa Madre de Dios* . . . He tried to keep Julia from entering the studio, but she pushed him aside.

The body of María Carmen was sprawled on the floor in a pool of thickening blood, her throat slashed from ear to ear. A piece of cardboard rested on her chest. The paintings on the wall had been cut to ribbons with a machete. Julia read the crude black letters on the cardboard: ¡ABAJO EL COMUNISMO! ¡VIVA EL ORDEN! Julia screamed.

★

"ORDEN is the new right-wing civilian vigilante outfit organized and bankrolled by some of the oligarchs and the G-2 of the National Guard," John Crespo told Julia. Still in shock, she had gone back to the Embassy and had asked Ann to call McVeigh to her office. Disjointedly, Julia tried to tell him about María Carmen. "And what is ORDEN?" she had asked. McVeigh said he would ask Crespo to join them; Jim Morgan was away, on a two-day trip to San Pablo, the Pacific Coast port, but the CIA Station was certain to have a line on it.

"ORDEN has been operating mainly in the countryside, terrorizing peasants," Crespo went on. "This is one of the few times they've struck in the capital that I know of. I suppose G-2 is getting nervous about Frente terrorism and wants to hit back with some terrorism of its own. And they must figure it's better to use civilian thugs rather than National Guard types for this kind of operation. And from what the Ambassador has just told us, they're pretty vicious bastards."

"But *why* María Carmen?" Julia asked. "What had she done?"

"I don't know," Crespo said. "Probably nothing. . . . But I'll make a guess. She was considered to be antirégime, and most likely close to the Left, as the majority of artists and intellectuals tend to be in this country. So somebody in ORDEN or in G-2 got the idea that she should be made an example of. What I'm afraid of now is a God-awful wave of terrorism both ways. María Carmen may have just been the beginning. . . . Yeah, this getting to be a new ball game, all right.''

"Tell me, John,'' Julia asked, "don't you people in the Station have some influence with G-2? Can't you get them to understand that this sort of savage violence will play in the end against them —and the government?''

Crespo glanced at Julia. "Madam Ambassador,'' he said, "I can't speak for the Station—nor should I. My boss is in charge of liaison with G-2. But if I were you, I wouldn't even bother to ask him that question.''

★

The day after Julia Savage returned to Malagua, General McCullen, the Director of Central Intelligence, was received by the President in the Oval Office, with only Tom Morelli present. Having been briefed by Colonel Duke the previous evening, McCullen had requested an urgent appointment concerning a "highly sensitive matter.''

The President greeted McCullen from behind his desk, motioned him to a chair, and said, "Please proceed, General.''

"Mr. President, I'm here on a most unpleasant mission, but I felt that I should inform you personally and immediately of a grave discovery made just a few days ago by our people. It concerns Ambassador Savage in Malagua.''

"What is it?''

"We have absolutely hard evidence that Miss Savage was involved a number of years ago as an accessory to the obstruction of justice by hiding a revolutionary Weatherman bomber who was being sought by the FBI and the police. It was during the antiwar movement in the mid-Sixties. I am concerned that a disclosure of Miss Savage's illegal activities may embarrass your Administration, sir. . . .''

The President raised his eyebrows. "Really?'' he asked. "But who is going to disclose it? You? The Agency?''

McCullen was taken aback. He had allowed himself to be convinced by Colonel Duke that the information about Julia Savage was of extraordinary importance—he had decided to withhold the part about Randolph Savage to protect the CIA—and now the President seemed to be treating it with insouciance.

"No, of course not, Mr. President," he stammered; "the Agency would never disclose it. But you know how stories of this kind get around Washington once somebody hears about it. If my people heard it, and the FBI has corroborated the basic facts, it's entirely possible that some reporter would also get hold of the story."

"Look, my dear General," the President said, "I don't mind telling you that I think this whole business smells of some kind of backstabbing. In the first place, I don't give a shit what Miss Savage did when she was a young girl. I don't think *anybody* cares about this sort of thing after so many years. But it would smear the reputation of an American Ambassador, and I won't stand for that."

"But Mr. President—"

"General McCullen, I continue to have confidence in Ambassador Savage, and I will hold you personally responsible if there are any leaks about this to the press or the Congress. As you say, the CIA came up with this information, so I insist that it keep it to itself. And believe me, General, I know very well how leaks work here. Since you have checked what you call your hard evidence with the FBI, I shall instruct the Director of the Bureau and the Attorney General to consider the matter to be highly classified. And thanks for coming in."

★

Later that week, Ann Mestre told Julia Savage that Manuel Schneider Belmonte, the president of Automotriz Schneider S.A., had asked for an appointment as soon as possible. Schneider was the MIT graduate Julia had met shortly after arriving in the country, and he had attended her August reception. She suggested that he come to the Embassy in the afternoon.

Manuel Schneider, tall and perfectly tailored, arrived punctually at three o'clock. He looked serious and worried, and he went straight to the point.

"Madam Ambassador, I am here to follow up on a conversation you had yesterday with a lady who is a mutual friend," he said in English. "Do I make myself clear?"

"Yes, Mr. Schneider," Julia replied. Silvia de Ferrer clearly wasted no time.

"I also have the authority to speak on behalf of a number of my friends in the Malaguan business community. The way my friends and I see it, the dictatorship can no longer be tolerated: Ferrer is destroying and robbing the nation. He is evil and bloodthirsty as well as greedy. On the other hand, the Frente, which includes many honorable patriots, is becoming dangerously infiltrated by Marxists and *fidelistas*. In fact, it may be taken over by the extreme Left, and after a terrible civil war Malagua will end up with another dictator. But my friends and I believe there is an alternative. May I tell you about it?"

"Certainly," Julia said. "Please go ahead."

"This alternative is the democratic center. You may not be aware that it exists politically, but I can assure you that it's very much alive. I am speaking of the new generation of businessmen, such as myself, of young and not-so-young professionals—doctors, lawyers and so on—and even of many intellectuals who are both anti-Ferrer and anti-Marxist. We have been organizing quietly for some time, and now I think we represent a potentially important force. I should tell you that we have contacts with factions in the Frente, with the non-Marxists, and we believe we can form an effective alliance with them. It is absolutely vital for us to have the support of the United States if we are to succeed —and save Malagua from wholesale murder and destruction. Without American support, the democratic center will be smashed by both Ferrer and the Marxists."

"I understand," Julia answered. "But what type of support do you wish from the United States?"

"It's very simple," Schneider said. "We want American support for a constitutional and peaceful transition to democracy. This can be accomplished, we believe, if the United States indicates to General Ferrer that it will cut off all forms of assistance to his régime unless he agrees to a popular referendum within six months. This referendum should be supervised by the Organization of American States, and Ferrer must commit himself to step down if he loses—which, of course, he will. Then a provisional coalition government would be formed, with the participation of democratic elements of the Frente, and free elections would follow as rapidly as possible."

"That's quite a tall order," Julia remarked. "I don't see General Ferrer agreeing to a referendum that will cost him his job, do you?"

"Not yet," Manuel Schneider said. "It will take pressure from Washington and it will take pressure from inside Malagua. For our part, we are prepared to apply pressure by paralyzing the economy. Ferrer can go on murdering people and sending out the National Guard after the guerrillas, but there's little he can do if we—the businessmen and industrialists—declare a general strike. It would be a novelty, a strike by capitalists, but we can shut down factories, big stores, banks, and so on. We can remain on strike indefinitely—the workers, of course, would go along with us—and this is something Ferrer cannot afford."

"But I thought that President Ferrer owns a good part of the commercial businesses in Malagua," Julia said.

"Of course he does," Schneider replied. "In fact, he owns forty percent of my dealership. My father had to give it to the Ferrers twenty years ago. But we are the managers, we can give the orders to lock out, and Ferrer cannot be everywhere at once. He can't have the National Guard operating banks and brewing beer—they're already swamped with police and counterinsurgency work. Yes, Madam Ambassador, the General *is* vulnerable."

"Don Manuel," Julia remarked, "what you've told me is extremely interesting. I can't give you any kind of answer today, as you must understand, but you can rest assured that I shall relay your views to Washington. Then we shall see."

After Schneider left, Julia summoned Mac McVeigh and Rick Anders to inform them of his proposals. "Well, it's the first fresh idea I've heard in a long time," McVeigh said. "I don't know how determined these businessmen are, but I'm inclined to take them seriously. What Schneider told you, Julia, fits in with other reports we've been hearing about the new mood in the business community. Yes, we should advise the Department immediately.''

Julia drafted a long telegram summing up her conversation with Schneider, adding that ''the Embassy has reason to believe that the businessmen have backing in high quarters of the Malaguan Establishment.'' McVeigh inquired what she meant by that cryptic comment, and Julia answered with a grin that ''This is something I'd like to keep to myself for the time being.''

★

In her study at the Residence, Julia sat up long past midnight scribbling on her yellow pad. It would be interesting to see Terhune's face when he read her telegram the next morning, she thought. And Marvin Black would, of course, see a copy. If nothing else, the Schneider move—or was it Silvia de Ferrer's move?—would reinforce Julia's recommendations for United States neutrality in the Malaguan affair. But, she wondered, was it too late? She wrote the word *Frente* on her pad, a question mark next to it.

Just then, Julia was hurled across the room by a powerful force, crashing against the wall of the study. An earthquake, she thought in a last flash of consciousness before everything went black.

BOOK FOUR

★ ★ ★

The Fighters

15

THE town of Jacaltec lies in the low yellow hills between the high *mesa* of Ciudad Malagua and the Pacific coast, but it is quite removed from the main highway linking the capital with the port of San Pablo. Jacaltec is just south of the Guatemalan province of Huehuetenango, and its people still speak the Mamean-Jacaltec dialect of the Mayan language, dating back more than two thousand years. Today, dusty and somnolent Jacaltec remains suspended between the Mayan period of disintegration and the Spanish conquest, but in the Classic Late Period of Mayan history, between the seventh and ninth centuries after Christ, Jacaltec was an important metropolis. It contained great *stela* monuments, the most famous of them unearthed by archeologists being the depictions of human sacrifices and the majestic Temple of the Jaguar.

Jacaltec had also been a major Mayan military center, the home of the bravest of the *nacom* warrior-priests. The *nacom* were elected for three-year terms to formulate strategies of war and were worshipped as deities. In the words of a contemporary chronicle, "The *nacom* could not, during these three years, have relations with any woman, even his own wife, nor eat red meat. He was held in great veneration and given fish and iguanas, which are like lizards, to eat. In this time he did not get drunk

. . . and no woman served him and he had but little communication with the people. . . . They bore him in great pomp, perfuming him as if he were an idol, to the temple, where they seated him and burned incense to him as to an idol.''

Rolando Asturias, the modern *nacom*—fighting priest—arrived in Jacaltec in the early afternoon of a hot day late in October. The rickety green bus stopped in front of the Jacaltec *pensión* on the main square, and he was the only passenger to step off. He was dressed in loose white pants and short boots, a white long-sleeved blouse, and a wide-brimmed hat that cast a shadow on his face. A revolver was tucked under his waistband. It had taken Rolando nearly twenty-four hours to reach Jacaltec from Ubique, changing buses three times and spending the night at a friendly priest's house in Tambic, a village below Ciudad Malagua. He carried a small canvas bag with a change of clothing and some *tacos*.

The square was deserted except for a disheveled rural policeman and a scrawny black goat. It was *siesta* time, and the town's few stores were closed. The bar, however, was open, and Rolando sat down at a fly-specked table, ordering a Cerveza del Rey.

A half-hour went by. Rolando drank the warm beer and ate a *taco*. He reviewed the stand he planned to take in the approaching confrontation—yes, he was certain it *would* be a confrontation—and relaxed in his chair. His thoughts, as they often did since the night at Santa Teresa del Monte, turned toward Julia Savage. Rolando had not seen her in a month, with the exception of the brief glimpse at Luis Merino's funeral, and he kept finding himself devising schemes for arranging another meeting.

It had been courageous of her to attend the Merino burial—in fact, it had surprised him—and it was on impulse that Rolando had sent the note with his blessing. But at this stage there was no reason to take the risks of another meeting. There was nothing further he could say about Malaguan politics, though there were many other things he wanted to tell her. For now, Rolando had to be content with thinking about her. And if he was the reincarnation of a Mayan *nacom,* he could not have relations with women for three years. Rolando laughed and finished his beer.

★

Rolando Asturias had not known of the bombing of the American Residence in Ciudad Malagua when he started on his trip from Santa Teresa del Monte to Jacaltec and beyond. He had returned to his highlands immediately after the Merino burial ceremony, spending the next two days in discussions with his guerrilla squad leaders—thus being out of touch with the outside world.

★

Julia had asked for him—repeating weakly, "Rolando . . . Rolando . . ." as she regained consciousness an hour or so after the explosion.

"What are you saying, Madam Ambassador?" asked the Embassy's Malaguan physician, who had been summoned by a Marine guard. "Oh, nothing, nothing . . ." she replied, now lucid, and worried that the doctor had understood her moans.

She was lying on a couch in the living room, a pillow propped under her head. She tried to move, and winced with pain. "But what happened—what's the matter with me?"

"A very powerful explosive charge, probably plastic, was set off by a timing device right after one thirty A.M.," Mark Starek told her. "Your bedroom is simply gone. The device must have been placed right against its outside wall. You know, it's a miracle you are alive."

Julia closed her eyes. She had planned to undress and work in her bedroom, but her note pad was in the study, so she had stayed there. There *must* be a God in heaven.

"Had you been in the bedroom," Starek went on, "you'd have been blown to bits. The steel doors at both ends of the corridor in your wing of the house helped to deflect the blast—though the steel door of your bedroom was torn off its hinges—and you were relatively safe in the study. The aftershock of the explosion knocked you against the wall. And you're okay: Dr. Mello says that all you have is bruises, nothing broken. You had the wind knocked out of you.''

"Any idea how the explosives were put there?" Julia asked, sitting up and reaching for a cigarette in the silver box on the coffee table. "I thought we had perfect security here."

"So did I," Starek said. "My best guess is that it was done by a part-time gardener or worker who belongs to a terrorist group. We had some maintenance work done on the outer walls and the garden when you were in Washington, and it's likely that's when the explosives were sneaked in. The Marines, of course, were watching the laborers, but it takes a minute or less to install a device of this type. And those guys are pros. I don't think you should blame the Marines. . . ."

"No, I don't," Julia said. "But someone went to a lot of trouble to plant the plastic or whatever it was on my bedroom wall. Someone wanted me dead. But I don't see what anybody would have gained by it. For the Frente, for example, it would have been senseless and self-defeating; and Ferrer isn't mad: he wouldn't have me killed because I recommended that we give him no arms. So why, and who?"

★

A battered blue pickup truck pulled up in front of the Jacaltec bar, and an elderly man in a straw hat got out. He looked like a small farmer, probably with a few *manzanas* of sugar and vegetables, and a few pigs and fowl. Spotting Rolando, he motioned to the truck outside, and said, *"Vamos."* The man drove in silence for several minutes, then smiled and said, "I forgot to introduce myself. I'm Padre Miguel, the parish priest from Agua Linda, which is where I'm taking you."

Agua Linda was a village some thirty miles northeast of Jacaltec, and it lay in the uplands at the edge of the jungle territory. The road was narrow and rutted, and halfway to Agua Linda, Father Miguel had to squeeze his truck to the side when they met a National Guard patrol jeep equipped with a radio and a .50-caliber machine gun. The soldiers looked over the two disguised priests, but did not stop and ask for their identification papers. Rolando carried a forged *cédula,* describing him as a farmhand, and it had passed Guard scrutiny three times on the buses from Ubique.

Father Miguel stopped the truck at the door of his church, a small structure at the entrance to the village. "Here we are," he said, "and your friends are waiting inside." In the semidarkness of the church, Rolando recognized Tomás Martínez, and the two men embraced. There were also two young men whom Asturias did not know. One of them said, "We'll have to wait until it gets dark; then we'll move on." Father Miguel asked his visitors to sit in the sacristy, and an old Indian woman in a black shawl silently served them a meal of stewed chicken and *tacos.* Shortly before eight o'clock, Norberto, the shorter of the youths, said, "Okay, let's go."

They left the church and walked several hundred yards to a peasant's hut, the three-quarter moon bathing the village in soft white light. There were no signs of life; villagers in Agua Linda went to sleep when darkness fell. There was no electricity, and kerosene was too expensive to be wasted in lamps. Behind the hut, Rolando saw four mules hitched to a post. Norberto wordlessly pointed to the animals, and the men mounted them.

Riding in single file, the two guides, Rolando, and Tomás took a tortuous, rock-strewn uphill path to the northeast. Then there was savanna, growing almost as tall as the mules, and, suddenly, the jungle, enveloping the riders in its nocturnal blackness. Rolando could barely make out the shape of the guide ahead of him, but the hard-breathing mules followed one another, and Norberto evidently knew his way. The jungle was alive, speaking the many voices of the night: chattering oukari monkeys that seemed to talk in their sleep, curassow birds calling each other high in the rain-forest canopy, a grunting peccary awakened by the rustle of the advancing mules, and *nahuyaca* snakes, hissing in the leafy ground cover.

The jungle above Jacaltec was completely different from Santa Teresa del Monte, and the Jesuit *nacom* felt lost, at the mercy of the silent guides. After they had climbed silently for well over two hours through the dense trees and foliage, Norberto abruptly stopped and dismounted. "Wait here," he whispered to the others, padding away noiselessly in his moccasins. Fifteen minutes later, he reappeared, saying, "*Bueno*. The way is clear. Let's go on."

The mules resumed their slow walk, and presently the group reached a large clearing in the jungle, a circle filled with flitting flashlights in the hands of a dozen armed men. They approached the riders, and a gentle voice said, "Rolando? Tomás? Is that you? It's Máximo. *Bienvenidos. . . .*"

★

Comandante Máximo Landino Sánchez, the supreme chief of the Ejército Guerrillero de los Pobres, led Rolando and Tomás to a large military tent that was pitched under the trees just outside the clearing. Inside, there were cots, a radio transmitter/receiver unit mounted atop a crate, a kerosene lamp providing a splash of light.

"*Compañeros*," Máximo Landino said to the visitors, "it's late and you've been traveling for long hours. Why don't you have a drink or two to warm you up—the nights are cool here—and something to eat if you want, and then go to sleep. Tomorrow we shall talk. . . ."

Rolando and Tomás slept late, and the sun was high over the tops of the mahogany, cedar, and *yaxche* trees around the jungle clearing when they finished their breakfast of maize gruel and bitter black coffee. Máximo Landino entered the tent and sat down on a cot opposite Rolando and Tomás. "Good," he said, "you look rested, so shall we start our conference?"

Now twenty-seven, Máximo had abandoned his law studies five years earlier to help organize the EGP; he had later moved to the mountains to recruit Indian peasants for guerrilla warfare. He was tall and thin and wore horn-rimmed glasses; without his rakish ranger's hat, which was his trademark, Máximo had a look of professorial mildness. He was clean-shaven, in contrast to his bearded companions, and his demeanor was mild and sad. He seemed out of place in the jungle, though he was entirely at ease with the West German G-3 submachine gun he carried in his left hand.

As a child, he spent his summer vacations in the *sierra* village of Manquinhiomo, where both his grandfather and father had been born, and Máximo knew the terrain like the back of his hand, having hunted armadillos, agoutis, deer, and even dangerous tapirs with the local Indians. Many of them remembered him from childhood. He spoke the Jacaltec dialect fluently, and he had Mayan blood in his veins: his great-grandmother and his grandmother were pure Indians, though the men in the Landino line came from old Spanish stock.

Máximo's father, who was eight years old when the General was murdered by the first Ferrer, was brought up by his mother, becoming a schoolteacher and marrying the daughter of a Landinist colonel killed in the same massacre. Young Máximo grew up in an atmosphere of hatred for the Ferrers—and for the Americans, who the family believed were behind the murder conspiracy. When Máximo acquired his guerrilla notoriety, his father was imprisoned by Juan Ferrer; he had now been held, without charges, for over three years.

The guerrilla commander had invited Rolando and Tomás, both representing the Frente leadership, for a strategy conference in his mountain redoubt. The dry season was about to begin, and it was necessary for all the revolutionary factions to agree on how to carry out the general offensive against the government planned for the coming months. All the groups were in agreement that the time was ripe for the big push, but deep political, ideological, and military differences existed among them. In fact, the split within the revolutionary ranks was reaching its most momentous point.

The so-called Centralists, represented chiefly by Rolando and Tomás, believed that the Frente was now ready for the "final" offensive, to be developed and escalated over a three-month period, from December through February. Both were members of the secret Directorate of the Frente.

The Directorate felt that the régime was in an advanced state of decomposition, and that it was imperative to shift from harassment tactics to open warfare. Urban guerrilla units in Ciudad Malagua and other cities and towns were quite well armed, and the Frente judged that they could engage the National Guard successfully in a battle for control of the urban areas. The *barrios* were seething with discontent, and the young fighters were ready to go. Rolando's guerrillas in the central highlands were prepared to move down from their hideouts and support the urban insurrection. Finally, the Frente had entered into secret conversations with a group of key Ciudad Malagua businessmen, who had agreed to stage massive lockout strikes before and during the urban offensive. This group was headed by Manuel Schneider, who a few weeks earlier had been invited to become a clandestine member of the Frente Directorate.

The Centralists were aiming at a national political-military coalition against Juan Ferrer. Rolando Asturias and Manuel Schneider, among them, also agreed that the "American dimension," Washington's refusal to go on supporting the dictator, was vital. But neither had mentioned their personal contacts with Julia Savage, there still being less than total openness between the different factions of the Frente Directorate.

Máximo Landino's attitude, however, was a serious problem for the Frente. For the offensive to succeed, the EGP had to participate fully. It was made up of hardened *guerrilleros,* and it had the best modern arms. The Frente believed that Máximo's troops had to engage the National Guard in their section of the country—Ferrer had to be exposed and vulnerable everywhere at the same time.

But this was not the EGP's strategy at the moment. Adhering to an extreme-leftist interpretation of the revolutionary process, virtually a Trotskyite interpretation, Máximo advocated what he called the "People's Prolonged War," resulting in time in Malagua's transformation into a full-fledged revolutionary state, based on an alliance of peasants and workers. He had contempt for the Frente's relatively moderate ideology, regarding its leaders as "deviationists" from the "true" revolution. He scorned the orthodox Communists in the anti-Ferrer movement, whom he accused of being stooges for Soviet "Stalinist" interests. Above all, he feared and detested the United States as Malagua's worst and most dangerous enemy. He would have no part of any arrangements supported by the United States, Máximo had often told Frente leaders.

★

Now, sitting in his command tent, Máximo was patiently restating his strategy. Rolando and Tomás had outlined for him the Frente's general offensive plan, emphasizing the importance of the EGP's full involvement, but Máximo remained unconvinced.

"Look, *compañeros,*" he said, "let's assume for the sake of argument that your strategic analysis is correct, and that Ferrer can indeed be overthrown by the actions you propose. I agree that it's not impossible. But, I must ask myself, what would be the ultimate result? Would it be a revolutionary Malagua where peasants and workers held the power and where there would be justice for all, including the poor Indians? No. I must conclude that the Frente's success would be no more than a *political* victory over Ferrer. The power would go to a bourgeois–leftist alliance, presumably blessed by the Yankees, who would be grateful that nothing worse has happened, and there would be no chance for a radical social transformation of the nation. You would gain a free press, elections, and all that shit, but the social *status quo* in Malagua would remain unchanged. This is not what the EGP has been fighting for in the last five years."

"You're wrong, Máximo," Rolando said. "You know perfectly well from the Frente's Program of Action that very profound social changes are contemplated after the victory. You know how I feel about it myself, that I'm as eager as you are for social justice."

Máximo interrupted him. "You talk like the liberal Jesuit that you are," he said with a grin. "I know. I was educated by the Jesuits too. You and your progressive friends in the Church— and don't think I don't respect men like you or Bishop Pepe Vargas for your courage—will fight the tyrant and the repression, and you will stand up for social justice, in which I know you believe. But won't you stop at the water's edge when it comes to the creation of the peasants–workers' state that we advocate? Am I wrong?''

"No, you're not wrong," Rolando replied. "The Frente is not trying to turn Malagua into Cuba or into Cambodia, and that never was the idea behind the anti-Ferrer struggle."

"Well, it's certainly *my* idea to launch a people's revolution," Máximo told him, "instead of a bourgeois-directed insurrection. That's why I believe in prolonged war; it takes time to inculcate political and revolutionary consciousness into the masses. We've done well with the peasants here in the northeast—all my fighters have a high level of political consciousness, and you know how good they are with the guns—but it may be another year or two before this consciousness spreads everywhere in the country."

"You mean before you can take over the Frente?"

Máximo laughed. "No, I'm not that ambitious," he said. "Not yet, anyway. When the masses are ready to move, a leader will emerge spontaneously. If it happens to be me, Rolando, I'll be ready."

Tomás broke in with a touch of impatient anger. "This is no time for ideological debates," he said. "What we came to discuss here with you, at your invitation, is simply this: is the EGP prepared to cooperate with the Frente in the general offensive against the tyrant? Yes or no?"

"Now, Don Tomás," Máximo answered, "let us be realistic. I don't have to tell you that the EGP has been fighting hard against Ferrer. We control the whole northeast of Malagua. This is liberated territory where the National Guard doesn't dare penetrate. It's a base through which quite a few weapons have gone down to the towns, including some of the weapons your own people are using. And the arms have been bought with money that the EGP has raised from kidnappings and bank expropriations, as we call them. We raise more money this way than any other revolutionary group. And as you know, we share it. The Cubans don't give us everything."

"Yes, I know all this," Tomás Martínez said.

"Fine. Then you should also know that the EGP will not sit idly in the mountains if the Frente launches a big offensive. You see, we do not confuse strategy with tactics. . . . Yes, I have a different strategic view as to how the revolution should develop. But it would be bad tactics for the EGP to undermine the struggle against Ferrer, and we're not crazy. If the Frente Directorate decides to mount a general offensive, we'll be with you—even if I think that it's politically premature. But if the offensive succeeds, the EGP must have a serious voice in the political decisions that will follow. This must be your promise and your commitment to us.''

"That goes without saying," Tomás told the *comandante*. "We have cooperated in the past. In this, then, everybody is equal, and naturally, you will have as much of a voice as anybody in the making of decisions when the time comes. But like everybody else, you'll have to take your chances politically."

"It's understood, then," Máximo said. "Your people can let us know when the offensive is to start, and we'll coordinate our actions with you. I can move down to Jacaltec, sever the main highway between Ciudad Malagua and the coast, and try to hold as much of the west as I can. And I think I can help your units to grab San Pablo."

"Sounds good, Máximo," Tomás said, extending his hand to the guerrilla leader. "We're shooting for the first week of December, but you'll get more precise dates in plenty of time."

"So we're in agreement," Máximo said, shaking hands with them. "Oh, by the way, what did you think of the bombing of the American Embassy? Our boys did a great job infiltrating the Residence area, even if they didn't succeed in killing the Ambassador. Well, the next time . . ."

"What are you talking about?" Asturias asked slowly.

"Didn't you hear? Oh, I guess you were traveling," Máximo told him with a proud smile. "An EGP unit was able to place plastic explosives—C-3 stuff—on the wall of the Residence, just outside the Ambassador's bedroom, and to hook up a timing mechanism. We had been observing her movements for some time, so we were sure she'd be asleep when the thing went off. But you can't win them all. The Ambassador stayed up late in another room of the house, and she survived."

"You miserable imbecile!" Rolando shouted, grabbing Máximo by the collar of his blouse and knocking off his ranger's hat. "You idiot . . ."

"Hey, what's the matter with you, Padre? Take your hands off me or I'll shoot you dead right here and now." Máximo shook Rolando's hands off his neck, pointing the G-3 at him. "Have you lost your mind?"

"You've lost *your* mind," the Jesuit shouted. Now the radio operator stood with his weapon behind Rolando, and three *guerrilleros,* attracted by the uproar, raced into the tent, guns at the ready.

Rolando was in a white fury. He yelled at Máximo: "Can't you see that this kind of terrorism is counterproductive and dangerous? We don't need to bring the Americans down on us. We don't need stupid, juvenile provocations to give them an excuse to rearm Ferrer. We had almost persuaded them to refuse him arms, and now you pull this kind of stunt. Also, the Ambassador is a woman. Don't you discriminate in your terrorism?"

Máximo Landino lowered his weapon and looked coldly at Rolando.

"No, we don't," he said. "Not when it comes to Americans. They and their *ferrerista* lackeys have killed enough of *our* women and children. Ferrer's *esbirros* didn't show any 'discrimination,' as you call it, when they assassinated María Carmen Escalante. Did you know that María Carmen and I were engaged to be married?"

"No. I didn't even know María Carmen was dead," Rolando said quietly. "I am sorry. But that's no reason to kill Julia Savage. It's the wrong kind of reprisal."

"It wasn't reprisal," Máximo replied. "It was a coincidence that the explosives at the Residence were set to go off on the same day María Carmen died. But, yes, it was part of the total war against Ferrer and the Americans. Anyway, I believe we've discussed all that we have to discuss now, I must attend to my duties. But you shouldn't start back until nightfall. Then Norberto will take you back to Agua Linda."

★

Asturias and Martínez reached Jacaltec in the early afternoon of the next day, driven from Agua Linda by Father Miguel. They had agreed to take different buses back to the central highlands and Ubique. But Rolando chose to wait for the last bus of the day to Ciudad Malagua, where he wanted to spend two days in clandestine meetings with Frente student leaders at the University.

Before they parted, Tomás said to the Jesuit: "You know, I still don't trust Máximo. I'm just not sure he'll move when we do. He may want to see us bloodied before he comes down from his mountains. It would make him stronger politically afterward. In my opinion, we should launch the 'Plan Zero' operation within the next week or so. Let Máximo be as surprised as Juan Ferrer."

"I suspect that you are right, Don Tomás," Rolando answered. "Yes, let's go ahead with 'Plan Zero.'"

16

"PLAN Zero" had been devised several years earlier by the Frente Directorate, but it had not been executed because the movement lacked sufficient strength and organization to carry it out, and because the political climate had not been propitious. Now conditions had changed, and at a meeting of the six-member Directorate in a dilapidated house in Ciudad Malagua's Barrio del Sur, shortly before Rolando and Tomás traveled to confer with Máximo Landino, a tentative decision had been taken to open the planned dry-season offensive with the spectacular "Plan Zero" blow at the Ferrer dictatorship. But the final go-ahead was delayed pending the result of their mission. If Máximo showed any doubt or hesitation about participating in the general offensive, the Frente would strike alone.

But apart from Rolando's and Tomás' reactions to their meeting with the young *comandante,* what forced the Frente's hand on "Plan Zero" was the unfolding of events in Washington that same day, events of which they were unaware as they went their separate ways from Jacaltec.

★

Malagua was the only topic on the agenda of the National Security Council's Special Coordinating Committee when it convened in the White House Situation Room on a chilly, rainy morning at the end of October. It was being chaired by Tom Morelli, the National Security Adviser, and all the principal foreign-policy players were present. Secretary of State Masterson had brought along Marvin Black, the Under Secretary of State for Political Affairs, who had recently developed a keen interest in Malaguan problems, and Terence Terhune, his Assistant Secretary for American Republics Affairs. David Lustig, the NSC staff's Latin American specialist, sat behind Morelli. Defense Secretary Creighton and CIA Director McCullen completed the group.

"The President wants an immediate decision on Malagua," Tom Morelli said. "You gentlemen have had adequate time to prepare your final positions, so there should be no further delays. The President feels that the situation has gotten completely out of hand—he is particularly disturbed by the bombing of the Residence in Ciudad Malagua—and he believes that the United States must finally take a stand. He told me earlier this morning that he's concerned about the stability of all of Central America —and about the impact of this unrest on Mexico and Panama. As you know, we are in the midst of delicate oil negotiations with the Mexicans, and their attitude has to be considered in whatever decision we take on Malagua; as you know, Mexico is on the verge of breaking diplomatic relations with the Ferrer régime. . . . The safety of the Panama Canal under the new treaties may also be affected by developments in Malagua. Let us first hear from the Secretary of State."

Masterson, who had a cold, coughed and blew his nose loudly. He shuffled papers in a folder in front of him, selecting the talking points prepared by Terhune. In an authoritative voice he said, "Our first concern is to prevent Malagua from becoming another Cuba. President Ferrer takes the view that he can put down the rebellion if he is provided with arms by the United States, and I gather the CIA concurs in this analysis. On the other hand, our Ambassador there, Miss Savage, is on record as opposing the supply of arms, and recommending American neutrality. She claims in a recent telegram that moderate non-Marxist opposition to General Ferrer is emerging in Ciudad Malagua, and that we should show some support for it. Ah, she calls it an alternative. . . ."

"Is she wrong?" Tom Morelli asked.

"In the judgment of the State Department—and the CIA— Miss Savage is wrong. There are only two power centers in Malagua: the Ferrer régime and the leftist revolutionaries. The rest, including the so-called democratic center, is marginal. Therefore, I must recommend that the United States grant arms to General Ferrer to help him quell the Marxist rebellion."

Morelli looked quizzically at Masterson. "I thought the State Department was trying for a *quid pro quo,*" he said. "What happened to that?"

"Well, I'm afraid that's dead," the Secretary replied. "Number one, Ferrer won't do it, and number two, it's too late in the game. Ferrer is fighting for his life."

"I'm afraid the President won't sign off on it, Ed," Morelli said. "The lines between Ferrer and the opposition are too clearly drawn now. The United States cannot be in a position of openly defending a dictatorship, and supplying guns to kill Malaguans, which would have to be done openly. Aside from the morality involved and the way the President feels about human rights, this would place us in an untenable position in Latin America. It could screw up the Mexican negotiations. And it's not politically tolerable at home. Are there any other ideas? Marvin, you've been giving a lot of thought to Malagua."

"The Secretary knows," Marvin Black said, "that I differ with him on this matter, and he has authorized me to state my dissenting views here. I happen to agree with Ambassador Savage, and with you, Tom, that it would be an error to send arms openly to Ferrer."

"Oh, my God," General McCullen sighed audibly. "What's the matter with you people?"

"Hold your horses, Henry, I haven't finished," Black said. "What I have in mind is a compromise that may satisfy everybody in this room. . . ."

"Will it satisfy the Malaguans?" Morelli asked flatly.

"Up to a point," Black told him. "There are no perfect solutions. I'm thinking of a face-saving plan. I propose that we tell Ferrer—that Miss Savage tell Ferrer—that it is politically inconvenient for the United States to supply him with arms. At the same time, we'll leak the word here that the President had said no to weapons for the dictator. That, I hope, will please the opposition in Malagua as well as our liberal constituency at home. Then we'll announce publicly that the United States is unfreezing some forty million dollars in *economic* aid to Malagua: we can do this because the human-rights legislation banning aid to violators, like Ferrer, allows the President to make a finding that it's in the national interest."

Black paused, looked around the room, and continued: "The announcement will say that these funds are being made available to alleviate the suffering of the people of Malagua, *et cetera*. The opposition won't like this part, but it will give Ferrer a sense that we aren't abandoning him altogether. We do want to keep him in the game. Of course, Ambassador Savage would inform General Ferrer of our economic aid at the same time as she gives him the bad news about the arms."

"Okay, but this doesn't really resolve the basic situation," Morelli broke in.

"No, it does not," Marvin Black replied. "But it may win some extra time for diplomacy. I would suggest that Miss Savage be instructed to open conversations with the moderates in Malagua to see whether they may indeed provide an alternative. But Ferrer has to be told about it. He may not like it, but it beats being thrown to the wolves. Briefly, what I'm proposing is setting the stage for a form of American mediation between Ferrer and the moderate opposition. In the end, a reasonably peaceful transfer of power should be the solution."

"Sure," General McCullen said, "but in the meantime, Ferrer may collapse and you ain't gonna have a peaceful transfer of anything. You'll have a Marxist takeover, that's what you will have. You've seen our intelligence reports on the shipments of Cuban weapons through Guatemala. And they keep coming almost every day."

"Right," Marvin Black told him. "This is the final piece of my scenario. I would urge the President to authorize a one-time covert operation by the CIA to supply a certain volume of small arms and ammunition to Ferrer so that the National Guard can keep fighting defensively. This too will help gain additional time for United States mediation. But Ferrer has to understand that this aid will be contingent on his agreement to accept talks with the moderate opposition. I'm sure the Intelligence Oversight committees in the Congress will go along with us if the situation is properly explained. Can you swing a Special Activity of this kind, Henry?"

"Yeah," McCullen answered. "I think you're proposing too little too late, but yes, I can swing it. We have access to some Chilean arms, and I can get them transferred to Malagua very discreetly. If any of these arms are captured by the rebels, they won't be traced to the United States."

"I don't like the CIA-arms aspect of your plan, Marvin, but I suppose we all have to compromise," Tom Morelli said. "I can probably sell the President on the package. Mr. Secretary, will you go along?"

Masterson blew his nose again. "I guess I will, but under protest," he said. "I would have preferred a clear policy of support for President Ferrer. I don't believe in half-measures."

"Secretary Creighton?" Morelli asked.

"I'll support it, but I too have reservations," the Secretary of Defense said.

"Then we seem to have reached a consensus," Morelli told the group. "The record will show the reservations."

"I want to make a point," General McCullen announced suddenly. "I don't think Ambassador Savage should be informed of the covert operation. She'll oppose it, and we'll have a new fight on our hands. Our Station Chief, who is very close to Ferrer, can clue him in."

"Christ, Henry, you can't undermine Julia that way," Tom Morelli protested. "After all, she has to conduct very delicate negotiations, and she should be in the know."

"Ambassadors don't have to know everything," McCullen

said. "We have used back channels before, as you well know. We've done other things behind the backs of ambassadors with the President's knowledge. Anyway, aren't you running policy out of the White House? You and Masterson can fine-tune the instructions, and Miss Savage won't be damaged. What she doesn't know won't hurt her."

"I agree," Masterson chimed in.

★

It was late in the afternoon in Ciudad Malagua when Ann Mestre handed Julia a long telegram over Secretary Masterson's signature. It had a pink SECRET cover sheet, and it instructed her to request urgently a meeting with President Ferrer to advise him of the Administration's decisions.

Julia read it slowly with a frown, then reread it to be certain she understood what Washington had in mind. Okay, Ferrer should be told that his request for weapons was being turned down. On this point, Julia felt vindicated: it appeared that she had won the big battle. But Ferrer was to receive, instead, $40 million in economic aid. She resented not having been consulted about this action, and she had strong doubts about its wisdom. She was ordered to maintain public secrecy over the arms refusal, presumably not to embarrass the General, but an announcement of the grant of economic aid would be made immediately after she had seen him. Julia shook her head—the reaction in the opposition would be extremely negative. Evidently Washington still failed to grasp the Malaguan situation, despite her frequent, lengthy telegrams and personal explanations.

But on the other hand, she was authorized to open negotiations with Manuel Schneider's moderates and to inform Ferrer of it. This was a plus, again vindicating her diplomacy. In fact, it was a major shift in American policy, ending decades of exclusive dealings with the dictatorship. Had Washington begun to see the light, or was it simply trying to please everybody at the same time? In any event, it instantly occurred to Julia that the lifting of this ban could be stretched to legitimize to some degree her clandestine dealings with the Frente through Rolando Asturias. The Frente itself was still taboo, but Rolando *was* a moderate. She decided she would try to get in touch with him—she missed him more and more—after her interview with Juan Ferrer.

On balance, Julia was not entirely displeased with her instructions, but she had the nagging feeling that something was missing in the puzzle. The instructions just did not hang together.

★

Jim Morgan arrived at the Presidential Palace at about midnight, roughly twelve hours after the decisions on Malagua had been taken at the White House. In midafternoon, he had gotten a call over his secure scrambler telephone line from Colonel Duke at CIA Headquarters with a detailed account of the session in the Situation Room. General McCullen had briefed Duke as soon as he returned to Langley, asking the Western Hemisphere Division Chief to relay the information at once to Morgan in Ciudad Malagua.

"It's not perfect, but we're back in the ball game," Duke said in conclusion. "You work out the details of the arms deliveries with Ferrer—I'll give you more information tomorrow—but he's got to keep it secret from the Savage dame. That means that he has to hold his own people on the leash so that the word doesn't reach her through the Defense Attaché or whatever."

Morgan grunted, putting down the scrambler phone. Over his direct line to the Guard's G-2 liaison officer at the Palace, he asked to see General Ferrer. The officer called back in a few minutes to say that the President expected him at midnight, after the dinner he was hosting for the visiting Vice President of Guatemala. Morgan said this would be fine, but requested a National Guard car to pick him up at home to make the visit inconspicuous. The important thing was for him to get to Ferrer ahead of Julia Savage. Meanwhile, he made himself a corned-beef sandwich and had two bourbons, watching on television an old American film with Spanish subtitles as he awaited the staff car.

Juan Ferrer was removing the bemedaled tunic of his gala uniform when Morgan entered his office. "Come in, Jim," he said, "come right in. . . . This Guatemalan is the biggest horse's ass in creation. I had to listen to his crap for four hours." He turned to the dwarf Fabio, saying, "Get a Jack Daniel's for Señor Morgan and the usual for me.

"What the hell's going on, anyway?" Ferrer asked Morgan as they sat down with their drinks. "First you want to see me in the middle of the night, then Ambassador Savage requests an urgent appointment for tomorrow—she's coming in at eleven A.M.—so I spend the dinner with that Guatemalan moron wondering what's happening. Are you guys declaring war on me, or something?"

"Not quite, Mr. President," Morgan said. "But I have some news the Director wanted you to get immediately. He wanted you to hear it from me, before you meet with the Ambassador."

"Shoot. What is it?"

"There was a big meeting on Malagua at the White House this morning. Three decisions were made. One, the United States will *not* give you the arms you'd requested from the Administration—"

"Why, the stupid cock-suckers," Ferrer said without emotion.

"Two, the Administration is unfreezing forty million dollars for Malagua in economic aid, but it intends to start talking to what they call the 'moderate opposition,' and you have to go along with it as the price," Morgan went on. "Three, the Agency was authorized to supply clandestinely a shipment of arms and ammunition for the National Guard on a one-time basis. This we can do immediately."

Juan Ferrer finished his drink, snapping his fingers for Fabio to refill their glasses. Then he broke out in laughter.

"You Yankees just aren't for real," he said in disbelief. "You can't make a straight decision one way or the other. It's always fucking compromises and covering your ass. . . . Do they really think in Washington that they can buy me off with forty million bucks and a lousy shipment of CIA arms? Is this the way I'm supposed to win the war against the Communists? Oh, for crying out loud."

Morgan shrugged. "I'm afraid that's the deal as it now

stands," he told Ferrer. "But as my boss says, we're still in the ball game. Besides, there are ways and ways of handling this sort of thing. Now that we're authorized to ship arms to you, we can stretch it out. I mean, nobody said how much we can give you and over what period. A one-time delivery doesn't have to be only one planeload. So you get a lot of flexibility there. Then, the forty million helps you to shift other funds to buy stuff on the open market, competing with the EGP and the Frente. Washington won't keep an eye on your bookkeeping."

"Yeah," Ferrer said, "forty million can buy a lot of hardware."

"Sure. And the Agency will help out in the procurement. But there's one more detail. Ambassador Savage is not being informed of the clandestine arms deliveries. It's essential that she doesn't find out about it. She got her instructions this afternoon to tell you that you're getting economic aid, but no weapons, and that she's been authorized to establish contacts with those moderates. I imagine it's the Schneider crowd; he was at the Embassy to see her the other day."

"That bastard. *We* made his family rich, and now he's biting the hand that fed him. . . ."

"The main thing, Mr. President, is that you act surprised when Miss Savage comes to see you tomorrow."

★

Julia Savage's sense of puzzlement over her instructions increased the next morning when she received a telephone call from Bob Robbins, the Malagua Country Director at the Department, just before she left for her appointment with Juan Ferrer.

"I take it that you've studied your new instructions and that you can live with them," he said. "But I thought I should read you a rather peculiar front-page story in this morning's *Washington Post*. This is what it says: 'In a twin move designed to deal more effectively with the worsening crisis in Malagua, the Administration has decided to refuse to provide arms to the dictatorial régime of President Juan Ferrer, but to offer him forty million dollars in economic assistance to alleviate the sufferings of the population, senior officials said yesterday. . . ."

"Jesus Christ!" Julia exploded. "Why are they leaking the part about the arms? It was supposed to be kept quiet. I'm on my way to the Palace to inform Ferrer that he's getting no arms and to try to get him to buy the business of the moderates. God, somebody's trying to blow me out of the water."

★

"Good morning, Julia," General Ferrer said heartily. "What good news do you bring me?"

"Well, Mr. President, a mixed bag of news, I guess," she replied as he motioned her to the sofa in his office. "I have requested this appointment on instructions from the State Department to inform you of decisions taken in Washington yesterday in regard to Malagua."

As she reached into her attaché case for the sheet on which the main points were summarized, Ferrer raised his hand.

"Let me be honest with you," he said very pleasantly. "I think I know in general terms what you're about to tell me. Just a little while ago I was called by my Ambassador in Washington, who read me the article in *The Washington Post*. He thinks the story is pretty accurate. Is it?"

Julia produced her best smile for the General. "In some respects it is," she told him, "and I must say I feel badly about its coming out before I had a chance to give you my government's official communication."

"Leaking stories is a way of life in Washington, they tell me," Ferrer remarked.

"In any case," Julia continued, "the Administration has indeed reached with the greatest regret the decision that this is not a suitable time to meet your request for arms. However, this decision was not going to be announced publicly, in order to make things less difficult for you at home."

"I appreciate the sentiment," Ferrer broke in.

"Therefore the State Department is most unhappy about this

leak. It's not helpful to either side. On the other hand, the United States is prepared to make forty million dollars available to Malagua on a grant basis to cope with humanitarian needs.''

Juan Ferrer looked speculatively at Julia. "You know, you people never cease to amaze me," he said. "I ask for arms, and you say no, even though my survival is in the interest of the United States. You'll regret this decision, but now obviously it's water over the dam. So I get no arms, and I do the best I can with my own resources. But then you zap me with an offer of economic aid, which I have not requested. Sure, Malagua can use the money, but that's not the point. What you're trying to do is please all your clients, and that's plain impossible. You undermine me by refusing me arms and you leak the story to make the Administration look good with the liberals, which does me double damage at home. The Frente and the EGP are the political beneficiaries of what you've just done. The economic aid—which I, of course, intend to accept—is a sop to me and my friends on Capitol Hill. To show that the mighty United States is not letting down its friends in Latin America. It's all nonsense, but there's not much I can do about it.''

"Ah, Mr. President, there's another element involved, which was not in the newspaper story," Julia said uncomfortably. "I am instructed to advise you that the Embassy in Malagua has been authorized to establish political contacts with moderates in the opposition groups.''

Throwing his cigar into an ashtray, Ferrer jumped out of his chair and paced up and down the room.

"How can the United States stab me in the back like this?" he shouted. "*Everybody* in Malagua will instantly know that the Americans are talking to my enemies. Don't you understand that you, the United States, are helping the Communists to finish me off, bit by bit?''

"I'm sorry, Mr. President, but these are my instructions," Julia replied stiffly.

"And I suppose that if I were to take a formal stand against these contacts, as you call them, I can say goodbye to the forty million bucks?''

"I'm afraid, sir, that you will have to draw your own conclusions in this situation—and I'm sure that you can do so," Julia said. She got up, and they shook hands.

★

Malagua's two daily newspapers, including *Clarín,* once edited by Nestor Cruz, splashed the news of the forty-million-dollar United States grant on their front pages. Both papers, *Clarín* now being run by a more docile editor, published in virtually the same words the announcement prepared the previous evening at the National Palace, although the Government Press Office had counseled them to make the stories appear as if they had been written by staff reporters.

American assistance, the articles said, was being provided in recognition of President Ferrer's untiring efforts to improve the living standards of Malaguans, demonstrating once more the confidence of the United States in the leadership of the Benefactor, the deep friendship between the two governments, and their unity of purpose in the struggle against international Communism. The National Assembly would meet within a short time to debate the American offer, according to constitutional provisions. Large photographs of General Ferrer in uniform and the President of the United States were printed alongside the articles. There were no references to the refusal of military aid and none to the lifting of the ban on contacts between the American Embassy and the opposition.

Rolando Asturias was staying in the Barrio del Sur house of José Manuel Limosna, a carpenter, poet, and Frente organizer. This was his second day in the capital, and he had already held several clandestine meetings with students whom he knew to be experienced urban guerrilla fighters. Although the full Directorate still had to ratify "Plan Zero," he was picking potential recruits for the operation, telling them only that a major action would soon be taken. Rolando hoped that the Frente command could meet before the end of the week: today was Wednesday.

He had finished his morning coffee when José Manuel Limosna, the owner of the house where he was staying, walked in with a copy of *Clarín*. "Look at this, *compañero*," he said in disgust, throwing the newspaper on the table, "just look at it. . . . *¡Gran carajo!* . . ."

Rolando scanned the page, his face turning red with outrage. "My God," he told José Manuel, "those Americans are demented! It is criminal to be giving money to Ferrer at this point. It will only prolong the war, because he will find a way to switch the funds around to buy more arms. So more of our country's people will die. We've got to do something about it—and quick."

"Sure," Limosna said. "I always told you the *yanquis* were good for nothing. That's what José Martí and Fidel Castro said in Cuba, sixty years apart. That's what our own Máximo Landino, may he rest in peace, said before they murdered him. Why, you even get this impression from reading Walt Whitman and Ralph Waldo Emerson."

Indeed they are good for nothing, Rolando Asturias thought. He had lived and studied among them; he had liked, respected, and even admired them; and in revolutionary Malagua, he had allowed himself to pin his hopes on them. But the Americans had once more betrayed Malagua. Julia was the American Ambassador, and therefore she had to share in the guilt, the treason. She must have been an accomplice to this latest crime. Everybody knew how the Yankees worked: they sweet-talked you about human rights—and Julia had done her part with the intellectuals in Malagua—but at the moment of truth, it was the cold steel of the sword between one's shoulders. And they were all in it together. *His* Julia too. God damn her to hell, Rolando said under his breath.

Now his anger left him. This was a time for cool deliberation, and the immediate task was counteraction to the American move. Rolando poured himself more bitter black coffee, pondering the options. But there was only one: the launching of "Plan Zero" as soon as possible. That was it, he decided. He would recommend immediate action to the Frente's Directorate, emphasizing that it would show both Ferrer and the Americans that the war was now really on. The effect of "Plan Zero" on Máximo Landino and the EGP had become secondary.

There was a knock on the door, and Rolando's hand went under the table to the revolver in his waistband. José Manuel stiffened and asked, *¿Quién es?* A young voice answered, *"Soy yo—Andrés."* The two men relaxed as a chunky youth, his face creased with concern, entered the parlor. Andrés had been Rolando's favorite student at the University, a twenty-year-old who knew the subtleties of the thought of St. Thomas Aquinas as well as the complexities of a G-3 machine pistol. They embraced cordially.

"Padre, you have read the newspaper today?" Andrés asked.

"I certainly have," Rolando replied. "I guess we should have expected it."

"Yes, but do you know about the rest of it? That the Americans have refused to give Ferrer arms?"

"What are you talking about, Andrés?"

"Well, that's what some of us heard last night on the radio, on the Spanish service of the Voice of America, quoting from some newspaper in Washington. That economic aid, yes, but arms, no. . . ."

"I don't believe a word of it," Rolando told the boy. "It doesn't make sense. It's just more Yankee propaganda—very clever propaganda—to give us a false sense of security. I'll bet you that American arms are flying to Malagua this very moment."

★

A muggy, misty dawn hung heavily over the Chilean Air Force base outside Santiago on this Wednesday when a propeller-driven DC-7 transport plane with the markings of Andean Air Services—AAS—roared down the runway. The craft was so heavily laden that the pilot lifted it off the ground with only a hundred feet of concrete to spare; he then headed straight out over the Pacific before executing a slow turn to the right to set his course. To the man at the controls, a pilot named Murphy, it was a routine takeoff: he had done it a thousand times or more, often in the midst of enemy fire from below, from more lousy airstrips in Vietnam and Laos than he cared to remember, when he had flown rickety Air America planes belonging to the CIA's secret aerial fleet in Southeast Asia. Murphy had gotten out of Vietnam just before Saigon fell in 1975, and he had spent the next few years doing odd flying jobs for the CIA wherever he was needed around the world. A year ago, the Agency had ordered him to set up housekeeping in Asunción, Paraguay, the headquarters of the newly organized Andean Air Services, a cargo airline consisting of three DC-7s that somehow were never available for normal commercial charter. And under the Stroessner dictatorship in Paraguay nobody asked too many questions about AAS. Most of Murphy's flights were between Asunción and Santiago, though occasionally he went to fields in the interior of Argentina, and a few times, to Panama.

This time, his orders were to fly the DC-7 to the U.S. Air Force Base in the old Panama Canal Zone, where he would refuel and receive further instructions. It was a rush job. Murphy had been told Monday night by the Station Chief in Asunción to take off for Santiago to load cargo, and be ready to fly again within twenty-four hours. At the Chilean Air Force base, Chilean Army trucks began bringing big wooden crates late Tuesday morning, and the loading of the aircraft was completed shortly after midnight under the supervision of three American civilians who did not identify themselves to the pilot. One of them told Murphy to gas up for a flight to Panama—there were to be no intermediate stops—and handed him a manifest describing the cargo as machine tools. Murphy was not interested in what the crates contained, nor did he know that for years, since the 1973 Army coup encouraged by the CIA, the Chilean military régime had been the Agency's most important foreign source of weapons for clandestine operations from Central America to Afghanistan.

At 5:10 A.M. on Wednesday, Murphy and his copilot, another Indochina veteran, were in the air, flying north along the Pacific coast of South America. Shortly before 2 P.M., a bit behind schedule because of strong headwinds, Murphy told the copilot to commence the descent. A few minutes later, he cranked up the radio frequency of the U.S. Air Force base in Panama, identifying himself as "Andean Air Services Flight Oh-Oh-One" and requesting landing instructions. The tower ordered him to park on a service runway, far from the main military terminal.

As Murphy cut the engines, a jeep driven by a young man in a blue *guayabera* shirt pulled alongside the DC-7, motioning to the pilot to step down. "You are to refuel and take off as quickly as you can," the man told him. "You need not carry too much gas on this leg, because your destination is Ciudad Malagua. You are to land at the Air Force base there. . . . Here's their radio frequency. They're expecting you."

★

Also on Wednesday morning, two twin-engine DC-3s left Harry S. Truman Airport in St. Thomas on a direct flight to Ciudad Malagua. The aircraft, part of the CIA's Caribbean air fleet, had been loaded the previous night. Because of the dangerously short runway in St. Thomas and the need to carry extra fuel for the crossing, the planes' heavy cargo had to be severely limited in volume—but not in quality.

Riordan Jordan, the chief of the CIA's St. Thomas base, knew exactly what to do when Jim Morgan called him on a secure radio circuit from the Ciudad Malagua Station to say that "Type A" military equipment had to be airlifted instantly to "my customers here." The St. Thomas base had a small arsenal of sophisticated hardware for its own operations, and Morgan told Jordan, "I want you to fill two planes with the best stuff you have on hand. I'll have it replaced real soon."

Jordan pulled together a half-dozen flamethrowers, several racks of small fragmentation bombs, ten crates of Israeli-made Uzi submachine guns and ammunition, six mortars, and twenty-five sets of special high-frequency field radio transceivers. The last were intended to ensure that the rebels in Malagua could not intercept National Guard radio traffic. The Major supervised the loading of the two DC-3s at the far end of the airport, telling the crews to race over the Caribbean to Malagua "as fast as you can" and turn around immediately.

★

Julia Savage, having also read the articles in the Malagua newspapers, spent much of Wednesday morning thinking how she could get in touch with Rolando Asturias. She had been shocked by the stories in the local press: to the uninitiated reader it looked as if the economic aid was unqualified United States endorsement of the Ferrer régime. The General had proved again that he was a masterly politician.

The problem now, as Julia saw it, was not only to convince Rolando Asturias and the Frente that American intentions were honorable—and that, indeed, a major breakthrough had been achieved by the refusal to give Ferrer arms and the decision to open official contacts with the opposition—but to make this point with the moderates as well. She had grudgingly accepted the economic-assistance gesture as a necessary bargaining chip with the General, but he had turned the tables on her by distorting the story in the newspapers he controlled. And Julia had to recognize that, given traditional Malaguan suspiciousness of the United States, most people would not put much stock in the leaked story that there would be no more American arms for the dictator. They were too skeptical for that.

In fact, Julia faced problems both with the opposition and with Ferrer. There was nothing she could do right now about Juan Ferrer, but she had to move quickly to establish her, and America's, *bona fides* with the opposition. And in the back of Julia's mind there was still the gnawing suspicion that she did not know everything that was going on. Summoning Rick Anders, the Political Counselor, Julia asked him to see Manuel Schneider at his office to arrange a meeting at the Embassy at his earliest convenience. Schneider, representing the moderate opposition in the Malagua business community, had to be brought into the picture without delay if Julia was to straighten out the political mess on her hands. He could be very useful in spreading the word that the United States had *really* turned down Ferrer's request for arms.

She again thought of Asturias, and she was fleetingly amused by the irony that new political requirements had created the necessity for them to meet again. But without Luis Merino she had no way of reaching Rolando. And their relationship had to be kept absolutely confidential. Suddenly, a possible solution occurred to her.

She walked over to McVeigh's office next door and said, "Do you remember that Peace Corps kid, Tom Flores? Okay, Mac, do me a favor. Arrange discreetly for Tom to come by the Residence this evening. He's not to mention it to anybody. And for now, please ask me no questions."

★

Enrique Palma Rioseco had arrived in Ciudad Malagua the day before to make his periodic visit to Comercio Internacional S.A. Although his blackmail attempt against Julia Savage had failed, there had been no disastrous repercussions. He had not heard from Jim Morgan since that night, and there had been no interference with his business. Pleasantly relieved that the Station Chief had not punished him for his failure, Enrique concentrated on his affairs. Having arranged a large cocaine shipment north from Cali, he flew to Malagua to pick up several million dollars from Dr. Lobo. Afterward, he telephoned Morgan from his hotel suite: it seemed like a good idea to mend his fences with the CIA.

"Hey, Jim," he said brightly. "I'm in town for a few days. Should we get together for a drink or something?"

"Nope," Morgan replied. "No need for that."

"Is there anything special you want me to do for you?" the Colombian asked.

There was a moment of silence, and then Morgan said, "Yes. There is. I want you to fly to St. Thomas as soon as you've finished your business here. Check in at the usual place, and somebody will be over to see you."

The line went dead as Enrique Palma stood with the mute receiver in his hand. Colonel Duke had told Morgan about the President's orders to keep secret Julia Savage's Weatherman involvement, and the two men had decided that Enrique had become a serious liability. *Latinos,* Duke had observed, can never be trusted to keep their mouths shut.

★

Late on Wednesday afternoon, Rolando Asturias left the house in Barrio del Sur for the Ubique highlands. He expected to find Tomás Martínez in the area, and he had sent couriers to the other members of the Frente's Directorate, in the capital and outside, urging an emergency conference in the next forty-eight hours. He planned to return to Ciudad Malagua for the meeting following talks with Martínez and his guerrilla leaders.

Dark clouds, the last vestiges of the rainy season, hovered over the city as Rolando walked through the *barrio*. Making a turn on the unpaved road, he came upon a group of people, perhaps fifty persons, at the edge of a vacant lot. They were quiet and solemn. Rolando slowed his pace, peering past the small crowd. He saw two men with shovels digging a grave, a large one. In the center of the lot lay six headless corpses, horribly mutilated. The Jesuit asked a man, hunched in his *poncho,* what had happened.

"Eh, *compadre,*" the man said, "this is a funeral without a priest. What you see is what remains of six very young *muchachos*. I don't know who they are, but a half-hour ago a truck of the National Guard dumped them here. Just like that, you see."

At that moment, a bolt of lightning tore the skies, eerily illuminating the fresh graveyard. Thunder rolled over the *barrio*. Rolando Asturias made the sign of the cross, not aware of what he was doing. An old woman, her head covered with a black kerchief, said, "In this land, it is a crime to be young."

17

Tom Flores was ushered into the Residence living room by Dudley as dusk was falling over Ciudad Malagua, the tropical dusk of early spring, quickly enveloping the Mixull volcano and darkening Lake Taxchilán. It was the first Saturday of November, and it was the birth of a new season.

"Tom," Julia Savage said, "I have a confidential mission for you, a mission in the national interest. Do you remember our trip up the hills, past Ubique?"

"No way I could ever forget it," the tall Peace Corps volunteer replied, grinning broadly.

"Okay. Tomorrow morning, drive up there in your Land-Rover, and try to contact Father Asturias, the priest who received us there. Tell him that it's absolutely urgent for him to get in touch with me. I'm sure you can talk your way past the *guerrilleros* there. They must remember you. . . . Now, the message *must* be delivered to Father Asturias personally, and none of his people must know what you have to tell him. If he isn't there, just forget it. Are you willing to do it, Tom? You know, I cannot order you to go there. . . ."

"You got it, Madam Ambassador," Tom said, "I'll be on my way the first thing in the morning. . . . I have brand-new tires on my Rover, so it should be an easy trip up the forest. Do you want me to report to you?''

"Yes, please come here as soon as you get back to town.''

★

Rolando Asturias looked around the kitchen table and said, "Then I take it that we're all in agreement on launching 'Plan Zero' on the day the National Assembly meets to approve the American aid.''

The others nodded and, one after another, said, *"Sí."* They were the Directorate of the *Frente:* Rolando, Tomás Martínez, Dora Merino, Manuel Schneider Belmonte, a young physician named Juan Carlos Reyes, and Hugo Estella, a pockmarked former National Guard major who had been imprisoned for criticizing the Ferrer régime but who had escaped and joined the guerrilla forces. He was the movement's *jefe militar.* Dora Merino had been named to the Directorate shortly before her father's death to represent the University, her predecessor having been killed in a shoot-out with the troops.

The Directorate was meeting that Saturday night in a safe house in the middle-class residential district, not far from the Merino home, to plan strategy for the dry season. "It's got to be now or never,'' Major Estella said as they sat around the large kitchen table.

"Right,'' Tomás said, "and my proposal, shared by *compañero* Rolando, is that the big push should be spearheaded by 'Plan Zero,' with all the other moves coordinated with it.''

The plan was discussed in detail, and Rolando insisted that it be timed to coincide with the National Assembly debate on the American assistance package. "It has to be absolutely clear to Ferrer and the *gringos,* as well as our own people, why this action is taking place,'' he said.

"Okay,'' Major Estella said, "let's do it. I think it's feasible. The next thing is to get it going.''

★

It was after ten o'clock on Sunday night when Tom Flores drove up to the Residence. He had been stopped several times by National Guard patrols, and the repeated questioning and checking of his identity documents had delayed him considerably.

"I'm sorry to be so late and to bring you bad news," he said.

"What happened?" Julia asked.

"Well, Father Asturias wasn't there. He's been gone for quite a few days, except for a quick visit two days ago, and the fellows there had no idea when he would be back or where he could be reached. I didn't want to ask too many questions. . . ."

Julia Savage sank into an armchair. "Oh, Lord," she said, "that *is* bad news."

★

In the bunkerlike command post in the basement of the National Palace, Juan Ferrer pored over a large relief map of Malagua, a gift from the U.S. Army. It was Monday morning. Three National Guard generals stood respectfully behind him. Jim Morgan and the dwarf Fabio leaned against a wall, near the bank of direct-line telephones and new field radio transmitters. Morgan had had the radios delivered and installed in the command post the previous morning.

"Well, *señores,* there are four basic areas of rebel strength that we must smash," Ferrer said, aiming the pointer at the map. "First, we have the northeast mountains where Máximo Landino's EGP is dug in. I have intelligence reports that he has been getting more Cuban arms from Guatemala, and that he may move down from the *sierra* soon as part of a coordinated rebel offensive. A brigade should be deployed immediately around Jacaltec to keep Landino from breaking out onto the *altiplano*. I would suggest some tanks and APCs as a show of force, but motorized infantry plus a howitzer company should be the backbone of the brigade. The infantry should have the flamethrowers we have just gotten from our American friends, and I want them used as soon as the first EGP son-of-a-bitch shows his face."

The General paused to light a cigar, and went on: "But we need some aggressive actions as well. The day after the National Assembly approves the American economic aid—it's meeting on November 11—I want the brigade's G-2 to round up about a hundred rebel sympathizers in Jacaltec. I'm sure G-2 can find enough plausible candidates there, and it would be a good idea to execute a half-dozen for illegal possession of arms, or whatever. The others can be penned up in that big cattle corral. That will cool revolutionary ardor up there, and the EGP may have second thoughts about risking an attack. Finally, let's spread some napalm from the air on Agua Linda and the other villages on the edge of the jungle. Is that clear?"

"*Sí, mi General,*" the Chief of Staff replied, jotting down notes on a pad. "I'll need seventy-two hours to get the brigade re-equipped and on the move to Jacaltec."

"Good," Ferrer said. "The next problem spot is the area around San Pablo and along the coast. G-2 tells me that the Frente has a few hundred well-armed urban guerrillas in the city itself, and that they may pull an uprising to try to take it over. I don't think they can swing it, but let's take no chances. I propose that a Guard battalion from the San Pablo garrison sweep through the poor *barrios* there, blowing up some houses, carrying out a couple of executions, and occupying the districts until we're satisfied the danger of an uprising has passed. The other battalion from San Pablo should run a search-and-destroy operation for, say, a week along the coast and on both sides of the main highway to Ciudad Malagua. Have them use flamethrowers to burn a few villages. The troops will get close ground support from the air; it will be napalm again. Understood?"

The three generals nodded, and Ferrer continued: "Now closer to home. I want two battalions from the capital to seal off the whole region around and above Ubique. The Frente has a respectable force there, but now we have the weapons to liquidate it. Ubique is to be occupied by armor, and infantry is to go up the hills to search and destroy. Of course, I'll provide air support there too. Okay?"

"*Sí, mi General.*"

"And most importantly, we have the question of the capital. I'm talking about the Frente's urban guerrillas. The two foci of infection are Barrio del Sur and the University. The time has come to eradicate them once and for all. Informers tell me that the rebels are contemplating some kind of uprising in Ciudad Malagua, timed with that in San Pablo, and I simply can't tolerate *that*. Therefore they must be disabled. This is how we'll do it: tanks and APCs plus infantry with recoilless rifles and flame-throwers are to occupy the entire Barrio del Sur. At the first sign of resistance—even a single sniper shot—armor and recoilless rifles are to fire point-blank at *barrio* houses, to destroy them. Flamethrowers will do well against wooden structures. And the troops are not to be afraid of killing people. The University is fairly easy to handle now that classes have been suspended for the balance of the year. A few tanks and armored cars on the campus will do just fine with the additional deployment of a few Guard companies and riot police."

Juan Ferrer looked at his digital wristwatch. "All this, natu-rally, is to be a coordinated offensive, to begin in all these areas at precisely 0500 hours on November 12. You have your orders, *señores*. And let's make sure all the commanders understand their missions."

The generals saluted and left the command post. Ferrer turned to Jim Morgan and Fabio, motioning to them to stay behind.

"There's one more thing that's necessary to make our plan work," he said. "I have decided that all the Jesuits are to be expelled from the territory of the Republic at once. They're a subversive lot and have been helping and advising the rebels. I know the Nuncio and the Vatican will raise hell with me, but it's got to be done before the offensive starts. Fabio, you're in charge of having G-2 locate all the Jesuits in the city and elsewhere and putting them on the first plane out. For the hell of it, let's send them to Mexico."

Ferrer laughed harshly and pointed his finger at Morgan.

"Hey, Jim, I'm afraid I have a problem with one of your Em-bassy people—or to be more precise, with a Peace Corps fellow. G-2 reported to me early today that a Peace Corps type—his name, I think, is Tom Flores—had been driving all day yesterday in the area of Ubique. I don't like it. A pro-Communist Jesuit, a Father Rolando Asturias, has a parish up in the hills above Ubique, and I have a feeling he's in cahoots with the Frente guerrillas. He's one of the Jesuits I definitely want out of circulation, but I'd like to know whether he's also involved with those crazy Peace Corps kids you've sent us here. You know, Jim, all of them are Marxists. Can you do something about it?"

Morgan had been listening intently, and now he cocked his head. "That's very interesting," he said slowly. "Flores turned up at our Residence late last night and spent a few minutes with the Ambassador. My sources inside the Residence couldn't hear what was being discussed. But you're damned right, General, I'm sure going to look into the Flores business. I'll let you know what I come up with."

"Do you suppose there's some kind of connection between the Savage woman and Flores and the priest Asturias?" Ferrer asked.

"I don't know," Morgan said. "I wouldn't put anything past her."

Ferrer turned to Fabio. "Listen, if you find this Father Asturias, don't waste time deporting him. Just have him shot through the head. We can blame ORDEN vigilantes. They don't like the Jesuits either."

★

John Crespo walked into Julia Savage's outer office, asking Ann Mestre if he could see the Ambassador right away, and apologizing for not calling ahead. Ann told him to go in: she was reading her mail and could be interrupted.

Crespo had made the decision to take matters into his own hands. He knew he was violating Agency regulations, but it was a matter of principle that, in his mind, overrode CIA loyalty and discipline. He belonged to the younger Agency generation, still in college at the time of Vietnam, and he was very much his own man. He had joined the CIA in the early 1970s, after graduating from a small college in California where he had majored in history and Latin American studies. In post-Vietnam years, the CIA was condemned by many young people, but John Crespo had concluded that it was the right place for him. His main interest was in analyzing and interpreting data, and he believed that foreign policy could probably be influenced better in this fashion from Langley than from anywhere else in the government.

The Agency, however, had other plans for him. Short on experienced personnel after the in-house purges of the Seventies, it considered that men like him were more needed in the field than in an analyst's cubicle at Headquarters. His command of Spanish was a factor in this decision. Crespo was sent to Mexico City for two years, to work with the Regional Command, then spent a year in Uruguay and a year in Panama, attached to the local stations. He showed promise, and when the deputy spot opened in Malagua, the WH Division assigned him there. Morgan posed no objections, believing that one deputy was as good, or as bad, as another. The Malagua operation, after all, was firmly in his hands. He never sought Crespo's opinions on political matters, and kept him informed of operations only to the extent the deputy had the "need to know" about them. Thus Crespo had the operational need to know about the arrival of arms from Santiago and St. Thomas because the CIA pilots had to be met and briefed.

Crespo had been at Ciudad Malagua's air base for nearly twenty-four hours the previous week, handling the planes. The more he thought about the implications of the secret CIA deliveries of arms to the Ferrer régime, the more disturbed he had become. His political sense had been critically aroused when Morgan warned him that nobody in the Embassy, specifically including the Ambassador, was to know of the shipments. This procedure was wrong, Crespo told himself. The Ambassador must not be sabotaged.

Now he faced Julia across her desk, saying, "Ambassador, as a matter of conscience, I have no choice but to violate Agency orders and inform you of something of utmost gravity. I assume, of course, that you will protect me as the source of this information."

"Naturally, John," Julia replied, taken aback by Crespo's visit.

"It is my view, Ambassador, that you should know that the CIA has been secretly delivering arms to the National Guard on orders from Washington."

"Are you sure?" she asked incredulously.

"Yes," Crespo said. "Last week, a cargo was flown in from Santiago, Chile, by way of Panama, and another from St. Thomas, in the Virgin Islands. There's some very sophisticated stuff in these shipments, and conceivably it could make the whole difference in the outcome in Malagua. Furthermore, it is my understanding that a high-level decision was made in Washington to prevent you from knowing about it. The reason I'm telling you all this, Ambassador, is that in my judgment it is dangerous, and not in the national interest, for you to be kept in the dark any longer."

★

She was furious. It wasn't possible that the CIA was again operating on its own. Julia knew from her White House days that the Agency *never* undertook a major covert operation without a Presidential sign-off. So Tom Morelli, her friend, had to be part of this decision in his capacity of National Security Adviser. It hurt that even Tom did not trust her enough to tell her the truth.

Okay, Julia told herself as she chain-smoked at her desk. She'd been had, she had been betrayed, she had been treated as no ambassador should be treated by his or her government. But fuming and feeling sorry for herself was not a practical way to deal with this problem. If Washington wanted to play its games with her, she would play her own game. Thus her first conclusion, after the first wave of her fury was spent, was to keep Crespo's information to herself. There was no sense in telling Washington what she had learned about the arms.

It was clear there was no point in attempting negotiations with Ferrer over power transition. The Administration had completely undercut her and had given him the upper hand. The General,

Julia reasoned, must have been informed of her ignorance of the arms transfers, which made conversations between them useless, at least for the time being. So let him enjoy what he thinks is his advantage, she decided.

The burning problem for Julia at this juncture was the anti-Ferrer opposition. If Ferrer had received sophisticated arms, he would immediately start equipping his forces with them. The opposition leaders would know of this development within days, and their deep distrust of the United States would be vindicated. Why had the people in Washington failed to anticipate it? Or was it that in the long run, they did not really care, because the actual policy was to keep Juan Ferrer in power at all costs? But the Administration's actions, she thought, would cause what was most feared: "another Cuba."

Julia had become convinced that the end of the Ferrer era was simply a question of time—she did not think that even the new CIA weapons would alter the course of Malaguan history—and that therefore the United States must not be cut off from the people who might well be the country's next rulers. If Washington did not understand it, then it was up to her, as Ambassador in place, to avert a disaster. It was absolutely essential to re-establish contact with the opposition. But her effort to find Manuel Schneider the previous week had failed: Rick Anders, who had called him to invite him to the Embassy, was told that the businessman was traveling for an indefinite period. And she was too realistic to expect Asturias to seek her out after the economic-aid announcement. God only knows, she said to herself, how he will react when he finds out about the new arms. All Julia Savage could do now was sit tight—and quietly curse Washington for its stupidity and duplicity.

★

Jim Morgan sat at home, drink in hand, pondering the situation involving Julia Savage and Tom Flores. His source at the Residence was a maid named Ramona whom he paid to keep him posted about visitors. Ramona was bright and alert, and when she did not know a person's name, she could describe the visitor well enough to give Morgan a fairly good notion of his or her identity.

Morgan remembered Ramona's saying that a tall priest had visited on the day of the shooting at the Cathedral, and he was annoyed with himself for not having given sufficient attention to this report. Now he wondered if that visiting priest had been Rolando Asturias. On his return from the National Palace, he had looked up the CIA file on Asturias, and the Jesuit, he concluded, certainly fitted the image of a Marxist priest.

From now on, Morgan decided as he poured himself another drink, Julia Savage and Tom Flores would be watched very carefully by the Station and its local agents. It would be a high-priority item for the Station: close surveillance of the Ambassador and the Peace Corps kid might lead to some interesting discoveries —such as a link between Julia Savage and the rebels. And thinking about Julia reminded Morgan of another priority item: Enrique Palma Rioseco. He picked up the telephone and put in a call to Riordan Jordan at the St. Thomas base.

"Riordan," he said, "how's the boy? . . . Listen, I told my traveling friend the other day to turn up at the usual place on your island. Have you heard from him? Good. . . . The thing is that I don't need him anymore. . . . Okay?"

"Yep," Jordan said. "I get you. We'll take care of it."

★

The St. Thomas *Daily News* is a tabloid newspaper which gives prominent coverage to local crime. Early in November, a front-page story under the headline MYSTERIOUS MURDER reported:

> The naked body of an unidentified white male was found yesterday afternoon by local residents near a garbage dump off the main road on Crown Mountain. . . . The body had been savagely cut up with what was believed to be a machete, and the parts were stuffed inside three plastic trash bags. . . . The authorities suspect that the victim may have been involved in the traffic of narcotics on the island. . . . The Governor's Office has issued a statement deploring this latest crime in the Virgin Islands, warning that this type of violence may gravely affect the tourist industry and the economic welfare of our Territory. . . .

Riordan Jordan clipped the story and mailed it to Morgan in a plain envelope.

★

Guests at the Malagua Inter-Continental Hotel on Lake Taxchilán—businessmen visiting the capital for a day or two, as well as American tourists stopping en route to Mayan temples and old colonial landmarks—filled the wide lobby late in the afternoon as the November sun was beginning to set over the Pacific. Most of the guest traffic was in and out of the hotel's three bars, where bartenders mixed rum drinks and musicians in Malaguan costumes strummed guitars and sang *malagueñas*. Suddenly there were bursts of gunfire outside, and a youth in jeans and a sport shirt rushed into the lobby through the open archway from the front garden, pursued by National Guardsmen.

Blood was streaming from his side as he ran in a zigzag through the lobby. The boy, not older than seventeen, began to falter, finally sinking to his knees at the entrance to the Papagayo Bar. The helmeted Guardsmen formed a circle around the fallen youth, their Thompsons pointed at him. Holding his side with his hands, the boy looked up defiantly at the soldiers. The commanding officer took a step forward, aimed his .45 Colt at the boy's head, and fired a single shot.

"My *God,* how could you?" an American woman screamed at the officer.

"Madam, this was for *your* protection," the handsome young officer replied in English with a courtly bow, replacing his gun in its holster. "He was a Communist terrorist, and the government of Malagua feels responsible for the safety of its foreign guests." He turned to the soldiers. *"Vamos, muchachos. . . ."*

★

The boy executed in the lobby of the Malagua Inter-Continental was a student at the National University, and his name was Eugenio Menéndez. He had belonged to the Frente for nearly a year and was a specialist in urban guerrilla activities, having learned a great deal about military matters from his father, a colonel in the National Guard and a Ferrer favorite. In Malagua, as in much of Latin America, the young rebels were often the children of the ruling elite.

Eugenio was among the students who had met with Rolando Asturias in the Barrio del Sur house, and one of those who had been ordered to be on standby for a special operation in the city. On the morning of the day he would die, Eugenio had received word to go to an address in downtown Ciudad Malagua, arriving there exactly at 6:15 P.M. Leaving his own home shortly before five o'clock, Eugenio had taken a bus to the Malagua Inter-Continental, from where he had planned to take another bus to his ultimate destination, the Frente practice being to move in circuitous fashion when on a mission in order to deflect possible surveillance. The only mistake he made was to carry a .22 pistol; the rule was that weapons were to be worn only when specifically ordered. When he alighted from the bus, he was stopped by a Guard patrol near the hotel. It was a routine check of identity papers to which young people in Ciudad Malagua were subjected more and more often. The lieutenant returned his *cédula,* finding it in order, but as an afterthought, started to frisk Eugenio for concealed weapons. The boy broke and ran, his .22 dropping to the ground. A bullet from a Guardsman's gun hit him in the left side, below the heart.

★

Fifteen fighters had been chosen to report that day to the old gray brick house on a narrow street behind Avenida Bolívar. Like Eugenio Menéndez, they were hand-picked for "Plan Zero." The house belonged to the Schneider family, and the previous week Manuel Schneider had informed the tenants that he was selling the property, and asked them to leave within forty-eight hours. He paid them a sum equivalent to six months' rent to expedite matters, and the police showed no particular interest when they left so abruptly. Everybody knew it was a Schneider house; no questions were asked.

Comandante Pablo, the Indian-featured guerrilla chief from Santa Teresa del Monte; Dora Merino; and a student leader from the University, a tennis player with a playboy reputation named Roberto Maxwell, had been designated by Major Estella as squad commanders for "Plan Zero." Pablo was in overall charge. Two days after the meeting of the Frente's Directorate, Major Estella and Dora Merino summoned Pablo and Roberto Maxwell to the carpenter's house in Barrio del Sur to brief them on the operation. Maxwell's reaction was joyful disbelief: ¡Qué fantástico! he kept repeating. Pablo said nothing, listening to the details and memorizing them.

"The three of you are to arrive at the Schneider house tomorrow afternoon at half-hour intervals, to avoid suspicion," Major Estella told them. "The door will be unlocked. Fifteen compañeros have been chosen for the mission, in addition to yourselves, and the team will be divided into three squads. Pablo, Dora, and Roberto will each lead a squad, though Pablo will coordinate all the moves. The compañeros will start arriving day after tomorrow, one every forty-five minutes until nightfall. None of them is to be told anything about the nature of the operation until three hours before it starts. Now, let's see: today is November 5. D-Day is to be November 11. So you will have four full days at the house, with everybody present, for silent weapon and hand-to-hand combat practice—and for getting to know each other as well as possible. This is very important if you are to operate as an efficient team. Supplies and equipment will be delivered to the house on a staggered schedule over the four days."

Pablo was the first to reach the Schneider house late on November 6. He was followed by Dora and then Roberto Maxwell. During November 7, fourteen young Frente fighters joined them, nine men and five women. At eight o'clock, Pablo said, "We're missing a man—Eugenio Menéndez."

When Eugenio failed to turn up the next day, Pablo told Dora and Roberto that "it looks as if we'll have to do with a total of seventeen instead of eighteen." The procedures established for "Plan Zero" prohibited any communication between the Schneider house and the outside; thus no request could be made for a replacement. "Anyway," Dora said, "if something happened to

Eugenio, the Directorate will have learned about it soon enough.''

By the evening of November 10, the three leaders decided that the team was in excellent shape. Weapons had been brought to the house on November 8, in a moving van in crates mixed with furniture and books. If an outsider were watching the house, it would look simply as if the new owners—a dummy company set up by Manuel Schneider—were moving in. Meanwhile, training in the handling of G-3 submachine guns, hand grenades, side arms, and knives satisfied the commanders that the team was combat-ready, though the weapons could not be fired inside the house. The women were as dexterous with the weapons as the men, and morale was superb. Though the fourteen fighters were eager to know the character and the timing of their mission, none of them asked questions. Because of Eugenio's absence, Roberto's squad had been reduced to five, including him, but this did not dampen the enthusiasm.

And time passed quickly. Military and physical exercises took up six hours a day. Three hours were devoted to political discussions, usually led by Dora, about the future of Malagua after the fall of the *tirano*. Then there was time for meals, cleaning up, and leisure hours for reading or card-playing. Three rebels were on guard duty around the clock in four-hour shifts, so sleeping time had to be rotated. The three commanders were the only ones authorized to listen to the radio: isolated as they were in the Schneider house, news broadcasts were their only link with the outside world. The important thing was not to be caught by surprise by an unexpected political or military event. Juan Ferrer was capable of anything.

★

At the Embassy staff meeting on November 10, Colonel Brown, the Defense Attaché, informed Julia Savage that there were strong indications of active preparations by the National Guard for a concerted offensive against the rebels in the coming days.

"The word I get," he said, "is that Guard units are being

shifted in a combat mode everywhere—from the capital to San Pablo. All leaves have been cancelled as of three days ago. I don't know what exactly the General has in mind, but it looks big. Very big. I also hear that the jump-off may be day after tomorrow, the day after the National Assembly acts on our economic-aid offer. My guys say that the National Guard has been getting some new equipment—good equipment."

"Oh, really?" Julia asked in a surprised voice. "Where do you suppose they have obtained it, now that the United States has turned down President Ferrer's request for arms?"

"Beats me, Ambassador," the Colonel replied. "Wherever they got it, it sure came here in no time flat. The officers themselves, even on staff level, don't seem to know. But they're very pleased, and they're bragging that now they can smash the rebels to bits."

"Well, that's certainly fascinating," Julia said. "We ought to find out more about it. Washington will be very interested. Ah, Mr. Morgan, can you tell us anything on this subject?"

"Not really," the Station Chief told her. "I hear pretty much the same thing as the Colonel here does, but not much more."

"My, my, and I thought we had a first-rate intelligence operation in this town," Julia remarked to nobody in particular. "I wonder what happened to it."

Jim Morgan lit a fresh cigar, staring at the ceiling with unconcealed boredom.

★

Back in her office, Julia asked Ann Mestre to take dictation. "I have a very special telegram I'd like to get off right away," she said, "and I want everybody in the government to read it." A half-hour later, Ann returned with the typed telegram for Julia's signature. It read:

ACTION 10-16
Fm AmEmb Malagua
To SecState WashDC Immediate 7134
   1. Embassy is informed National Guard plans series of

coordinated attacks countrywide against anti-GoM rebels starting 12 November. Information comes from Embassy/DAO sources and is regarded as highly credible.

2. Indications are President Ferrer hopes to destroy military potential of rebel movement as a result of planned operations. However Embassy is unable to predict outcome.

3. DAO sources report National Guard has been reequipped with modern arms in recent days although origin cannot be ascertained at this time. Embassy is marshaling all resources to establish origin, volume and type of arms, and hopes to report as soon as possible.

4. Embassy would appreciate any DOS assistance via third countries in determining origin of arms supplied to National Guard.

5. National Assembly meets at noon tomorrow—11 November—to approve US Gov economic assistance package. Ambassador plans attend sessions. Ends.

SAVAGE

18

A T nine o'clock on the morning of November 11, a Friday, the telephone rang at the Schneider house. It was a prearranged call, the only one received during the stay of the assault team. When Dora Merino picked up the receiver, an old woman's voice said, "This is your aunt Clarita. I would very much like to have the children come to lunch at noon today as we discussed it the other day, my dear. And to make it easier, I shall send transportation for you all. *Hasta luego.*"

Dora hung up, and turned to Pablo and Roberto Maxwell. "This is it," she said: "it's at noon today. God, I was so scared that something would go wrong, that they would cancel or postpone it. So we have two hours to get ready."

Roberto was all excitement. "*¡Fantástico!*" he shouted. "*¡Fantástico!* I just hope the old bastard will be there."

Pablo cut in: "Let's get the troops together in the downstairs living room. The mission has to be explained to them."

★

At ten o'clock, Juan Ferrer, in field uniform, strode into the command post in the basement of the National Palace, followed by Jim Morgan and Fabio. General Amador Mujica, the National Guard's chief of staff; the acting chief of G-2; and all the brigade commanders were already assembled in the bunker. They stood at attention to receive the President.

"*Bueno,*" Ferrer said. "Is everything ready?"

"*Sí, mi General,*" the chief of staff answered stiffly. "The Guard is ready to go into action at 0500 hours tomorrow in all the sectors. The new equipment has been issued to the units, and the troops have been confined to barracks. The Third Brigade under General Roberto Bauch-Barriga, with tanks and APCs, is in a staging area about fifty kilometers from Jacaltec, and it will begin advancing at midnight. The Air Force is standing by for support missions."

"Well, gentlemen, this is a historic moment," Juan Ferrer declared. "*Por Dios y Patria* . . . for God and the Nation, we shall conquer—for here we are kings." He looked at Morgan and repeated: "*Aquí somos reyes*—right, Jim?"

"Yes, sir," Morgan agreed.

"And by the way, have you come up with anything on your Ambassador and the Peace Corps kid?"

"No, not yet, but I'm working on it."

"I hope you're doing better than my friend Fabio here. He hasn't been able to find this priest Asturias I want liquidated. I'm absolutely sure that there is a connection between Savage and the Marxist priest. My instincts are never wrong. I'd like to declare her *persona non grata,* but it's probably the wrong time to antagonize your President. Anyway, Jim, do you want to join me upstairs to watch the National Assembly session on television? It starts at noon, and Fabio can fix us a couple of drinks to celebrate."

★

At eleven o'clock, Julia Savage asked Ann Mestre to have Salvador get the car ready to take her to the National Assembly.

"Since the business of the day is to approve our aid package," she said, "I'd better be there on time. If I don't keep my eye on them, they're liable to run away with it and approve twice the amount we're offering them."

"Julia, don't forget that you have a luncheon at two o'clock with the Minister of Agriculture, what's-his-name, at the Residence."

"Don't worry, I won't forget. This thing at the Assembly can't take more than an hour. How many speeches can they make to say that they're accepting our dough? Besides, the Minister will be there."

★

At ten minutes past eleven, Rolando Asturias, Major Estella, and Manuel Schneider went down to the cellar of the house of José Manuel Limosna, the poet-carpenter, in Barrio del Sur. The cellar, with a radio/transmitter receiver set, was the command post for "Plan Zero." Tomás Martínez and Juan Carlos Reyes, the physician, were in the basement of a villa on Lake Taxchilán, manning the backup command post with their two-way radio. Dora Merino, the sixth member of the Frente Directorate, was with the team at the midtown house, with the third radio set. All three portable sets were on a high VHF frequency, and special codes had been devised for secure communications in emergencies.

"Less than an hour to go," Major Estella said. "The vehicles should be on their way."

"God willing," Rolando Asturias replied.

★

At 11:35 A.M., two olive-drab panel trucks with the markings of the National Guard turned right from Avenida Bolívar onto Calle Bilbao and then made another right turn into the narrow Alameda San Bernardo. They stopped at Number 24, the Schneider house, and the uniformed driver of the first truck sounded his horn twice. Dora Merino came out of the house, looking up and down the Alameda. It was empty, and Dora whistled softly. Comandante Pablo and seven hunched figures, each carrying a package wrapped in heavy brown paper, ran out and climbed into the back of the first truck. Dora was the last to jump in, slamming the door shut. Simultaneously, Roberto Maxwell and seven others got into the second truck. The two vehicles pulled away at once from the gray house.

It was now 11:43 A.M., and the panel trucks made their way back to Avenida Bolívar, joining the flow of late-morning traffic. Inside the two trucks, the men and women hastily donned the National Guard uniforms and combat boots that had been stacked on the floor, Comandante Pablo, Dora Merino, and Roberto Maxwell putting on blouses with officers' insignia. The brown-paper parcels were opened, and G-3 submachine guns, ammunition belts, clips, pistols, hand grenades, and knives were passed around. Within eight minutes, each of the rebels was fully armed and uniformed. They could not have risked donning the uniforms while still in the house: there was always the danger of a sudden police or G-2 raid.

Pablo checked his wristwatch. "We are allowing between twelve and fifteen minutes to reach our objective in this traffic," he said. "That means we'll be disembarking between noon and twelve oh eight P.M. We'll need three or four minutes to move into position. The attack must start no later than twelve twelve P.M."

"Correct," Dora answered. "We're exactly on schedule. And I think the most difficult part is behind us. I mean getting into the vehicles without being spotted." Pablo grunted, examining the safety catch on his G-3.

In the second truck, Roberto Maxwell told his group: "You have less than fifteen minutes to prepare yourselves for the biggest adventure of your lives. . . . The most important thing is to avoid confusion. Now, remember that there are eight of us in here, but three of the *compañeros* belong to Squads A and B, which are in the first vehicle. We are Squad C—five of us, including me. Make sure that you join your own squad after we get there. And good luck, *chicos* and *chicas!*" Roberto Maxwell laughed merrily, his blue Irish eyes shining hungrily. The others smiled tensely.

★

The black Chrysler of the American Ambassador stopped at the entrance to the National Assembly at 11:50 A.M., Julia Savage noticing the time on the clock over the broad staircase leading to the gleaming modern building. Gonzalo, her bodyguard, and the security men from the escort cars surrounded her as she mounted the stairs to be greeted by the waiting Chief of Protocol, Señor Moreno. It was hot, but she was comfortable in her dark print cotton dress.

Gonzalo had asked Julia whether he should accompany her inside the Assembly. She said no, it would not look right for the American Ambassador to be attending a ceremonial occasion with an armed man behind her. Gonzalo made a face, and said unhappily, "Don't you remember the Cathedral, Madam Ambassador?" Julia laughed, patting his arm. "Nobody is going to shoot me inside the Assembly. Look at all the cops and soldiers around here."

Rows of National Guard Military Police in white helmets and white gloves, their side arms in white leather holsters, lined the sidewalk in front of the National Assembly, and scores of riot policemen filled the street for a block in each direction. The Assembly building, erected by Juan Ferrer four years earlier as a sign of his dedication to representative democracy—he insisted on quadrennial elections, with hand-picked candidates from the two officially sanctioned political parties—was located at the end of Avenida Ferrer, beyond the embassy residences and the Malagua Inter-Continental. It was set on a large section of choice land between the Avenida and Lake Taxchilán and was surrounded by elaborate gardens. The *malagueños* called it "El Mausoleo."

Señor Moreno kissed Julia's hand and led her to the diplomatic gallery on the second floor of the building. The gallery was above the terraced public seats, overlooking a large hall. The 120 deputies were seated in a well in the front of the hall, opposite the elevated rostrum where the chairman and vice chairmen of the Assembly had their long marble table. A marble-faced lectern from which legislators spoke—they were not allowed to speak from their seats—stood in the center. The Malagua hall resembled the General Assembly Building of the United Nations in New York, and in fact, Juan Ferrer had ordered that its design be based on that building's. The ground floor and the third and fourth floors of the Malaguan Assembly were given over to legislative and executive offices.

In the gallery, Julia greeted the ambassadors from three Central American countries and Paraguay, the only other diplomats on hand. All the deputies were in their places, and the public seats were filled with government employees, who were pressed into service on occasions like this. Television cameras were poised to transmit and record the event. Glancing down idly, Julia calculated that there were already at least seven hundred persons in the hall—and more were arriving.

At noon, the Chairman of the National Assembly, Laureano Vega y Vega, and the two vice chairmen entered the hall, self-important in their dark suits, and the deputies and the public rose to applaud them. The ambassadors in the diplomatic gallery clapped their hands without rising; a television camera caught Julia Savage in a long-shot close-up. Vega y Vega took his seat behind the marble table, gently banging the gavel. The session of the National Assembly of the Republic of Malagua had come to order.

★

At 12:02 P.M., the two olive-drab panel trucks drove along Avenida Ferrer, slowing down as they approached the National Assembly. The first vehicle turned left on the ramp leading to the east side door of the building on the lower level; the second took the ramp for the lower west side entrance. The MPs paid no attention to the Guard trucks.

The first truck stopped a hundred yards from the east door. Comandante Pablo; Dora Merino, her black military beret in place; and the seven other rebels jumped out onto the narrow sidewalk. Pablo barked an order, and the group fell into single file, marching behind him, their G-3s at the ready. Two policemen were guarding the door, submachine guns casually slung over their shoulders. Approaching them, Pablo rasped, "El Jefe is coming," and pushed open the glass door, leading the team inside. Suddenly, one of the policemen became suspicious and started to shift his weapon. Pablo wheeled with the speed of a jaguar and plunged his knife into the man's heart. Andrés, the exemplary philosophy student, simultaneously stuck his knife into the back of the second policeman. The two men sank to the ground soundlessly. *"Adelante,"* Pablo whispered, running up to the inner staircase.

Roberto Maxwell and his seven *guerrilleros* had an even easier time at the west door. There was only one policeman guarding the entrance, and Roberto shot him through the chest with his silencer-equipped .45 Colt. Pablo had stressed that if action was required at lower-level doors, only knives or silencer pistols were to be used. Premature gunfire had to be avoided at all costs, he had repeated over and over during the final briefing session at the Schneider house earlier that day.

The operational blueprint devised by the Frente Directorate for the takeover of the National Assembly—this was "Plan Zero"—called for the two attacking groups to penetrate the building unobtrusively through the side doors, reach the second floor by the inner staircases, and converge from both sides on the rear foyer leading to the diplomatic and public sections of the main hall. Architecture students from the University had provided detailed floor plans of the structure, and they were studied first by the Directorate, then by Pablo, Dora, and Roberto. They were shown to other members of the attacking force only after the morning call from "Aunt Clarita," and then they were burned.

The first phase of "Plan Zero" was completed at 12:07 P.M., when the two teams burst into the second-floor foyer. Their National Guard uniforms provided them with an extra edge of safety as they raced up the staircases: the few Assembly employees they encountered on the stairs simply stepped out of the way. In fact, nobody in the crowded building suspected that it had just been seized by Frente rebels.

★

In José Manuel Limosna's cellar, Rolando Asturias turned on the television set a few minutes before noon. "We might as well watch our own show on the tube," he said to Manuel Schneider and Major Estella. "It will be an unforgettable spectacle for the whole nation, courtesy of the National Television Network. . . ."

As the Chairman of the National Assembly was seen entering the hall, Rolando laughed, but stopped short when the close-up shot of Julia Savage filled the TV screen.

"Jesus and Mary," he exclaimed, "the American Ambassador is there!"

"What's wrong with that?" Major Estella asked drily.

"Everything, everything," Rolando Asturias replied. "She mustn't get hurt, no matter what happens. We must get word to Pablo."

★

In the second-floor foyer of the National Assembly, Pablo tied a black-and-red kerchief around his face, only his eyes showing over the colors of the Frente. The sixteen other *guerrilleros* followed his example, and at a signal from him, the team split up into three squads. Roberto Maxwell and his four companions placed themselves so that all the entrances to the foyer were within the range of their guns. This was the protective-screen squad, Squad C. Squads A and B, the first one headed by Pablo and the second by Dora, rushed into the Assembly hall from the right and left entrances.

Vega y Vega was in the middle of a flowery sentence when a burst of submachine-gun fire from Pablo's and Dora's G-3s sprayed the huge coat of arms of the Republic of Malagua on the wall behind the rostrum. Plaster and chips of marble flew into the air. The Chairman froze, his mouth wide open. A woman in the public seats screamed. Pablo and Dora each fired another burst into the coat of arms, carefully aiming over the heads of those in the hall. Then there was total silence—a moment of paralysis.

Dora Merino raised a bullhorn and shouted: "*¡Abajo el tirano!*
¡Viva la libertad! The National Assembly has been taken over by
the fighting forces of the Front of National Liberation. This is the
first step in the offensive of the people of Malagua against the
tyrant and usurper Juan Ferrer Berrio. Other forces of liberation
are moving elsewhere at this very moment. All of you are our
prisoners; you are hostages. Guns are aimed at you. We do not
wish to kill anybody, but we shall not hesitate at the slightest
provocation. Our orders are that these events in the Assembly
continue to be televised to the nation as long as we consider it
necessary. If the broadcast is interrupted, lives will be lost. Our
terms for your release will be made known by us at the proper
moment. For now, nobody is to move."

Chairman Vega y Vega struggled to his feet, his face crimson
with rage. He was an important landowner, and he had served as
a colonel in the National Guard. He was not accustomed to defi-
ance. "This is an indignity!" he roared. "Who are you? How
dare you?"

A burst from Dora's submachine gun hit the wall behind the
Chairman. "Shut your mouth, you filth," she told him over the
bullhorn.

★

Juan Ferrer watched the television screen in his office. He was
silent and motionless as Comandante Pablo and Dora Merino
fired their weapons in the National Assembly hall and as Dora
announced the takeover. After a long moment, Ferrer said to
Fabio, "Refill my glass."

He tasted the whiskey, put down the drink, and walked over
to his desk. Picking up a telephone, he said flatly: "I want the
chief of staff of the Guard and all the top officers now in the
capital to report to me at the command post at the Palace within
a half-hour. . . . Get the G-2 to provide me as soon as possible
with a list of all the deputies and government officials held at the
National Assembly."

"What are you going to do?" Morgan asked.

"Right now," he replied after a long pause, "absolutely nothing. I'm going to let the terrorists stew in their own juices. Let them sit there, waiting for my move. When I'm ready, I'll show them who is boss here. One thing I can promise you, Jim, is that they won't get away with it.''

"And if they start executing the hostages?''

"That's okay with me,'' Ferrer said. "Most of the people inside are expendable. If I have to, I'll appoint a brand-new Assembly tomorrow morning. In the meantime, for each hostage killed I'll have a prisoner shot in the jails. When I've run out of prisoners, we'll start picking up Frente people and shoot them. I can wait longer than they can, and I'm planning a surprise, possibly for tonight. If they want to execute hostages on television, that's just fine. Let the world see these bloody jackals for what they really are.''

"Yes, General, but there are foreign ambassadors among the hostages. The American Ambassador is there.''

"That's tough. Besides, I didn't know you cared that much about her well-being, Jim.''

"I don't, but the Administration in Washington does. You're supposed to be responsible for the safety of diplomats in your country.''

Juan Ferrer shrugged and drained his whiskey glass. "Let's go down to the command post,'' he said. "We've got to get organized.''

★

At the American Embassy, John Crespo saw the Frente's takeover of the National Assembly. After calling CIA Headquarters over the Station's secure line to inform the watch officer at Langley of the events, he raced down the flight of stairs to McVeigh's office. The DCM was on his way out to lunch when Crespo stunned him with the news.

"My God,'' he exclaimed, "it might turn into a slaughter, and Julia is there!'' He shouted to his secretary to put in a priority call to the State Department, then turned on his television set. The cameras were pointed at the rostrum of the Assembly, a long shot, and the TV reporter, his voice hysterical, was saying,

". . . and I repeat, nobody has been harmed as a result of this extraordinary occurrence."

Within three minutes, McVeigh had the State Department's Operations Center on the line. "This is McVeigh, the DCM in Malagua. Rebels of the National Liberation Front have just captured the National Assembly building. They're holding hundreds of hostages, including Ambassador Savage. We'll keep you posted, but I need urgent instructions."

★

After the first shock—the realization that she was, incredibly, a hostage and that she could be killed—Julia quickly became calm. Whatever the demands of the Frente commando, she reasoned, immediate and wholesale killings of hostages were unlikely. They must want something; therefore they must be prepared to negotiate, and each prisoner—alive—was a bargaining chip. This was the normal pattern of hostage-taking, and she did not think the Frente would act differently or irrationally. Especially when it came to foreign ambassadors. Julia wondered briefly if she knew any members of the assault team. Rolando Asturias certainly was not among them, but there was something familiar about the carriage and the voice of the woman with the bullhorn, her face covered with a kerchief and wearing a black beret. Then she realized it was Dora Merino.

The ambassador from Guatemala, a thin elderly man in a dark suit who sat next to her, was wringing his hands and whimpering like a child. Julia touched his arm. "Embajador," she said soothingly, "relax . . . all will be well." The Guatemalan ignored her. The Honduran and Costa Rican ambassadors were rigid with fright, staring ahead, unseeing and unhearing. The Paraguayan envoy, a plump man in a morning coat, was unruffled. "It's a sticky thing," he told Julia, "but they won't keep us forever. . . ."

★

In Washington, Secretary of State Masterson telephoned the President of the United States to inform him that Ambassador

Savage was a hostage in Malagua, but the White House had already received word from the CIA. Within the hour, Masterson joined Tom Morelli in the Oval Office.

"It's the policy of the United States not to give in to the demands of kidnappers," the President said, "but here we're faced with a special situation. Obviously, the government of Malagua has to do the negotiating, and I suppose we have to be as supportive of them as we can. Any ideas?"

"No, Mr. President," Masterson replied. "We're waiting to hear what the demands are."

"Tom?"

"Nothing I can suggest right now. . . . However, just to be on the safe side, I would recommend that you quietly authorize alerting some military units, perhaps the Special Forces in Panama and the Air Force. The thing that worries me the most is the rebels' finding out about that CIA arms transfer to Ferrer."

"Maybe it wasn't such a hot idea after all," the President remarked.

★

Inside the National Assembly, Comandante Pablo was redeploying his small force. Numerically, the team was at an almost incredible disadvantage: seventeen men and women seeking to dominate what he estimated at well over nine hundred hostages, most of them in the hall, but many elsewhere in the building. These too had to be brought under control—rapidly.

Pablo calculated that there must be several hundred National Guardsmen and police outside the building, and Ferrer could bring in hundreds more in reinforcements. However, "Plan Zero" was based on precisely such a scenario. Its key elements were astounding daring, total surprise, and the team's firepower. People, Pablo knew from long experience, did not argue with submachine guns. Seventeen rapid-fire guns, strategically deployed in the hall, could hold the nine hundred or more hostages in check. Just one burst could kill scores.

As planned, Squad A, led by Pablo, moved down to the Assembly's rostrum area. The rebels positioned themselves so that the presiding officials and the deputies were in their range of fire, and they also covered the ground-floor entrances to the hall. Pablo stood behind Vega y Vega, his back to the wall. Dora Merino's Squad B remained at the top entrances to the hall, just above the diplomatic gallery, placing the diplomats, the public, and the deputies in a crossfire pattern between their guns and those of Pablo's group below. Roberto Maxwell's Squad C, a force of five guerrillas, continued to occupy the foyer. Maxwell had opened the doors to the two inner staircases, securing them in such a way that anyone trying to go up or down could be instantly machine-gunned. He had brought the building's two elevators to a stop at the foyer level, the doors open, cutting off this escape route and preventing Guard troops from using them. Major Estella had considered the possibility of soldiers' being landed on the Assembly's roof by helicopter, but with Maxwell's squad holding the foyer entrances, they would be unable to gain entrance to the hall.

At the rostrum, Pablo poked Vega y Vega in the ribs with his G-3. There was one more problem to be solved.

"Listen, pig," he said to the Chairman, "I understand that you can activate a building-wide public-address system with one of those microphones in front of you. I want you to switch it on, instructing everybody in this building, those who are upstairs and downstairs, to come to this hall. They are to enter the foyer from the staircases in single file, fifteen meters apart. If you don't do this at once, I'll shoot you through the head."

Trembling, Vega y Vega turned on the public-address microphone, relaying Pablo's orders. Within minutes, men and women, their hands above their heads, began entering the foyer from the staircases, covered by the guns of Maxwell's squad. From the foyer, they were pushed, one by one, into the hall, where Dora's group directed them down to the well. It took fifteen minutes to shepherd some two hundred persons into the hall. The total of hostages under the rebels' direct control had grown to close to one thousand.

"Good," Pablo said into the microphone. "I want everybody where I can see them. If you all follow orders, nothing will happen to you."

★

Her G-3 in hand, Dora Merino walked slowly along the carpeted passageway that separated the diplomatic gallery from the public seats below. Looking up, she spotted Julia Savage leaning forward in her seat. Although it had not been unreasonable to expect that Julia would attend a session dealing with American aid, this was the only contingency for which the Frente planners had not been prepared. Now Dora was cursing herself for it. It was an unnecessary complication, and they should have anticipated it. Walking past Julia a second time, Dora signaled to the Ambassador to follow her. Julia left her seat and went behind the armed woman. Dora stepped inside the entryway into the foyer, pushing Julia to the side.

"I assume that you recognize me, Ambassador," Dora said softly. "My designation in this operation is 'Number Two'—the *comandante* down below is 'Number One'—so I must ask you not to address me by my name in front of the others."

"Dora . . . Oh, my God. What's going on here? What are you people doing?"

"You heard what I said a little while ago over the bullhorn. Your government's decision to provide economic assistance to the régime forced us into this action, but I'm sorry that you've gotten caught here. I remember that you had the courage to come to my father's funeral."

"What will happen to me?" Julia asked. "What will happen to the others?"

"As far as you're concerned," Dora replied, "I will do my best to protect you from harm. But the final decision has to be made by the *compañeros*. As for the others, it will depend on their behavior, and especially, on how the tyrant responds to our demands. Now please go back to your seat."

★

Juan Ferrer, surrounded by his commanders and with Jim Morgan and Fabio at his side, watched the television set at his basement command post. It was two o'clock in the afternoon, and the dictator had ordered a redeployment of his military units. He had directed General Bauch-Barriga to abandon the Jacaltec operation and to bring his brigade back to the capital, and he had instructed the Guard's elite battalion to seal off Barrio del Sur. Other units from the Ciudad Malagua garrison were spread out around the city, blocking the Pan American Highway and all the other access roads. Ferrer's strategy was to prevent an all-out attack on his capital.

"The way I see it," he told Morgan, "the action will be right here in town. This is where the war will be won or lost—but I'm the one who's gonna win it. I can outwait, outlast, and outkill those sons-of-bitches. Hey, look at this."

The rebel commander, who had been standing behind Vega y Vega, now faced a television camera, submachine gun in one hand, a sheet of paper in the other. The lens brought him into a close-up.

"I am Number One, and I shall read the list of the Frente's demands, which are the conditions for the safe release of the hostages of the Revolution," Comandante Pablo said in a flat voice, distorted by the bandana over his face.

"We wish our entire nation to hear our statement," he continued, "and therefore I warn that the Chairman of the Assembly will be executed if there is interference with this transmission. We have radio contact with *compañeros* outside who are monitoring this radio and television broadcast.

"Demand Number One: The tyrant must immediately release all the political prisoners in the territory of the Republic of Malagua. This must be completed within the next twenty-four hours.

"Demand Number Two: The tyrant must immediately confine all units of the National Guard and riot police to their barracks. They are to remain there for the duration of the negotiations for a political solution to the crisis in Malagua.

"Demand Number Three: The tyrant must announce his irrevocable intention of surrendering power and leaving the territory of the Republic of Malagua. He must agree to a peaceful transfer of power to the authorities of the Revolution under international supervision. The Frente will guarantee the tyrant's safe exit from the country, with his family, because the revolution is not vengeful.

"Demand Number Four: The transfer of power must be effected within the next seven days. The hostages will remain under our control in the National Assembly until the tyrant has left Malagua's soil. Preparations for the transfer of power must start not later than tomorrow. Failure of the régime of the tyrant to meet any of our demands will result in the death of a number of hostages."

Comandante Pablo finished reading the list of demands, folded the sheet, and put it in his breast pocket.

At the National Palace command post, Juan Ferrer said to Morgan: "This guy is out of his fucking mind. Did you hear that? The 'tyrant' must resign? Political prisoners are to be released? The Guard is to be confined to the barracks? He's got to be kidding. Wait till he sees what I have in mind tonight for his friends. We'll teach them a lesson they'll never forget. Damned shit-eaters. . . ."

★

In her sitting room in the National Palace, Silvia Palos de Ferrer had also listened to the statement by the rebel commander. She had not watched the actual takeover of the Assembly, learning of it when her husband called her from the command post. After thinking about it for a few minutes, she asked her social secretary to put her in touch with the American Ambassador.

"But *señora*, the Ambassador is among the hostages," the secretary said.

Doña Silvia thanked her. Then she made a telephone call herself, received a call back, made another one, and finally, lit a candle in front of a gold-framed image of Our Lady of Malagua. "Please pray for us," she murmured.

★

It was midafternoon in the mountains above Agua Linda when the radio operator abruptly tore off his earphones, rushing outside the tent to where Máximo Landino stood with three bearded guerrilla leaders.

"Comandante, Comandante," he shouted, "the forces of the Frente have captured the National Assembly building and have taken hundreds of hostages. They are demanding that the tyrant leave Malagua."

"What *are* you talking about, man? Come to your senses," Landino snapped.

"But it's true, it's true," the operator shouted. "I heard it on the National Radio just now. It was a broadcast from the National Assembly."

Landino went into the tent and called the Agua Linda church on the radio. Father Miguel kept a wireless set in the sacristy to warn the EGP guerrillas in the jungle hills of any sudden National Guard movements in the area. Landino spoke into the transmitter: "This is Blue Bird to Armadillo—can you read me? Please advise what's happening in the capital."

"Armadillo here," Father Miguel answered. "I read you okay, Blue Bird. The news in the capital, as I just saw it on television, is that the Frente have seized the National Assembly, and their *comandante* has read a statement that Ferrer must resign and meet a number of other demands, if the hostages are to be spared."

Landino switched off the transmitter, humming pensively to himself. It was his habit when he was considering a major decision, his favorite melody being the Ode to Joy, which he hummed off key. He walked out of the tent, looking up at the sun, still high in the spring sky.

"Tonight, the Ejército Guerrillero de los Pobres, our glorious EGP, will march down from the mountains to take Jacaltec and to deal the final blow to the tyrant," Máximo announced to a half-dozen of his associates who awaited him in the clearing.

Each of them was the leader of an EGP column, and they had come up during the previous night for their weekly meeting with Landino.

★

In the course of the afternoon, National Guard units encircled Barrio del Sur. Sherman tanks and APCs stood on the main streets leading to the slums, and infantry squads set up road-blocks, amidst decaying garbage, in the foul-smelling alleys. By nightfall, nobody was allowed to leave or enter. Frente couriers, barefoot children of the *barrio,* quickly spread word of the Guard's movements among block leaders in the slum. One of the leaders ran to the house of José Manuel Limosna to warn him that the whole area was surrounded. Since the start of the preparations for "Plan Zero," the Frente security system had provided for all information to be channeled through the poet-carpenter. Limosna barred the front door from inside, and went down to the cellar to pass the news to Major Estella, Rolando Asturias, and Manuel Schneider.

"Well, it looks as if Ferrer is spoiling for a fight," Major Estella said, spitting on the floor.

At that moment, Sherman tanks began firing their cannon point-blank into the *barrio.* Incendiary bullets from heavy machine guns mounted on APCs rained on the slum in long red ribbons. The wooden shacks caught fire at once, and screaming inhabitants poured out into the narrow alleys. Infantrymen picked them off with automatic rifles as they raced for cover, the soldiers laughing at every hit. All around, boxlike concrete structures were collapsing under the impact of cannon shells.

Rolando Asturias looked at the television set in the corner of the cellar. Juan Ferrer, in full uniform, was addressing the nation, the rebels having ended the transmission from the Assembly after their demands were read.

"I speak to you tonight, my dear fellow citizens, from my office at the National Palace," Ferrer said. "As you know, Marxist terrorists have succeeded in temporarily taking over the building of the National Assembly, holding nearly one thousand innocent people, including foreign ambassadors, at the point of their mercenary guns. It is my duty as constitutional President of the Republic of Malagua to inform you that your government will not tolerate such acts of terrorism, nor will it negotiate with Communist gangsters. Fire must be fought with fire if our Christian values are to be preserved. Therefore the valiant soldiers of the National Guard—your brothers—under my personal command are engaged at this very moment in a mopping-up operation in Barrio del Sur, where other Marxist traitors are hiding out. I am aware that this operation may endanger our brave hostages. The gangsters may retaliate by executing them inside the National Assembly. Well, so be it. Let the blood of innocent people be on the hands of the Communist traitors. This is the moment of truth for every proud *malagueño,* the moment of sacrifice for the Motherland."

★

In the basement of the National Palace, in the section where the G-2 operated its private prison, the dwarf Fabio sat in a chair in the center of a large cell, languidly observing two emaciated prisoners undergoing electric-shock treatment on their genitals. It was the third pair of men brought before him that evening, and the dwarf squealed with delight each time electrodes were applied to their penises, the smell of burned skin and flesh filling the cell. The men screamed inhumanly. To Fabio, the stench was like incense, and for the third time he felt uncontrollable desire and excitement mounting inside him.

When the first prisoner lost consciousness on the surgical table to which he was tied with leather thongs, the dwarf leaped forward and sank his bared teeth into the man's scrotum, biting off his testicles. Then he turned to the second prisoner, repeating the savagery. He sighed with abandon, and a dark spot grew slowly on the crotch of his trousers. Silently, the dwarf Fabio left the cell, exhausted but fulfilled. In ancient Mayan superstition, sickness is always caused by dwarfs.

★

At the National Assembly, at the other end of Ciudad Malagua, Comandante Pablo had heard General Ferrer's speech over a portable transistor radio. He grabbed his walkie-talkie, calling Dora Merino and Roberto Maxwell.

"They're attacking Barrio del Sur," he said quietly. "I propose we start the executions here. Do you agree?"

Dora Merino answered over the walkie-talkie, "We have to proceed with the greatest care. Why don't we consult the *compañeros* of the Directorate?" When Roberto Maxwell agreed, Pablo hesitated and then said, "I suppose you're right."

In the cellar of the carpenter's house, in the heart of the torched *barrio,* Rolando Asturias received the radio message over Dora's portable VHF set, as did Tomás Martínez at the lakeside villa. "We have just heard the tyrant's speech," she said, "and we wish to have your opinion on how to proceed with the hostages. It has been proposed that we begin executions in reprisal."

The Jesuit exchanged glances with Major Estella and Manuel Schneider. They shook their heads. "No," he answered, "we counsel patience for the moment." Across Ciudad Malagua, the voice of Tomás Martínez chimed in: "Correct. This is the time for patience." The consultation had lasted less than a minute— not enough time for the National Guard to locate the transmitters by triangulation.

19

BARRIO del Sur burned brightly through the night, and many hundreds of people died—some incinerated in their houses, others mangled by cannon shells or torn apart by machine-gun bullets—but there were no executions at the National Assembly.

Curled up in her seat, Julia Savage had dozed intermittently. She was hungry and thirsty, and she ran out of cigarettes. Late in the afternoon, the Red Cross, responding to a request from Comandante Pablo, delivered some food—sandwiches—and water to the Assembly, but it could not provide enough on short notice. The sandwiches and bottled water were placed at the east entrance, where two rebels picked them up and took them inside. But like others, Julia did not get enough to eat and drink. Around midnight, Dora Merino walked past the gallery, offering her water canteen to Julia; it did not quench her thirst, but she was grateful to the young woman.

★

Antonia Llosa de Schneider was also spending a sleepless night. One of Malagua's great beauties and the wife of the president of Automotriz Schneider S.A., she was known as an outstanding hostess in the capital's high society and as a patroness of the arts. María Carmen Escalante, the murdered painter, had been one of her friends, as were most of the city's artists and intellectuals. Because of the Schneiders' standing in Malagua, the secret police tended to overlook these friendships, normally suspect in the present atmosphere. But Antonia was not considered to be politically minded—she seemed too busy with her lunches and dinners and charity balls—and she was known to be very close to Señora de Ferrer, with whom she often took tea at the Palace.

In fact, Silvia Palos de Ferrer had placed a quick and discreet telephone call to Antonia after the takeover of the National Assembly. "The time is now," Malagua's First Lady had whispered. Dashing to her blue Mercedes-Benz convertible, Antonia had spent the late afternoon and much of the evening driving to the homes of her husband's fellow businessmen. She started every conversation by saying that Manuel was out of town on a "business trip," but that she had been instructed to pass on the message that "the time is now."

From her bedroom in the elegant Schneider mansion on Avenida Ferrer, Antonia watched the fires burning in Barrio del Sur, and she listened to gunfire. She prayed for Manuel's safety.

★

The bombardment of Barrio del Sur stopped at midnight, and on the morning of November 12, a Saturday, Ciudad Malagua awoke to great silence. The city's streets were empty. All the private banks and large downtown stores failed to open. No workers came to the industrial plants in the suburbs for the Saturday shifts. No buses were running, and even the aggressive taxi drivers had stayed away. When a *bodeguero* or café owner, ignorant of what was happening, tried to raise the shutters over his establishment in the morning, someone would sidle over, saying quietly, "*Paro general*. General strike. Go home, if you know what's good for you."

Antonia Llosa de Schneider had done her job well. After the Cathedral massacre, a number of key Malagua businessmen had made up their minds that Juan Ferrer must go, Manuel Schneider being the principal moving force behind this resolve. Their conclusion was that the country would become totally radicalized—and be plunged into civil war—if the dictator was not removed. Unexpectedly, they found an ally in Silvia Palos de Ferrer. A deeply religious woman, she had long been horrified by the bloody excesses of the National Guard and the secret police. She had gradually come to realize that she loathed her husband and everything he stood for.

At first, Silvia de Ferrer felt ashamed of these feelings, and she took counsel with Don Pepe Vargas, the fiery bishop from the highlands, and several of her Jesuit friends in the capital. They told her that, yes, even in the eyes of the Church her loyalty belonged to the people, not to her husband's régime. And imperceptibly, Malagua's First Lady slid into conspiracy. Antonia was her link to the group of businessmen in secret opposition to the government, and as time went by, Doña Silvia turned out to be a precious ally. She knew which of the National Guard's generals and colonels could be counted upon to coldly switch sides at the right moment, aware that they were opportunists, unwilling to go down with Juan Ferrer. Two or three of them were decent, sickened by what Ferrer was forcing them to do.

Following the Cathedral tragedy, Schneider and his friends—none of whom was aware of his membership in the Frente Directorate—agreed that a general strike by business and labor together could quicken Ferrer's overthrow if the armed rebels struck in force against him. Antonia was instructed to inform Doña Silvia of the plan, which they discussed softly over coffee after dinner at the home of the Foreign Minister. The final decision was that the First Lady would give the signal for a general strike after satisfying herself that the time was ripe and that enough Guard commanders would assume at least a stance of neutrality in an open challenge to the dictator. Suddenly, she was one of the chief strategists of the opposition.

With the takeover of the National Assembly, Doña Silvia knew that the right moment had arrived. She called the wife of the Guard general commanding the Ciudad Malagua garrison, asking her, "How does Marcos feel?" This was a prearranged code, and the wife of General Marcos Pacheco Lutz was back on the phone within three minutes to say that "Marcos is fine, and he sends his warmest regards." This meant that he would be neutral in the developing confrontation. Doña Silvia then called Antonia. The general strike for the next day was set in motion, the message being conveyed by business and factory owners to their managers and labor leaders. The war was on.

★

The first reports of the general strike reached Juan Ferrer shortly after nine o'clock in the morning at the basement command post where he had spent the night. His response was instant: "I want the owners and the managers of all the establishments on strike—banks, stores, plants, and so on—arrested at once," he barked over the phone to the acting chief of G-2. "And pick up the labor leaders, too."

At ten o'clock in the morning, word reached the command post that the EGP had taken Agua Linda and nearby villages at dawn and was moving toward Jacaltec. Ferrer swore loudly, and instructed the Guard's chief of staff to have General Bauch-Barriga, his best and toughest commander, turn around and race to Jacaltec. "Tell him that Jacaltec must be held and that he must prevent the rebels from cutting the main highway," he shouted. "I'm sending the Air Force after the Landino columns with napalm and fragmentation bombs."

A half-hour later, the Guard commander in San Pablo reported that riots had erupted in the port city's slums and were spreading. "Use maximum force," Ferrer told the general. "I don't care how many people are killed. The more the better."

★

At noon, Monsignor Luigi Bansa, the Papal Nuncio, got through by telephone to Comandante Pablo at the rostrum of the National Assembly.

"I appeal to you to spare the hostages," he said with emotion. "Give us time to negotiate. I am trying to establish contact with General Ferrer."

"I shall make no promises," Pablo replied, "but for us, you

are the wrong negotiator. You're too close to the reactionary hierarchy. Find someone else, and don't waste time, because our patience is wearing thin."

"With whom would you negotiate?"

Pablo thought it over. "We'll talk with Don Pepe Vargas," he said. "But in the meantime, I want the Red Cross to deliver more food and water on a regular basis for my people and the hostages. There's no telling how long we'll be here. And don't try any tricks."

"We'll call the bishop, and the Red Cross will be prodded," the Nuncio told him.

★

In Washington, another urgent meeting on the Malagua crisis was being held in the White House Situation Room late Saturday afternoon. Tom Morelli, the National Security Adviser, listened as General McCullen, the CIA Director, read the latest reports from Ciudad Malagua, then said:

"Clearly, we should have paid more attention to Julia's reports, but to hell with hindsight. A civil war is raging in Malagua, and our Ambassador is a hostage. The President wants action, both to stop the war and to get Julia out. Any suggestions?"

Secretary of State Masterson and McCullen looked at each other; both shrugged helplessly. Terence Terhune stared at an ashtray on the conference table.

"Okay," Morelli said, "let's talk business. There seems to be only one avenue open to us, and that's mediation between the parties. The first step is to convince Ferrer that he must negotiate with the rebels through an intermediary. If he agrees, half of the battle is won, because the Frente will see it as a major political breakthrough."

"Yes, I suppose so," Masterson said, "but who could the intermediary be? The rebels have rejected the Nuncio, and I just can't imagine Ferrer dealing with Bishop Vargas. Besides, as far as I'm concerned, the Bishop is too close to the Left. We could wind up with a Cuban-type régime."

"For God's sake, Ed," Morelli told him, "can your Cuban

obsession for a couple of minutes. The Communists are not the only opposition force in Malagua—as your own Ambassador has been trying to explain to you for the last four months. My choice for the mediator would be Julia, who has credibility with the opposition and to whom Ferrer has to listen as the American Ambassador—if we could only spring her loose. . . ."

"And how do we do *that?*" McCullen asked, not concealing his irritation.

"I'm not sure. I guess by persuading the Frente to let her go. After all, she was caught by accident in the National Assembly —they were not after her. But of course, we have no contacts with the opposition—that's the price we're paying for that idiotic policy of putting all our eggs in Ferrer's basket. So I think the only feasible approach is for the United States to go public with a proposal that if Julia is released, she will act as mediator. The Frente could do much worse, and I suspect they might buy it."

"I have no objections, if you assume the responsibility," Masterson said.

"The President will assume it," Morelli answered. "But first, we need a formal acceptance of the principle of negotiation on Ferrer's part. Without it, the rebels may refuse to free Julia. Now, General McCullen, I understand that your Station Chief in Malagua is a friend of Ferrer's. I would like him to make a pitch to Ferrer immediately. Would you please instruct him accordingly?"

★

The takeover of the National Assembly was in its third day. Comandante Pablo was under instructions from the Frente leadership to continue refraining from violence against the hostages —they communicated briefly by radio once a day—in anticipation of political negotiations. The Directorate was encouraged by the success of the general strike that had paralyzed Ciudad Malagua; they knew that Landino's EGP columns were moving toward Jacaltec, and that there was fighting throughout the country between the Guard and rebel bands.

"We have to stand firm to win a political victory without a

terrible bloodbath," Rolando Asturias told Manuel Schneider and Major Estella in their cellar in Barrio del Sur. "There've been enough killings already."

"War means death, and we're at war," the Major said placidly. "But it would be good if we could get the tyrant to negotiate and shorten the suffering in our country."

Inside the Assembly building there was suffering too. After two nights of confinement, tempers were becoming frayed, fear giving place to abrasiveness among the thousand hostages herded together in the lower part of the hall. The air conditioning had broken down on the second day, and the air was hot, heavy, and fetid. The food and water supplied by the Malaguan Red Cross was insufficient, and the hostages pushed and jostled each other to grab the rations. There were fistfights, shouts, and curses. Only two toilets were accessible to the prisoners; they were at the far end of the hall, by the entrance doors, and the hostages had to wait their turn for hours in two single files guarded by armed rebels. People slept fitfully in the aisles or in their seats.

In the upper gallery, the five captive diplomats enjoyed a measure of privacy and space, but they too were experiencing cabin fever. Julia Savage, her dress sticking unpleasantly to her body, found the boredom and inactivity almost intolerable. From Dora Merino, who occasionally stopped by the diplomatic gallery, she learned about the bombardment of Barrio del Sur, the general strike in Ciudad Malagua, and the fighting elsewhere in the country. Although intensely fatigued—the rebels took turns catnapping—Dora still radiated enthusiasm and optimism. "We finally have the tyrant on the run," she told Julia.

During one of their quick chats, Julia asked Dora if she knew where Rolando Asturias was. The girl smiled mischievously, and said, "I really cannot tell you, but I wouldn't be surprised if you heard something interesting about him before too long."

★

It was late evening of the third day of the crisis—Sunday— when Jim Morgan finally succeeded in talking with Juan Ferrer after repeated phone calls to the bunker command post. His orders from Langley were to see the dictator with the greatest urgency, but the Guard duty officer insisted throughout the day and into the night that El Jefe was in conference and could not be disturbed. Driving to the Palace after dark, Morgan was stopped at the gate, a new experience for him, and informed by an officer in battle dress that he could not proceed any farther. Following calls from the gate to the bunker, the Station Chief was admitted under armed escort to the Palace grounds. He was kept waiting for another hour, still under guard, in a room adjoining the command post.

Juan Ferrer was tired and on edge. The news had been bad for the last twenty-four hours. The attack on the slums the first night had failed to force the release of the hostages, and since the end of the bombardment, the troops surrounding the *barrio* had been under sniper fire. Only periodic salvos by tank cannon succeeded in silencing the invisible snipers, but the Shermans could not keep up a sustained barrage. They were short of ammunition. North of Jacaltec, a battalion of the Third Brigade had been ambushed the previous night by EGP guerrillas. Using 81mm mortars concealed in the woods above the town, Landino's forces had surprised Guard troops with a rain of ordnance fired with deadly accuracy. The battalion broke and ran, leaving behind at least two tanks, three APCs, several howitzers, and uncounted heavy machine guns. Now Máximo Landino had acquired considerable firepower, posing a serious threat to the Ciudad Malagua–San Pablo highway. At first light, two C-47 gunships bombed and strafed Jacaltec, killing a number of inhabitants, but Landino and his freshly reequipped columns had vanished. Meanwhile, the capital remained paralyzed and sullen.

Turning away from wall maps he was studying with his aides, Ferrer said brusquely to Morgan, "Yes, Jim, what is it?"

"Well, Mr. President, I came to see you on instructions from Washington. With Ambassador Savage held as hostage, it was decided that I should deliver an official message to you."

Leading him into a small adjoining office, the General said, "Okay, let's have it, and make it snappy. I'm fighting a war, you know."

"I hate to be the one to tell you this, Mr. President," Morgan began. "The United States Government wishes you to suspend military operations and enter into negotiations with the rebels, with the assistance of the United States, in order to obtain the release of the hostages and to explore modalities for a political solution of the crisis in Malagua."

Juan Ferrer's eyes narrowed, and he said slowly, "I see . . . the fucking rats are abandoning a sinking ship. Isn't that it?"

"No, not really," Morgan replied. "What is proposed is that you announce that you accept the concept of mediation by the United States if the Frente, for its part, releases our Ambassador. Then Washington will officially designate her as the mediator. Look, Mr. President, this is a ploy: once the Savage woman is free, you can do any damned thing you please. You can stall on the negotiations, you can reject mediation under any pretext, you can resume your military operations. That's not the formal instructions I received, but that's the way I interpret it."

"Great," Ferrer told him in disgust. "Just great. You get your Ambassador back, but what's in it for me? I don't give a shit if Miss Savage is a hostage for the next hundred years or if they cut her throat tonight. And come to think of it, it would be a plus for me if the Communists killed her. Then American public opinion would swing behind me. So why should I go through this charade?"

"Because, sir, you need the United States," Morgan said, "or at least, someone in the United States, to help you out. To be precise, you need arms if you're going to win this war."

"You're not making sense, Jim. If the Americans want me to say that I'm ready to negotiate, which I am not, why should they give me arms?"

"You know perfectly well, Mr. President, that there are all kinds of Americans. Some of them may be in a position to give you a break—unofficially, you understand. If your actions result in the release of the Ambassador, then you can expect reciprocity from your friends. If she remains a hostage, there isn't a God-damned thing we can do for you."

Juan Ferrer took a cigar from his breast pocket and bit off the end.

"Let me see if I can understand you," he said. "You're saying that if the CIA can claim credit—internally—for engineering the Ambassador's freedom through the good offices of the President of Malagua, then it can get away with 'unofficial' military aid to us? But how long can the CIA ship me arms?"

"As long as necessary," Morgan replied. "As long as you have soldiers to fire the guns."

★

At the Embassy, Jim Morgan reported to McVeigh, the Acting Chief of Mission, that he thought General Ferrer would agree to announce his readiness to negotiate with the Frente to try to defuse the crisis, but principally as a gesture of friendship toward the United States, to secure the release of the Ambassador.

"It took a lot of persuading," he said, "but I think I've succeeded. However, it would be wrong to assume that the President is ready to cave in. If there are negotiations, they will be very tough."

Over the secure telephone line to Langley, the Station Chief provided his superiors with a fuller and more accurate account of his conversation with Ferrer. "And I assume there's more stuff available in Santiago and elsewhere for rapid delivery here," he added. "This guy needs help desperately."

★

In the late morning of Tuesday, the fifth day after the seizure of the National Assembly, Juan Ferrer went on radio and television for the second time since the events of November 11. In Washington, the State Department spokesman had just issued an announcement that the United States would mediate in Malagua if the rebels released Ambassador Savage. Ferrer spoke solemnly to the nation:

"We *malagueños* are compassionate and humanitarian as a people. We deplore fratricide and bloodshed. In the present crisis, the Government wishes to encourage a peaceful solution. It also wishes to reaffirm Malagua's tradition of hospitality toward foreigners living among us, especially diplomats, who, under international law, enjoy full immunity. For these reasons, I have taken the decision to enter into negotiations with the forces now occupying the building of the National Assembly. Such negotiations will be conducted under the auspices of the Government of the United States, a traditional friend of Malagua. Only one condition is attached to my readiness to embark on the talks. That is the immediate release of the foreign diplomats held in the National Assembly. My enemies are invited to designate their negotiators at the time of the release of the diplomats.''

★

"All this is extremely interesting, but I don't trust Ferrer,'' Manuel Schneider said to Rolando Asturias and Major Estella after watching the dictator on television. "He must have some trick up his sleeve. By negotiating with us, he legitimizes us, and I don't see him doing that out of the goodness of his heart.''

"I agree that it sounds too good to be true,'' Major Estella commented. "But the Frente has to respond in some fashion. What do you think, Padre?''

Rolando stroked his chin pensively as he paced. "We must *always* assume that Ferrer has something up his sleeve,'' he said. "Still, we have nothing to lose by releasing the ambassadors. The very fact that Ferrer used the word 'negotiations' is, in my judgment, a net gain for us, a very important one—no matter what happens afterward. I say, let's free the diplomats.''

Schneider and Major Estella considered it, and told the Jesuit they were willing to take the chance. Rolando then contacted Tomás Martínez and Juan Carlos Reyes at the lakeside safehouse to advise them of the conclusions reached at the *barrio* command post and to request their views. Tomás Martínez replied that he and Reyes were of the same opinion. He then urged Rolando to become the Frente's negotiator, because of "your American connections." He added, however, that Rolando must be offered full guarantees of immunity and safety during the negotiations.

Radioing Comandante Pablo and Dora Merino at the National Assembly, Rolando said that if Dora, the sixth Directorate member, agreed, the commando team should take preliminary steps toward the release of the ambassadors. Quickly, Rolando explained the procedure the Frente had in mind.

★

After hearing Ferrer's speech, McVeigh drove to the residence of Monsignor Bansa to suggest that the Papal Nuncio communicate with the rebels at the Assembly. Though Comandante Pablo had initially refused to negotiate with the Nuncio, McVeigh felt that Bansa, as Dean of the Diplomatic Corps, was the best channel now that a mediation effort was taking shape. Besides, Bishop Vargas had not yet been located: he was somewhere in the highlands, perhaps on his way back to the capital. McVeigh thought that they had to move fast, and the Nuncio agreed. Morgan was instructed to stand by for a meeting with Ferrer.

Bansa telephoned Comandante Pablo at the Assembly rostrum. "Have you heard the President's announcement?" he asked.

"Yes," Pablo said. "The Frente is prepared to let the diplomats go. But there are several conditions."

"What are they?"

"First, the ambassadors will be turned over to Don Pepe Vargas and to no one else."

"No problem. We expect the Bishop in the capital any moment."

"Second, the release of the ambassadors will be timed exactly with the arrival of the designated negotiator of the Frente at the National Assembly building. He is to be under your personal protection, as Dean of the Diplomatic Corps, and you must escort him here from Barrio del Sur."

"I am positive that can be done."

"Third, the subsequent political negotiations are to proceed under the *joint* auspices of the American Ambassador, Don Pepe Vargas, and yourself—as Dean. The three of you will be responsible for the safety of our negotiator. If anything happens to him, I shall start executing the hostages. Understood?''

"Yes," the Nuncio said. "I'll get back to you as soon as I've discussed these points with the parties concerned."

McVeigh, who had been listening to the conversation on an extension, now telephoned Morgan at the Embassy, instructing him to tell Ferrer that the United States expected him to accept the *comandante*'s conditions. Then he called the State Department to dictate a message for Secretary Masterson.

★

Early in the afternoon, Morgan returned from the Palace with Ferrer's assurances that he would go along with the rebels' proposals. McVeigh went back to the residence of the Nuncio, who again contacted Comandante Pablo.

"Your conditions are acceptable to all concerned," he said. "When and where am I to take your negotiator under my protection? And who is he?"

"At exactly 1700 hours you are to be at the principal National Guard checkpoint at the entrance to Barrio del Sur. The negotiator will be accompanied to the roadblock by several colleagues, and he will identify himself to you. But I repeat: if anything happens to the negotiator, the whole deal is off, and I shall proceed with execution of the hostages."

Upstairs in the Assembly hall, Dora Merino walked over to the diplomatic gallery. "Keep your fingers crossed," she said to Julia Savage. "If all goes well, you will sleep in your own bed tonight; and you'll have a surprise, too."

★

The Nuncio's black limousine, the yellow-and-white Vatican flag flying on its right fender, arrived at the Barrio del Sur roadblock at ten minutes before five in the afternoon. The commanding officer of the Guard's elite battalion stood waiting at the side of a Sherman tank. The two men shook hands silently, and Monsignor Bansa checked his watch. Looking down the *barrio* street, he saw burned-out and smashed houses, rubble mixing with garbage on the ground.

At one minute before five o'clock, a small band of armed men came into sight on the *barrio* street, walking briskly toward the checkpoint. Fifteen meters from the Sherman tank, they stopped. A tall figure in a white shirt and *vaquero* trousers embraced each of his companions and then walked alone toward the Nuncio and the colonel.

"I am Rolando Asturias," he said smilingly to Monsignor Bansa. "I am the designated negotiator for the Frente. And by the way, I am also a member of the Jesuit Order, educated in Rome. I am placing myself under your protection."

Escorted by police motorcycles, the Nuncio's limousine reached the National Assembly fifteen minutes later. The sun was beginning to set over Lake Taxchilán when Rolando stepped out of the car and into the arms of Don Pepe Vargas. "Bless you, my son!" the Bishop exclaimed. He had just arrived in Ciudad Malagua.

An emergency telephone had been installed in a National Guard truck in front of the Assembly building, and Monsignor Bansa used it to call Comandante Pablo.

"Your negotiator is here, and so is Bishop Vargas," he said. "We are ready whenever you are."

"In ten minutes," Pablo answered. "At the east side door."

★

Dora Merino and another woman guerrilla, automatic rifles in hand, strolled over to the diplomatic gallery. Addressing the five ambassadors, Dora said, "Please come with us." The diplomats were led to the entrance to the foyer, where Roberto Maxwell and his squad waited. Dora turned to Julia. "Good luck," she said. "Maybe we'll meet again before too long." Impulsively Julia embraced the girl and said, "Please take care of yourself."

Roberto Maxwell and a member of his squad took Julia and the Latin American ambassadors down the inner staircase. The two rebels hung back, and Julia pushed the outer door open. Don Pepe Vargas spread his arms, a huge grin on his tanned face. *"¡Bienvenidos!"* he cried. "You all look healthy and well . . ."

The Bishop showing the way, Julia and the four ambassadors walked up the ramp to the broad avenue. The Guatemalan was muttering imprecations against the rebels. The others moved in silence. Squinting in the sunlight, Julia saw McVeigh standing in the middle of the street with a group of other people. He ran forward, shouting, "Julia, Julia! Thank God." They kissed emotionally and moved toward the group. Then Julia saw Rolando Asturias, looking immensely pleased. Her defenses collapsing, she trembled and burst into tears. Rolando approached and took her hand. "The bad part is now over," he said softly. "The good part starts now. You and I will be seeing a great deal of each other—and openly."

Book Five

★　★　★

The People

20

AFTER a long hot bath, Julia Savage joined Mac McVeigh in the dining room of the Residence, and he brought her up to date as they ate. Just as they finished, the President called Julia from the White House. "You're doing a great job there, Julia," he told her. Then Tom Morelli came on the line to say the same thing, adding that it was urgent for her to get the mediation under way —"as soon as you've had some sleep." Secretary of State Masterson phoned a few minutes later. "Julia, we are proud of you," he said. Terhune from ARA was next, warm and friendly. He too told her how proud she had made the Department and "all of us in the ARA shop."

"God," Julia said to McVeigh, "why do I have to get captured before people show the slightest recognition that I've been doing a decent job all along?" She had received, of course, intensive attention from the media, all three American television networks covering her release from the Assembly earlier that afternoon. Swarms of reporters descended as soon as she had reached safety, but Julia felt that because the political situation was so delicate she should make no public statements. She even refused to talk on the phone to her favorite Washington columnist and friend (with whom she had once almost had an affair), Claude Suzet.

The next morning, Julia found a long telegram of instructions awaiting her at the office. The policy, as set forth by Washington, was to create a "framework"—this was currently a favorite State Department word—for a peaceful transition of power from Juan Ferrer to a "democratic" group that would ultimately become the new government. Julia, according to the telegram, was to achieve this objective within six weeks through negotiations with Ferrer and the "moderate opposition." She was to convey to Ferrer the view of the United States that the time had come for him to yield power voluntarily to forestall a radical takeover.

This was a very tall order, Julia thought as she scribbled notes on the margin of the telegram. The Frente and the EGP were doing well in their offensive, and it might be difficult to persuade them to agree to mediation. Ferrer, for his part, was fighting for his life. The weapons the CIA had been secretly giving him were likely to encourage him to think that in the end he could win the war, and Julia again marveled at the Administration's ability to run entirely contradictory policies. The reality of Malagua was total polarization. But her orders were to mediate.

The first step had to be the freeing of hostages at the National Assembly, and this could be accomplished only through talks with the Frente, which meant Rolando Asturias. Julia dictated a telegram to Washington requesting specific authority to deal with him. Though the Frente had designated him as the official negotiator, Julia wanted the clearance in writing. She had to be extremely careful.

In the meantime, a meeting with Juan Ferrer was necessary. Julia had to sound him out as to whether the mediation process could start with the freeing of political prisoners from Malaguan jails. She had Ann call the National Palace to request an appointment, and word came back that she was expected within the hour.

★

Ciudad Malagua was deserted, except for tanks along Avenida Ferrer and at the approaches to the Palace. The general strike had the capital in its vise, and few people ventured out in the streets. Bluish smoke hovered over Barrio del Sur.

Ferrer received Julia in his office, looking gaunt and tired. "So, this is the start of the American mediation?" he asked sarcastically, shaking hands with her.

"I hope so," she answered. "My government expects that a peaceful solution can be found before too long. We pray that Malagua may be spared a bloodbath."

"That's nice of your government, Julia," Ferrer said. "It's nice to pray while stabbing us in the back, which is exactly what you're doing with your mediation. You are legitimizing Communist rebels, in case you don't realize it."

Julia chose to ignore his remarks and said: "Mr. President, you have publicly agreed to negotiations, and as you know, I have been named to conduct them on behalf of the United States. I think we should concentrate on the release of the National Assembly hostages, but there are conditions posed by those holding them. Evidently, you will not meet all the conditions. Still, the deadlock must be broken, and I would like to approach the other side with some concessions on your part."

"Such as what?"

"I believe the freeing of political prisoners should be one of them. Another helpful concession would be the confining of your troops to barracks while the mediation develops. It goes without saying that the United States does not expect you to announce your intention to resign at this stage."

"That's very considerate of you," Juan Ferrer said, laughing unpleasantly. "I may consider releasing the prisoners, but on conditions of my own: one is that they be flown out of the country, together with the guerrillas at the National Assembly. You can't ask me to let all those people run loose in Malagua. I'm not suicidal, you know. The other condition is the immediate cessation of the general strike. And I will pull my forces back to the barracks *only* when the terrorists call off their attacks. This is my best offer, and you can take it to the Communists. And make no mistake: I'm *not* surrendering."

★

The State Department telegram authorizing Julia to negotiate with the Frente, and specifically with Rolando Asturias, arrived late in the afternoon, though with the cautionary note that no commitments to the rebels were to be made in the name of the United States. Julia had decided to assign Rick Anders, the Political Counselor, to assist her in the mediation work, and now she asked him to set up a meeting with Rolando.

Because the Frente had insisted that the Papal Nuncio, the American Ambassador, and Bishop Vargas be jointly responsible for Rolando's safety, it was agreed that the Jesuit would remain at Monsignor Bansa's residence throughout the negotiations. It was neutral territory, and Rolando was guaranteed freedom to communicate with the Frente leadership. Bishop Vargas had also accepted Monsignor Bansa's invitation to stay temporarily at the *nunciatura,* but he declined his offer to be accompanied by Vatican diplomats whenever he went outside. "I must be free to move alone in my own country, among my own people," he told the Nuncio. "The people are my best protection."

Rick Anders told Julia that the Nuncio had proposed a working dinner that evening at his residence, and she said, "That's fine . . . let's not waste any time."

Two tanks were parked at the entrance to the Nuncio's residence, and scores of heavily armed Guardsmen were deployed along the street as Julia arrived for the dinner. Greeting the Nuncio at the door of his residence, Julia told him that she would demand that Ferrer remove the tanks and the troops from the area: "We are not going to negotiate with guns pointed at us." Monsignor Bansa nodded agreement and led her and Rick Anders to the living room. Bishop Vargas and Rolando Asturias rose as they entered.

"Madam Ambassador, I believe you met the Bishop and Father Asturias yesterday outside the National Assembly," the Nuncio said. Julia smiled and shook hands with them. Rolando held her hand a moment longer and a little harder, their eyes locking for an instant of eternity. He was wearing slacks, a sport shirt, and a light jacket, and Julia realized again how attractive he was. Asturias thought she was the most marvelous sight he had seen in a very long time.

At dinner, after the Nuncio had murmured a prayer, the five of them spent a few minutes exchanging pleasantries. Then Julia suggested they get to the matter at hand. Speaking in Spanish, she addressed Rolando, who sat opposite her on the Nuncio's left. "Tonight, I want to assure you, Father Asturias, that my government will approach this mission of mediation in a completely neutral fashion. In other words, we favor neither side. We hope to assist in a solution that would end bloodshed in Malagua, but we believe that in the end, the people of Malagua must decide their own future. Now I must ask you, Is your side willing to accept our good offices?"

Rolando Asturias looked at Julia, and she thought she detected a flash of amusement in his eyes.

"Does this mean that the United States no longer supports the Ferrer dictatorship in Malagua?" he inquired.

"It means that we are neutral," Julia replied. "But before we can move on to political discussions, we must, in my judgment, arrange the release of the hostages at the National Assembly. So long as they are there, I doubt much progress can be made in other areas."

Rolando said, "It may be so, but we *are* at war, so I must ask you, then, What's in it for us?"

"Fair enough," Julia told him. "I am authorized by General Ferrer to inform you that he is prepared to free all the political prisoners in Malagua if the hostages are released, although he insists that the liberated prisoners be flown out of the country together with the commandos at the Assembly. Furthermore, he agrees to confine his troops to the barracks if your side halts military operations against his forces. In other words, we are talking about a truce. In my opinion, Father Asturias, such a state of affairs would be highly favorable to you. It would open the way to political negotiations for a peaceful transfer of power."

Rolando's eyes narrowed. "Are you telling me that the United

States would *actually* support a transfer of power away from Ferrer? That sounds like a new policy. . . ."

"Let's say for now that we are not ruling anything out," Julia said.

"This is something to think about," Bishop Vargas remarked, "if it can bring freedom, peace, and justice to Malagua."

Rolando turned to the Nuncio. "Monsignor, would you mind if the Ambassador and I had a few words in private?"

★

In the Nuncio's library, under a benignly smiling portrait of John Paul II, Rolando and Julia embraced silently. Then he let her go, taking a step back.

"You look more beautiful than the last time I saw you," he said softly. "That was at the cemetery, remember? And more beautiful than at Santa Teresa del Monte."

"I wasn't all that beautiful yesterday," Julia answered. She was conscious of being foolishly coquettish in the most improbable of circumstances.

"Oh, *that,*" he whispered. "That doesn't count. You did look sort of awful, but lovely at the same time. There's so much I have to say to you, and I will say it soon, I promise. But right now you're Madam Ambassador and I'm the Frente negotiator, so we must talk of less pleasant things. First, I am in favor of United States mediation, and second, I think the hostages ought to be released soon. But I can't take decisions alone—even as a member of the Frente Directorate. You didn't know that, did you?"

"No, I didn't. I thought you were just a fighting priest."

"I am that too. Still, all our decisions are taken collectively. And Máximo Landino is now very much in the picture since his columns came down from the mountains. They are fighting very hard, and we can't ignore them and their voice so long as the war goes on. With Ferrer in power, we must remain united."

"I understand."

"Anyway, I have to consult with the *compañeros* of the Frente on all these points. We can probably resolve alone the question of the hostages if Ferrer does release our prisoners. But I don't know about the truce. That is where Máximo and the EGP come in, and it could be quite difficult. And I'm not convinced that Ferrer is ready for a truce, either. He still has a lot of firepower, and he has to be bloodied quite a bit more before he's prepared to talk seriously. You have a tough job ahead of you, Julia."

"I know," she said, "but I have to start somewhere. That's why I want a quick solution on the hostages. When can I have an answer?"

"Perhaps tomorrow or the day after. I'll communicate with you through the Nuncio as soon as I can."

Rolando kissed her lightly on the lips.

★

Accompanied by Monsignor Bansa, Rolando Asturias drove up to the tank-guarded checkpoint at the entrance to Barrio del Sur. It was the morning after his meeting with Julia, and the Jesuit had made arrangements to return to the Limosna house for several hours for consultations with Major Estella and Manuel Schneider. He had made several telephone calls during the night, speaking in code, and word was passed on to the safe house to expect him after daybreak. An armed escort was sent out to the checkpoint to await Rolando, the men hiding in the alleys until the Nuncio's limousine came into sight. The National Guard had remained outside the *barrio* since its attack the previous week, and the rebels now felt fairly secure in the labyrinthine slum. The Nuncio had notified Ferrer's office that he was bringing Rolando Asturias for a brief visit to the *barrio;* the Guardsmen on duty were ordered not to interfere.

In the cellar of the poet-carpenter's house, Rolando gave Major Estella and Schneider a detailed account of his conversation with Julia at the *nunciatura.* "I think 'Plan Zero' has been quite successful so far," Rolando concluded. "It has accomplished a number of things. Most importantly, it has shown Ferrer's vulnerability. I think the overall situation has been altered drastically—in our favor."

"In that case," Major Estella said, "why should we negotiate?

As you say, the momentum is with us. So let's keep the hostages indefinitely, and let the military operations proceed—with both Frente and EGP forces. We can defeat the tyrant on the battlefield, even if it takes weeks or even months, and we'll have a clear victory. To hell with negotiations.''

"You're overlooking the political aspect, Hugo,'' Manuel Schneider said. "American support is crucial, and I agree with Rolando that it might be worthwhile to make a deal over the hostages to keep the United States on our side. You are right that military pressure should be maintained, but at the right moment we'd want the Americans to give Ferrer the final push. Besides, we have to think of Máximo Landino and the problems we'll have with him in the future. You know that Máximo is determined to be the new *jefe,* the new Fidel.''

"Bueno," Major Estella replied. "I see your point. But the decision ought to be unanimous. The other *compañeros* of the Directorate have to be consulted. And we must establish permanent liaison with the EGP for military purposes.''

"Absolutely,'' Rolando Asturias said. "If you give me your agreement on the negotiations, I'll get in touch at once with the others.''

★

With the tanks and National Guard troops removed from the area in front of the *nunciatura*—Juan Ferrer had agreed to order them away after a call from Julia Savage—it was easy for Rolando Asturias to slip unnoticed in the dark into the American Embassy's Chrysler. He squeezed himself between Julia and Monsignor Bansa in the back seat, while Bishop Vargas sat in the front between Salvador and Gonzalo.

The Chrysler with its escort cars proceeded down Avenida Ferrer to the American Residence. Inside the Residence grounds, Rolando transferred to a waiting black Embassy sedan next to Rick Anders, who was behind the wheel. As Julia, the Nuncio, and Bishop Vargas entered the Residence, Rick Anders pulled out into the Avenida and, directed by Rolando, turned right. Within a few minutes, they reached a lakeside villa, and Rolando said, "This is it." Rick parked the car, and the two men walked to the door. The Jesuit rang the bell four times, and a young girl servant let them in. Tomás Martínez and Juan Carlos Reyes, the physician, stood in the hallway, submachine guns cradled in their arms. Recognizing Rolando in the dimness of the foyer, they relaxed.

"Why don't you have a drink here while I chat with my friends," Rolando told the American. Rick nodded and sat down as the others disappeared into an adjoining room. It had been decided by Julia and the Nuncio that the safest way for Rolando to meet with Martínez and Reyes at their hideout was for Anders to drive him over to the villa. To a passing patrol, the presence of a parked sedan with diplomatic license plates would suggest simply that an American official was visiting friends on the lake, a normal occurrence. The régime knew that members of the Frente command operated from somewhere in Barrio del Sur, but it obviously did not suspect the existence of a safe house in the expensive residential district. And Rolando wanted to keep it that way.

He briefed Martínez and Reyes on his initial contact with Julia Savage and on his consultations earlier that day with Major Estella and Manuel Schneider. The two Frente leaders asked a number of questions and then gave their assent to the proposed negotiations. "I suppose we have nothing to lose," the physician remarked.

"There are two more things," Rolando Asturias said. "One is to consult Dora Merino and Pablo inside the National Assembly. Don Pepe Vargas will be escorted to the Assembly by the Nuncio, and he will explain the situation to them. The other matter is liaison with Máximo Landino. I would like to ask *compañero* Tomás to undertake this mission. I realize it's very dangerous, but he's the only one who can carry it out properly. Máximo doesn't care much for me. Are you willing to go?"

"Yes, of course," Tomás Martínez replied. "But where do I find Máximo, and how do I get there?"

"No problem," Rolando said. "You will be picked up by somebody tomorrow morning and you will be taken there. Just be sure to carry no weapons on you."

★

Back at the Residence, Rolando rejoined Julia, the Nuncio, and Bishop Vargas, who were talking quietly in the living room. Don Pepe had been telling stories of his childhood in the highlands and of his early years as a priest. A short, dark-complexioned man, he was vivacious and full of good humor.

"Ah, here's the next Foreign Minister of the Republic of Malagua!" the Bishop explained as the Jesuit walked into the room.

"You flatter me, Don Pepe," Rolando said. "But just in case you're right, you must let me practice some quiet diplomacy. Do you mind if the Ambassador and I have three minutes alone?"

Julia led him to the library, closing the door behind them. She put her arms around Rolando and kissed him gently. "There," she said, "you've earned it." He kissed her back, slowly and sensually. Julia marveled at how comfortable she was with him, more comfortable than with any other man she had ever known.

Rolando said, "I have something to tell you. Today, I formally renounced the priesthood. Don Pepe has accepted my renunciation in the name of the Church: he understands my problem of faith. Of course, to make it legal, I still have to petition the Holy See for my release, and that may be refused. But I'm prepared to live with that fate—my way."

"Oh, Lord," Julia breathed.

★

As Rolando Asturias was driving to the lakeside villa, a heavily loaded DC-7 landed at Ciudad Malagua's Air Force base. Murphy had left Santiago, Chile, at dawn, refueled in Panama, and reached his destination in excellent time, pushed by strong tail winds. "Let's have a beer and hit the sack," he told his copilot as they taxied to a stop. "We're taking off at first light for St. Thomas to pick up another cargo."

John Crespo was at the field to check in the DC-7 and supervise the unloading by Malaguan Air Force troops. He called Jim Morgan at home from Operations to advise him of the plane's arrival, hating himself. The Station Chief grunted, put down the phone, and went out to his car. This time he had no trouble entering the National Palace and making his way to the bunker command post.

"Okay, Mr. President," he told Juan Ferrer. "My plane just came in from Santiago with a lot of good stuff for you. Mortars, flamethrowers, and that sort of thing. Also ammo. We'll have another shipment tomorrow from the Virgin Islands. You see, we keep our word."

"Just in time, just in time," Ferrer said. "Tomorrow is the big day. Watch us zap the sons-of-bitches."

A tall, thin man in the uniform of a National Guard general was leaning against the wall. His skin was pockmarked, and one cheek was slashed with a deep scar. Shifting into Spanish, Ferrer said: "Look here, Bauch-Barriga, a planeload of equipment was delivered tonight. You can send some of it to the brigade at Jacaltec, and keep the rest in town. We can use it here for something special I have in mind."

He pointed at the tall general, and told Morgan in English: "This is Roberto Bauch-Barriga, the best fucking general I have. I've put him in overall command of operations. He doesn't speak a word of English, but he's a real tiger."

Morgan said, *"Mucho gusto,"* but Bauch-Barriga did not reply.

"By the way, Mr. President," the Station Chief asked, "how's the negotiation going?"

"Your Ambassador was here yesterday with her pretty little speech about concessions and American mediation and all that bullshit. I wouldn't worry about it, Jim—so long as you keep sending the goodies."

★

A fine spring drizzle was falling on Ciudad Malagua as the Papal Nuncio and Don Pepe Vargas arrived at the National Assembly building at ten o'clock in the morning of the next day, a

Friday. Guardsmen stepped back to let Monsignor Bansa's limousine through. The Nuncio left the car and walked over to the Guard truck with the special telephone to the rostrum inside the Assembly.

"Bishop Vargas is here to see you," he told Comandante Pablo. "He'll come in through the east side door."

Don Pepe made his way to the lower-level entrance, and two *guerrilleros* let him into the building. They greeted him effusively and led him to the upstairs foyer. Dora Merino and Pablo awaited the Bishop there. After exchanging embraces, Don Pepe explained that he had come in the name of the Frente's Directorate to ask for Dora's agreement to the negotiations proposed by the United States.

"Ambassador Savage will conduct the negotiations," he said. "Your companions hope you will accept. Personally, I favor it."

Comandante Pablo began to protest, but Dora Merino cut him short. "Excuse me, Comandante," she said, "but this is a matter for Directorate decision. And if the Bishop says that the others approve and that he is in accord too, then I say yes as well. The release of our prisoners is very important. And I have very good reasons for trusting the American Ambassador. She was my father's friend. . . ."

In the limousine, Don Pepe said to the Nuncio: "I would appreciate it if you could drop me at the Cathedral, Monsignor, if it isn't out of your way. I shall be saying Mass at noon, as I do every Friday."

★

Late in the morning, a television-repair van stopped outside the lakeside villa. The driver, wearing a coverall and a light cap, stepped out and rang the doorbell four times. The maid motioned him inside.

"I am to take you to Jacaltec," the man said to Tomás Martínez, handing him a faded coverall. "Please put this on. You will find an identity *cédula* in one of the pockets. You will be safe with me."

★

Julia Savage was at her desk at the Embassy, drafting a telegram to the State Department on her meeting with Asturias the previous evening, when John Crespo entered unannounced at a few minutes before noon.

"Morgan is out somewhere," he said, "so I thought I'd drop in to let you know that another shipment of arms for Ferrer arrived from Chile last night. And another one is due in later today from St. Thomas."

Julia banged the desk with both her fists. "God damn them!" she burst out. "The bastards! How dare they? Do they realize what they're doing?"

A series of explosions, one after another in rapid succession, suddenly shook the building. From the window Julia saw three helicopters wheeling away from Barrio del Sur, tall columns of smoke rising behind them. Then she saw cannon-muzzle flashes around the *barrio*, and more black smoke.

"They're bombing and bombarding the *barrio*," John Crespo said in an unnaturally quiet voice. "They're out to smash it to smithereens."

★

Don Pepe Vargas had arrived at the Cathedral at eleven forty-five. After donning his vestments in the sacristy, he walked toward the small altar of San Antonio, stopping here and there to bless the *pordioseros*, among whom a new dwarf had appeared, and to exchange greetings with the faithful, young and old, who were gathered for the Mass. People always came to his masses, even on weekdays, as much to pray with him as to listen to his homilies about social justice and political freedom.

The bishop bowed deeply before the statue of San Antonio, and genuflected. As the clock in the tower began to strike noon, Don Pepe heard the deafening explosions over the barrio and, at the same time, felt a sharp pain in his back. He turned around and, as through a mist, saw the muzzles of two submachine guns still firing at him, riveting his body with bullets. His lips moved with the last great effort of his life: "May God forgive . . ." And Don Pepe Vargas slowly crumpled in front of the altar.

An old *pordiosero* bent over to kiss Don Pepe's inert right hand.

21

JUAN Ferrer had always been a realist, a player who knew how to adjust to new and changing situations. But now the Malaguan dictator was losing control of events—and of himself.

He had agreed to announce his willingness to negotiate with the Frente under United States auspices only when Jim Morgan promised him more CIA arms. Ferrer was cunning enough to have made the deal, but he had no intention of going through with any further negotiations—and Morgan had encouraged him to break his commitment as soon as Julia was free. The dictator believed that with the CIA's help, he still could win the war. And with new CIA shipments arriving in Ciudad Malagua, he was ready to strike again.

Thus at noon of that Friday late in November, the National Guard again attacked Barrio del Sur with planes, helicopters, tanks, and artillery under the command of General Roberto Bauch-Barriga, while another offensive was being launched simultaneously in the northeast. This time, the purpose was not to punish, but to destroy Juan Ferrer's enemies once and for all. The slum was in the hands of the Frente, so it had to vanish. In Jacaltec, the EGP was the threat, so it had to be liquidated.

★

The bombardment of the *barrio* lasted two hours. First, C-47 aircraft flew low over the vast slum area, at less than 1,000 feet, dropping hundred-pound demolition bombs. Then Alouette helicopters made banking passes, spraying napalm and antipersonnel fragmentation bombs. Sherman tanks and APCs, deployed around the *barrio*, fired steadily into the shantytown at point-blank range. Nobody knew how many *malagueños* lived in the slum, but a hundred thousand was a good guess, and many thousands of them were killed in these two hours of fire rain. Most of the remaining buildings collapsed or were burned to the ground.

One of these was the house of José Manuel Limosna, the poet-carpenter, where Major Hugo Estella and Manuel Schneider had been hiding for more than a week. When the first bombs exploded in the *barrio,* Major Estella rushed to the VHF radio in the cellar to call the Directorate members at the villa on Lake Taxchilán and Dora Merino at the National Assembly. "We are under air attack," he said quietly, "and I think there's a lot more to come." At that moment, a bomb scored a direct hit, and the cellar ceiling crashed down on Hugo Estella, killing him instantly. The carpenter and his pregnant wife were buried in their kitchen when the whole roof caved in. Manuel Schneider was standing in the alleyway outside, guarding the house, and he was thrown clear by the blast. Bruised and lacerated and with a broken collarbone, he was the only survivor of the *barrio* command post.

At two o'clock in the afternoon, General Bauch-Barriga, directing operations from a staff car a half-mile away, ordered the infantry of the Guard's elite battalion to advance into the slum behind tanks. "Shoot to kill anyone you see on your way in," he radioed his company commanders.

The order was followed without hesitation or mercy. Troops emptied their submachine guns at the men, women, and children who were fleeing from burning houses, and at the wounded who lay moaning in the streets. There were no exceptions for women or children. Manuel Schneider escaped death because he lay motionless in front of the carpenter's ruined house when a Guard platoon swept past him. At three o'clock in the afternoon, the occupation of the *barrio* was completed, and black *zopilote* birds replaced the planes and helicopters in the sky over the slum, circling lower and lower—hungrily.

★

Elsewhere in Ciudad Malagua, inhabitants hid in their houses when the bombardment of the *barrio* started, fearing that the unleashed Guard might storm other quarters of the city as well. Thus word of Bishop Vargas' murder did not spread throughout the capital until later in the day, when people began to emerge cautiously into the streets. The *pordioseros* and the faithful at the Cathedral, who alone knew the terrible truth, waited out the *barrio* war inside the House of the Lord, staring at Don Pepe's blood-drenched body, which rested peacefully before the altar.

★

Julia Savage picked up her direct-line telephone and dialed the National Palace. "This is the Ambassador of the United States, and I demand to speak to the President."

After a minute's wait, Juan Ferrer came on the line.

"You have broken your agreement to negotiate, and you have violated the truce," she said without preamble. "Your troops are killing innocent people. In the name of my government I insist that you halt this bloodshed. Otherwise I shall recommend to Washington the suspension of diplomatic relations with Malagua."

"Hey, take it easy, Julia!" Ferrer exclaimed. "I haven't violated anything. This was nothing but a limited police action to clear the *barrio* of some of the rebels and criminal elements. There was no bloodshed. I'm still ready to negotiate under your auspices."

"Mr. President, you are not telling the truth," Julia replied coldly. "I saw your helicopters bombing the area. I must repeat: if you value relations with the United States, you will put a stop immediately to your 'police action.' . . . I am informing Washington of what is happening in Malagua.''

★

Julia slammed the receiver down hard, her body heaving with anger. She pressed the intercom, and told Ann Mestre: ''Get me the White House, please. I want to talk to Morelli.''

Her phone rang two minutes later. ''Julia? What's the matter?'' the National Security Adviser asked with alarm. ''Are you all right?''

''I am, but Malagua is not,'' Julia said. ''Tom, have you any idea of what's happening here? Do you know that Ferrer has bombed the hell out of the biggest slum in this town with planes, helicopters, and tanks? That there are probably thousands of casualties?''

''My God, we haven't heard a word.''

''And Tom, are you aware that Ferrer has been receiving, and is still receiving, arms from the CIA?''

There was a brief silence at the other end. Then Morelli said, ''You know this is not a secure line. We shouldn't be discussing this sort of thing over it.''

''I don't give a damn,'' Julia snapped. ''All I know is that thousands of people are dying here because of those arms.''

''Well, Julia,'' Morelli said, ''it's a little complicated. But yes, there was authorization for a single delivery a few weeks ago.''

''And I wasn't informed? Why? I *am* the Ambassador here.''

''No, you were not informed for complex national-security reasons.''

''Okay,'' she said. ''But what about the shipment that came in last night, and one that's arriving today?''

''I give you my word I know nothing at all about that,'' Morelli told her. ''And I'm positive the President hasn't authorized it. Let me find out what's going on. We'll stop whatever is on the way.''

''Tom, I want you to know one thing. If you can't put an end to the shipments, you will leave me no choice but to resign—and go public.''

★

Arriving at the Nuncio's residence, Julia found Monsignor Bansa and Rolando Asturias sitting in silence in the living room. After her telephone conversations with Ferrer and Morelli, she felt it was urgent to contact the Frente. She was afraid that the attack on the *barrio* might have destroyed her mediation efforts. And she had to be sure that Rolando had not been hurt—or killed. Seeing Rolando in the room was an immense relief. But before she could speak, he raised his hand.

"Julia," Rolando said in English. "Something terrible has happened. Don Pepe Vargas has been murdered. He was gunned down at the Cathedral just as he was preparing to celebrate Mass —exactly when the attack on the *barrio* was starting."

Julia sank into an armchair, dizziness coming over her. Tears rolled down her face. "Don Pepe," she whispered. "Oh, my God, why? Who did it?"

"I don't know their names," Rolando said harshly. "There were two of them. With submachine guns. All I know is that Don Pepe's blood is on the hands of the tyrant. They were his gunmen. Nobody else in Malagua—nobody—would have touched a hair on his head. He was loved by our people."

"You're right, I'm sure," Julia said weakly. "But what happens now? I telephoned Ferrer at the Palace to protest the bombardment, and I threatened him with suspending diplomatic relations if he didn't stop the killings in the *barrio*. I didn't have the authority to do it, but I said it anyway. Christ, what else can I do?"

"Get your government to back you up on it," Rolando answered. "Malaguans are being killed with American weapons, and if the United States doesn't come out firmly and clearly on the side of the people of Malagua now—right now —we shall have to go our own way, and you know what that means."

"I understand," Julia said. "I'd better go now and see what I can do, but we mustn't break off contact."

The Nuncio bowed, and Rolando walked Julia to the door. He

pressed her hand. "You and I will never break off, no matter what happens," he said, kissing her quickly on the forehead.

★

It was evening when the panel truck veered off the main highway, taking the road toward Jacaltec. Several National Guard trucks full of soldiers coming from the town passed Tomás Martínez and his companion on the narrow road, but they were not challenged. In the distance, they heard the rumble of artillery fire, and planes roared low overhead. Ten minutes later, the driver made a sharp turn onto a rutted forest lane and switched off the truck's lights. "We'll be there in a few minutes, *compañero*," he said.

A weak light blinked ahead, and the truck stopped. Several men surrounded the vehicle, and a flashlight shone at Tomás Martínez and the driver.

"Get out and come with us," one of the men said. "Comandante Máximo is waiting for you."

Landino stood in the doorway of a darkened farmhouse, a submachine gun over his shoulder and four *guerrilleros* at his side.

"Welcome, *compañero*," he said. "I don't have much time, because several of my columns are engaged in heavy fighting with the Guard just north of here, and I must get back to the front line. First, tell me, Why did you and Asturias not let us know that you were going to spring the National Assembly coup?"

"Because it hadn't been quite decided yet, and because you didn't seem very much interested in coming down from the mountains to join the Frente in an offensive."

"*Bueno*—I'll accept that for now," Máximo said. "But as you can see, we *have* come down, and we are fighting. And doing very well, too. We inflicted heavy losses on the Guard last night and captured a lot of good equipment. I have a whole brigade pinned down around Jacaltec. I hear that another brigade is moving against us from the east—we had some air attacks today—but we can handle them."

"That's good news. But I'm here to ask you a question: Are we going to fight this war together or separately?"

"Oh, we're in it together, *compañero*. Unity against the tyrant is essential."

"Okay. Now I have a follow-up question: Is the EGP prepared to join with the Frente in forming a democratic government after the victory?"

Máximo Landino thought it over for a moment.

"I'll be honest with you, Don Tomás, because of my deep respect for you," he said. "Yes. The EGP will participate in a government with the Frente, but only on the clear understanding that we shall maintain our separate political identity. In the end, the people will decide what form of government they wish to have in Malagua. We must be prepared for disagreements. However, I promise you that we shall be quite open about where we stand. It is the only way for us."

★

Saturday, November 19, was one of the most beautiful days of the Malagua spring. People commented on it—ironically—as they began leaving their houses early in the morning from one end of the capital to the other. First singly, then in pairs, finally in groups that swelled from block to block, they marched from all directions toward the Cathedral. It was like a procession on the day of Our Lady of Malagua—everyone in holiday attire: men in dark suits or shirts, women in black dresses, children in the best finery their parents could afford. Many carried flowers, single blossoms or little bouquets. Others carried candles. The march, however, was silent and somber, not festive. The mood was sad and angry and defiant as the people of Ciudad Malagua went to honor Don Pepe Vargas, the martyr.

Curiously, nobody had summoned them to do so. There had been no special communication among the families the previous afternoon and evening when everybody had learned, it seemed at the same time, that the bishop from the highlands had been murdered at the altar of San Antonio, a revered saint who had performed important miracles in the course of Malaguan history. It was a spontaneous decision, by each family, to take final leave of Don Pepe, although no funeral or Mass had been planned for that day. It was not even certain whether the body of the murdered priest still remained at the Cathedral: and it did not truly matter. The *malagueños* wished to pay him the last tribute.

★

Doña Silvia Palos de Ferrer awoke shortly after dawn, the sun already brightening her bedroom in the National Palace. She had learned of Don Pepe's death from the servants the evening before, and asked her husband about it when he appeared briefly in the upstairs apartments to change for dinner.

"Yes, the Bishop is dead," Juan Ferrer had told her impatiently. "And don't you go blaming me for it."

"God will punish you," Doña Silvia whispered.

Now she put on a black dress, selected a single rose from a vase on her dresser, and picked up the telephone. She dialed a number and said, "Tell Marcos that I'm going out, that I'll be there, that the people of Malagua count on him."

Then Doña Silvia took the private elevator to the ground floor and walked alone out of the Palace into the courtyard. Passing the saluting guards, she went through the iron gates into the tank-filled plaza.

★

By ten o'clock, the square around the Cathedral was filled with mourners, silently standing in the hot sun in absolute silence. The side streets were becoming impassable as the crowd grew larger and larger. Guard and police patrols had fallen back from the area, disoriented and frightened. A G-2 officer telephoned the bunker command post at the Palace and said with alarm: "*Mi General,* you have at least one hundred thousand people around the Cathedral. They aren't doing anything: just standing there."

Juan Ferrer called General Marcos Pacheco Lutz, the commander of the Ciudad Malagua garrison at the barracks on the southern outskirts of the capital, beyond Barrio del Sur.

"Listen, Pacheco," he said, "There's quite a crowd at the Cathedral, probably because of the dead Bishop. Bauch-Barriga is tied down holding the *barrio,* and I want him to stay there. Your units are the only troops I have in reserve in the city. You are to surround the whole area, then start breaking up the crowd. Bring some tanks in as close as possible, then have the infantry advance in wedges. Tear gas and bayonets ought to do it, but you are free to open fire with everything you have, if necessary. I trust your judgment."

★

A half-hour later, the garrison battalion reached the Cathedral district, General Pacheco riding in a jeep ahead of the tanks. A short, compact man with an authoritative air, he was greatly liked and respected by his officers and troops. His battalion was the Guard's tactical reserve, and it never participated in the search-and-destroy operations against the guerrillas in the mountains around Ciudad Malagua. Instead, it had considerable contact with the inhabitants of the southern section of the city and had something of a sense of kinship with them.

Suddenly, the silence in the Cathedral square was broken by a chant, at first timid, then rising in a great rush of sound toward the spires of the church and the blue sky. The crowd was singing the national anthem: ". . . In the shadow of our volcanoes . . . On the shores of our lakes . . . Free Malagua will live forever. . . ."

General Pacheco's second-in-command, a young colonel, asked nervously, "What are the orders? What shall we do?"

Pacheco looked at him and said, "Nothing."

"But General—"

"I said, nothing. There is no law against singing the national anthem."

The strains of the song trailed off in the still air of the morning, and a hush descended on the square once more. But the crowd had established a common identity—a sense of oneness—and a purpose. Now the crowd had to act in some fashion, to assert itself, and every person in the square knew that it would be so—

as if electric impulses had flashed through their minds and psyches.

Silvia Palos de Ferrer, a black *mantilla* on her head, felt this spirit as she stood near the Cathedral's steps. So did beautiful Antonia Llosa de Schneider, who had had no news from Manuel, her husband, for over ten days. Esteban Arismendi, a pharmacist whose shop was behind the Cathedral, felt it, as did John Crespo, who hovered discreetly on the far edge of the crowd—not on an assignment for the CIA Station, but to satisfy his own needs.

A woman's voice rang out, loud and clear: *"¡Tirano! . . . ¡Asesino! . . ."*

Instantly, the crowd picked it up as a choir responds to the first notes of the soloist, repeating the theme in a rhythmic chant: *TI-RA-NO . . . A-SE-SI-NO . . . TI-RA-NO . . . A-SE-SI-NO . . .* It swayed with the chant like a ceiba forest in the wind: *¡A-SE-SI-NO! . . . ¡A-SE-SI-NO! . . .*

Troops of the Guard's garrison battalion heard the threatening chant at their positions on the outer perimeter of the crowd. The men stiffened, safety catches clicking off on their weapons, tear-gas grenades being fitted into launchers.

The young colonel touched General Pacheco's arm. "Now?" he asked. "Now shall we move?"

Pacheco took a cigarette from a silver case. He lit it and watched the smoke curl upward. "No, Colonel," he answered, "we are *not* moving anywhere. Not yet."

"But the Jefe has ordered that the mob be dispersed. If we don't attack, it will get out of hand."

"So let it," Pacheco told him. "This battalion will not massacre *malagueños* so long as I am in command." He drew his .45-caliber Colt from the holster, pointing it at the colonel. "You understand?"

★

On this Saturday, Julia Savage stayed at the Residence instead of going to her office. She too had a presentiment of things to come. Don Pepe's assassination, Juan Ferrer's *Blitzkrieg* in the slums, and Rolando Asturias' warnings had convinced her that Malagua was about to explode.

Julia and McVeigh had agreed that in the event of a major disturbance in the city, the Residence would become the operational center: she could not risk being trapped at the Embassy building. McVeigh and Colonel Victor Brown, the Defense Attaché, manned the office while Rick Anders of the Political Section and Mark Starek, the security officer, joined Julia at the Residence. Jim Morgan could not be found. Starek had ordered most of the Marine contingent to the Residence, the men breaking out their M-16 rifles and shotguns.

In a series of calls to the White House and the State Department the previous evening, Julia had told Washington that the crisis in Malagua could be coming to a head in the next forty-eight or seventy-two hours. About midnight, Terence Terhune phoned her with a "new set of instructions." It was absolutely essential, he said, for the Embassy to establish contact with the Frente—"just in case." Julia was too tired to laugh, saying only, "Yes, Terry, I'm aware of it." She did not bother to remind him that the Department had authorized her earlier that week to negotiate directly with Rolando Asturias, whom she had described as a member of the Frente's Directorate. Then Tom Morelli called to inform Julia—sheepishly—that he had discovered "some irregularities" in "certain shipments," and that the President had ordered "appropriate authorities" to prevent a recurrence. "The President was hopping mad," Morelli told her.

By midmorning, McVeigh advised Julia from downtown that huge crowds were gathering around the Cathedral, and she passed the information on to the State Department's Operations Center in Washington over an open phone line from the Residence. A few minutes later, Rick Anders ushered the Nuncio and Rolando Asturias into Julia's study.

Monsignor Bansa said, "Father Asturias wanted to speak with you urgently, so I brought him over. I'll wait in the living room while you two talk in here."

Smiling tensely, Rolando kissed Julia on the cheek.

"Things may be happening very rapidly from now on," he said. "The situation at the Cathedral is uncontrollable, and I can't predict what the people will do next. But this may be *it*. I want you to know, Julia, that the Frente and the EGP—we are now in touch with Landino—are prepared to form a provisional government to take over from Ferrer the moment he collapses. I must know, therefore, what will be the reaction of the United States. What the United States does at this juncture will influence future events."

"All I can tell you now," Julia replied, "is that I am instructed to maintain contact with the Frente—with you—and that I'm in permanent contact with Washington. Let's deal with the situation as it develops. But we can act very quickly at the right moment. Trust me, Rolando. And please—be careful."

★

Juan Ferrer was pacing up and down his bunker command post like a caged panther. He had been told by G-2 a few minutes earlier that the crowd at the Cathedral had erupted in shouts of *"Tirano—Asesino"* and that the Guard garrison battalion had failed to move. Ferrer had tried to get Pacheco on the radio, but the General refused to answer.

"I'm being betrayed," Ferrer bellowed. "This *comemierda* Pacheco is ignoring my orders. I always suspected he was pro-Communist. God, I should've relieved him of his command and slammed him in prison long ago. I'll kill him as soon as I get my hands on him."

Jim Morgan, sitting in a corner of the room, chomped silently on his cigar.

"And you know what else?" Ferrer yelled. "That God-damned wife of mine has disappeared. The guards say she left the Palace early this morning. What is she up to? The fucking rats are abandoning the ship, but this ship ain't sinking yet, I promise you. I'll get even with every stinking son-of-a-bitch if it's the last thing I do. Jim, when is the next shipment coming in? I may be running low on ammo."

"It's not coming," Morgan said quietly. "The White House ordered us to lay off."

★

At the Cathedral square, a new chant swept the crowd: *¡Muerte al tirano!* and *¡Abajo Ferrer!* The roar, like thunder, rolled from thousands of throats. Then, from somewhere in front of the church, still another cry arose: *¡Al Palacio!* . . . *¡Al Palacio!* . . . And this too was picked up by the multitude in a rhythmic chorus. The Frente's black-and-red flags appeared over the heads of the crowd as it veered away from the Cathedral and into the narrow street linking the square with the Palace plaza on El Cerro.

The human torrent poured down the ancient street between colonial buildings, slowing down only briefly when the tanks and APCs guarding the Palace opened fire. Thirty or forty people in the vanguard of the column fell, but hundreds and then thousands rushed into El Cerro, overtaking and surrounding the tanks, and advancing on the Palace gates. Silvia Palos de Ferrer, propelled by the mob, was among them. She thought it was a strangely new way to be returning home from the Cathedral. Troopers in the Palace courtyard took aim at the advancing mass.

In his jeep, less than a quarter of a mile away, General Pacheco lifted his radio microphone and called Juan Ferrer in the bunker.

"Presidente," he said, "this is Pacheco. My troops are on the side of the people of Malagua. I no longer take orders from you. Please instruct your forces at the Palace to cease firing at once. Otherwise, I shall bring up my armor and infantry to protect the people."

The young colonel in the jeep reached for his gun, and Pacheco shot him through the heart. The soldiers shouted their approval: *¡Viva Pacheco! ¡Viva Pacheco! ¡Guardia con el pueblo!*

★

Juan Ferrer radioed General Bauch-Barriga to race his tanks to the Palace.

"I don't know if I can," the General replied. "My troops in the *barrio* are under intense sniper fire, and I need the tanks."

"Fuck the *barrio*," Ferrer screamed into the microphone. "Get over here on the double."

Now the great crowd had reached the iron gates of the Palace, and gasoline-filled bottles with flaming wicks sailed over the fence, crashing in the courtyard, where men of Ferrer's personal guard began falling back, though still firing intermittently. Then four tanks turned around in the plaza, pointing their guns at the Palace. They had been taken over by Frente students in the crowd, their crews disarmed and beaten to death. From behind the Palace, General Pacheco's tanks appeared, black-and-red flags flying from their turrets, and they smashed through the rear gate.

General Pacheco again took the radio microphone in hand. "Presidente," he said, "your Palace is completely surrounded. I urge you to capitulate now, instructing your forces everywhere in the territory of the Republic to lay down their arms. I am assuming overall military command in the name of the people of Malagua. You have five minutes to hoist a white flag before I order that the Palace be assaulted. Your personal safety will be guaranteed."

Pale as a ghost, Ferrer turned around to look at his command post. Only Jim Morgan and the dwarf Fabio remained there. His generals and colonels had fled.

"It looks like you have no choice, Mr. President," Morgan remarked. "You'd better have Bauch-Barriga surrender too, before his troops turn on him—and on you. Now, I think, it's every man for himself. And as for me, I'm leaving. It wouldn't do for me to be found here by the new people."

★

The Palace guard dropped their weapons, the men raising their hands over their heads as Pacheco's troops and the roaring crowd broke into the courtyard. Then a white flag appeared in a Palace window, and within minutes General Marcos Pacheco Lutz entered the basement bunker at the head of a squad of submachine-gun-wielding soldiers.

"Mi General," Pacheco told Juan Ferrer, "I declare you under arrest. You will remain here under the protection of my men until the new government decides your fate."

Juan Ferrer removed his pistol from the holster and placed it on the map table. In a corner of the room, Fabio furtively took a pill from a pocket and put it in his mouth. His body was shaken by convulsions, and he dropped to the floor—dead. Ferrer noticed nothing.

★

At the Residence, Julia Savage was on the phone to Tom Morelli at the White House. John Crespo had called a few minutes earlier to say that the Guard's garrison battalion had turned against Ferrer and was assaulting the Palace, with tens of thousands of civilians behind its tanks.

"Ferrer seems to be finished," Julia was saying to Morelli. "And . . . Wait a minute, Tom . . . there's something on television . . ."

A Guard general appeared on the screen and began to speak: "My name is Marcos Pacheco Lutz. I am the commander of the Ciudad Malagua garrison, and I am speaking to you from the Presidential Palace in the capital. The Palace is in the hands of the armed nation, and General Juan Ferrer Berrio is under arrest."

Pacheco paused, and went on: "As of this hour, Malagua is free again. My forces will maintain order in the Republic, and I will turn over the power to civilian authorities once a provisional government is formed. Meanwhile, I appeal to the people to remain calm and to refrain from reprisals against members of the deposed régime. Those who have committed crimes will be judged by the courts of the Republic. *¡Viva el pueblo! ¡Viva Malagua!"*

"Ferrer has fallen," Julia said to Tom Morelli in Washington. "The revolution has triumphed, and for now, a General Pacheco is in control. The United States must immediately announce where it stands.''

★

Within minutes of General Pacheco's speech, Ciudad Malagua was swept by the greatest celebration within memory. Strangers embraced each other in the streets as happy throngs chanted, *Se cayó . . . se cayó*—"He has fallen . . . he has fallen." Black-and-red Frente flags appeared everywhere; Pacheco's troopers put on makeshift black-and-red armbands, and ecstatic Malaguans kissed and hugged them.

Manuel Schneider telephoned his house from downtown—he had left the *barrio* when the assault ended—to say that he was alive and well; Antonia had not returned home yet, but now the message awaited her with the servants. The lakeside villa where Tomás Martínez and Juan Carlos Reyes had been hiding was transformed into the headquarters of the Frente Malagueño de Liberación Nacional. Rolando Asturias rushed there in the Nuncio's limousine to join his companions. Prisons in Ciudad Malagua opened their doors, and political prisoners streamed out into the sunlight. One of them was Máximo Landino's father. At the National Assembly, Dora Merino and Comandante Pablo announced over loudspeakers that the occupation was over and "all of you are free to go. . . ."

In the plaza on El Cerro, in front of the Presidential Palace, Red Cross workers and volunteers tended to the wounded and removed the dead. One of the bodies, torn by machine-gun bullets, was that of Doña Silvia Palos de Ferrer. Someone had placed a black *mantilla* over her face, and a wilted red rose was clutched in her hand.

"Señoras y señores—y compañeros," General Marcos Pacheco Lutz announced stiffly to several hundred men and women assembled in the vast reception hall of the National Palace. Most of them were Frente militants, and they had been urged by their leaders to come to the Palace. "Yesterday the dictatorship of the Ferrer dynasty came to an inglorious end, and the proud date of November 19 will be remembered by our future generations. Now we face the task of reconstruction, the task of creating democracy in our country, the task of instituting social justice for all. This, however, is the responsibility of the civilian leaders of Malagua—not of the military."

Applause and shouts of *¡Viva Malagua!* swept the hall, interrupting the stern-faced general. Pacheco had never before spoken in public—except to his soldiers—and he was ill at ease addressing the festive crowd at the National Palace. He had memorized the speech—making it a bit flowery in the Castilian political tradition, yet short and to the point. The audience loved it: the short General, still in battle dress, was declaring the dawn of a new age for Malagua. The leaders of the revolution and many of those who had fought and conspired with them against Juan Ferrer were gathered at the Palace to see their hopes and dreams at last come true. And all Malagua watched it on television.

Pacheco raised his hand for silence, and went on self-consciously: "Yesterday, I announced that the armed forces would step aside when a civilian government was constituted. I am ready to fulfill my pledge. Inasmuch as agreement has been reached on the formation of a *junta,* I herewith present to you Compañero Tomás Martínez, the head of the Junta."

The General smiled, and made room in front of the microphone for Tomás Martínez, the former prisoner of the dictatorship.

★

On Saturday night, while Malagua, intoxicated with joy, was celebrating Juan Ferrer's fall, the Frente headquarters at the lakeside villa, guarded by young armed rebels in ragtag uniforms, had been the center of frenzied political activity. Tomás Martínez emerged as the senior figure in the nightlong conferences. He was the oldest, the most experienced politically, the only surviving founder of the Frente; and above all else, he commanded absolute respect.

Rolando Asturias and Juan Carlos Reyes, the physician, had set the political process in motion. Through Saturday afternoon and evening, they made innumerable summoning telephone calls to their friends and associates in the opposition movement and sent out couriers to others. Manuel Schneider refused to go home despite his broken collarbone, and was brought to the meeting in a National Guard jeep. Antonia joined him immediately. Dora Merino, Comandante Pablo, and the entire assault team from the National Assembly arrived in a truck, cheered wildly by a crowd gathered in front of the villa. Young businessmen who had directed the general strike, university and labor leaders, and *barrio* fighters who had lived through the final Ferrer offensive came to the villa one by one or in groups.

At Tomás Martínez' request, General Pacheco had sent a C-47 transport plane to Jacaltec for the EGP representatives, and in midmorning, Tomás Martínez, Manuel Schneider, and Máximo Landino had gone to the National Palace to confer with Pacheco.

By noon, a seven-member Provisional Junta of Government had been formed. Tomás Martínez was designated its chairman.

The Frente was represented by Rolando Asturias; the EGP by
Máximo Landino; the business community by Manuel Schneider;
the University by Dora Merino; labor by Eusebio Villas García,
a leftist union leader; and the armed forces by General Pacheco.

Persuading Pacheco to serve on the Junta had been most difficult. He had argued that his place was back in the barracks,
reorganizing the National Guard and purging it of officers and
men guilty of crimes during the Ferrer era. He had already detained General Bauch-Barriga, the chief of G-2, and a half-dozen
other senior officers, holding them for trial. In the end, however,
Pacheco succumbed to the pressures of the revolutionary leaders: national unity, they told him, was of overwhelming importance, and the General was needed to help cement it as well as to
integrate Frente and fighters into the armed forces. "In this revolution," Tomás Martínez had said, "there should be no victors
and no vanquished—and no vengeance. Only proved criminals
will be tried and punished. Malagua must stand united."

★

The first decision taken by the Junta was to send Juan Ferrer
into exile. Landino wanted him to stand trial, but General Pacheco demanded that Ferrer suffer no reprisals. He had guaranteed the safety of the deposed dictator, he said—his honor as a
soldier was at stake. He also insisted that Ferrer's continued
presence in Malagua would only create problems. Finally Landino shrugged and said, "Do what you want with that bastard."

As the new government was assuming power at the National
Palace on Sunday, Juan Ferrer, with two aides and his son Pedro,
a Guard officer, were on their way to Malagua International Airport inside a military truck, guarded by heavily armed soldiers of
the garrison battalion and Frente guerrillas. The truck pulled up
behind a hangar where a transport plane of the Malaguan Air
Force awaited Ferrer, the pilot revving up the engines. Without
a look backward, Juan Ferrer, wearing a dark suit, went aboard
the aircraft. The door was closed; the C-47 taxied to the runway,
turned around, and raced for takeoff.

The last thing Ferrer saw from the plane's window was the

Mixull volcano, brightly lit by the setting sun. His destination was Guatemala: there he would be an honored guest as well as *memento mori* for the generals still running that country.

★

Each member of the Junta was assigned a specific responsibility in addition to participation in the overall decision-making. Thus Rolando Asturias was named Foreign Minister, his immediate concern being international recognition of the new Malaguan government.

On that first day, Rolando paid two visits. Leaving the National Palace after the ceremony, he asked his driver—an official car had been placed at his disposal—to take him to the *nunciatura*. There, he informed Monsignor Bansa, the Dean of the Malagua Diplomatic Corps, of his appointment, and thanked the Nuncio for his help during the crisis. Then he told the driver to go to the Residence of the American Embassy on Avenida Ferrer —which *malagueños* had already rechristened Avenida Libertad, tearing down the signs with the name of the detested dynasty.

Julia Savage was in her study with Mac McVeigh and Rick Anders, working on a lengthy reporting telegram on the day's developments, when Dudley knocked and opened the door.

"The Foreign Minister is here to see you, Madam Ambassador," he announced. Julia and the two men looked at each other in surprise.

"Yes, ma'am—the Foreign Minister. He's waiting in the living room."

Rolando bowed with mischievous exaggeration, flashing a happy smile at Julia. He was wearing *vaquero* boots, blue jeans, and a red polo shirt.

"I may not look the part in these clothes," he said, "but I really *am* the Foreign Minister of Malagua. I'm not here in an official capacity. I'm here to pay my personal respects to a friend who stood by us in our hour of need."

Julia ran over to him across the room, her face radiant. She embraced him and drew back to look at him.

"Oh, Rolando," she cried, "how wonderful! I just wish Don Pepe were with us today to see his prophecy come true."

"Well, nobody else wanted to worry about dealing with you Americans, so they let me have the job."

They laughed, and Julia led him to the study, calling out to Dudley for a bottle of champagne and two glasses. The toast to Rolando having been drunk, they stood for a long moment with their arms around each other, kissing deeply and avidly. Julia felt light-headed and full of love. Finally, she broke away from him.

"Enough of this foolishness," she said firmly. "The American Ambassador can't just stand here kissing the Foreign Minister. Sit down and tell me about the new government. Let's get serious."

"Okay," Rolando replied. "First of all, you must bear in mind that the Junta is a hybrid. It's a product of compromises among different revolutionary forces and other groups in Malaguan society."

"But would you call it a leftist or leftist-inclined government?"

"Lord, you Americans always want to place precise labels on things! Even you, Julia. Life just isn't that way. It's not helpful to have us typed ideologically within hours of Juan Ferrer's overthrow. Don't push us."

"I understand, Rolando, but you know damn well that that's the first question I'll be asked by Washington and by the American press."

"Well, if you put me up against the wall, I suppose I'll have to say that on balance, the Junta is left-inclined, or left-of-center, or whatever you want to call it. But this is a natural political development in a small, underdeveloped country which has been in the grip of a dictatorship for fifty years. You wouldn't expect a right-wing régime to take the place of Juan Ferrer, would you?"

"No, of course not. But how does the Junta break down?"

"This way. Tomás Martínez, as he told you himself in Santa Teresa del Monte, is a Marxist, but he isn't a Communist. I'd say he is a European-type Marxist of the old school, probably fitting into the Socialist International. In my opinion, that's good for Malagua, so let's not start calling us 'Marxist-controlled Malagua.' You know how that would play in Washington. The point is that as a Marxist, Tomás has good credentials with the others on the Left, and this will be very useful when the real power struggle develops.''

"Do you expect one? With the extreme Left?''

"Sure,'' Rolando Asturias said. "It's just a question of time. But let me go on. Tomás is the chairman of the Junta, but he isn't the absolute boss. The Junta is more of a collegial arrangement for the time being. Now, going down the line. Dora Merino is definitely on the left, quite close to the Cuban view in terms of the need for a radical social revolution in Malagua. She's the new generation. . . . Eusebio Villas, the labor leader, is on the same ideological wavelength. Máximo Landino is a Trotskyite, a hard-line revolutionary who thinks Fidel Castro is a traitor to Marxism-Leninism. On the non-Marxist side, you have your friend Manuel Schneider. He's in charge of the economy, which makes him a crucial player, and I think he will try to steer a moderate course, though he is certainly not a member of the right wing. And finally, there's General Pacheco. He's nonideological, a patriot who simply wants his country to prosper.''

"And what about you, Rolando? Where do you fit in?''

He laughed, and took her hand. "I knew this was coming,'' he said. "Well, I'm obviously concerned with social justice, and if you need a label for me, I guess you could say I am a democratic socialist. I am comfortable with Tomás Martínez' line without being a Marxist myself. The last thing I want for Malagua is a dictatorship of the Left, with or without Cubans. We'll have to face the ideological problems and fight it out sooner or later with Máximo Landino, Dora Merino, and the people who share their different revolutionary views—and there are quite a few of them. I think that American support for the Junta will be tremendously important to the survival of democracy in this country. You have to be subtle in dealing with a situation as delicate as ours.''

★

Jim Morgan had escaped from the National Palace just ahead of General Pacheco's troops and the attacking crowd. Leaving

Ferrer's bunker command post, he made his way out by walking through the deserted building into the back courtyard. He went to the rear gate, which a Guard officer he knew unlocked for him. "I hope *you* make it, Señor Morgan, because we are finished," the officer said.

The street behind the Palace was empty, but Morgan, hearing the rumble of Pacheco's approaching tanks, hid in the dank doorway of a decrepit house until the battalion passed him by. Then he blended with the crowd advancing behind the soldiers and carefully made his way to the Embassy. There he picked up his passport—he always kept one at his office and one at home—and several thousand dollars in cash from his safe. In the basement garage Morgan took one of the Station's cars, and in it he drove to the airport.

Morgan reached the airport three minutes before the departure of a flight to Panama, being the last passenger to board. He drank three Bloody Marys between Ciudad Malagua and Panama City, arriving in a state of pleasant relaxation. After spending the night at the home of the local Station Chief, Morgan went on to Washington. Waiting for a cab at National Airport, he shivered in the cold November wind from the Potomac.

On Monday morning, Morgan sat in General McCullen's spacious office at Langley, explaining to the Director of Central Intelligence what was happening in Malagua. He had read the Station's overnight cables on the situation in the wake of Ferrer's collapse, on the formation of the Junta, and on the general mood in the capital.

"There's no doubt in my mind that Ferrer's fall is disastrous for the United States," he said. "The leftists are solidly in control, and the only question is when the extreme elements will complete the takeover. And if we are to prevent it, we must act at once."

"What do you have in mind?" McCullen asked.

"Covert operations to discredit the God-damned Communists and shake up the place a bit. I think we still have the necessary assets for that," Morgan replied. "In the meantime, there's a related problem that should be taken care of."

"Which is?"

"The same one that's been bothering us for months—Ambassador Savage. She's too close to that Jesuit, Rolando Asturias, whom they've appointed Junta member and Foreign Minister. He's a fucking Communist, you know."

★

Secretary of State Masterson was furious. "I knew it all along," he sputtered at Tom Morelli, who was chairing a meeting of the White House Special Coordinating Committee to review the events in Malagua. "I knew that we would have another Cuba on our hands. Why, Hank McCullen here was just telling me that the Reds are completely in control of the Junta. Why did we listen to Savage and refuse arms to Ferrer? If we had okayed real military aid, instead of that half-assed CIA delivery, Ferrer would probably still be in power and the Left would have been crushed once and for all."

"We listened to her because her arguments convinced the President; it's that simple, Ed," Morelli said. "And I agree that the CIA business was half-assed: not because of the one-time delivery, but because the Agency took it upon itself to send additional arms without proper authorization. That made it possible for Ferrer to stage one more massacre at a time when he no longer had a chance of surviving, and to trigger the final uprising. And now we have to live with it."

"Oh, shit," General McCullen broke in.

"Anyway, the problem is: where do we go from here?" Morelli went on. "The President has read Ambassador Savage's cable recommending that we grant recognition to the Junta, and he agrees. So the proposal here is for us to announce our recognition right away, and have the spokesman at the State Department say the right sort of things about our faith that Malagua will become a democracy and so on. . . ."

"I suppose we have no choice," Masterson snapped. "But I would be in favor of recalling Ambassador Savage and naming a real tough Foreign Service officer in her place after a while."

"Why?" Morelli asked. "What's the sense of doing that?"

"Hank McCullen says that the CIA is worried that she has too many close friendships with the new crowd, especially with that priest, whatever his name is, who's been made Foreign Minister. The danger is that she will be their advocate."

"That's right," McCullen said. "The boys think she's bad news."

"Well, the President doesn't think so," Morelli said.

★

In the weeks following the overthrow of Ferrer, the Junta's internal splits deepened, and in mid-December a front-page headline in *Clarín* proclaimed: MALAGUA IS PARALYZED.

The article gave a list of the problems deadlocking the Junta. They ranged from its inability to decide whether and when presidential and congressional elections should be held to disputes over the method of distributing confiscated Ferrer family land and the reorganization of the armed forces and the police. *Clarín* proceeded to describe the Junta's difficulties in working effectively with business, industrial, and labor leaders because of lack of agreement on basic policies. "We bask in the glory of our new democracy, but we want the government to function as well," the newspaper declared.

The fundamental division within the Junta was between the Left and the moderates. Dora Merino, Máximo Landino, and Eusebio Villas were pushing a hard revolutionary line, while Rolando Asturias, Manuel Schneider, and General Pacheco were holding out for evolutionary policies. Tomás Martínez sought to act as an arbiter, though shying away from asserting his authority as the Junta's chairman—not only because of the ruling body's collegial structure, but also because the memories of power being exercised by a single man were still too fresh and raw in Malagua. Besides, as he confided to Rolando, he feared that the fragile political balance of the Junta would break down if he took sides too forcefully.

Matters came close to an explosion when the Junta met in the middle of December to take up the matter of the armed forces. Although it had been agreed in the beginning that the Frente's and the EGP's forces would be integrated, together with "clean" elements of the old National Guard, into a new army, Máximo Landino simply ignored this arrangement. He had redeployed about one-half of his guerrillas in the northeast mountains while keeping other units in Jacaltec and at the barracks of the former Ferrer elite battalion in Ciudad Malagua.

Landino's *comandantes* were instructed not to accept orders from officers of the new army commanded by General Pacheco; these officers, in fact, were not even permitted to enter EGP encampments. In Jacaltec and the surrounding countryside, the EGP had established its own, and highly militant, political organization, recruiting peasants into "action committees" and holding indoctrination meetings and classes. Landino himself spent as much time in Jacaltec and his mountain headquarters as he did in Ciudad Malagua. For all practical purposes, he had carved out a separate state in the northeast region of the Republic.

At the session of the Junta, General Pacheco finally forced a showdown with Landino. The EGP leader had returned to the capital the night before from his latest visit to Jacaltec, where he had delivered speeches, rich in revolutionary rhetoric, to his troops and gatherings of peasants. The call was for a unity pact between the EGP and the rural population; Landino's new slogan was EGP-PUEBLO.

"This just can't go on," Pacheco told the Junta. "We can't have two separate armies in Malagua, one of them being a private revolutionary army belonging to Comandante Landino. It is imperative that the integration of the armed forces be carried out and discipline restored."

"The EGP reflects the will of the people," Máximo Landino replied airily. "The people do not wish the EGP to sacrifice its identity, and I have to respect that desire."

"Do you realize that you're playing with fire?" Pacheco asked. "Don't you see that you may provoke a second civil war? Most *malagueños* don't want your kind of politics. They want peace and democracy and progress. You are depriving them of it."

"That's a matter of opinion," Eusebio Villas remarked. "A lot of people want a genuine popular democracy, not a 'Made in

U.S.A.' imitation that some of the *compañeros* here are propounding. Like our Foreign Minister, who is a devoted friend of the American Ambassador.''

Rolando Asturias stood up. "I suggest that we refrain from personal attacks and innuendos,'' he said angrily. "Things are bad enough as it is. At this rate, our democracy will be stillborn.''

"If *this* government is the Frente's idea of democracy, Padre,'' Máximo Landino told him, "it may be just as well if it is stillborn.''

★

Julia Savage requested an appointment with Rolando Asturias the day after the meeting of the Junta. She had been instructed by Secretary Masterson to express to the Foreign Minister the concern of the United States over the growing intensity of anti-American propaganda in Malagua. Masterson had cited speeches by labor and University leaders as well as by Máximo Landino and his *comandantes,* the circulation of pamphlets accusing the United States of complicity in Barrio del Sur massacres in the final days of the Ferrer dictatorship, and editorial attacks in a half-dozen leftist publications that had sprung up in recent weeks.

All these incidents the Embassy had daily reported to Washington in meticulous detail. Julia herself had noted in a telegram a week earlier that the anti-American campaign was becoming increasingly disturbing, but had to be placed in the context of the rising battle between the extreme Left and the moderates. In fact, Julia added, this leftist offensive underscored the need for active backing of the moderates by Washington, including economic aid for reconstruction. Rereading her own telegram, she had a feeling of *déjà vu;* for the second time in the space of six months she was pleading Malaguan moderates' case. But now the moderates had a new enemy, and the State Department seemed, as usual, to be missing the nuances.

Her first reaction was to tell Masterson that it would be a waste of time to protest to the Foreign Minister a situation over which the Junta had no control. On reflection, however, she decided to obey the instructions and go through the motions with Rolando. There was no sense in antagonizing Masterson. Only a few days before, Tom Morelli had told Julia to be cautious, saying "The long knives are out for you."

At the Foreign Ministry, an ill-kept mansion, Rolando Asturias greeted her with grave formality. When they sat down and Julia delivered the Masterson communication, he shrugged. It was the first time she had seen him dispirited and depressed.

"Why don't you just tell them that I expressed my regrets over this whole business and promised that the Junta will try to do something about it?" he said. "I won't even bore you by saying that it's a bit hypocritical of the United States Government to be complaining about anti-Americanism in Malagua after all it did for the Ferrers. Oh, the hell with it. I have more serious problems."

"Such as?" she asked.

"Oh, everything, Julia," Rolando sighed. "It's been barely a month, and the taste of victory is already turning to ashes. . . . I'm beginning to wonder if we're not losing the fight with the Left —Máximo Landino and the others. Christ, why is it that the Marxists can always get their act together, and we, the bleeding-heart democrats and liberals, can't? We threw out Ferrer, and now we may be thrown out in turn. Would you believe that I was even accused of being a 'devoted' friend of the American Ambassador and, in effect, of fronting for the United States?"

Suddenly, Rolando brightened, his mischievous smile again on his face. "Hey, Julia," he said. "We both need a rest. Why don't you join me and Tomás Martínez for Christmas Eve and Christmas Day at the government guesthouse on the coast, near San Pablo? It will be perfectly proper: Don Tomás will be the chaperon; we will swim and get some sun, and the world will look a hell of a lot better. What do you say?"

In the weeks since the Junta had replaced the Ferrer dictatorship, Julia and Rolando had developed a discreet, but increasingly deep relationship. Julia called on him at the Foreign Ministry several times a week, and the fact that Rolando was her best source of political assessment on the Malaguan situation made her visits professionally legitimate. Washington demanded in-depth reporting on Malagua, and her chats with Asturias provided her with valuable material. But she always stayed a bit longer than strictly necessary, and gradually, their conversations had acquired a very personal tone.

Julia and Rolando had not had a lengthy personal conversation since the night at Santa Teresa del Monte, and now they were beginning to know and discover each other. He told her more and more about himself—his youth, his studies, his priesthood, his family, and his spiritual evolution—and Julia spoke to him of her marriage and the years that followed in a way in which she had never discussed them with anyone. She felt very close to Rolando. Occasionally, he visited her at the Residence—ostensibly on Junta business—and they spent time together on the patio where they had first talked together after the affray at the Cathedral. Once in a while, they stole a moment for a quick embrace, a fleeting kiss; but they had to be exceedingly careful about their relationship, so vulnerable were they both as public figures in the uncertain atmosphere of new Malagua. Julia was completely in love with Rolando, and he with her, and they both knew it without words.

Now Rolando's invitation to spend Christmas together on the coast was irresistible to Julia. She knew that the next step in their lives was inevitable. She kissed him lightly, and said, "I'd love to go, if you think it's such a good idea after those accusations of your being my devoted friend and an American stooge."

★

Jim Morgan flew from Washington to St. Thomas by his usual route: to San Juan by airliner and on to the Virgin Islands aboard a CIA light plane. It was the preholiday season, and St. Thomas was awash with tourists. There were seven cruise ships in the harbor, and the streets were jammed with traffic. It took the CIA's yellow taxi nearly an hour to get up to the base on the mountain, Morgan cursing obscenely all the way. For one thing, he was dying for a drink: the plane from Washington had been so crowded that he could get only an economy-class seat, and cabin service was nonexistent on the Boeing 747 out of Dulles.

At the base, Riordan Jordan gave Morgan a bottle of bourbon, ice, and a glass. Then Morgan went off to the apartment that was always kept ready for him, to take a shower and change into sports clothes. In a half-hour, he was back at Jordan's office, pouring himself a fresh drink.

"Listen, pal," Morgan said. "I've got a mission for you. Very sensitive and high-priority, but right down your alley."

"Shoot," the Major told him.

"I want you to go to Ciudad Malagua as soon as possible. In fact, you should leave tonight. I have some unfinished business there, but I'm too well known to get back in. But nobody knows you in that shit town."

23

ON the morning of December 24, Rolando Asturias drove up
to the American Embassy Residence in the black Foreign Ministry limousine to pick up Julia Savage for the trip to the coast.
Comandante Pablo, now a deputy defense minister, and a Frente
security guard were in the car—each armed with a submachine
gun—but at the insistence of Mark Starek, the Embassy security
officer, Salvador and Gonzalo were to drive behind in Julia's
Chrysler. "A little extra protection won't hurt," Starek had said.

She had requested the State Department's authorization to
spend Christmas out of town with the Chairman and the Foreign
Minister of the Provisional Junta, and it was granted by Masterson without any questions. Julia wanted this to be regarded as an
official trip, formally approved by the Department. Remembering
Tom Morelli's warning, she was taking no chances.

Jumping out of the limousine, Rolando informed Julia that
Tomás Martínez had been delayed at the Palace, but would fly to
San Pablo and meet them at the guesthouse for dinner. She noted
with pleasure that Rolando was relaxed and obviously delighted
over the prospect of spending two days with her away from Ciudad Malagua. And his delight matched hers: this would be the
longest time they had ever spent together—even if others were
to be with them.

It was Julia's first trip to the coast. Since her arrival she had left Ciudad Malagua only to visit Rolando at Santa Teresa del Monte, and that seemed to have been a century ago. Now she chatted airily with Comandante Pablo, reminiscing about their first meeting in Rolando's church, and teasing him about his role as her captor in the takeover of the National Assembly. The laconic Pablo enjoyed her company, and turning to Rolando, he said, *"Mi prisionera favorita."* They laughed.

On the way to the coast, Rolando treated Julia to a running travelogue, commenting on the towns and villages they passed along the dusty road, telling her where ruined Mayan temples and *stelas* were located in the area, and where famous battles had been fought by Mayan warriors. As they drove south of Jacaltec, he said to Julia: "See those mountains in the distance on your right? That's where our friend Máximo Landino and his army are encamped. I wonder how he will be spending Christmas."

By late afternoon, they reached San Pablo, a somnolent port city smothered in the humid heat of the lowlands summer, and turned north on a narrow coastal highway. A half-hour later, they arrived at a large estate on the Pacific Ocean. Two armed guards in military uniforms with black-and-red Frente armbands saluted as the limousine drove through the open gate.

"This is *our* territory," Rolando said. "Here we are snug and safe."

The guesthouse was a sprawling single-story structure, built of stone and Malaguan redwood.

"It's lovely," Julia said. "Was it a Ferrer house?"

"Yes," Rolando replied. "It was one of his playpens where he entertained American congressmen and business tycoons with bevies of dancing girls. Tonight, I am entertaining the American Ambassador with the Chairman of the Junta—and myself—as the principal attraction."

★

Riordan Jordan arrived in Ciudad Malagua at noon on Christmas Eve. He identified himself to the Immigration officer as an

American businessman in town for just a day, and rented a car to drive to the capital. Checking a map of the city, Jordan found his way to Avenida Bolívar, parking the car in front of a Chinese restaurant. Crossing the crowded street, he went into an electric-appliance store and said a few words in English to the owner. The man nodded, and led him into the back office. There two men, one of them tall and thin with a straw hat on his head and the other fat and squat and bald, were waiting for Jordan. He shook hands with them, sitting down at a table littered with beer bottles, half-empty glasses, and overflowing ashtrays.

"Do you speak English?" he inquired.

"Enough to understand what you want," the tall man rasped.

"Okay," Jordan said. "Then let's get to the point. I have a job for you, as you were told by our mutual friends."

The two men exchanged glances, and both inclined their heads in assent. Jordan then gave them the instructions he had received from Jim Morgan at the St. Thomas base. And Morgan had been absolutely precise about what he expected to be done in Malagua.

"The name of the game is to turn Malaguans against the Communists who now control the new government," he had told Jordan. "This is the policy of the Agency. And the way to do it, as I see it, is to create a major political and psychological shock that would unite enough people in Malagua against the Left. A top-level political assassination should get things rolling, and that's what I want you to organize."

"Whom did you have in mind?"

"The new Foreign Minister. A priest named Rolando Asturias Puix. He's extremely popular with the middle class and lots of other people who think he's a moderate, although we have reason to believe he's really in cahoots with the Communists. The killing of Bishop Vargas helped to bring down General Ferrer, and the killing of Asturias, another priest, may help to overthrow the Provisional Junta. Besides, Asturias is the principal conduit between the new government and our Ambassador in Malagua, that woman Savage. Once he's gone, it will be hard for her to keep pushing their cause."

"Sounds good," Jordan had said. "How do you propose to do it?"

"We'll use a couple of hit men from ORDEN—that's a paramilitary organization that supported General Ferrer. They did some good things before the revolution, and we used to help them a little bit. I hear that they still have their shit together and would love to taste some action. I have some hidden assets in Ciudad Malagua, and I'll set up a meeting for you with the ORDEN people. You'll have to explain the operation. The most important thing is that Asturias' murder has to be arranged in such a way that everything will point to the Communists, or the Left in general, as the killers. And it has to be reasonably credible. Asturias and some of the other so-called moderates have been fighting publicly with the extreme Left in the Junta, which in my opinion is a maneuver to mislead public opinion, and it would be believable for the leftists to want to get rid of him. You understand?"

★

Now, in the back room of the electric-appliance store on Avenida Bolívar, Riordan Jordan finished outlining Morgan's plan to the two men sitting with him at the dirty table.

"Can you do it?" he asked them.

"Yes, we can," the man in the straw hat replied. "But do we get paid, and how? Things aren't easy here anymore."

"Of course you'll get paid," Jordan said. "We have channels for that. And you know from experience that you can trust us. We may want to do more business with you."

"Muy bien," the straw hat told him. "Consider it done."

Jordan again shook hands with the men. He left the store, returned to his car, and drove back to the airport. He left on a flight for Panama forty-five minutes later.

★

As promised, Tomás Martínez made it in time for dinner, which was served on the candlelit patio overlooking the ocean.

After coffee was brought, the butler placed a bottle of champagne on the table.

"I want you to know," Martínez told Julia, "that this is the last bottle from Ferrer's cellar here. It was overlooked by his caretakers when they fled with the loot on the day of the revolution. We were saving it for a special occasion, and I can't think of a better one than a visit by our favorite ambassador."

"Why, thank you, Don Tomás," Julia said. "But you must let me propose a toast to you, and Pablo, and Rolando—and of course, to the success of democracy in Malagua."

"You know, it's not simple to make democracy work," Martínez said pensively. "I'm surprised at how hard it is to deal with little everyday realities. For example, I'm responsible for running the police force, and I feel queasy about it. I spent most of my adult life fearing the police and hiding from them, and now I find myself the chief policeman of Malagua. I even find it hard to give orders to the man in charge of the traffic police. And we have to convince the people, after fifty years of fear, that the police are here to protect them, not to repress them."

"And that's not all," Rolando broke in. "We have to change people's lifetime habits, their whole cultural pattern. *Malagueños* believe that to get any response from the government they must know someone or bribe the right bureaucrat. Our people don't understand that the government's function is to serve them, not exploit them. And needless to say, we have incredible manpower problems now that so many of Ferrer's officials had to be removed and others, the ones with bad consciences, have simply disappeared. I had to ask Costa Rica to lend us Immigration and Customs officials for border-crossing points and the airports until we can train our own personnel."

"Right," Tomás Martínez said. "Then we have *compañeros* with the greatest goodwill in the world, but no idea how to get things done. The other day we had to apologize formally to the mother of a Frente volunteer from Panama whose body was sent back in a large fruit crate instead of a coffin. Nobody has any experience in anything."

"But how are you dealing with Ferrer's National Guard soldiers who cannot be integrated into the new army?" Julia asked. "Don't you have quite a few of them in prison?"

"Let me answer that," Rolando Asturias said, "because Don Tomás is too bashful to tell you the real truth. First, the worst types, the Guardsmen who know they would be tried for crimes against the people if they were found, have made their way to Guatemala, which is fine with us. Others, about whom we aren't sure, have been imprisoned, but my friend Tomás is extremely softhearted about them. Did you know that he's been going to prisons, having the men lined up in the courtyard, and releasing them if they are willing to shout 'Long live free Malagua'?"

"To tell you the truth, I think Don Tomás is being too kind to this rabble," Comandante Pablo interjected. "Let them suffer a bit, I say."

"Well," Martínez said, "there's been too much suffering already. I spent three years in prison and I know how it feels. I'd rather have a criminal on the loose than an innocent man behind bars. Have you noticed, Julia, that our revolution hasn't produced any acts of violent vengeance?"

"Of course I have," Julia Savage answered, "and I think it's most admirable. But aren't you afraid that if you have too many Ferrer followers running around, you may have trouble on your hands? What about ORDEN, for example?"

"Oh, I think we can handle them," Rolando told her. "They would be crazy to attempt anything serious. They know there is no way they can bring Ferrer back."

"And if I worry about anything," Tomás Martínez added, "it's the Left . . . Máximo Landino and his crew. And we have to set the example of how a decent government should be run. If we do it well, the Left will be less of a threat."

"Tomás *does* set the example," Rolando remarked. "The other day he went to a prison and came across the G-2 officer who had tortured him during his time in a Ferrer jail, and who had been wounded during the fighting. He decided that the man wasn't getting proper medical treatment, and had a doctor called from the outside. I may be the priest, but Tomás is a true Christian."

★

On the afternoon of Christmas Eve, the tall thin man in the straw hat called the Foreign Ministry.

"I have urgent business with Señor Ministro," he said to a secretary. "It has to do with the arrival next week of a trade mission from Mexico. Can I catch him today?"

"I'm afraid the Minister is out of town," the woman replied. "He'll be back the day after Christmas."

"Could you possibly tell me where I can locate him, perhaps by telephone? It really is very important. The Minister has asked me to confirm the dates for the mission as soon as possible."

"Well, in that case, I can tell you that the Minister is spending the holiday at the government guesthouse on the coast. The telephone number there is San Pablo 3285."

"*Muchísimas gracias,*" the caller said. "And a Merry Christmas to you."

★

On the patio of the guesthouse, Tomás Martínez stretched and yawned. "My God, it's bedtime for me. I've had a long day and I'd better get some sleep. I hope you sleep well, Julia . . . and Merry Christmas."

Comandante Pablo rose too, saying the champagne had made him sleepy. Julia and Rolando were alone.

The three-quarter moon cast its cold light on them. Rolando stirred uneasily in his chair, immensely conscious of her nearness. He leaned toward her, kissing her softly, lovingly on the lips. Julia put her arms around him, savoring his kiss, then responding hungrily.

"Oh, Rolando, my darling," she whispered, "I love you so. . . . And I want you so . . ."

Rolando stood up and took her by the hand. The war was over, and he, the *nacom*—the warrior-priest—was at last free of his vows. Julia followed him across the patio and into the darkened house. He pushed open the door to her bedroom, off the foyer, leading her to the bed. The rays of the moon shining through the window were long shafts of light riveted to the floor.

Rolando gently took off Julia's silk evening gown, murmuring, "I love you, I love you." When she lay naked on the bed, he tore off his own clothes, sliding his burning body next to hers.

"Make love to me quick . . . don't wait," Julia heard herself say. Her hand sought him out, guiding him into her.

"Oh, yes, oh, yes . . . I'm going inside you, completely inside you . . . all the way . . ."

Julia experienced a frightening, powerful tremor inside her whole being. It lasted a lifetime, many lifetimes.

Afterward they rested in each other's arms, relaxed and happy, until the passion returned, and they made love again and again.

"I must leave you now, but I love you, Julia, I love you as I've never loved anyone before," Rolando whispered. "But I won't be far; I'll be in the next room, dreaming about you."

"I love you, my Rolando."

★

The white Fiat hurtled down the deserted highway through the night, and early on Christmas Day it came to a halt a few hundred yards from the guesthouse. The driver, tall and thin, his head covered with a straw hat, eased the car into a clump of bushes off the coastal road, and he and his fat companion moved noiselessly over dark sand dunes to the beach. They padded north along the waterline to a point opposite the house. It was still dark as they walked up from the beach to the patio. They slithered from window to window, peering inside, until they found the room they wanted. A sleeping figure was stretched on a bed beneath the open window. The tall man directed his flashlight for a moment at the face on the bed, and nodded in satisfaction. He took a silencer-equipped pistol from his waistband, aiming it carefully at Rolando Asturias. The fat man removed a piece of stiff cardboard from his jacket pocket, placing it on the window-sill and weighing it down with a stone.

Julia could not hear the whoosh of the silencer gun as the bullet caught Rolando square in the face. Asleep in her bedroom, she was deep in a dream: she and Rolando were walking along a beach, holding hands, and the warm sun was shining on them. But the instant the shot was fired, Julia came suddenly awake with a paralyzing sense of horror and foreboding. She ran to Rolando's room, too late to see the last words forming on his lips: "Our Father . . ." He was dead when she reached his bed. Julia let out a scream.

The two sallow men escaped unnoticed. Their message, written in Spanish and neatly printed in red ink, read:

THE EXECUTION OF THE TRAITOR ROLANDO
ASTURIAS PUIX,
THE LACKEY OF U.S. IMPERIALISTS,
WAS CARRIED OUT BY COMMONDO NUMBER ONE
OF THE PEOPLE'S REVOLUTIONARY ARMY OF
MALAGUA.
LET IT BE A WARNING TO OTHER TRAITORS.

24

TENS of thousands of Ciudad Malagua's citizens turned out for Rolando Asturias' funeral, defying the oppressive heat that marked the day after Christmas. His body had been brought back to the capital from the coast aboard a military helicopter, and the Provisional Junta had decreed a day of national mourning, Tomás Martínez having proclaimed on behalf of his colleagues that the murder of the Foreign Minister had dealt a powerful blow to Malagua's nascent democracy.

On the proposal of Dora Merino, the decision was made to bury Rolando Asturias in a grave next to that of Professor Luis Merino, her father, at the Main Cemetery, the cemetery of the poor people of Ciudad Malagua, beyond Barrio del Sur. "That's where he belongs, with his friends," she said.

A memorial Mass for Rolando Asturias was held at noon at the Cathedral, with Monsignor Bansa, the Papal Nuncio, the celebrant. The casket was then placed in a hearse, escorted by Frente fighters with black-and-red armbands, and taken very slowly to the Main Cemetery. In absolute silence, the cortège wound its way through the narrow streets of the city and past the charred ruins of Barrio del Sur, followed by columns of mourners stretching over long kilometers.

Julia Savage chose not to attend the Mass. Instead, an hour

earlier, she had gone to the Nuncio's residence to pray with him. She said her farewell to her friend and lover in the room where such a short time ago Don Pepe Vargas had jocularly predicted that Rolando would become the Foreign Minister of Malagua. It was in this house, Julia remembered, that she and Rolando had embraced for the first time. Now she had lost him.

Flying in the same helicopter as Rolando's body—with Tomás Martínez and Comandante Pablo—Julia had arrived in Ciudad Malagua on the afternoon of Christmas Day. McVeigh had already informed Washington of the murder of the Foreign Minister, noting that the American Ambassador had been present in the guesthouse when it happened, but Julia made a point of dictating her own reporting telegram on the event and the details. She was totally composed and impersonal, although at one point she remarked to Ann Mestre, who was taking down the telegram, that the Foreign Minister had been a "personal friend." Then she decided to incorporate this phrase in her cable. Julia reported on the cardboard sign found on the windowsill of Rolando's bedroom, but commented that she believed the killing had not been perpetrated by the extreme Left, but by "another, as yet unidentified organization."

Reading the telegram, McVeigh asked, "What makes you think so, Julia?"

"Common sense," she replied, "and instinct. This was a professional killing, arranged by someone who knew exactly what he was doing. The leftists had nothing to gain from the assassination—on the contrary, it would be immensely harmful to them—so I have to conclude that it was either vengeance by Ferrer followers or a provocation on the part of those with an interest in putting the blame on the Left, undermining the Junta, and embarrassing the United States in its relations with Malagua. Do you remember the murder of Colonel Saavedra that Ferrer had ordered? Well, this is the same pattern."

★

Late in the afternoon of Christmas Day, Secretary Masterson telephoned Julia from Washington. "I'm calling you from my home," he said, "to express my shock over the killing of Foreign Minister Asturias, my Malaguan colleague, and to say that I hope you are well after this ordeal, which must have been terrible for you, being in the same house."

"Thank you, Mr. Secretary," Julia said, "I am quite well."

"I also want you to know that the Department is issuing a statement in my name deploring this cowardly murder and expressing the confidence of the United States that this act will not affect the democratic process in Malagua. And the President instructs you to convey his personal condolences to the Junta and to the family of the Foreign Minister."

"Yes, sir," Julia said numbly.

"And finally, I'd like you to come home for some rest," Masterson added. "You've been through an awful lot lately."

"I think it's a good idea," she replied. "I shall turn the Embassy over to Mr. McVeigh after the funeral, which is tomorrow, and I shall come home."

★

In her car on the way to the cemetery, Julia decided that she would resign her ambassadorship on her return to Washington. The horror of Rolando's murder made her want to flee Malagua. She doubted she would remain in government service. The months in Malagua had been bitter. All her work, all her battles with her superiors had accomplished nothing.

Yes, Julia told herself, the moment had come to give up diplomacy and her dreams of diplomatic glory, and to refashion her life in a new way. She could not face more drama and tragedy in faraway places. For the first time, she gave way to self-doubt and depression.

At the cemetery, Julia was escorted to the gravesite by Foreign Ministry officials, young people in casual attire whom Rolando had recruited. Tomás Martínez and the five other members of the Junta stood in the front row of the mourners as if awaiting her arrival to give the signal for the start of the ceremony. Suddenly, Julia felt like the widow at her husband's burial, seemingly the center of bereaved attention under the ceiba trees of the park of death. Sun filtered through the foliage in intricate patterns, and Julia remembered the burial of Luis Merino. Today, however, Rolando Asturias wasn't reading from Scriptures for a departed friend; today they were read for *him*.

Tomás Martínez put his arm around Julia's waist and held her closely as the coffin was slowly lowered into the grave. Other ambassadors accredited to Malagua stood several paces behind the Junta, Julia, and Rolando's mother. Comandante Pablo was a hundred yards away with a squad of Frente fighters. When the coffin was settled into the ground, he raised his right arm, shouting the order of *"¡Fuego!"* The men fired a volley, and Pablo let out a howling sob of despair, tears flowing down his hard Mayan face.

Walking back to her limousine with Tomás Martínez, Julia said, "Don Tomás, I'm leaving for Washington tomorrow. For a long leave. I don't know when I shall see you again."

Martínez stopped. He looked into her eyes for a long moment. "Julia," he said harshly, "you *must* come back to Malagua. For yourself. For Rolando."

★

In Washington, Julia requested an appointment with the Secretary of State—she wanted to advise him personally that she was about to resign—but Masterson was away on a week's vacation in California. She had moved in with Tom Morelli and his wife after a day at a Foggy Bottom hotel, the National Security Adviser insisting that she must not be alone for the balance of the holidays. After dinner on her first evening at the Morellis' house, Julia told him that she did not wish to go back to Malagua.

"I just don't think I can be very useful there anymore," she said, playing with her cognac glass. "I've done what I could before and during the revolution, and now it's time to send someone else, a good career officer. It's going to be very tough in Malagua now that Rolando Asturias is dead. The battle between the moderates and the extreme Left is only beginning, and what you need there is a professional to monitor the events and recommend policies. Not me. I can't fight anymore."

"I think you've taken leave of your senses," Morelli said evenly. "If there was any time when you were really needed in Malagua, it is now. . . . You understand that God-damned place, you have contacts and friends, you are liked and respected there. Why, the President will never accept your resignation—not if I have anything to do with it. . . ."

"Tom, you're very sweet, and I appreciate what you're saying," Julia answered, "but I know myself. I've got to get away from it all. Let's say I have personal reasons to return to private life."

"My advice to you, Julia, is to spend a few weeks resting here —you know the house is yours and we both love having you with us—without making any decisions. Think it over calmly; then let's talk again."

★

Pedro Herrera Samper was a nineteen-year-old University student from a poor rural family, who supported himself with odd jobs. Shortly before Christmas, he was hired to help out with the holiday rush at an electrical-appliance store on Avenida Bolívar. He had been a Frente courier during the revolutionary period, and he read with horror the newspaper stories about Rolando Asturias' murder. The more he thought about the assassination, the more he was bothered by something that had stuck in his mind, something he had observed in the store, but given no particular thought to at the time.

Finally, Pedro Herrera decided to contact the Frente leader in Barrio del Sur with whom he had worked in the war against Ferrer. The man listened to him in silence and then said, "What you're telling me, Pedro, may be extremely important. I think we'd better get in touch with the authorities."

The next day, Pedro was received by Comandante Pablo at the Defense Ministry. "I'm not sure what to make of all this," the student said, "but let me tell you what I've seen. During the holidays, I was working in a store on Avenida Bolívar, owned by a man who had very strange friends. . . . Several times a day, one or two of them, sometimes more, came into the store, and were led by the owner to an office he has in the back. They never said anything in front of me, but they looked sinister—you know, like thugs or something. But maybe it was just my imagination."

"Go on, Pedro," Comandante Pablo encouraged him. "Don't omit any details."

"Okay. On Christmas Eve, I guess late in the morning, two of these men walked in—I remember that one of them was tall and thin and wore a straw hat, and the other one was short and fat. I think he was bald. They went right into the back office. Then, a little later, a *norteamericano* whom I'd never seen came into the store. He said something to the owner and was taken to the back room. After half an hour or so, the foreigner left, and the tall man and the fat man walked out a few minutes later. Is any of this important?"

"I don't know," Pablo said. "But it's good, Pedro, that you came to tell me about it."

Within the hour, the owner of the electrical-appliance store was brought to the Defense Ministry by a military investigatory team that specialized in tracking down Ferrer-era criminals. The owner was a sullen elderly man who had been a minor official in Ferrer's Liberal Party, and he refused to answer any questions about the comings and goings in his shop.

"You know, *señor,* we don't torture people here anymore," Pablo told him, "but under the circumstances, you are a candidate for preventive detention pending various investigations. If you prefer, you can sit in jail and decide if you want to tell us anything. I'll call a judge right away to get a warrant for your formal arrest."

"You don't have to do that," the merchant said. "I can't afford to sit in prison. I have a business to run and a family to support. What do you want to know?"

Over hours of interrogation, the store owner admitted that he belonged to ORDEN and that his premises were used by ORDEN militants to receive instructions from leaders who were hiding somewhere in the city. He said he had received a telephone call from one of them the night before Christmas Eve telling him that an American—"one of our good friends"—would be visiting the next day to meet with two ORDEN militants who often came to the store to pick up messages and receive payments. He was one of the paymasters for ORDEN, he said, but he never knew what orders were being given or carried out. He remembered that the tall man was known as Carlos and the fat man as Arturo, and he provided detailed descriptions of them.

"Do you expect them again?" Comandante Pablo asked.

"I suppose so. They have to come to get the money for whatever job they did."

Carlos and Arturo were arrested two days later at the store as they were receiving a sheaf of bank notes from the owner. At first, they claimed they did not understand why they were being held, that they were innocent of any crimes, and that the store owner was a friend whom they visited occasionally for a couple of beers. But they could not explain why they were receiving the money. The interrogation went into the night. Finally, Carlos and Arturo acknowledged that they belonged to ORDEN, and they repeated for Comandante Pablo the conversation with the *gringo* who had come to see them on Christmas Eve. They had been ordered by their *jefes* to carry out whatever the American wished.

"Did you kill Foreign Minister Asturias?" Comandante Pablo asked as the dawn was breaking over Ciudad Malagua.

By midmorning, Pablo had their signed confessions and the names of ORDEN leaders with whom they communicated. By evening, the ORDEN men had been rounded up and jailed. Tomás Martínez, informed by Pablo, said, "Of course, they will be tried in court—but must we always live with evil and violence in this damned country of ours? Will it ever be over?"

Epilogue

On a cold afternoon in early January, Tom Morelli called Julia Savage from his White House office and told her he had to see her immediately. She was there within an hour.

"It seems that the Foreign Minister was killed by members of a right-wing terrorist organization called ORDEN," Tom said, "and furthermore it appears that they were acting on orders from an unidentified American citizen."

"My God!" Julia exclaimed. "I can't believe it!"

"Well, you better believe it. The Junta in Malagua has passed all the information on to McVeigh, requesting the cooperation of the United States Government. We may be on the verge of a tremendous crisis with Malagua. So I think it's absolutely urgent, Julia, that you go back to Malagua at once."

"But I can't, I can't. I've already told you that."

"I know, but you simply have to change your mind. The national interest requires your presence in Malagua. The President wants you to remain as Ambassador in Malagua."

Julia Savage sat silently for a moment, then shook her head.

"No, Tom, I won't go. From what you tell me, the Asturias murder may have been arranged by Agency people."

"Yes, that thought has occurred to me too."

"And I can't face my friends there if that's true. How can you expect me to convince the Malaguans that this was the action of a few demented CIA officers who operated on their own, without the knowledge of the Administration? I'm not sure *I* can be convinced of it.''

"Christ, Julia, you know that this President wouldn't authorize anything like that. . . . The immediate problem is to persuade the Junta, especially Tomás Martínez, not to go public with accusations that the United States was behind the Asturias killing, to give *me* time to investigate. And you're the only person who can do it.''

"I'm sorry, Tom, I just won't clean up the Agency mess.''

★

Several days later, Julia Savage went to lunch at the Cosmos Club with Terence Terhune. They discussed the Malagua situation—Terhune made only a passing reference to the possibility that "some American" might have been involved in the Asturias murder—and then talked about how she was spending her Washington leave. Julia thought that Terhune was just making pleasant conversation, trying to be friendly in his own awkward way. She wondered whether he suspected that she would be submitting her resignation to the President and Masterson the following day. It would please him, she thought. There was one loose end that bothered her, and over coffee, she asked him: "By the way, Terry, what ever happened to Morgan? He never surfaced in Malagua after Ferrer's fall.''

"Oh, haven't you heard?'' Terhune said. "Well, just the other day Jim Morgan was appointed Chief of the Western Hemisphere Division over at Langley. Colonel Duke is retiring. And Morgan, as you know, is a good man, so I'm sure we'll work well together.''

Fury tore through Julia, and she fought to repress a scream of savage protest. If indeed the Agency was behind Rolando's assassination, Jim Morgan had to have been part of it. Malagua had been his fiefdom—and he would have wanted to have the last word in the Malaguan drama. And the promotion must have been his reward. Now he would subvert, and suborn, and kill, when necessary, all over Latin America.

To Terhune, she said matter-of-factly, "No, I hadn't heard the news about Morgan." It was time to leave, their coffee finished.

Strolling out of the club on Massachusetts Avenue, Terhune asked if he could drop Julia anywhere on his way back to the State Department. Fine snow whitened the pavements and the trees.

"Why, yes," she answered. "At the White House, please. I have some unfinished business there. I just remembered."